CrackerJack!

SHĒA ROSE

authorHOUSE®

AuthorHouse™
1663 Liberty Drive
Bloomington, IN 47403
www.authorhouse.com
Phone: 833-262-8899

Published by AuthorHouse 06/18/2021

ISBN: 978-1-6655-2946-4 (sc)
ISBN: 978-1-6655-2944-0 (hc)
ISBN: 978-1-6655-2945-7 (e)

Library of Congress Control Number: 2021912283

She wanted to be tussled. Why? She didn't know. But the thought persisted. There must have been a reason. Recessed in the cavern of her mind lurked the answer…

1

Let Me Be... Just Let Me Be

C INDY GOT UP AT 6:30 a.m. religiously. She'd been at her regimen almost ten years. The routine and the mundane were simply her norm. Never anything new. Life was boring. She had never come across anybody who thought life to be an exhilarating journey. But deep within Cindy knew something for her was out there on the ocean. She just couldn't fathom how or when her ship would arrive.

Cindy Jack, stenographer, twenty-nine years old, five-feet seven-inches with the most adorable dark brown eyes imaginable, received her weekly job assignments from the private firm with various state government contracts. Cindy would go out and record commentary and testimonies from the diverse local government agencies charged with the duty of "in the public interest" protection thing. Day after day, Cindy would sit there, nonchalantly recording the verbiage from the mouths of the public servants or the concerned and/or offended public participants. An awesome stenographer indeed, Cindy was fast, typing a tad more than 300 spoken words accurately per minute! The only breaks she took would typically be to ante up the paper in her stenography machine or an infrequent ladies' room visit. But Cindy had trained her bladder to behave and usually not require relief.

Monday morning, June 26 at 6:45 a.m., Cindy was done with her shower. Her mane-like towel-dried hair circled her lovely almond-complexioned face as she slid into her terrycloth robe. On her way to the kitchen to quickly brew up a cup of java, being mulatto, the thick texture of her long dark curly hair and succulent color of her skin

1

culminated into a perpetual healthy glow. Nothing was unusual about the morning, just another Monday. But Cindy felt something different as one incessant thought kept circling around in her head… 'I want to be tussled; I'd *really* like to be tussled!'

"I'll finish my coffee and get dressed. Maybe the day will offer something new," she thought aloud, "and since I want to be tussled maybe I should look up the word since I don't even know what it means." She playfully smiled and finished her coffee. On the way back to her bedroom to scan her closet for the day's attire she stopped to look up the word…

'Tus-sle (tus'el). v.-sled, -sling.n.-1. To struggle or fight roughly, -n. 2. Any rigorous struggle'.

"So why on earth would I want that?" Her immediate thought was how disconcerting it was to be bothered by such a strange thought. She continued aloud, "Uh, probably just a word I heard somewhere in passing. So now knowing what it means, I can simply dismiss it. But maybe it wouldn't be too bad if I'd be *tussling with a man!*" Sheepishly smiling she went on with her routine.

Back in her bedroom rummaging through her closet she picked out a black fitted skirt that gracefully touched just below her knee, a white tailored blouse, and a sexy red teddy undergarment she liked to keep on a hanger. An off-black pair of pantyhose would complete the ensemble. Her verbalized thoughts continued amidst a self-indulgent flight of fantasy, "Victoria ain't the only one with *secrets* today! While I'm sitting there typing that boring bullshit, nobody will know but me that I'm wearing my sizzling red-hot teddy and I'm ready to be tussled! I got *two secrets* today, Vicki. *Yes!*" She laughed while gyrating a sexy dance move back to the bathroom.

While blow-drying and styling her lengthy locks, she got the pressing feeling that time was not on her side. She quickly finished her makeup, checked her bedroom clock confirming her suspicion. Now 7:37 a.m. and running late, she needed to head out within the next few minutes. Quickly dressing and sliding on a pair of black square-toed low heels, she grabbed her shoulder bag off the doorknob, gathered her other paraphernalia, and left. Traffic was not on her side either. Not more than a few minutes later than usual, Cindy sat in what seemed to be a stagnant parking lot. And the relentless 'I want to be tussled' thought was back.

Checking her watch made for more tension since most of the hearings she was assigned to record usually started at 10 a.m. She would need about thirty minutes more for travel time to the State buildings where the proceedings were held. But first, and especially on Mondays, she would need to get to the office and pick up her weekly assignment register.

Cindy had made it to the Casten Agency parking lot at 8:52 a.m. Twenty-two minutes late was not a travesty but certainly enough to cause concern on a Monday with so many things to cover before take-off again. And still she'd have to get from the parking lot to her office, punch in, and get acclimated; perhaps another ten minutes added to the infraction, "*Shit*," she grimaced.

9:08 a.m., Cindy, scurrying to her desk to plop her briefcase atop a pile of papers awaiting her return, was aiming to attend to her office affairs and be on the road again. She had to walk past her supervisor's office who unbeknownst to Cindy was somewhat awaiting her arrival. Claudia Hoosier, peering over her husky bifocals blurted out, "Cindy! Cindy, come in my office. I need to speak with you. Even though you're late this is important."

Cindy put on the brakes full force and backed up to Claudia's doorway. "Sorry, Claudia, yes I am running a little late. Traffic and all, you know? I didn't mean to rush past you." A bit rattled, Cindy was trying desperately to be polite to the personality known as Claudia.

But Claudia, a bitter divorcee, was none too empathetic. She had a capacity to cut one off at the knees and reprimand them for having the unmitigated gall to bleed and feel pain. "You rushed by like a bat outta hell! You're late. You need to watch that, dearie. You're a good stenographer, Cindy, but your arrivals at the proceedings must be timely. If you're not on time here, you can't possibly be on time there! What is it with you young ladies? You're out too late on weekends? And Lord only knows what you're doing and who you're doing it with." Claudia's facial expression and vocal tone were totally off the wall. Her usual bitterness was always distasteful, and cold disposition bone chilling. At fifty-five, Claudia's personality served to make all the firm's younger women wonder if that age was worth achieving. Claudia had been with Casten since its inception thirteen years ago. Being part of the founding gave her executive privilege even though she'd never been promoted to executive status.

Cindy replied, "I wasn't out late at all just hung up in traffic. Just takes a few minutes off schedule. Left about ten minutes later than usual."

"All the details are not necessary," Claudia retorted. "We ensure our clients that our stenographers are on time. Excuses are irrelevant. We can't tell the Hospital Rate Review Commission that *traffic* caused our stenographer to be late and disrupt their proceedings. Would you suggest we do that?"

"Not at all. But that's the truth." Cindy's instinct told her to stop talking while she was still breathing since Madame Hoosier was now leering at her as if she'd soon be roadkill.

Changing the subject, Claudia continued, "Your assignments. Margie is going on maternity leave in two months and I'm switching you over to the Hospital Rate Review Commission. They're always scheduled for 9:30 on Monday morning of the fourth week of the month. A new reason for timeliness. You're second to Margie's seniority so I figured you'd be best to replace her. And since you already have the Joint Hospital Payer Task Force this one will work well for you. I've told Margie I want both of you here by 4:00 on Fridays from now until she leaves so you can spend time together discussing that Commission. Word has it there's going to be a major issue coming up for them in about three months over a threatened labor strike. You don't need those details, but I do want you versed on HRRC's mission and the players. You may have to work more days for them if needed. This could be a biggie! By the way, any issues last week I should know about?"

"No," bluntly said Cindy. "If that's all, I need to get to my cubicle and prepare some scrolls for transcription. Can I have my schedule for this week? Pretty much the same?"

Calmer, Claudia replied, "Same for now. Ten o'clock for this entire week is your charmed time. Fate must be with you. And don't forget to be back here on Friday at four."

"Will do. Have a good day." Cindy proceeded on to her desk, took

4

care of her routine duties and pressed on towards her assignments. She was headed to the Pharmaceutical Aged Assistance & Oversight Council (PAAOC) at ten o'clock; the Joint Hospital-Payer Task Force Committee (JHPTC) at one o'clock, and as fate should have it, they were both in the same vicinity. The agenda summaries she got from Claudia gave an overview of what the proceedings would cover. Rising prescription costs for the elderly was a concern and political platform for the PAAOC; the Department of Health's growing concern with regulation versus deregulation of the State's hospitals was the focus of the JHPTC. "All these acronyms suck," Cindy thought aloud, "they don't even form a decent word to say." The rest of the week would be no different. The acronyms were the same unclever first initial descriptors and the agendas essentially the same…political platforms for those who could grandstand best.

Having arrived for the PAAOC at 9:40 a.m., she promptly set up her apparatus with five minutes to spare. There was a set-up of coffee and tea in the rear of the room to which Cindy hastened to get her percolating for the morning session.

Precisely at 10:00 a.m., the Council Secretary made a motion to engage the proceeding.

"This is an official meeting of the Pharmaceutical Aged Assistance and Oversight Council. Adequate notice was posted in surrounding local newspapers regarding today's proceedings. Any public representative should now acknowledge themselves if they wish to testify about the issues being represented today. Please stand and identify yourselves if you wish to give testimony for the record. We will acknowledge your standing and ask each of you to speak in designated order."

Cindy's fingers rapidly worked her machine recording every word the speaker said. She would next record every word from those who wished to be heard. Assuming the public participants in attendance were versed on the matter, Cindy aptly recorded five audience members who stood up to be acknowledged.

The Council Secretary continued. "State your name and affiliation. Speak slowly and spell your last name for the recorder please."

"Gerald Mignela, Grey Panthers member. M-i-g-n-e-l-a."

"Thank you, Sir. Next."

"Mary Osborne, Medicare recipient. O-s-b-o-r-n-e."

"Thank you, Ma'am. Next."

"Ronald Siburn, Insurance Company Agent. S-i-b-u-r-n."

"Thank you, Sir. Next."

"Rose Cadella, Medicare recipient. C-a-d-e-l-l-a."

"Thank you, Ma'am. Next."

"Gregory Hayes, representing my elderly father, Jackson Hayes. H-a-y-e-s."

"Thank you, Sir. You have all been recorded as desiring to give testimony today. First, the Council members will present their views. Then we will proceed to take the comments from the public who want to express their opinions. Our recorder today is Ms. Cindy Jack of the Casten Agency. We shall begin with Mr. Warren Lein, Deputy Commissioner of the State's Health Department." There were six PAAOC official and ex-officio members, including the Council Secretary. Seated on a raised platform in a panel-like configuration, all the Council members had inscribed nameplates and official looks etched upon their faces.

"Thank you, Mr. Secretary. The issue of rising prescription drug costs to the elderly is a pressing matter. I don't believe there's anyone who doesn't share the sentiment that as the greying of America proliferates the costs increase too. I have elderly parents facing the same dilemma. The State offered a subsidy with income limits to help but unfortunately those income limits are low and not meeting the people's needs. This is a State budget issue at best, a humanity issue at large, and an inflationary matter for real. I don't have any concrete answers to ease the burden, but I do have two ears. I'm willing to listen to any reasonable ideas towards a solution."

"Thank you, Deputy Commissioner Lein. Ms. Feen, Chairperson of the Aged and Disabled Work Group, your comments please."

"Thank you, Mr. Secretary. I share Deputy Commissioner Lein's sentiments, but I do think the State can do more. Those income limits for starters could be raised. Single elderly individuals with monthly incomes of $1500 or less; couples with combined incomes of $3000 are seriously outdated. Some elderly people require about $1500 a month for prescription drugs alone with no money left for other expenses like rent or a mortgage, food, utilities, car expenses, insurance payments. Because one is sixty-five or older does not mean they should be expected to live off a less than humane income level. Without adequate assistance for these rising drug costs, there's not much point to the greying of America. Who wants to live to seventy, need medication to sustain their life, and can't afford it? Medical technology has made the greying of America possible; inability to afford the medications to sustain those lives is a critical downside. We all need to work hard to find a solution. We're all headed there, folks."

"Thank you, Ms. Feen. Mr. Damion Spears of the Public Advocates Office, commentary please."

"Thank you, Mr. Secretary. This feels like being caught between a rock and a hard place. While I sympathize with Ms. Feen's comments, I defer to Deputy Lein's statements. Coming from the Public Advocates Office, several issues have pressing urgency. For example, what about funding deteriorating roadways potentially contributing to fatal accidents in the State? What about the educational system needing cash infusions to prepare our youth for the challenges of tomorrow? What about those needing legal assistance who've been victimized by unsavory businesses or crimes they did not commit and can't afford their right to legal defense? What about environmental protection efforts to fund clean air initiatives so we can all just breathe? Then there're personal protection initiatives that need funding so that criminals don't feel as though they have more of a safe harbor than do honest law-abiding citizens. From my perspective, I must *add* the rising cost of prescriptions for the elderly to all those considerations I just named. And that wasn't even an exhaustive list! What I conclude is that it's not just a budget issue, it's an appropriations issue. When there are so very many issues requiring so much additional funding, being elderly is not the qualifier. Quality of life for all is the qualifier. I'm not suggesting that the prescription costs to the elderly is less than a big-ticket item. I'm saying that it's up there with all the other big-ticket items. And no one to date has been able to reasonably or rationally conclude that any one item takes precedence over another. That's the dilemma ladies and gentlemen. That's the dilemma."

"Thank you, Mr. Spears. Mr. Roland Green, public member testimony."

"Thank you, Mr. Secretary. While my co-Council members' testimonies have been compelling, I remain convinced that more can be done if there is a desire to. And whereas I don't intend to jump in the ring with the Public Advocate, I think it should be recognized that appropriations come from some body of people, somewhere, based on something, who've decided to put one issue above others *and fund it.* After all, isn't that the basis of appropriations? Therefore, I conclude that some body of people, somewhere in this State, because there is a suffering segment of the State's population, decide to put this issue at the forefront of the political agenda. Then this elderly prescription cost issue might become a bigger-ticket item than it seems to be on the political totem pole right now. Then and only then might come the desired funding that everybody *claims* they want to happen."

Cindy was aptly recording and listening to what she felt was heart-wrenching. So much verbiage and sentiment but no call to action other than the public member's eloquently delivered pitch. The meeting soon concluded after the public audience's comments she'd aptly recorded. At 11:48 a.m. Cindy was packing to go.

Entering the Broad Street Commerce Building's cafeteria, the tussled thought was back. Mindfully she replayed the proceeding wondering if she should avail herself to the elderly's tug-of-war and seemingly concerned State representatives' and public participants' tussle. She thought again, concluding, nope, not her forte.

In line with her tray and turn to order, "May I help you, Miss?" The attendant was diligent but not overly personable. Just matter of fact.

"Yes. Tuna on rye, please. Do you have soup today?"

"Vegetable," he replied.

"I'll have a cup of that too. Oh, and a bottle of water."

As the attendant whipped up Cindy's order, she found herself gazing into the seated pool of State workers and others from various walks of life led there for lunch.

The attendant handed over her order. "Will that be all, Miss?"

"Yes. Thank you."

"Five dollars, twelve cents," he said.

Cindy gave him a ten-dollar bill, took her change, her food, and headed to an empty table. Sitting alone, she watched other people … eating alone, or with another person or people, conspicuously engaged in work-related doldrums or personal conversations.

Suddenly a friendly voice, "Cindy! Hello! How are you? I thought that was you. I just heard some news about you and like a flash of lightening here you are," he enthusiastically said.

As he walked closer to her table, she was becoming excited and a bit anxious. "*Hello, Alonzo Prier*! How are you? It's been forever since I last saw you! And excuse my ignorance but what news are you talking about?"

"The agency you work for. Casten, right?"

"Yes."

"I hear you're replacing Margie Wyndam while she's on maternity leave. I'm the Health Department's Senior Counsel for the Hospital Rate Review Commission. When they switch you over, we'll be seeing lots of each other. It was good to hear that we'll be working together again."

"Goodness! You're Senior Counsel for the Hospital Rate Review Commission? *Awesome!* I had no idea! The last time I worked with you was probably five years ago when you were attending some proceedings for the Attorney General's Office, and I'd just become a stenographer."

"Even as a newbie you were an excellent stenographer, Cindy. I always looked forward to reading the transcripts when you'd taken dictation. Always one hundred percent accurate. If I wanted to know what I'd said at a particular hearing or anybody for that matter, I remember thinking, just get the transcript… especially if Cindy was the recorder." He was smiling. His smile gave Cindy the biggest boost she'd had in months. Someone that she'd earnestly admired was paying her one of the best compliments she'd received in a while. He could not be a love interest as he had no capacity to be as a veteran of married life with three young children, but he was certainly a man to be taken seriously. He was tall, dark and handsome, early forties, and operated from a discernable basis of integrity. He was revered for his IQ and very much respected for his compassionate but non-compromising style. Practically every female had the hots for Alonzo Prier. But he had a reputation for not fooling around.

Alonzo's parting comments disrupted Cindy's intimate thoughts. "Well, I'm joining some other folks for a brief lunch meeting here or else I'd join you. It was great seeing you and I'm looking forward to working with you again. Take care, Cindy."

Little did Cindy know that as rumor had it, Alonzo would soon be off to another venue having spent so much valuable training time in State servitude. He'd worked so successfully on various high-profile cases for the Attorney General, that many of the Fortune 500 law firms were courting him heavily. Cindy couldn't help but revisit her tussled thought with him in mind. 'If I could be tussled by Alonzo Prier, I'd go for it! Pronto!' Hurrying through her tuna on rye and nearly cold soup, she collected herself and her thoughts towards her next move.

Cindy took the essence of Alonzo Prier with her to the Joint Hospital Payor Task Force Committee. Could it be that this was the man that she could be tussled with? "I shouldn't even be having that thought about that man. He's married but he's just so damn hot with a boatload of charm. There's no way a man like that would get hung up in some illicit State affair! *Or would he?*" She silently mumbled about Alonzo all the way to her next meeting.

Parked in a rather central location to both proceedings for the day she found it best to leave her car where it was and head off by foot. She pulled her strapped in stenography apparatus on its two-wheeled steel cart with her left hand, cross-body bag positioned from right shoulder and with clutched pocketbook in right hand she scurried to the South Broad Street building. It was 1:01 p.m. when she entered the room. She'd attributed her meager one-minute lateness to her unexpected encounter with Alonzo Prier.

Cindy noticed the JHPTC Secretary staring at her. She was a little uneasy realizing she should have at least arrived at twelve-fifty-five versus one-oh-one! But Cindy was in her glory fantasizing that Alonzo would stand up for her if any controversy over minutes ensued. Cindy deliberately stared back at the rather unattractive balding Commission Secretary for about three seconds. The silent thoughts zooming her mind were juxtaposed, 'I've got on my red-hot teddy; I'll soon be working with Alonzo Prier. Fuck you!' Cindy precociously smiled at the JHPTC Secretary and proceeded to quickly set up for the session. She was ready to go at precisely seven minutes after one. All the Committee members had still not arrived. By one-thirteen, they were underway.

"This is a formal meeting of the Joint Hospital-Payor Task Force Committee. Adequate notice has been posted throughout the State via local newspapers. Any audience members in attendance at today's session may express their concerns if so desired. At this time, we wish to recognize those individuals. Would you please stand and state your name and affiliation please. Also, spell your last name for the record."

No audience participants stood. This would be a relatively closed session. Private hospitals were there to discuss whether Big Brother's oversight was necessary or not; a select few public hospital participants, invited at the request of the privates, where there to share their views on the imposing nature of total State intervention and regulatory oversight. The overriding gist for the task force formation, urged by the quasi-regulated private hospitals, was that if there was an opportunity to come from under the umbrella, it should be taken, and not taken lightly.

The State Health Department was also willing to explore letting go the reins. The invited State hospitals provided a little nuance for those private hospitals that were uncertain as to which way to vote. Deregulation versus regulation? That was the question. Will State intervention become more burdensome over time? Yet another question. What route would be chosen and what all hospitals would ultimately decide? Those were the ultimate questions.

After having given adequate time for mulling over the fact that there would be no public participants, the Committee Secretary continued, "We shall officially begin with the Task Force member hospitals, joined by their invited public hospital guests. Please state your name, title, and hospital affiliation for the record."

Again, Cindy's fingers were in rapid stride. There would be no name spelling since there were no public audience participants and the round-table speakers all had nameplates. The purpose for the vocal introductions was to get on record what the guest public hospitals would be offering to the plight. The Secretary looked to his immediate left, and the introductions began.

Six private hospital members representing the state's hospitals with a bed-capacity of five hundred or more were in attendance. Number of hospital beds was a major factor for being elected to the JHPTC by the State's Hospital Association for the deciding of the regulation versus deregulation issue. The reimbursement level from the State to the representative hospitals was the other major selection criteria. The greater the level of State assistance to the hospital, the greater the reporting challenge to the hospital. Ultimately, it was deemed that only the State's largest hospitals getting the most State financial assistance could best represent the burden that quasi-regulation was placing on the hospitals' human and financial resources. It took a lot of time, people, and money to run the hospital reports the Health Department required in response to its regulatory oversight responsibilities. The hospitals felt as though they were beginning to buckle under the pressures with somewhat antiquated computer systems, reimbursement issues surmounting from insurers, and cash shortfalls that kept occurring with self-pay patients. And that wasn't all! Dealing with the other State system of Medicaid tracking and Federal Medicare accountings made for further rough waters.

The three guest public hospital members were next. The public hospitals would not be voting since they would always remain regulated no matter what. The public hospitals were totally dependent on the State for revenue since they essentially catered to the needs of people without money or insurance. That dependency gave the State a right to know that its money was being handled and accounted for appropriately. But the three public hospital non-voting members were there to offer opinions and share the woes of their strenuously regulated scenario. And if deregulation was the outcome, the public hospitals would shift down to a quasi-regulated status versus the full-blown one they presently did not enjoy. The Committee Secretary turned to his immediate right, and the public hospitals' introductions began.

That concluded the hospitals' representations. Next up would be the three representatives from the State Health Department, followed by the Independent Consultants hired by the State to assess the feasibility and plausibility of deregulation.

"With all members identified, we shall begin today's proceedings.

I am Timothy Matthews, Secretary for the Joint Hospital-Payor Task Force Committee. Today we begin with the same issue as we've been in deliberation over for the past thirteen months. Should the Department of Health continue quasi-regulatory oversight over the private hospitals in the State? We'll start today's proceedings with opening remarks from the private hospital representatives. Mr. Emerson, would you begin, please?

"Yes. Thank you, Mr. Secretary. As most of you know, I'm responsible for a six hundred-bed hospital. The market area we serve is upper middle class and most of those residents are gainfully employed. The insurance reimbursements are typically in place for those who utilize our hospital. But we have our share of Medicare beneficiaries and to a lesser degree, Medicaid. Our dependence on the Health Department to assist us periodically with rate relief is not necessarily something we can do without. We experience significant shortfalls occasionally. While I don't want to candidly take the position that we don't need State intervention, I don't want to conclusively say we do. But I also know that if we're going to look to a hand to feed us, we're going to have to justify why that is. I want to hear more from my counterparts as to what their challenges are before coming to a definitive position towards deregulation or not."

"Thank you, Mr. Emerson of Jamesburg Valley. Mr. Waterston of Maytown. Your comments please."

"Thank you, Mr. Secretary. Point blank, my hospital cannot continue to hold up under all the reporting pressures that the Health Department requires. It's out of control. Our systems are old, we've got a major debt financing tab, and the last thing we need to do is upgrade systems just to be able to report sideways and any other way but loose, what the State wants to know! Yes, we're one of those hospitals that relies on the State for relief; instantaneous relief at times, but so what. There's a cycle to life. You sow; you reap. You gain; you lose. You build; you break down. I don't see this hospital cycle of life to be any different. The excessive reporting required is overkill, burdensome, and required quarterly. There's no magic to what we do. We provide lifesaving and/ or life-sustaining services. Sometimes we don't get paid. To always be on the carpet pleading our case for the Health Department's financial assistance is harsh medicine that we shouldn't have to take."

As Cindy continued to rapidly record all the boring dialogue, she recalled being in her red-hot teddy bringing a momentary smile to her face. Adding Alonzo to the equation, her thoughts peaked towards climax, as she silently wondered, 'What would Alonzo do if he were to notice my blouse unbuttoned and I slipped out of my skirt right in front of him? Would he ignore it, or would he ravage me? Suddenly realizing she was beginning to lose touch with the speaker's commentary, her silent thoughts shifted, '*I need to focus!*'

Gary Numan, CFO of Harrington State General Hospital now speaking, was certainly able to keep Cindy's attention. He was rather explicit about the Health Department's excessively burdensome overkill reporting requirements and intrusive regulatory oversight. "They have you searching for damn blasted pennies in those cost reporting categories! We're in the business of health and healing; trying to promote initiatives to better serve our patients, and they've got us running rampant trying to justify every dime we make and cent we spend! You private hospitals, even though it's not as tough for you, have most of the same reporting challenges we do! Deregulation would put an end to most of those damn meaningless questions and reports!"

'Whoa, he's pissed,' thought Cindy. 'I wonder what'…

"Ms. Jack. Ms. Jack! We're going to take a twenty-minute recess!" The Committee Secretary was clearly disturbed as he was trying to get Cindy's attention as she seemingly appeared preoccupied. "I just stated for the record that we're taking a ten-minute recess. I was informed that another public hospital speaker will be replacing Mr. Emerson who's not here yet. Please update the record. Is everything alright?"

Somewhat embarrassed and annoyed by the intrusion, Cindy replied. "Sorry. I'll update the record. I'm fine."

Out in the hallway with no one to talk to, Cindy watched the folks come and go from various directions in the South Broad Street Building. All the men in meetings attendance were usually too unattractive or too married to even give an engaging smile. 'This is such a boring job, such a boring life. I wonder what I should have for dinner tonight. Dining alone is such a boring thing. I wonder what the Monday night movie is?' As she was wading through her nothing-much-to-think-about thoughts she saw a familiar face.

"Hey Gina! What's up? I heard you got married about six months ago?"

"Yeah! Cindy—hi! I certainly did! What are you doing here?"

"My usual stenography thing. How's married life?"

"Fine. And baby on the way is soon to make three. We didn't plan it though. I'm happy in a sense but I wanted to spend more time with hubby before the diapers arrived. But it didn't work out."

"What about birth control? You are aware."

"Totally. But the pill started giving me problems, and when you're married, condoms and rubbers are curse words!"

"Then you'll just be the next Mr. and Mrs. Alonzo Prier."

"Alonzo Prier! Damn, he's fine. You'd worked with him before, right? But why would we be the next Mr. and Mrs. Prier?" Gina was obviously perplexed by that odd remark.

"Oh, it's just that I saw him today—by accident—we happened to be in the same cafeteria for lunch. He's married with kids. Must have started early too, I suppose."

Cindy's response was somewhat suspect. Gina looked curious and took the opportunity to make a pleasant but pointed statement. "I see. He's certainly one hell of a hunk! And adding to his charisma is that he's totally not available."

"I'm sure," Cindy unenthusiastically replied.

"Well, it was great seeing you, Cindy."

"Yeah, Gina. Let me give you my home number. I'm sure you've lost it by now. And I'd love to come to your baby shower. Let's keep in touch, okay? We used to have so much fun!"

"Absolutely! I'll give you my number too."

As Cindy walked back towards the Committee area, she remembered the bygone days when she and Gina spent hours talking about the facts of life...men, to be specific. Gina was thirty-four years old, currently a Secretary for the Department of Environmental Protection Commissioner, with a great sense of humor. They met five years ago when Gina was Executive Secretary to the founder of the Casten Agency. She'd left Casten about two years ago for her current position. Gina's thought process was somewhat more grounded than Cindy's since Gina was more mature. Gina would always think things through and analyze a situation. Cindy on the other hand, was always seeking adventure, sometimes throwing caution to the wind. When Gina met her husband Dan, she no longer had availability for Cindy.

Back inside the Committee hearing and poised to continue, Cindy now caught herself leering at the Secretary as she privately thought, 'I don't know what it is about him, but he gives me the creeps.'

"Ms. Jack, our proceedings will probably be over a little earlier than usual since Mr. Emerson's replacement didn't show."

"Would you like me to take that down—for the record?" Cindy sarcastically asked.

"Not necessary." He replied. And the proceeding was underway again, and the session dragged on and on to its long overdue end.

Cindy packed her apparatus and quickly left. It was 3:45 p.m. It was too early to end the day and too late to tax her brain for something even slightly entertaining. On her way to her car quite coincidentally she spotted Alonzo again. This time they were walking in opposite directions on the same side of the street. Alonzo was with a man she slightly recognized.

"Lightening striking twice?" In approaching, Alonzo had also spotted her and was none too hesitant to remark.

Cindy quickly replied, "I guess. And that's a good thing too. Isn't it?"

"Depends," Alonzo replied, "if it takes you out, guess not. If it lights up your life, guess so!" He then flashed that sexy smile leaving Cindy to wonder what he was thinking. Whatever his thoughts, they certainly weren't apparent as he and his associate never broke stride.

Unreasonably annoyed, Cindy now thought, 'would he fuck me or not? If he would, he should let me know. If not, he shouldn't bother to say anything to me. I don't know what to think!' Her alter ego suddenly arrived bringing her back to reality. 'Get a grip! Your imagination is running wild and you're making more of this than it is. You're over the edge. It's not his fault you ain't exactly Greta Garbo.' In the 1930's, movie starlet Greta Garbo was deemed to be every man's fantasy mistress. She was the bomb! "That's a weird thought," Cindy thought aloud.

She decided to head back to Casten. Although not needing to be there until Friday, she'd at least have something to do until everybody else was headed home from work. Then she could sit in traffic like the rest of the humdrum.

"Cindy! What's the problem? Was there an urgent development that I should know about? Why are you here?" Back at Casten and headed to her desk, Claudia, in her usual obnoxious manner cut Cindy off in passing. She was visibly nervous and anticipating the worst.

"Nothing's wrong, Claudia. I just got done with the JHPTC meeting earlier than usual since some replacement person didn't show. I decided to come back here and check on whether my last week's jobs had been transcribed and see if I had any voicemails. No problems."

"Well, you usually check your voicemails from the road and since when have you started to be concerned about your transcriptions? Office Support girls do a great job getting them out without the stenographer's assistance. And you know that. I sense something is wrong."

There was plenty wrong that Cindy felt no compulsion to share. Feeling somewhat out of synch shouldering the weight of a rekindled crush on Alonzo Prier; a little resentful over her long-lost friend Gina's newfound happiness; and an innate desire to be tussled—whatever that meant, she just kept focused on what she'd returned to Casten to accomplish—all of nothing much but nonetheless something to kill time.

It started to rain in route to her apartment complex. She was going to stop and pick up some chicken cutlets at her local grocer but decided on a TV dinner she'd had for months. 'I hope that shit's still edible. It's raining too damn hard to stop anywhere for anything.' She also thought about perhaps going to a local restaurant even though she'd have to battle the rain but wouldn't have to hassle with any food preparation. A final thought occurred— 'go home and take a breather from yourself!'

Cindy succumbed to her last thought. In her kitchen tossing up a salad to compliment her antique TV dinner, the phone rang. "Hello?"

"Cindy? Hi. It's Gina. Hope I didn't catch you at a bad time."

"Catch me at a bad time? That's funny. When I'm home with absolutely nothing to do but heat up some bullshit and make a salad it's always a bad time. Gina my life is the pits right now. I'm overjoyed for the interruption."

"Damn. I would have never expected to hear that from you. Cindy you're so pretty! You're intelligent, witty and fun! Why haven't you found a man yet?"

"How the hell should I know? There're just none. The men I'd want are all married—like Alonzo!"

"Give it a break, Cindy. You've got to find somebody who's right for you. Alonzo is married, not available, not into you, and whatever else. Don't get yourself caught up in desiring a married man. That's nothing but trouble."

"I'm sure you're right and saying that since you're married now. You wouldn't want any other woman looking at your property for a little whatever."

"Damn right! And when you get married, you'll feel the same way. There're plenty of single men out there. Get Alonzo off your mind. Anyway, I didn't call to discuss him. Dan is out coaching his little league baseball kids and I was thinking about running into you today. It was great to see you! How often are you in that building? I work there for the DEP Commissioner. I miss our talks and good times too! I was thinking that maybe we could do lunch on the days you're there."

"Cool! I'm at that Joint Hospital Task stuff on the second and fourth Mondays of the month. The meetings start at one o'clock. How come I've never seen you in that building before?"

"I have lunch from twelve to one. I was on my way back from my obstetrician appointment today. That's why you saw me. I'm usually right back at my desk promptly at one since I go down to the building's cafeteria. Straight down by elevator; straight back up. Public service life is so damn boring. All you do is go up and down, and all around, in the same damn circle. That's a form of a screwing within itself."

"I'll second that motion. Anyway yeah—I'll meet you over at the South Broad Building cafeteria on the second Monday of July. I believe that's July tenth. We'll plan our standing schedule from there. Thanks for calling. I really didn't think you were going to give me a second thought. I'm so glad you called. I've really missed you, Gina."

"I've missed you too, Cindy. But being married puts a different dimension in a life. I apologize, but I just couldn't hang out like we used to.

"I understand. No worries. Glad we're back, Gina."

"Same here, Cindy. And if nothing comes up, I'll see you on July tenth at noon for our first standing lunch date."

"We've got a date. Thanks again for calling, Gina."

"No problem, girlfriend. Bye."

Despite Gina's words of wisdom, Cindy's mind was back on Alonzo. It had just occurred to her that when they spotted each other on the street, he and the man accompanying him were headed in the direction to the South Broad Building she'd just left. It also occurred to her that the man he was with was possibly the Attorney General. 'Why were they going there? The Albertson Justice Complex, where Alonzo and the AG work is on the other side of town. Umm.' Her thoughts ceased momentarily as she stared into blank space. 'Gina's right. I have got to get this man off my mind. Pretty soon my thoughts will have me sitting in his lap naked, and then he'd probably have me arrested!' With that, Cindy concluded her unfancy-feast preparations, gathered it all together, and entered her living room to watch television. She turned to the Golden Classics cable movie channel, and ironically Greta Garbo was staring in "A Woman of Affairs"; a 1928 silent feature with a new orchestral score, about a reckless socialite taking on the burden of making good on her late husband's thefts. Douglas Fairbanks Jr. was also featured in the all-time golden oldie. The title alone and her earlier thought that day about how she was no Greta made it a "must see". At 10:30 p.m., the show was over. Cindy went to bed in anticipation of tomorrow, though it would probably be only another boring day.

Rough…. Some Like It Rough

THE CHALLENGES OF LIFE HAVE always separated the wheat from the chaff, the strong from the weak, the bottom-line survivors from the face down and dead in the water. When Cindy came upon people who flourished despite life's issues by coping with difficulties, searching for solutions, and tackling obstacles—she found herself at a heightened respect for those people. These were the 'world is my oyster' people aiming to find the pearl inside.

And then there was another categorization of rough and those who wallowed in it. They grew up in rough neighborhoods, exposed to tough times and undeniably poor conditions, challenged by merely trying to survive. They became so accustomed to negativity that they remained ensconced in the discomfort at hand versus moving towards the good worth seeking. These were the 'life stinks' people aiming for nothing.

Cindy and her two radically different sisters grew up in a Brooklyn neighborhood. Cindy's disposition and mindset were best described as somewhere in the middle of two extremes. Her two sisters each fell squarely into one of the categories above.

Bess was blessed. Thirty-seven, married to a prominent vascular surgeon lived in Sag Harbor where folks were of affluence. For some reason life had been overwhelmingly good to Bess. Maybe it was because she had the strongest resemblance to a full-fledged Caucasian. Whatever the reason, Cindy felt excluded from her world and rarely reached out.

Eve on the other hand was blessed with two children and cursed with a self-centered cheating husband. They lived in New Jersey about an hour's drive from Cindy. Cindy was not partial to visiting because of the negativity of that household. Eve, who was usually not operating on a real-time basis would frequently view Cindy as her villain, someone who was vehemently not accepting of her. Cindy cringed at Eve's assessment but also desperately tried to understand her sister's deficits and disillusionment. From all the marital disappointments and frustrations and trying to rear two young children, Eve had turned to alcohol in search of sobriety. 'An interesting parallel,' thought Cindy. 'Get drunk to drown the disgust while the drunkenness perpetuates the disgust.' "And who you gonna' call?" In recalling the one-time popular song, Cindy thought perhaps "Ghostbusters" would be appropriate. But Ghostbusters wouldn't work either. Nothing and nobody worked for Eve. Eve was the middle child, who inherited the strongest resemblance to an African American. Eve was thirty-three years old.

Their parents, who would have been in their mid-seventies were dead. Although born and bred in the U.S., Dad was Irish. Mom was Black. Cindy and her siblings were clearly the products of milk in the coffee. Their parents died from a horrific automobile accident two years ago in route to retirement prospecting in Florida. Driving down Interstate 95, Cindy's Dad fell asleep at the wheel somewhere in Virginia. Cindy suspected that he was probably bored since Mom had most likely fallen asleep during the long monotonous drive. With no one to talk too, keeping his mind alert, Dad fell victim to road hypnotism. He veered off into the highway railing, skidded along about a quarter mile, was somehow sucked back into barreling down traffic right in the nick-of-time to collide with an unsuspecting silver-bulleted 18-wheeler. Cindy recalled the police reports and horrific pictures. She quickly jumped out of bed, ran to her bathroom, and violently vomited.

And this was all at 4:50 Tuesday morning. Why had she suddenly been awakened to an accounting of her life's devastating times and tragedy? Now, what was going wrong? She put a cold compress to her head and climbed back into bed. She wasn't sick, just disgusted. Upon second thought, maybe it was that nightmare-of- a- TV- dinner she ate. Overall, the disgust with boredom, humdrum, and no sex to ease the tension was beginning to take toll. She had to do something. She continued to lay there in silence trying not to think at all, until her clock radio sounded-off at 6:30 with Luther Vandross singing 'A House is Not a Home'.

"Just what I need. Luther on the radio telling me that my little shitty abode just ain't no big deal. Well at least I've got a place to lay my head and hang up my clothes. Fuck you, Luther!" She slipped out of her little cotton nightshirt and headed to the shower. Repeating her usual morning routine, she would be out of the house on time since she wouldn't be engaged in tracking down a nagging word. But in the few minutes she gifted to her morning coffee, she began entertaining a new nagging thought…Greta Garbo.

Back in her bedroom, she turned off the radio in need of some peace and quiet from either the shitty love songs or depressing life-saga songs. In search of another ensemble for the workday, she decided on a soft pink weightless satin blouse with an off-white satin collar. A pair of off-white trousers and low-heeled sandals would complete the outfit. Of course, her undergarments were always a consideration. No teddy today. A skimpy black thong and a push-up bra would keep her most intimate apparel's secrets perched. "Who needs panty-lines etching one's ass? Wouldn't a man just rather see the whole enchilada—uncut? Ha-ha!" Cindy liked flirting with herself. Quickly dressing and moving on she started planning her after work time. She had mysteriously become acquainted with Greta Garbo. Since the Golden Classics cable channel was featuring Greta's silent movies during the week, she believed it was a compelling call for her to see Garbo's silent classics. This was a good thing, so she thought. Greta gave her someone else to focus on to keep her mind off Alonzo. But Cindy's subconscious behavior was all accredited to her obsession with the man. That wasn't a good thing. Not knowing if he was even attracted to bi-racial women, Cindy surmised that Greta could certainly get her in touch with her Caucasian ingredient.

At 8:15 Tuesday morning, Cindy was out the door and on her way to her scheduled Alcoholism and Rate Setting Council (ARSC) session. "Another fucking acronym not to be said. I'll be on time though. Wish I could somehow get Eve in on this as a live showing for the horrors of alcohol abuse. Maybe they'd look at her and offer some help." Even if she thought Eve could benefit from the ARSC, it was not the forum for resolving Eve's problem. Cindy innately knew that. Eve needed personal counseling and alcoholism therapy. They were a council seeking sustainable and reasonable reimbursement levels for the facilities helping alcoholics.

Driving towards her destination, Cindy thoughtfully rationalized her thoughts. 'My desire to have everything work is just not working. Sometimes things are just what they're supposed to be, like it or not. Eve is a basket case and so am I right now. We'll both be fine in time.' Cindy began hoping that she could take herself through a clearing, a terminology she'd picked up in a former meditation class she'd attended. Clearing was a cleansing of the mind. It was a way of releasing negativity so one's path would be open to positivism. Cindy at that point recalled that she'd only attended one class. "It all seemed like bullshit then. Now I wish I had hung in there. Now I feel like I could use a clearing and don't know where to start. One good thing is that I know enough to know it's what I need." Travelling down the road she turned on the radio to drown her thoughts.

She arrived at the War Memorial Building where the ARSC proceedings were held. Of all the public agencies' sessions she recorded, she found herself somewhat interested in this one because of Eve. Other than believing that Eve at least needed counseling, there would possibly come a time that she'd need residential treatment. Who would take care of her kids? Cindy hardly visited Eve and was not the aunt who could just pick up where mom left off. She also didn't like the way Eve's husband Paul would openly flirt and admire her. Eve didn't like it either. And that was yet another good reason for Cindy to keep her distance—Paul had issues.

Now seated behind her stenography machine patiently watching the public attendees and the council members arriving, Cindy tried desperately not to think of anything negative. She was insistent upon trying to evoke a clearing to let the sunshine in. 'This does feel somewhat better', she thought, despite her efforts to not think.

The meeting was now underway. The ARSC Secretary had read his opening public address and notification remarks and introduced the council members. He continued with a briefing of the day's agenda.

The main feature would be a discussion about treatment settings and the fact that the return-rate amongst alcoholics was *exponentially* high.

Mr. Gleamer, representing the State Department of Human Services was up first.

"They're almost like social clubs! For the kind of money you're wanting, these places should all be privately owned and supported by those who can afford it. And there's a big problem with that! But we all know the State is not going to pay the entire tab on these kinds of facilities. The costs are outrageous!" His voice resounded as if he was getting angry.

Mr. Jay Kindler, representing the Fair Meadows privately owned facility responded, "It's just not the well-to-do or those who can afford it that have substance use problems! We see all people from all walks of life who need appropriate treatment modalities." Mr. Kindler's response seemed desperate.

Mr. Evert, from the State Insurance Department, spoke next. "That's because you have an outpatient clinic too, and most insurances cover about a month's worth of outpatient visits. I guess you do see people from all walks of life. Some can only afford to walk in and walk right out! There's not enough money in the system to put them up overnight at your rates!" Mr. Evert was clearly perturbed.

The meeting was getting a little out of hand. Cindy was recording and listening. The bantering back and forth continued for two hours. Some were in favor of continuing to seek higher reimbursement rates from the state and insurers versus those who were in favor of primarily outpatient visits. Clearly, these treatment facilities were viewed as social clubs banking on the high return rate of alcoholics and substance abusers.

'What a mess,' she thought as the session ended and she packed to go.

For as long as she'd been working for Casten, rarely did anyone at those meetings ever speak to the stenographer. 'It's like we're just there to clean the toilets. And once we've got everything spic-n-span we can take our lowly asses up outta there. We're not really appreciated for sitting there taking down all that gobbly-gook those bastards try to out-smart each other with. Alonzo was the only person that I somewhat got to communicate with. Maybe that does mean he's interested. At least he did communicate with me.' Cindy had come full circle back to Alonzo. Making her way to the elevator in the War Memorial Building, headed down to the cafeteria, she would order her usual tuna and soup combination. She had a Health Care Payor Cooperative (HCPC) meeting scheduled for one-thirty about fifteen minutes away. Peering into the lunch crowd as usual and noticing two other stenographers from Casten, she headed over to their table.

"Hey Becky. Hi Carol. What's on your plates' today? I'm not interrupting, am I?"

"Oh no! How're you doing, Cindy? Carol and I were just talking about the wicked witch of Casten."

Cindy rapidly joined in. "Becky, I couldn't have thought of a better description of her, other than what her mother named her. She's definitely a C-l-a-w-d-i-a. Always scratching down to the bone to find whatever she's looking for. She gives 'bitch' a whole new meaning."

"Yeah. Look up bitch in the dictionary and you see Claudia's face." Carol was the newest stenographer, having been with Casten for about nine months but had quickly picked up on Claudia's not-to-pleasing personality. "How does she get away with being so—nasty?"

"Cause she's been there forever. I think they just feel sorry for her. Her husband ran off with a young woman about three years ago. Claudia had a nervous breakdown and been fucked-up ever since. She went digging around for dirt on him and when she found out, it landed her in the hospital for two weeks and out of work for four. Her boss knows she's a pisser, but she kisses his ass. So, her job's safe. Bitch just makes everybody else miserable." Becky had pretty much sized up the Casten-Claudia connection. "I think she's so hard on everybody else because she's so hard on herself. You know she blames herself for her former husband's shitty-ass behavior."

"That's what women do." Cindy responded feeling a twinge of melancholy realizing her sister could be headed in Claudia's footsteps. "A woman will blame herself for a man's loss of desire for her. Why can't it be that there's just something wrong with that man? Maybe he's a dog-dick, a womanizer, or just searching for self-aggrandizement through conquering women."

"Wow, Cindy, sounds like you either know a woman who's going through that or a man who's very fucked up," Carol replied.

Cindy simply said, "Both." All three women recognized that it was time to get through lunch and be off to their next sessions. Their discussion had taken on a feeling of gloom, the very thing Cindy was aiming to avoid.

"Thanks for your company ladies. It's bad enough that nobody we work for talks to us, and then most of the time we eat alone too. Isn't that the pits? Oh! Guess who I ran into yesterday? Gina! Gina Perella now Mrs. Gina Falcone."

"Really?!" Becky knew Gina—Carol, had no clue. "How is she? Her husband is so cute! She married Dan, right?"

"Becky, the girl is pregnant! She didn't waste any time. She said, 'and baby on the way makes three'. She's happy!"

"Great. If you talk to her again tell her I said hello and best wishes." On that note, Becky, Carol and Cindy parted ways.

Headed over to the Public Works Building, Cindy vigorously inhaled the fresh air. It was about a fifteen-minute walk, but she felt the exercise and free breathing would do her some good. The HCPC session would last for about two hours and forty-five minutes, making it about four-fifteen when she could be off, and on to her next assignments. Personal assignments. She would stop by her local library to track down biographical information on Greta Garbo and stop by her local grocer to pick up the chicken cutlets the rain had dissuaded her from Monday evening. She also knew she'd be on a reasonably inflexible schedule since she most definitely wanted to be in position to watch the nine o'clock golden classics movie. Greta would be on again, featured in yet another silent film. Cindy liked Greta in A Woman of Affairs. She also likened her own statuesque appearance and well-structured pretty face to Greta's. There was a striking similarity there!

The HCPC session was off and running at exactly 1:30 p.m. The meeting droned on and on until finally it was 4:00 p.m. Seemingly everybody had had enough and was ready to end it all.

"If there're no more comments on the inflationary components of our members' health coverage programs, I suppose we can conclude this meeting. May I have a motion to conclude?" The HCPC Secretary was a bit more soft-spoken than any of the others.

And that was still another reason why the HCPC meeting was more taxing than the other long-winded monotonous meetings. Cindy would always strain to hear what the Secretary was saying. Cindy raged silently, 'I wish somebody would give that man a damn microphone!' But glad it was over and happy to be headed out, Cindy was now on her way to study her next subject, smiling to herself seductively, she softly said, "I'm going to get to know...Ms. Greta Garbo!"

Pulling into the small parking area behind the library, Cindy noticed only three other cars in the lot. "People sure don't read much these days. Or if they do, they sure don't do it at the library. But it's too early for working folks to be at the library though. Maybe there'll be school kids in here who wouldn't be driving anyway."

Rarely did Cindy have occasion to visit the library. Whenever she did, it would be to check out something on the Internet since she didn't have a home computer. "That's it!" Cindy blurted out, undaunted by whether anyone was in earshot, "I'll check out Greta on the Internet! What a time-saver! Yes!" And once inside the golden silence of the main area Cindy spoke to the attendant about using the computers.

On her way to the Internet, determined to find all she could within about a dedicated hour to Greta, she would still need to get to the grocer; get home and cook; get situated; and ultimately get in front of the television to get some more Greta.

What she'd gleaned from the web was interesting. The first site she happened on presented a full-faced shot of Greta exposing one bare shoulder. The look on her face appeared pensive, as she wore an expression that only a classic beauty could sport. Her well-defined face was both stern and sultry. Her hair, straight as an arrow from the top down turned into a full flip at the bottom, accentuating the structure of her bold but beautiful face. The inscription above the portrait was, "Life would be so wonderful if we only knew what to do with it."

'Ain't that the truth! My sentiments exactly, Greta.' Cindy was back to her earlier thoughts of how boring life was...particularly her life. And now she had found a dead bombshell who at one time in her life had expressed the same longings for adventure. 'This is too much of a coincidence to be overlooked. What does this all mean? Is it possible that Greta is trying to return through half of me? Why do I seem to be picking up on the essence of Greta Garbo? This is enough to freak me out for life!' But it wasn't enough to keep Cindy from continuing to explore the life and theatrical times of Greta Garbo. Next, she read her bibliography capturing some other riveting facts for future reference.

In a nutshell, Greta Louisa Gustafsson was Swedish. Born September 18, 1905, she grew up in poverty. Her father died when she was age 13. She worked in a local Barbershop for a while, and then secured a job in a local department store which featured her in a promotional advertisement. From the ad, Maurice Stiller, a great Swedish Director, discovered her. Stiller became her mentor towards the golden age of film. In 1924, when Stiller was made an offer by Louis B. Mayor—an offer he couldn't refuse—he parlayed to bring Greta along for the ride. Mayor reluctantly agreed. The rest is undeniably.... history!

Cindy was now paralleling herself against what she had just read. She wasn't necessarily born in poverty, but she sure wasn't born in wealth. Both Cindy's parents died when Cindy was twenty-seven; Greta's father, with no mention of Greta's mother, reportedly died when she was thirteen. And last, but most definitely not least, Greta had a mentor. Alonzo Prier was certain to be Cindy's mentor— especially if the fates were to let Cindy decide. Conclusively, there was just no doubt about it—at least in Cindy's mind—she was tapping into the essence of an all-time movie starlet. And one who could help her play up her Caucasian part too!

Continuing to visit the various websites offering commentary, classic movie purchase bargains, and pictures, Cindy hung out with Greta until six-thirty. Recognizing it was probably time to hang it up, she logged off, and in walking towards the exit, she bumped into the attendant. "Did you have a productive search?"

"Yes, actually I did. I've been researching the life and times of Greta Garbo. She was thought of as every man's fantasy mistress. Did you know that?"

Smirking somewhat, the elderly attendant who appeared to be in her mid to late sixties, hastily replied, "Well that's because every man probably saw a little of himself in her. She was a lesbian, you know."

Shocked, Cindy was now stopped in her tracks. "How do you know that?"

"Because it was a publicized fact of her life. Just keep searching. You'll stumble across it. I don't have anything against the woman. I obviously never met her, but my generation wasn't too accepting of that sort of thing. I guess you kids today are not fazed by it though."

"Whatever."

"Have a good evening. Come back again." The elderly attendant was rather pleasant. She also had no idea that Cindy was trying to align her persona with that of Greta Garbo's.

And Cindy, who was taking all this stuff too much to heart was now feeling as if some major infraction had been perpetrated against her. 'My God, does my obsession with this woman mean I'm going to discover I'm gay? I hate the thought of women in that way!

That's a bit ridiculous. If I were a lesbian, I certainly wouldn't wantta bed down Alonzo. Besides, what does that old library broad know anyway? Maybe Greta was a lesbian, but she was a beautiful and stately lesbian. So...*so what!*"

Moving off from her parking spot the next stop was the grocery. Four chicken cutlets and a large container of spring water completed that mission. It was now almost 7:30; she still had to slip into something comfortable, start and finish her dinner, check her mail, and write some checks for bills. Barring any unforeseen interruptions, she would still be ready to settle down for television around 9:00 p.m. That was plenty of time for her planned golden oldie.

The Tuesday night special was a one hour and thirty-six-minute presentation of The Mysterious Lady. Understandably so, Cindy again found the title to be intriguing in deference to the whole Cindy-Greta connection as mysterious within itself. The silent feature was about an Austrian soldier falling in love with a beautiful woman, unaware that she's a Russian spy. "I wonder if he'd found out she was a lesbian, the spy thing would have been a moot point? Ump! Some crazy-ass men like that kind of kinky shit." Nonetheless, Cindy was still awed by the way Greta carried herself, and how she struck poses for the camera. Not only was she beautiful, but she also had a certain style that reeked confidence.

With the movie's end, Cindy changed the channel to the news already in progress. "A twenty-two-year-old man and his eighteen-year-old live-in girlfriend were fatally shot today in Brooklyn. New York police investigations have concluded that the pair were the victims of a drug-heist gone wrong. The man currently being held for questioning in this..."

Cindy cut the commentator and the television off. "Every time you turn on the news there's some more horrible shit to hear about! Where does this end? Sometimes I just wonder what I did wrong to end up here in this mad ass world! I'm going to bed. Maybe I can have a pleasant dream."

In her bedroom having undressed, she fell nude upon her bed. She reached over and tapped the alarm button pre-set to wake her at six-thirty to the tune of anybody the WBLM lite-jazz and soul station chose to play. Her head rested upon her pillow. Aiming for clearing, she drifted off.

"Ugh...Natalie Cole and Nat King Cole's Unforgettable" duet, Cindy moanfully expressed. "I should throw this damn radio out the window! At 6:30 in the morning us single lonely-hearts wake up to musical reminders that ain't shit happening in our miserable lives. Yeah! *Un-for-get-table! Alonzo. That's what you are*! Now just what the fuck would you suggest I do about that, Natalie and Nat? Just what I expected—no answer!" She shut up and headed to the shower.

The beginning of Wednesday all the way through the end of Wednesday would be no different from any other Wednesday—or Tuesday, or Monday, for that matter. Simplistic little twists and turns here and there, but nothing drastic to disrupt the all-too-familiar routine monotony. Gloriously, she would tune into yet another Garbo silent classic on Wednesday night, still another on Thursday night, and overwhelmingly yet and still another on Friday night! There was the hint of a thrill she got from that which she'd invented by way of the suggestive movie titles. The last of the week's silent three; The Temptress, Love, and The Kiss, all provided Cindy with some parallel to either position her body against Alonzo's, or some striking pose for future reference to lure him with. However, there was one little blip that offered a bit of a stir in Cindy. It happened on Friday at Casten because Claudia had demanded that she and Margie meet up to discuss Cindy's transitioning to the HRRC.

Acquiescing to Claudia's rule, Cindy entered Casten's parking lot at 3:55 Friday afternoon. She pulled up next to Margie's car arriving momentarily before Cindy. They slowly walked to the building together, pace set by Cindy, as this was the perfect time to pick Margie's brain about Alonzo. Cindy and Margie didn't know each other well, even though Margie had been with Casten about two years prior to Cindy's arrival. Margie bordered on the more serious, studious, and very-married-with-two-children type, gravitating to the other married women at Casten, whereas Cindy's personality and single status kept her in league with females like Gina before her nuptials. Becky, being married too, was also more of Margie's Casten comrade.

"So, Margie, you're doing the baby thing for a third time, huh? It really must be nice. I just ran into Gina, who's now married and pregnant."

"Yeah, I heard she's pregnant. I went to her wedding. Were you there?"

"No. We'd sort of lost touch for a while." 'Damn,' thought Cindy, 'this is not the conversation I want to have with this woman. Let me redirect this back to Alonzo.' "You know it's interesting. The acronyms I like usually say something. Like Mothers Against Drunk Drivers. You know, MADD. That makes sense. I get it! But these State acronyms suck. You can't even pronounce them, like HRRC. How do you pronounce that?"

"You don't. I simply say H.R.R.C. Doesn't bother me," Margie nonchalantly responded.

"There's no other choice. And all I really know about the HRRC is that Alonzo Prier is Senior Counsel for them."

"Yeah. That's right. He's wonderful too. He's so good-looking and knowledgeable. He knows all those hospital rules and regulations, and when he speaks, everybody listens. He's not easy though. Reminds me of somebody who rules with a velvet whip; smooth, but tough."

"Really? How did you find him to work with—as a stenographer?

31

Was he friendly?" Cindy was searching for whether there had been any personal exchanges between Margie and Alonzo. Not from a romantic stance but from a basis of 'did you ever fantasize about doing him?'

"You know those people hardly say anything to the stenographers. But there was one interesting encounter I had with Alonzo. I would've thought it would have been awkward for him, but he played it off. He's a smooth operator."

"What happened? Can you tell me quickly? We're near Claudia's office."

"Oh yeah. Are you nervous about working with Alonzo?" Margie had picked up on something but wasn't sure what. By now they had reached and stopped at Margie's cubicle positioned about fifty feet from Claudia's office, positioned in a manner that Claudia would have to stand in her doorway to determine if Margie was in or not. This was a workable scenario. If Claudia were to visually peruse the area, she'd see Cindy and Margie conversing and their conversation inevitably would be about the HRRC.

"No. I'm not nervous about working with him. I briefly worked with him years ago. But he was in a different job then. Nowhere near what he does now. I just want a pulse on him."

"No problem. Like I said, he's so cool—or better yet, hot! What happened was, the HRRC had to reconvene for Executive Session at five o'clock. And you know, all those Executive Sessions for their administrative business are closed to the public and usually long. Anyway, the way they were seated, Alonzo was on the end, and I was set-up right next to him. While everybody had taken a moment to read a memo, he leaned over and whispered to me to please ask for a paper change break. Seems like he'd received a message on his cell. Said he needed a moment to step out. He sort of chuckled and had a devilish smile on his face. After the meeting he told me he was going to Washington for a Health Care Conference, and he'd forgot one of his overnight bags. Said he was glad cause he got to see his wife before he left."

"What did you do other than ask for a paper change break?"

"I covered for him. I took an extended five minutes, and he still wasn't back. You know it only takes us two minutes to put in a new paper roll."

"Then what?" Cindy's curiosity was at an all-time high.

"I excused myself for the ladies' room. I wasn't going to let him down. When I got in the hallway, Alonzo was about ten feet away giving his wife one hell of a kiss. He was lost in the sauce! A silver-screen moment! If I hadn't come out there, I think he would have taken her panties off. And she's beautiful. She's got regal beauty. She is gorgeous." Margie was giggling relaying the scene.

Cindy's heart was now pounding as her face contorted into a scowl. In having pushed to dig up dirt on Alonzo she now felt like 'C-l-a-w-dia' looked— awfully bad. She was so disappointed in having been confronted with the reality that Alonzo still had the hots for his fantasy lady. But still in excavation mode, Cindy continued. "How could he be so passionate in a State building with employees around? How do you know she was his wife?"

"First of all, it was about 5:20. You know those State workers are out at five on the dot! The building was vacant except for us. And when she noticed me approaching, she sort of backed him off. A mistress would have kept on going."

"What did he do when he saw you?"

"Nothing! He played it off and introduced her. He first said, 'My wife does this to me all the time, such a bad girl.' Then he smiled and said, 'This is the love of my life, my lovely wife, Shawna.' She smiled and said hello. He then picked up his bag and walked her to exit where her car was parked. I went to the ladies' room. When I got back to the session, he was back at the table. He looked at me, winked, smiled, and said thanks."

Cindy's enthusiasm for the details had diminished upon the completion of Margie's recounting. Cindy was a little concerned with the thought that perhaps Margie had sensed there was a sensitivity there but didn't feel close enough to her to comment. Being more mature and sensitive enough to the overall situation, Margie was able to offer something of validity spiked with candor.

"You know, Cindy, mostly all women who meet Alonzo find him so appealing that they develop a little crush on him. Hell, he is a hunk, and I think that's the night I went home and got pregnant, thinking about him and that passionate kiss! But you know, Cindy, bottom line is that when you find your own man, the thrill of the possibility with someone else's goes away. From what I saw, he is clearly into his wife and makes it known. And another thing I've heard is that a lot of single women have come away disappointed in trying to get with him. In his position, a mistress would cost him way too much. We better get into Claudia's. It's 4:08."

"You're right on all counts, Margie." Feeling somewhat subdued, Cindy really wasn't in the mood to sit through Claudia's must-do session. "So, let's get this no-party started," concluded Cindy as they headed to Claudia's office.

"It's about time you two decided to let me in on your private conversation about the Hospital Rate Review Commission hearings. I'm only your boss." If Claudia was trying to be funny, nobody laughed. If she was trying to be witty, she'd missed the mark. Cindy concluded that Claudia was just being her usual 'trying and prying' self.

"So, Cindy, since you and Margie have undoubtedly started conversing about the HRRC, what do you think?"

Cindy unprepared to respond, Margie chimed in saving the moment. "Well, Claudia, first I gave Cindy a rundown of the Executive Sessions the HRRC usually hold. They're long, and I had my family to get home to. But Cindy, on the other hand is single, so if she's comfortable with the long hours she'll be fine."

"Excellent point, Margie. I'd totally overlooked that! Well, Cindy, are you prepared to deal with the fact that sometimes these Executive Sessions won't end until about six-thirty or seven?"

"Absolutely, Claudia. What else do I have to do? I'm single and free. As a matter of fact, I'd welcome the opportunity to do a little overtime. What's the overtime scale?"

"Time and a half. If they need you on a weekend, it's twice your hourly rate."

"Then I'm fine. There's a class I was thinking about taking up again—of course when I'm free."

"Really? What is it?" Claudia boldly inquired.

"Umm—a yoga class. Good for one's body, mind and spirit. I've done some reading on it, and with the HRRC overtime, I can generate some extra cash for yoga." Cindy was reluctant to say the word, but it was a meditation class versus a yoga class that she sought.

With what had now deteriorated into a not worthwhile discussion, Margie interjected. "Well, we still have a lot more ground to cover. Not so much about the substance of the HRRC recordings; Cindy will be fine with that; but they've discussed at recent Executive Sessions to hold these meetings twice a month. Right now, the HRRC is only once a month. The twice-a-month formal sessions are in addition to the Executive Session overtime."

'Jackpot—Cha-ching!' That was Cindy's immediate non-vocalized thought! Alonzo amplified! She'd also cash in on being in Alonzo's presence more than once a month.

"Cindy, if you're comfortable, then I'm fine with having you replace Margie. I was recently thinking about giving this to Carol since she's relatively new and not all that overburdened. But she's not as seasoned as you. I might have to change one of your other assignments though, considering this new expanded HRRC session possibility. Let's talk about it next Friday. If you get any thoughts of your own on this, call me and let's arrange to talk prior to Friday. If not, see you both back here next week, earlier than today though. I want both of you in my office at no later than four unless a client meeting holds you up. Understood?"

"Yes, Claudia," Margie politely replied.

"Sure, Claudia. We understand." With Cindy's underhanded sarcastic comment, Claudia silently snarled.

"Well, Cindy, we survived the Claudia encounter. Have a good weekend."

"Yeah, you too, Margie. Thanks for the Exec Sessions rundown. I really appreciate being able to talk with you before I replace you. Are you coming back after the baby?"

"I'm not sure yet. My son is eight and my daughter is six. They're well-adjusted but with a new baby, I'm going to have to see how they react. I've heard—and probably more so with younger children—when a new baby comes, the other children go through sort of a relapse. They act up for attention. So, I'm playing it by ear for now."

"That's quite understandable. Anyway, have a nice weekend. See you next week."

"Same to you, Cindy."

Cindy went over to her desk and checked her in-box and voicemail for messages. There were none so she quickly left. With no specific plans for the weekend, she winged it. On her way home she happened back by the library to search out Greta's lesbianism, and to also get a handle on whether any meditation classes were being offered in her vicinity. She did come upon a write-up on Greta alluding to her disappearance from the silver-screen was attributed to the discovery of her lesbianism. On a brighter note, there was a transcendental meditation class offered at the local high school scheduled to start July third. The cost was two hundred twenty-eight dollars, and would last six weeks, with two classes per week. 'Oh, how I really need a clearing now! I've got to make sure I haven't pulled too much of Greta into my psyche. To each his own, but I'm praying her desire for women stays dead and buried!'

For all intents and purposes, Cindy's weekend was surely dead. Not only didn't she have any plans; she wasn't even on anybody's radar for the possibility of sharing in someone else's. It was usually that way. Cindy had almost become reclusive. She had the requisite desire to be involved with a man; she was rather attractive; outgoing and witty; but tended towards being maliciously sarcastic at times. But the sarcasm certainly wasn't what was forcing her to be a shut-in. Everyone has his or her own cross to bear—getting a handle on sarcasm was hers since that trait could turn people off. But to believe that was the reason her life and times had seemingly been placed on indefinite lock-down was to believe in the perpetuation of the ridiculous and the sublime. The entire weekend she reflected over her recent past, searching for when and where she'd fallen off the map realizing that the nuances of life's twists and turns are often so subtle it's only at the road's end comes the realization that the course changed somewhere.

She wondered, 'Is this how fate operates? A person is right where they're supposed to be, having gathered enough of whatever to unwittingly move on in a different direction.' Cindy was only cognizant of what she knew and wanted at the moment…Alonzo's body; Greta's essence…dead end, dead meat. Cindy was presently circling the dead zone. Having arrived at that underwhelming conclusion, she felt the overwhelming need to revitalize and spring back to life with the determination to use Greta for something.

Golden Silence

JULY THIRD, 6:30 MONDAY MORNING, was different. The night before, Cindy pre-set her clock radio to allow for only the alarm to sound. She could no longer tolerate the songs the disc jockey selected for wake-up calls. The thought of changing the station occurred but WBLM was her favorite. No matter what, she still didn't want to start her day predisposed towards life because of a song she'd heard that morning. "So there! Beep-beep-beep is not as bad as Michael Bolton singing his heart out in some silly-ass love song." With that, she was up for a new workweek. In preparation, she revisited what she'd gleaned from the silent Garbo features, believing she'd made a vital connection. Cindy asserted aloud, "Since my introduction to Greta was through those classic silent movies, and I liked her style, that was probably my signal to use her style. After all, us stenographers have a silent role. We don't speak, we just sit there and type. People overlook us. Umm. So, I'll be like Greta in those flicks. Silent, sassy and seductive. If I'm sitting there behaving like Greta, Alonzo will notice. I don't care how beautiful his wife is. He's still a man and he's no dead man, either."

Cindy's mood was generally flirtatious. If only that were a consistent mood thing, embellished by a man, her core desires would be met. If only she could work the law of attraction to bring anything and anyone into her life at will, she'd have it all! She certainly wouldn't need a meditation class. Her thoughts were now running the gamut and running amuck.

Fully dressed and on time, out the door she went. Having ensured that her business gear was securely placed in the trunk she jumped in her car and headed off to Casten. Even the thought of Claudia wasn't too repulsive. Cindy was beginning to see a ray of light at the tunnel's end. Was she about to be tussled? That thought still menaced her.

Cindy made a point to stop at Claudia's office in passing. She didn't enter; just stuck her head in the doorway with a greeting. "Morning, Claudia. How are you? Did you have a nice weekend?" Not sincerely interested but this was her way of showing up as the new and improved Cindy.

"Not particularly. Just another weekend. Why do you ask?" Claudia didn't bother to look up. Engrossed in paperwork she just kept on working through Cindy's small talk.

"Well, mine wasn't particularly delightful either but life is what you make it." In having recognized that Claudia would regard her well-intended comment as sarcastic, she quickly followed up. "I mean, sometimes we just have to take the lemons and make lemonade."

Claudia, now thoroughly annoyed snapped back with, "Do you have anything specific on your mind, young lady? If not, just come in and pick up your register. Yours is the one on my chair." Her face was scowl-like accentuated by her blustery voice. The husky bifocals did no justice either.

Cindy sauntered in and retrieved her weekly register. She'd refrained from saying anything else, but her silent thoughts were back as usual. 'I wish I could have my way with you in the parking lot. I'd run your boney ass from one end to the other.' With that, Cindy picked up her register, smiled and offered Claudia a sarcastic, "Have a good day."

"Remember what I said about you and Margie being back here on Friday at four."

Cindy chose not to respond and kept walking. At her desk and quickly scanning her assignment register she noted one itsy-bitsy change. All the unclever acronyms for the first week of July aligned with those she'd encountered the first week of June. The little change was a venue change for her Children's Relief Fund Committee (CRFC). The CRFC, usually held in the same building as the PAAOC, was going to be held in the Albertson Justice Complex.... where Alonzo was!

'Damn! I don't know that I look good enough to run into Alonzo today. *Shit*! I want to be at the height of Garbo when I see him again. Well, too late now. If I see him, I'll just ignore him. Won't be easy but he doesn't exactly hang around when he sees me anyway. So, I'll be alright. I probably won't even see him.' Noticing that the mailing list for her transcripts from the prior two weeks' sessions was on her desk she filed it appropriately and took off.

Entering the Albertson Justice Complex she was nervous. A bit uncharacteristic but reasonable considering the improper thoughts she secretly harbored about Alonzo. She really desired at least one night in the throes of passion with that man. She wanted to know what it would be like to sexually experience a well-respected and revered handsome man at his peak of sexual prowess. She imagined the athletic virtuosity of his pelvic thrusts. She really wanted to know if she had the feminine wiles to get him off like his wife apparently had...and had.... many, many times. The only disruption to her wicked and steamy thoughts came upon her approaching the guard stationed inside the entrance of the building midway the entrance and the escalators. So lost in thought, she almost obliviously walked through the guard's desk.

"May I help you, Miss?"

"Oh! Yes. I'm from the Casten Agency. Stenographer, Cindy Jack. Umm, one second, my ID is in my wallet."

"No problem, Miss. Take your time."

So discombobulated, Cindy felt as though the guard had read her secret Alonzo thoughts and was probably laughing at her. "Here it is. I'm here to record the Children's Relief Fund meeting."

"Oh yes, the CRFC. We're playing host for them today. Some other meeting put them out of where they usually meet. Take the elevator since you have your equipment there. Third floor; follow the signs to the CRFC meeting. Can't miss it."

"Thanks."

Cindy quickly moved on aiming to get out of view and behind the closed doors of the business for which she was there. Once inside the room she scurried to set up and await the arrival of all the CRFC participants. By now it was five minutes before ten. Most of the people where there. Throughout the session, Cindy stayed on the edge of her seat, haunted by the thought that Alonzo could possibly peak in at any time. Not that he had a reason too but just because stranger things have happened. Two hours later, she was again scurrying to pack up and get out of Dodge.

Upon leaving, she didn't see Alonzo. Instead, she came upon two men discussing him at the elevator. "We'll go down to the cafeteria, grab lunch and wait for Alonzo to get back." The man speaking seemed to be in his mid-fifties, well attired, and spoke in a straight-to-the-point manner.

The other man asked, "Where did his secretary say he was?" He had the same look as the other, only a little shorter.

The first man replied, "Department of Health. More than likely he's with the Commissioner. I thought this would be a good time for you to meet Alonzo Prier. He commissioned our firm to handle the independent evaluation and analysis of the deregulation versus regulation matter, and now he's considering adding the proposed labor strike to our plate. He's smart and well-respected; made a lot of strides within the last few years."

"Yes. I'm looking forward to meeting him."

Cindy had positioned herself closely behind the men to better hear their conversation. And just as she was feeling relieved in not running into Alonzo was when the elevator doors opened and there he was. He stepped out with a huge legal folder securely tucked under his muscular arm. He had a perfect V-shape masculine physique, and without a jacket, his well-toned manly form was something to behold. He immediately shifted the folder to his left arm and extended his right hand.

"Charlie Monahan! How are you?" Alonzo's ruggedly handsome face donned a smile.

Charlie Monahan was the first man speaking about Alonzo when Cindy arrived at the elevator. Charlie responded, "Fine! Fine! We just came from your office and your secretary ..."

The other voices all around started drowning out Charlie as all three men began walking away from the elevator and continuing to chat. Cindy had her own maneuvers to make. She had been standing a few feet behind the two gentlemen, and unless Alonzo had known to deliberately search her out would have easily not noticed. With people now moving off and on the elevator, Cindy deliberately lost herself in the movement breathing a sigh of relief thinking… 'Close call! I really didn't want him to see me today. I'm not ready yet. I've got to study Greta more. I need some of her movies where she had talking roles. I want to hear her voice to see how she handled herself while talking.'

Rushing through the lobby, Cindy got herself out of the Albertson Justice Complex and back to her car. She decided to go somewhere far for lunch hoping to not see Alonzo again until the time was right.

Cindy's behavior for the remainder of the week was just as bizarre as in the beginning of the week. Possessed by Greta and obsessed with Alonzo, she rented movie after movie featuring Greta Garbo in talking roles. The 1930's was an unfathomable era, but it had produced a revered actress. If Greta was mysteriously reaching out from beyond, she'd vowed to do her justice by at least updating her style to that of the 1990's. Cindy thought that reasonable since she died in 1990.

Tuesday, Wednesday and Thursday offered nothing more than she'd anticipated. She was getting into the silent poses that she'd witnessed via her silent movie viewings, cultivating another personality effect in deference to the "talkies". It was comical though. Cindy, at the public State sessions trying to play a magnanimous sexy, seductress over a blatantly non-sexual little recording contraption. Fortunately, one of her biggest offenses became her greatest defense. Luckily, nobody paid attention to the stenographer—and especially now—at the height of Cindy's golden moments. She wasn't merely striking keys she was now striking poses too.

Friday afternoon around 3:50, she pulled into Casten's parking lot on time for Claudia's hosting of the transition meeting. Margie's car was already there with no sight of Margie in view. Cindy parked, exited her car, and proceeded onward. Once inside, she hastened to her desk to drop off her belongings. Noticing that Margie was already seated in Claudia's office in passing, Cindy made sure to make a beeline back to Claudia's den.

"Well, I see we're all doing better with timing." Claudia remarked before Cindy could even greet anyone.

"If you say so, then I guess it is so." Cindy disliked Claudia immensely and her comments served to confirm that fact.

"Well, I say so, and so be it! So have a seat and let's get to what we're here for," snapped Claudia.

'Damn', thought Cindy, 'that old bag should be shot.' Taking a seat, the three were now ready for caucusing.

Claudia began, "I was just saying to Margie, it's official. The HRRC meetings, starting in September, will be held twice a month. Apparently, Alonzo Prier, Section Chief of the Attorney General's Office and Senior Counsel for the Health Department, met with the Commissioner earlier this week and it was decided that they should accelerate those sessions. They're doing this because of the regulation versus deregulation proposal and the proposed labor strike. I understand that Alonzo wants to get as much off the table as possible and look at all these hospitals closely in case they're let loose by the State. I hear he's quite the maverick. They say the Governor admires his knowledge and style too. Is that so, Margie?"

'Damn', Cindy thought again, 'Alonzo really has power over women. Even Claudia's old tough ass softens up in talking about him. I wonder if she's ever met him?'

Margie continued, "I've heard the Governor admires him too. But I really don't know. I know when the Health Commissioner attends some of the more controversial HRRC meetings she always sits with Alonzo and usually asks him for advice before she speaks for the record. So being that she relies on him and reports to the Governor, I guess she does talk about him favorably."

It was now Cindy's turn to be silent and take it all in. She was intently listening and watching Claudia, as Claudia for some odd reason was seemingly trying to get a feel for Alonzo. 'You old bat!' Cindy silently grimaced.

"Cindy, I'll be transitioning you over beginning with the August schedule. Like I said last Friday, I'm going to make a change in your assignment register to accommodate the HRRC. So, I'm taking you off either the PAAOC or the HCPC. I haven't decided yet. And if you have any thoughts on either, share them with me. I don't see as where any of your other assignments may conflict. As a matter of fact, it's good that you have the JHPTC, since that correlates with the concerns of the HRRC." Claudia was good at her job. She knew how to juggle those lack-luster acronyms and demanding schedules. She also knew the capability levels of Casten's stenographers. She usually made solid choices and with all due respect, deserved recognition for that. "Do either of you have any concerns or problems with what you covered this week?"

Cindy replied first. "Nope. Not me."

Margie replied next. "Me either. I'm just getting a little tired now and lugging all my stuff around isn't too easy in my condition."

Claudia reconfirmed, "I'm sure. You're going out on maternity leave the third week of August. Correct?"

"That's right. I'll be eight months and 3 weeks and I really appreciate you transitioning all of my assignments well." Margie was rather reserved.

Claudia was uncharacteristically composed, "No problem, dear. I figured it would be good to have you in the office and off your feet. This way if the girls needed to reach you for anything, you'd be readily accessible, and you can clear up and close out any of your files before you're off for the blessed event."

"I really appreciate it, Claudia. Thanks."

Cindy's thoughts were on the warpath. 'I don't know what the hell she's thanking Claudia for. That's part of Casten's maternity leave policy. Give 'em some weeks in-house before they're scheduled to leave to clear up any shit; and be available to the unsuspecting and newly transitioned. Margie knows that. Hell, she's already had one baby on Casten! Merry Christmas, Nitwit! Love, Claudia.' Cindy suspected Claudia was just role playing and insincere.

"If there's nothing else then I'll see you both Monday morning. Have a good weekend."

Both ladies responded in synch, "You too, Claudia."

And off to start another boring weekend, Cindy headed out. On the way to her car her thoughts accelerated to Monday since she'd begin her standing bi-monthly lunches with Gina. 'Maybe this is life's way of giving me back one little golden nugget. Gina and I used to talk about any and everything—and everybody! It will be so good to have my partner-in-crime back again. I hope she hasn't changed too much—being married and all. But some change is to be expected, I guess. I've changed—I'm almost Greta Garbo now! Ha-ha! Umm. I wonder what Gina thinks of Greta Garbo. We'll just have to find out.'

Cindy's bizarre thoughts were engaged all the way home. She was feeling delightfully euphoric in response to her impending HRRC transitioning. She had even decided to tone down her sarcasm recalling how Margie—who obviously knew the particulars of Casten's maternity leave policy—responded to Claudia's feigned concern and pretentious bullshit. Claudia was a little nicer to Margie though. 'Ump! And I always thought it was because Margie was noticeably quiet, homely looking, and someone even Claudia wouldn't envy—even though she was married with children and a husband not about to run off. But on second thought maybe Claudia tolerated her better because she was polite to her. I'll try it.'

Truth be told, Claudia was less receptive to younger, vibrant and attractive single females. After her husband ran off with one, all females who could be described as such, Claudia resented. It was sad because her bitterness had taken its toll. Any older man that could have possibly found Claudia to be worth at least an exploratory first dinner would more than likely have left her at the table after salad. Her facial scowls were indelibly etched, and her husky black bifocals against her pale white skin added no value. And she was scrawny.

Having pulled into her apartment complex parking lot, Cindy circled around and drove right back out. 'I'm going to get a real treat for dinner. Guess I'll go to the deli and get a salad and pastrami on rye. Then I'll head over to the strip mall and rent some more movies.'

The local delicatessen had the best sandwiches and salads imaginable. It had been a while since she had been there, but that place was truly unforgettable. She ordered her pastrami and salad, paid and moved onward. Her next stop would be to rent more of Greta's talkies. Entering the Movie Masters rental place, she ran into one of her neighbors.

"Hey, Cindy. How are you?"

"Fine, Carlos. How are you?"

"Not too bad. My wife has one of these bad summer colds so she sent me out to round up a stack of movies for her."

"Oh, sorry to hear that. Guess plenty of hot tea with lemon and honey, huh?"

"That and bed rest," Carlos replied.

"Well, give her my regards. See ya." Cindy had no interest in continuing that humdrum conversation. Carlos, although not too bad on the eyes had a little crush on Cindy but the feeling was not mutual. He'd always want to stop and hold a long, worthless conversation that was nothing more than a waste of time. Cindy had developed a knack for cutting him off and leaving.

Over in the "Classics" aisle, Cindy looked and looked for anything featuring Greta Garbo that she had not already seen. The first three talkies she'd rented were all from MovieTime, and that's all the Greta they had. Rather frustrated since she found nothing in Movie Masters' Classics section, she approached the attendant. "Do you have any Greta Garbo movies that she made in the 1930s. I don't want any of the silent ones—the ones where she has talking roles are what I'm looking for."

"Do you have any titles, Miss? We catalog our movies by titles, not stars."

"Oh no. I don't. Why wouldn't she be in the Classics section?"

"For one, our Classics section doesn't quite go back that far. But we might have one or two Garbo movies in some other sections. That's why if you had a title, I could better help you."

"Oh. You know, I do!" Just at that point Cindy remembered her list of Greta's talking features was still in her briefcase, as she'd used it for the first three talkies she'd rented. "I'll be right back!"

Rambling through her briefcase's rather organized folders she found the Garbo computer listing in her "Miscellaneous" folder. Back inside, she started running down the list of movies for the attendant to search out. He didn't have Camille, he didn't have Mata Hari, she'd already seen Conquest, Two-Faced Woman, and Grand Hotel—but he did have Ninotchka.

"Great! I'll take it. What section?"

"Comedy Classics."

"Thanks so much." With that, Cindy was on her way to search for Ninotchka. 'Shit—now it's a fucked-up name that looks like an acronym that I can't pronounce!' Having searched and found it, Cindy was back at the desk for checkout.

"Is that it, Miss?"

"Yes. Can you pronounce this title?"

"No. That'll be three dollars and it's due back Sunday." The attendant wasn't rude, just matter of fact. His response didn't bother Cindy though. She was undaunted by personalities like that as she sometimes responded the same way.

"No prob-lem-o. See ya." She rounded the other side of the counter, received her movie and departed. At home, she'd enjoy her food and feature. The mood and the madness were all that mattered.

Of all the Garbo talkies she had seen, Ninotchka turned out to be her favorite. It was the comedic story of a Soviet official who went to Paris on government business but succumbed to romance. Melvin Douglas was the man who put the move on Greta's Ninotchka character and got to take her panties off too.

"Wow!" Cindy spoke out. "Alonzo Prier is my Melvin Douglas! The theme fits. And now I can even pronounce that Russian name 'Ninotchka'. Actually, it's robustly sexy! Yeah. Come to think of it, that's how Greta came off. She was robustly sexy. And witty. I like that!" Cindy was now laughing aloud in reflecting over Ninotchka, a 1939 production winner, having received four Academy Awards nominations. "And I like her voice too. It's direct and stern but sensual. I can see why she could have been a lesbian. There was something man-ishly demanding about her. Interesting."

She re-wound the movie and decided to busy herself with something else. She'd sort her laundry for Saturday's visit to the Laundromat and do whatever else necessary to accomplish her typical weekend chores.

With housework and mind games, Cindy busied herself until about eleven o'clock. She thought about turning on the news but quickly changed her mind towards possibly hearing any horrific events. To the peaceful sound of golden silence, she manicured her nails. Nothing noteworthy occurred from Saturday morning through Sunday night. Having struggled through yet another boring weekend, Monday morning was now manifesting as a Godsend.

Monday morning she woke up feeling a sense of purpose. Her alarm's beep- beep- beep, she'd likened to Marvin Gaye's *Let's Get It On*. And that was workable! Besides, it was Monday, July tenth! She was scheduled to re-connect with Gina at noon.

Out of the house and on the way to Casten's to retrieve her weekly roster, her mood remained elevated. This was the first time in a long time that even the boring weekend hadn't dampened her spirit. Cindy was viewing herself as 'being on to something', and for the most part, all she could imagine was that the 'something' was 'someone'. And that someone of course, Alonzo.

Arriving on time and now in Claudia's office, Cindy offered a non-intrusive greeting. "Good morning, Claudia. Since we spoke Friday, I'll just take my weekly roster."

"Fine. By the way, I've decided how to revamp your schedule to accommodate the HRRC. The PAAOC has to go since that one directly conflicts with the HRRC, and from the way it appears, the proposed second HRRC meetings will conflict with your ARSC meetings. So, beginning with the fourth week of August, instead of the PAAOC on Monday at ten, you'll have the HRRC from 9:30 until noon. Then in September, the following Tuesday, instead of the ARSC at ten, you'll be back at the HRRC from 9:30 until noon. That's the way I understand Mr. Prier wants these meetings conducted. Full continuity. He's really fast-tracking this stuff. I hope he finds what it is he's looking for." Claudia was giving the impression that she was concerned about what was going on. She was certainly revamping Casten's stenographers to handle the fallout of the Health Department's and the Office of the Attorney General's plight. Cindy still couldn't help but wonder if Claudia also had a secret crush on Alonzo. This time, she asked.

"Claudia. Uh, have you ever met Mr. Prier?"

"No. I've never formally met him, but I have seen pictures of him in the newspaper with the Health Commissioner. He's a handsome man."

Wantonly smiling, Cindy replied, "Yes, he is."

"He's also a married man—with children—I've heard."

"Yes, he is. See you Friday, Claudia." Deciding not to pursue Claudia's deliberate "don't even think about it" subtlety, Cindy left her office with her assignments in hand.

She arrived at the PAAOC meeting and set up her apparatus with about fifteen minutes to spare. She'd made unusually good time in getting to the meeting that day. As she sat waiting for the meeting to begin, she reflected over her three-year stint with that committee.

True, little or no progress had seemingly been made. Three years and still running without any discernable milestones, but she'd become somewhat partial to the way all of the State's representatives articulated their positions. She liked their philosophical viewpoints and the way they expressed themselves. Oddly enough, she recognized that with the prospect of moving on, she was going to miss the PAAOC's final deliberations. She wouldn't be there for the outcome of the rising cost of prescription drug plight.

With the meeting now in motion so was she. Typing and posing away. These meetings were the practice runs for forming her new Greta appeal. Again, some of her moves were hysterical and looked totally ridiculous but no one was watching anyway, so she thought.

At 11:40 a.m., the PAAOC secretary called for a motion to end the meeting. With the motion made and meeting over, Cindy was packed and raring to go at 11:48. 'Great! I'll rush over to the South Broad Building and meet Gina in the cafeteria,' she said to herself.

It was about ten after twelve when Cindy rushed into the South Broad Building's cafeteria. Gina had taken the liberty to order Cindy's lunch. Upon mutual sightings, Gina beckoned her over. "Hey! Girl, it's so good to have lunch with you again! I ordered for you. Sit down. I knew you'd be in a rush."

"Thanks, Gina! And yeah—it's great to be back with you too! How much do I owe you?"

"Nothing. This one's on me. But we'll do it like this. Since you're pushin' your ass off to get here, I'll get your lunch and you just leave your money with me afterwards. Just make sure I always know what you want me to order you. Deal?"

"Deal. You're still the best. You know, I don't have any girlfriends that amount to the friendship we had. As a matter of fact, I don't have any girlfriends at all!"

"Well, what in the hell do you do with yourself?" You're not dating anybody either, right?"

"Right. Nothing. This is the worst. And I don't understand it! It's like I've been left out of the game of life."

"You must do something—sometimes, huh?" Gina had cut straight to Cindy's chase.

"What do you think about Greta Garbo?"

"Greta Garbo? What? Who? What the hell would you be thinking about Greta Garbo for? Isn't that some dead actress from years ago?" Gina was now questioning Cindy's curve ball from left field.

"I've—umm—I've—uh—picked up on a hobby, I guess. I'm getting into movie classics and classic movie stars. She was supposedly every man's fantasy mistress. I'm not even on any man's mind. So, I figured I'd find out what worked for her and work some of her for me."

Gina, visibly stunned by Cindy's explanation, candidly responded. "Cindy, you really have too much time on your hands. Why don't you just hang out with some of those single women at Casten on Friday nights and meet some eligible guys. Remember? That's what we used to do. My goodness, it hasn't been that long!"

"You know, Gina, there's something else. In the back of my mind, I keep having this thought that I want to be roughed up a little. Like being riled up so I can fight back! Like tussled—maybe?"

"And dead-ass Greta Garbo is supposed to get you roughed up a little? That's crazy—really, Cindy. Get a grip. You need something and someone to occupy your mind and your time. If I wasn't pregnant, I'd hang out with you. Now I'm feeling bad that I haven't been there for you with you talking all crazy and shit! You damn sure weren't talking about some long-forgotten movie star when we were hanging out. I just think you need a girlfriend—or better yet, a man! And once you get a man, you'll be fine. But in the meantime, get a girlfriend!"

Although Cindy didn't let on, that was precisely one of her biggest fears. A girlfriend? Would people assume she was a lesbian like her idol if she chose a girlfriend? No! Now was not the time to start cultivating a new female relationship. "I don't really want a girlfriend. I'm a firm believer in the fact that you can't look back. You and I were great girlfriends. That's not necessarily something you can recover through somebody else. It's either there or it's not."

"Yes, but Cindy, you've got to start somewhere with somebody. You and I didn't start out thinking that we'd be the best of friends. It happened over time. But you need to start putting yourself in motion to get some new people in your life— not dead ass movie stars! Couldn't you choose somebody that's alive? What about Pricilla Presley? Elvis' wife. Shit. There you'd have the best of both worlds. Dead-ass superstar Elvis, and his gorgeous very-much-alive ex-wife!"

Recognizing it was time to pay a little more attention to their lunch, Gina and Cindy became less talkative. Gina was analyzing Cindy's odd thought process; Cindy was caught up in analyzing herself in relation to Gina's comments. Nonetheless, it was a good thing that Cindy and Gina had re-connected. Cindy needed a point of reference for grounding.

With a needed subject change and time-out to eat, Cindy regenerated their conversation with, "So when's the baby due?"

"My doctor says around the first week of January."

"You've got five months to go! Gina, you know I want to be there for you."

"Thanks, Cindy. I certainly appreciate that. Dan has two sisters, and they're wonderful too, but if you're there that's all the better. Speaking of sisters, how are your two?"

"I don't have the foggiest. The three of us are so radically different. One on Sag Harbor, the other on a sagging harbor. I'm in the middle. We hardly ever communicate."

"That's a shame. Since you're not all that busy these days why don't you reach out?"

"I admit it. It's tough. Neither of them wants to be bothered for different reasons—I don't want to be bothered for my own reasons."

"Cindy, I'm convinced. Your life is rather unusual."

With that, their hour lunch break was over. They both needed to get on with the next half of their separate and distinct afternoons. As they left the cafeteria, Cindy decided to surreptitiously try Alonzo on Gina...again. "Oh! I'm being transitioned over to the Hospital Rate Review Commission in August. That's the one that Alonzo Prier is Senior Counsel for. Can you imagine? I get to work with him again!"

"A fate worse than death, huh Cindy?"

"What? Why would you say that?"

"What I do know is that Alonzo Prier is in love with his wife, and his three kids. All women that go after Alonzo end up as dead birds. Hey! Maybe that Greta thing of yours is right on! She's dead. Keep following in her tracks and on Alonzo's trail. You'll be a dead duck too—emotionally. Cindy, I keep warning you. Don't go after a married man who has no interest in being gotten. Don't go there!"

"And you know that how?"

Almost whispering, as they were now on the crowded elevator, Gina's parting remarks to Cindy were, "He's my boss's best friend. I know a lot more about him than you do. And I don't know all that much. We'll talk Cindy, but please, don't go there. For your own sake! Call me—we'll talk. I'll need to get your order for next time too. See ya."

Cindy left the elevator for her JHPTC meeting, while Gina continued upwards. Cindy's floor was also host to the concession stand where all frequenters of the South Broad Street building could stop and buy anything from breath mints to newspapers. Walking over to where she'd be recording the JHPTC's public session, she'd recalled how she spotted Gina walking towards the elevator. Gina had a definitive walk, as well as a definitive position on life.

She checked her watch. 12:57 p.m. Cindy moved swiftly into the room where the JHPTC meeting was to be held and immediately beheld the likes of the Task Force Secretary. He was sitting at the U-shaped table, head down, flipping through a barrage of papers. As Cindy walked down the long aisle to the table's end where she usually positioned her stenographic set-up, a few public participants were already dispersed throughout the room. The little balding secretary was usually in place no matter what time Cindy arrived. In nearing the table, he looked up and spoke.

"Hello, Ms. Jack. How are you this *fine* day?" He placed a detectable emphasis on the word fine, which Cindy chose to overlook and play on, at the same time.

"Fine." That was her immediate response, followed by an insincere smile. Her immediate thought was, 'You sure aren't fine.'

He never expressed anything sexual, but Cindy could sense that he was thinking something sinful. 'I know what it is that I don't like about him. He gives me the impression of a dirty old man. He just looks creepy!'

He continues speaking, "You arrived a little earlier than usual today. Any reason why?"

"No." Cindy responded emotionlessly as she busied herself in set-up of her apparatus.

She gave him the cold shoulder, so he elected to not comment any further.

A few minutes later, the Secretary was making his usual introductory statements for the record. Cindy was typing and posing away. In betwixt and between his all too familiar canned speech, he was paying close attention to Cindy. She was also displaying her newly adopted sultriness, making it difficult for Mr. Secretary to keep his eyes off her. As the participants of the JHPTC were amid their heated discussion, Mr. Secretary was in somewhat of a hot seat himself, as the task force members kept watching him too.

Cindy somehow picked up on the feeling that she was being stared at, when abruptly their eyes met. Cindy's silent thought at that moment was— 'And just what in the hell are you looking at? The word man is wasted on you! You're just a male—at best.' Without further silent commentary, Cindy noticeably rolled her eyes away and kept typing.

Seemingly captivated by Cindy, Mr. Secretary was having difficulty in appropriately monitoring the meeting. The participants; a few times, had to get his attention to move on to the next speaker.

"And if there are no further comments, may I have a motion to conclude this meeting?"

John Waterston, CEO of Maytown Memorial made the motion to conclude. Jim Fisher, COO of St. Charbel's Medical Center, seconded the motion. It was three forty-five p.m.

As Cindy was packing up, the Secretary was making his way over. Although appearing nervous, he spoke anyway. "Ms. Jack, may I interest you in a cup of coffee?"

"No."

Trying to cover up his all-too-obvious interest and save face, he quickly retorted. "I just mean the coffee that's in the back of the room from the meeting. I don't think anyone drank any today. I wasn't asking you out if that's what you thought!"

Cindy was just listening to him babble. 'Yeah, right', she thought. "Thanks for the clarification. I still don't want any coffee." Silently thinking again, 'and why would I drink that coffee that probably tastes like shit by now?'

Dejectedly, the man walked away.

IV

Brass Tactics

MEANWHILE, AT THE ATTORNEY GENERAL's Office, Alonzo, in concert with the Health Department staff, were in preparation for the acceleration of the Hospital Rate Review proceedings. If the State were no longer going to tightly hold the monitoring reins, all ninety hospitals, public and private, would require a closer look before the State would feel comfort in letting go. It was within the scope of the Health Department's and the Office of the Attorney General's duty to ensure public protection. They had to know; far beyond a reasonable doubt, whether the hospitals were financially viable or not. The ones that weren't, the State would have to make special concessions and provisions for, until they became financially viable. If any were in too bad a condition, the State could revoke its license. At any rate, review of all ninety hospitals' financial status, up through fiscal year 1998, had to be achieved. To date, only thirty-five had been placed under the microscope, and granted a clean bill of health. And this was all happening while the hospitals were having nursing staff problems. The nurses throughout the State had bonded in the bewilderment of more dread and highly contagious disease exposure requiring longer shifts, with no commensurate raises in pay!

It was now four o'clock, time for Alonzo's emergency staff meeting. He'd excused himself from his earlier meeting to update his staff on the urgency of the matters at issue. Six Deputy Attorney Generals, responsible for the business of the Department of Health and the Department of Insurance, reported to him as Section Chief.

"This is a late breaking meeting, Alonzo. We must be onto something serious again." Debbie North, thirty-eight years old, was one of Alonzo's most senior people, whom he admired, for her work ethic.

"Whatever it is, we'll get through it. We always do." Thom Reily, thirty years old, was another strong performer in Alonzo's camp.

"Yeah, folks. This is big. Is everybody here? Yep." Alonzo was getting ready to go into full effect as Section Chief hovering over a few rather serious issues for the Governor, the Health Department and the public-at-large. "Damn near everybody in the State as a resident or as an employee is potentially affected by this one. You guys have heard all the buzzing and by now I would suspect that you all know the gravity of both the deregulation issue and the proposed labor strike. Is there anyone here who is unaware?"

None responded, Alonzo continued. "Great. That brings me to the purpose of this quick meeting. I met with the Health Commissioner earlier this week and we're beefing up the HRRC scheduling. I'm not going to be as available to you all since most of my time will be spent in ensuring that we send these hospitals off, if deregulation happens, in good standing. Even if deregulation happens, it won't be effective until one year after the date of the vote. But, if we find hospitals that are financially impaired, we'll either devise a corrective action plan or possibly revoke licenses. We can't allow any hospital to be operating under financial duress and stumbling around in a non-regulated environment. That's possible disaster to any person who may be a patient in such a hospital. And at least three of you know; those who are working the Health and Insurance issues with me, that, I've got some minor concerns with two of the thirty-five hospitals reviewed so far. But there's one other hospital—a State hospital—that I'm extremely concerned with. There're enough outstanding financial and reporting issues there that I'm probably going to call an investigation. The Health Department brought them to my attention recently."

"Which hospital, Alonzo? I've been noticing some irregularities that consistently show up on Harrington State General's financials." Lindy Jewel, thirty years old, was Alonzo's third and final stellar performer. She would always go above and beyond the call of duty, and the call she'd just made, proved that fact. Lindy was also the one that Alonzo would ask to review the matters that he held closely, such as those very same HRRC matters. Lindy, Debbie and Thom were Alonzo's Health and Insurance Deputies. The other three were his Insurance Only Deputies, assigned to property/casualty business. They pretty much remained silent during the meeting.

"That's the one! Harrington State General has problems. Big problems too. And they're not forthcoming about them either. There's something wrong there. I've already spoken with Dr. Morris about Harrington. She suggests we do what we've got to do." Dr. Gwendolyn Morris, forty-nine years old, was the State's Health Commissioner.

"So, guys…Greg, Tyler, Steven, if you need me, I'll be mostly on Health and hospital business. But if you really need me for property/casualty issues, I'll be there. Try and handle them yourselves first though. Debbie, Lindy and Thom, I'm going to be leaning on you guys a lot. Our plates are going to be extremely full researching, investigating, reviewing, fact-finding, and working with Independent Counsel and Financial Consulting Firms. Lindy, Charlie Monahan from McCarther and Parks will be contacting you for further issues' analysis. Charlie is a Senior Vice President with M&P and will be heavily involved with the statistical and financial projections vis-à-vis deregulation. Debbie, Michael Neely, a Vice President with M&P, will be calling you within a week to discuss the labor strike concerns from our perspective. So, let's schedule a lunch meeting Thursday so I can brief you. Questions anyone? Speak now. Okay, if there're no questions, that's it then. Progress reports due Friday. No exceptions; no excuses."

"No problem. Have a nice evening." Debbie commented and exited.

"Sure thing, Alonzo. Whatever you need, you got it!" Thom followed suit.

"Let the games begin! I can just feel it. You're gearing up to ride herd over Harrington! And you know what, I think they deserve it. When I looked at those numbers, I said 'they can't be serious.' Those financial reports they submit are ridiculous." Lindy was still on the case.

"Lindy, I want to do lunch with you too next week. Have Anna check my schedule and schedule you in." Anna was Alonzo's secretary.

"Will do," Lindy replied smiling.

"Just one last thing for the property/casualty side of the house.

Guys, do your homework, no shortcuts. If you make a mistake on a technicality that's reasonably understandable, I'll support you. If you make a mistake because you were shooting from the hip, I'll fire you. Forewarned is forearmed." Alonzo had covered all the bases.

None of the about to exit three said a mumbling word, but they all got the message. And with that, Greg Mathis, Tyler Cordon and Steven Bowman filed out, with Steven offering a tad of a comment. "Gee, I wish the property/casualty business had a little more kick. Seems like you guys are on to something that could make headlines with that Health Department business. Best wishes, Mr. Prier. Let me know if I can help." Steven was a go-getter type of guy, and a hard worker, but unseasoned. He was the youngest of the Deputies, being twenty-nine years old.

Smiling also, Alonzo replied, "And thanks for your support, Mr. Bowman."

Alonzo looked at his watch. It was 4:40. He would have quite enough time to make an exploratory phone call to his best friend and colleague. He exited the small conference room where he and his staff usually assembled for meetings. He rushed past Anna's desk, into his office, closed the door and headed straight to the phone.

"Good afternoon. Commissioner Garretson's office. Gina Falcone speaking."

"Hey there, Gina. This is Alonzo. How are you?"

"Oh, hello, Alonzo! I'm fine—getting more pregnant every day, though."

"Just hang in there! The big day will soon arrive. Is my buddy Ted around?"

"Yes. He's in his office. I'll tell him you're on the line. Hold on please."

"Ted, Alonzo is on your line. Can you take his call now?"

"Sure, Gina. Thanks."

"Alonzo, I'll put you through. Nice speaking with you."

"Thanks, Gina."

"Hey, Azo! What's up?" Theodore "Ted" Garretson was the Governor's choice for the Department of Environmental Protection Commissioner. He and Alonzo attended and graduated law school together ten years ago. As a matter of fact, it was because of Ted that Alonzo "Azo" Prier met and married his beautiful wife, Shawna Vaglione. Shawna was Ted's wife's cousin, and she and Alonzo met at Ted's wedding eight years ago. It was love at first sight, and he'd married Shawna six years ago.

"I've got a State hospital that's in serious trouble. They aren't exactly being up front about what's happening there, so I've decided to go on an exploratory expedition before I start a formal investigation on them. There're a couple of questions I need you to answer for me first though."

"Sure. Umm, what are you doing tonight? Want to grab dinner so you can fill me in?"

"Yeah, sounds good. Let me call Shawna first and make sure my home-front is okay."

"Fine. I'll give Jan a call too. I'll call you back in about ten or fifteen."

"Thanks, Ted." Alonzo quickly dialed Shawna's cell phone.

"Hello?"

"Hello, sweetheart."

"Hi, honey. Everything okay?" Shawna had a sexy sweet voice that always tended to give Alonzo a warm fuzzy feeling.

"Yeah, Baby. I'm fine. Kids, okay?"

"Yep. Right now, we're at your parent's house, just getting ready to leave when I heard my phone. What's going on with you?"

"Listen, stay over there, you and the kids have dinner with them tonight. I've got to meet with Ted about a troublesome work-related issue; so, he and I are having dinner tonight. I'll be home about nine. Okay, Love?"

"Sure. No problem. See you then."

"Oh, Shawna, put Mom on please."

"Hold on." Shawna was a great wife. Probably because she knew how to handle her great husband. She knew exactly how to juggle the roles of wife, lover and mother. She also looked like and had the body of a sultry seductive model. But with all of that, she was demure and not vain nor demanding, all of which added to their healthy, supportive, mutual respect and trust for one another.

"Nan, Alonzo wants to speak with you." Nan, short for Nana as per the kids, Nannette, being her given name, was Alonzo's mother.

Receiving the phone, Nan was happy to hear from her younger son. "Hello, stranger. If it weren't for Shawna's lovely self coming by with my grandchildren occasionally, I wouldn't even remember that I had a son, Mr. Alonzo Prier." Nan was pleasant about it, but Alonzo could have stood to visit his parents a bit more.

"I know, Mom. It's just that I'm so busy and on the weekends, I try and get Shawna and the kids in. Before the summer's end, we'll have a barbecue. My yard. You and Dad stay over with us that weekend. We'll have a blast! Anyway, Mom, I've got to run. If it's not too much of a bother, would you mind Shawna and the kids staying for dinner? I won't be in until late tonight."

"Not at all! You know they're welcome anytime, Alonzo. I wish you could join us. Your dad would be ecstatic. Your brother comes by with his two girls all the time. But you know your dad—he's more partial to those boys of yours. Reminds him of when you and Wallace were growing up."

"Thanks, Mom. Love you. See you soon."

"Okay, dear. Do you want to speak with Shawna again? Never mind she's changing Chloyee's little underwear. She's growing so fast—eighteen months now! My how time flies. She's even wearing those little pull-ups. Oh, how adorable!"

"Right, Mom. Gotta go. Bye." Feeling comforted about his family's dinner plans, he waited for Ted's return call and began reviewing more of Harrington General's financial documents heaped atop his desk. "This just doesn't make sense. None of these numbers make any damn sense at all! What is going on there? What in the hell are they doing?" Perplexed and concerned, Alonzo was speaking aloud—something rather uncharacteristic for him. Just then his telephone rang—his private-line button was blinking.

"Azo, I'm okay at home base. What about you?" 'A-zo', was Ted's nickname for Alonzo, that had spread like wildfire amongst close friends and family members. It sort of implied that the man was always in the A-zone of whatever he'd sat out to accomplish.

"Squared away too. What about The Brewsky Steak-N-Ale? A few beers and a London Broil should do it."

"Absolutely. Meet you there at six."

"Cool."

V

And Never The Twain Shall Be

A s Cindy entered her apartment complex, she couldn't get her mind off her lunch conversation with Gina. 'It was great reconnecting with Gina, but we still have some unfinished business. Like her telling me she knows Alonzo better than I do. What's that about? How could she know him better than I do? I worked with the man. She didn't. I need to call her. I've got to find out what in the hell she's talking about. Oh, but, if I do, she'll just tell me how much I'm obsessing over him. Maybe I am. So what! Besides, it was a Monday when she'd called me—Dan's at that little league shit, and Gina could use a rap session. I'm calling her.'

Finishing up another makeshift dinner she got comfortable to call. 'Gina should be game for gab right about now.'

"Hello?"

"Hey, Gina. It's Cindy. I just wanted to tell you how much I really enjoyed lunch today. If this works for you, I'll certainly keep pushing my ass to get over there. It's the perfect spot for us."

"Oh! No doubt! It was great—just like old times. And guess what, Cindy? Alonzo called my boss today. Oh, I haven't told you anything about him yet. Did I ever tell you his name?"

"Your boss? No."

"Theodore Garretson. Everybody calls him Ted. He's another one that the Governor adores. And he's great to work for. He's about forty-five, has one cute son, about seven years old; he's very married— wife's

62

a stockbroker—and he and Alonzo are best friends. Oh, Alonzo called him this evening right before I left."

"So that's what you meant by knowing Alonzo better than I do?"

"Sort of, yeah."

"Well—what else?"

"Ted's the reason that Alonzo met his wife Shawna. Ted's wife Jan is Shawna's cousin. They met at Ted's wedding. Ted always teases Alonzo about how he freaked out when he saw Shawna and hasn't been back to earth since."

"Really?"

"Really. And Ted has a picture in his office of the four of them at the Governor's mansion together, taken with the Governor. Shawna is beautiful. No wonder Alonzo went crazy when he found out she was available. She is gorgeous!"

Cindy was flabbergasted. This was now the second time she'd heard about Shawna's awesome pulchritude. And to make matters worse, she was being noticed and described by other women! An unheard of. Only men are supposed to notice and talk about the overwhelming beauty of a woman—not other women. Trying to be caviler, Cindy replied, "Well I bet she's got some flaws, just like the rest of us human underlings."

Right on the mark, Gina came back with, "Maybe. But your man Alonzo damn sure doesn't see them—and Cindy, that's all that counts!"

"Well what else is there?"

"They've got two boys, ages five and three, and an eighteen-month little girl. Her name is Chloyee. She's *so* cute! I don't know the boys' names. Ted is Chloyee's godfather. I had to run out and get Chloyee a card from Ted for her baptism a few months ago. He started her off with a $500 savings bond."

Cindy had had enough. Alonzo's life was so sweet it was sickening. How could she ever fit into his equation? Even Greta didn't seem like enough anymore. How disappointing. There were seemingly no cracks in the Alonzo/Shawna schematic for Cindy to seep through.

Picking up on Cindy's silence, Gina continued, "I keep telling you, Cindy, Alonzo is not the man for you. He's locked up tight with his gorgeous woman—the wife and mother of his three kids. The man does not have affairs. He has *four* reasons not too! Cindy, I love you like a sister, and I'm only trying to spare you some pain. Alonzo, as a lover, is not going to come through for you. Quit while you're ahead and nobody knows but me."

"Thanks, Gina. I truly value your friendship and your advice. I just really wanted to touch bases tonight to say what I said… lunch was great. You know—I'll call you next week with my meal request. Thanks. I love you Gina—gotta go. Gotta fix dinner. Bye." Cindy had already eaten dinner. She lied to Gina to save face from having her Alonzo yearnings totally exposed. Giving into her emotions, tears streamed her face. She'd finally realized that she had a crush on Alonzo from the first day she saw him. He was married then. But she never got close enough to give credence to his band of gold. She was so mesmerized by his presence that she only looked into his eyes and up to him. She should have looked down at his left hand and observed what had already transpired.

And then again, somewhere along the timeline, she had heard that he was married with children. But no longer in proximity, she'd pushed him into the recesses of her mind as the most memorable and admirable man she'd ever met. So, when she happened upon him again and he remarked about her excellent stenographic skill, she wanted to believe he'd possibly kept a secret yearning for her.

Her thoughts continuing aloud, "It's almost nine o'clock. There're no movies I want to watch, I don't want to see the news, and I'm not in the mood to listen to music. Maybe I'll give Bess a call. She never calls me though. Never mind, that's just another dead end. What would we talk about anyway? Her mansion and her dog named Fee-Fee. Everything is about money—twice over with them. She and her prominent vascular surgeon husband. She even named their damned dog to confirm it! I can just hear her now, 'Oh, Fee-Fee, I like chasing money. So, if you're going to chase cars, make sure they're Mercedes, Bitch. I'm going to bed."

Now alone in bed, she realized she'd retired for the night way too early and having difficulty falling asleep. She succumbed to her mind's aimless wandering…again. Having heard about Alonzo's three children, and moments earlier thinking about her childless sister Bess, she'd latched onto a couple of thoughts about her other sister Eve.

'Maybe I do need to reach out to Eve. I've reconnected with Gina, and it's great. I could start by calling and finding out when dog-dick isn't home. That should be often. I'd get to know my niece and nephew. Like Gina said, my life is rather unusual. Maybe I do need some family in my life so at least I'd appear to be normal, like everybody else—appears to be.' And with those thoughts, Cindy finally drifted off.

It's 9:21 p.m. when Alonzo pulls into his driveway. Tapping the garage door opener and parking alongside Shawna's new silver Volvo, he twisted around in his immaculate high-end BMW to retrieve his briefcase from the back seat. He realized at that moment that he'd made the decision to do Shawna when he got home, not more work. She'd intuited as much. Upon entering their semi-palatial home, Shawna was awaiting her husband's arrival. Their oversized marble-mantled fireplace was glowing from an inside grate holding twelve lit candles. A bottle of chilled wine sitting in a wine-chiller accentuated by two golden etched wine glasses graced their Oriental-styled living room coffee table. Sade's Greatest Hits CD was softly playing in the background, and the sensual essence of aromatic fragrances wafted romantically about the house. Shawna donned a silk emerald green see-through teddy, with four tiny buttons slinking down the crevice of her voluptuous breasts. In perfect timing with him walking in the house, she was seductively sauntering down their spiral staircase. Alonzo stood almost mesmerized at the bottom of the staircase, watching her long-sexy legs approaching by the dim living room light. She was a well-put together young woman who'd captivated her husband.

He looked up into her dark beautiful eyes. Her full lips parted to sensuously greet his. She softly asked, "Hey, how's my man?" She smiled.

"Umm, all good now. Couldn't be better," he replied. Where're the kids?"

"Boys at your parents, Chloyee sound asleep. I'm all yours for whatever."

Music to his ears. "So, let's get busy, Baby." His voice changed to a subdued sensual tone, "Life has a way of pulling us through challenges.

But it all comes in crystal clear in the end though. And this is a good night's end. I love you, Shawna." Aroused by her and the ambience, Alonzo was in full effect.

Not knowing what he was particularly referencing didn't matter. Yet another one of her qualities. She had a knack for knowing what and what not to question. Not the time to get him worked up over work. She loved pleasuring and being pleasured by her fine man. She replied softly in his ear, "I love you too. Busy me, Baby."

Tuesday morning arrived at the sound of beep, beep, beep. Off went Cindy's alarm. Showering, she tried to recall if she'd ever heard a song about Tuesday. "Didn't the Beatles write something about Tuesday? Whatever." Not expressly focused on the day's attire she decided on a simple beige denim skirt and pullover top. "I don't feel sexy today, I just wantta be comfortable."

By 9:47 a.m., she was pulling into the parking lot of the building hosting the ARSC meeting. Being careful not to think aloud she internalized her next series of thoughts. 'I'm on time again; this is another meeting that I'm going to somewhat miss, and it's sad. I think the ARSC gave me some insight about Eve. I never realized alcoholism is an illness until I started taking dictation for ARSC. But I'm not willing to stay on this ship when I can be aboard Alonzo's luxury liner. So, it is bon-voyage, ARSC!'

Cindy couldn't help but laugh to herself as the ARSC discussion became lively and heated. Betwixt and between striking keys and striking poses she fought to hold back laughter. Some of the commentaries were off the wall.

"What did you say, Mr. Kindler? Why in the world do you believe that the Insurance Department should *require insurance companies to pay more and offer more benefits for overnight stays?* Why are you looking for us to help line your pockets? Whose gonna line mine? And why would we fight your battle? It's not even statistically credible!" Commentary from Mr. Evert of the State Insurance Department.

"Care to respond to that, Mr. Kindler?" Mr. Secretary was seemingly riling up the participants in asking Mr. Kindler representing Fair Meadows Alcoholism Treatment Center to respond.

"I sure would, Mr. Secretary! I cringe to even dignify that comment with a response! But for the record, I must! Why should anyone *line your pockets, Mr. Evert, for doing your job and doing the right thing!* People that come to our facility need the help we provide!" Mr. Kindler boldly countered.

Mr. Evert boldly replied, "And who says you're doing the right thing? All the numbers suggest that you're pretty much running a beach house! Your recidivism rates are horrible! In and out, in and out, in and out is all that's happening there! How are people getting viable treatment if there's no efficacy, no substantive results? And for that, you want your reimbursement rates raised? *Poppycock!*" Mr. Evert threw his hand up in the air and waved it in disgust.

Cindy was silently smirking at these folks as it was becoming clear that the Secretary was unprepared to handle the dissention, timidly calling for the meeting to end. He uttered, "If there are no further comments, would someone *please* make a motion to conclude this meeting."

"There are further comments and there will be no conclusion of today's meeting until everyone who wants to express their opinion is heard! Is that clear, Mr. Secretary? It's only 10:45 for goodness sakes!" Another angry committee member hurling his remarks directly at the Secretary didn't bother to state his name of affiliation for the record.

The meeting continued at fever pitch until noon. All the yelling and screaming left participants somewhat hoarse by the end. One member in leaving expressed his overall dissatisfaction in heightened volume. "Mr. Secretary, you need to better control these meetings and diffuse these angry people! Isn't that part of your job?" Mr. Gleamer of the Department of Human Services was seemingly concerned with the propensity for these meetings to continue with personal attacks rather than substantive fact-finding. He didn't give the all-too-shaken Secretary a chance to respond. He just made his point and walked out.

The week progressed along to Thursday without much ado in anybody's camp, except for Alonzo's. He was busy rounding up the troops to do battle with what was looking more like an enemy of the State's structured hospital system. Wednesday, the formal environmental report Ted had promised was delivered to his office, but Alonzo, having been in New York that day for briefing sessions with McCarther and Parks, hadn't gotten the opportunity to review the document that Ted had sent via special delivery. Thursday morning upon nearing her desk, Anna interrupted his usual good morning greeting and continuing stride to his office. "Morning, Alonzo. This came hand-delivery for you yesterday afternoon. Looks like a package you'd want to review first thing."

"Thanks, Anna. Will do." Alonzo retrieved the goldenrod envelope stamped CONFIDENTIAL and proceeded into his office. He closed the door signaling the desire for uninterrupted privacy having noticed that the package was from the Department of Environmental Protection, Commissioner's Office. Attentively studying the contents and reading Ted's notes carefully, Alonzo now knew beyond a shadow of a doubt that Harrington could never play the "*it's the toxicity of the area that's causing our patients to be sicker than anywhere else in the State*" card. Just as Ted had previously said, the Compton County air could never be blamed for Harrington's excessively sick patient population because that was not an issue. After about fifteen minutes in deliberation over the information, Alonzo called Ted.

"Commissioner Garretson's office. Gina Falcone speaking. May I help you?"

"Hey there, Gina. Alonzo. Is Ted there?"

"Hello, Alonzo. Yes, he is. Hold on please."

"Azo! You read my report?"

"Yes, sir! Thanks a million, man. One door closed. I've still got two others to check before I hammer those clowns. But you called it before you researched and documented it! And like you pointed out, even the surrounding counties are clean. Thanks again. Shawna's going to give Janice a call about that barbecue. Invite your parents too, mine will be there. Gotta run, be in touch."

Ted ended with, "Yep. Keep me posted."

With that, Alonzo was on to his next move. He depressed the button on his phone clearing the line to immediately dial Lindy. "Lindy Jewel speaking."

"Lindy, Alonzo. I need you in my office, now please." He hung up the phone before she could respond. She soon arrived to his still closed office door. Looking at Anna for direction, Anna shrugged as if to say, if he called knock on his door. She did.

He responded, "Come in."

"Good morning, Alonzo. Everything ok?"

"Things are beginning to look more suspicious but at the same time there's a lot more clarity. Close the door please and have a seat."

Lindy was the consummate professional. She'd always arrive with pen and notepad in hand.

Alonzo continued, "I asked DEP Commissioner Garretson for an assessment of Compton County, Harrington hospital's local. Environmentally, that's one of the cleanest counties in the State so they can't claim their unusually high Average Length Of Stay days are because of excessive toxic and carcinogenic levels in the area, something that they'd been alluding to when asking the Health Commissioner for emergency cash infusions. Even the surrounding counties are clean. There are a couple of other things I want to check and if I'm right, it's three strikes and they're on their way to a formal investigation."

Lindy added, "And that's not all. Even with those high ALOS days, their financials don't indicate that their supplies or meds are being depleted in correlation to those unusually high inpatient stays. Plus, I've noticed that some of their other variable costs, like utilities for example, are not rising either. If they have so many sick patients for extended lengths of time, wouldn't' they experience higher overhead costs too?"

"Of course. But we're dealing with the bizarre and absurd here. I'm going to have you do some additional fact-finding with the Health Department. If they've got legitimate reasons for what appears to be so strange, I'm all ears. Give Candice Bremmer a call, she's the Health Department Analyst who handles Harrington. You know her, right?"

"Yes."

"From Candice, find out when the last time their data systems were serviced; if they've hired any new data entry/data retrieval staff; if they've implemented any new reporting formats which could conceivably impact the integrity of the data they're required to submit to the Health Department; and if they hired any new personnel, I want hire dates and qualifications of those people. Also, get their drug costs over the last three years in concert with the specificity of the surgical procedures and any other high-end medical treatments done there too. Check for whether they had any new professional fees recently, and if so, for what. I want all of that documented for our files."

"Got it!"

Alonzo continued, "Those are just some of the peripheral questions before we get to the more technical and serious one. I'm looking for the smoking guns first. I know they're also on the Joint Hospital-Payer Task Force. What in the hell they're doing there only God knows. They should be busy properly running that hospital. Instead, Gary Numan's running his mouth on that task force.

"I'll get right on it, Alonzo."

"Thanks' Lindy." As she turned to leave, another thought came to mind. "Lindy, just a word of advice. Make sure you juggle your other assignments accordingly. This Harrington business is urgent and so are a few of your other cases. I don't want anything falling through the cracks."

And they all pressed on. Lindy started conversing with Candice Bremmer in tracking down the detail Alonzo had requested; Debbie was becoming more familiarized with the labor strike issues to meet with M&P; and Thom was gearing up for Alonzo's expanded scheduling of the HRRC meetings in concert with the appropriate Health Department staff. They had a long way to go, but they were all capable of going the distance.

VI

Be Anxious For Nothing

THE END OF THE FOURTH workweek of July hit like a ton of bricks. Friday morning, she was in her shower with steamy water cascading from the top of her head to the tip of her toes. She caught herself screaming to herself, *"Why have I been left out of the love game?!"*

Drying off she decided upon a new course of action. She'd go out and do something although unsure what. Anyway, in the kitchen for her coffee and quickly back to her closet for the look of the day, she thought aloud, "Since this is a Claudia encounter day, I'll just look drab. Besides, I want to save my sexy duds for when I'm in front of Alonzo again! Monday, August 28, nine-thirty sharp, I'll be taking down every word he says. And starting with those September sessions, I'll see him Mondays and Tuesdays for a very long time. *He's mine now. Jack*-pot!"

By day's end she was exhausted from the heaviness of the thoughts upon her heart and head; the droning of the day's meetings; and the tenseness her body was feeling from striking poses and trying to maintain while striking keys. She was beginning to do Greta justice with each passing State session and time.

At three-fifty, she was back at Casten. Margie had already arrived. In Claudia's office, they discussed a few details that were mostly Casten's administrative considerations. Not that Cindy needed to know, but Claudia was on a role discussing the changes she'd made to the stenographers' assignments in deference to Margie's leaving. "So, if Carol or Becky need to call while you're home, is that okay?"

"Sure, Claudia," Margie replied, "I doubt they'll need me, but I'll certainly be glad to help."

Cindy was thinking that Margie was just being gracious. With no other business, Margie, Cindy and Claudia said their farewells.

Driving home, Cindy had decided to go shopping on Saturday. She'd spice up her wardrobe with what she'd liken to *nouveau Greta*. Sometime on Sunday, she'd reach out to Eve. Those were the major weekend plans.

And so it was. Saturday was the shopping spree of the year. Cindy bought Victoria Secrets, Liz Claiborne, Dana Bachman, Ellen Tracy and a few other fabulous designer creations. Her credit card approached the limit with a whopping nine-hundred-seventy-five dollars charged! She couldn't help but wonder if that shopping spree was worth it but suddenly realized she'd never know if she hadn't done it. She graciously accepted her purchases in the ultimate knowing that the deed was done, and time would tell.

Sunday morning around ten and after coffee, she made a beeline to the phone having decided to call Eve. "Hi, it's Cindy."

"Cindy? My long-lost sister *Cindy*? And just how are you?" Eve's voice sounded strange. It was 10 a.m. and Eve sounded a bit sloshed. Her speech was somewhat slurred; her attitude seemingly condescending.

"I'm okay, Eve. It's been a while, true. I feel like we need to re-connect and get back to family ties. I miss you."

"You miss *me*? Come on, Cindy. You and I never had a damn thing in common, never got along. Now suddenly you miss me. Who the hell are you kidding? What do you want? And what is this family ties shit? Mom and Dad are dead! There are no more real family ties. Why the hell didn't you call Bess? Don't you always see yourself as more like Bess?" Eve was clearly imbibed.

"Eve, can you bury the hatchet? I called because I've been thinking about you, thinking about all of us lately and I want us to build the bond we should have always had as sisters, especially with Mom and Dad gone. I know we had our problems but we're older now. We should get together. I don't even really know my nephew and niece. How are Corey and Noel?"

"Corey's nine, and Noel –is um, seven. They're kids—like any other damn kids their ages. Anything else?"

With a commanding tone, Cindy said, "Eve, please! I didn't call you for a confrontation or for bullshit either. I love you. We're sisters. We should behave like sisters and be there for each other. Is that so distasteful to you?"

Eve had simmered down long enough for Cindy's words to penetrate. "I'm sorry. This is the absolute worst time of my life! Paul and I live like we're divorced; the kids are pains in the ass; and my life stinks, Cindy. My life fuckin' stinks! But what about you, *Miss Sunshine?* Do you have a fabulous story to tell and that's why you're calling?" Eve was becoming riled again.

No, Eve. Quite the opposite. My life is fucked up too, in a different way though. I have no love life; no girlfriends to speak of or hang out with; and I don't even have a pet. Shit, I don't even have a plant to come home to. And what's worse, I have two sisters I don't even communicate with. So, I'd like to change that."

"Quite commendable, Cindy. I applaud you."

"Eve, lose the sarcasm. I'm exactly like you in that way so I can call you out on that."

"You're right, Cindy. I've always thought of you as having everything, but I guess the only one of us who really does is Bess. And maybe she's not even happy. Who knows? But I can say sorry for my behavior and attitude. You're my little sister! My God! *You're my little sister.*" Eve started crying, slinking into the depths of depression without warning.

"Eve don't cry. Please stop crying. I called so we could get ourselves back together--- not break down. Let's get together. Um—let's start with lunch next Saturday or Sunday – alone. You're only about an hour away, or if you want, come to my house. I'm always alone."

Sobbing and in trying to make a better sounding of herself, Eve responded, "Okay. Umm – I don't drive much so umm, you come here, and maybe we can go out for lunch somewhere? I need to find out when Paul can be here to look after the kids or maybe the neighbors can. I'll call you back. Okay?"

Feeling like crying herself, Cindy ensured Eve had taken down her home and job cell numbers correctly by having her repeat them.

Knowing that Eve was in an altered state at 10 a.m. she could only image how the rest of Eve's alcohol impaired day would go. Eve clearly needed to be rescued—from Paul, the children, and most importantly, herself.

Eve hung up the phone realizing that she did want to see her sister. She'd felt a certain warmth inside emanating from someplace other than the reservoir of alcohol her body typically stored.

"Who was that Eve?" Paul was entering the kitchen as she had ended her Cindy conversation and now looking for a glass.

"It wasn't a woman looking for you! Surprised? It was for me! *That's right!* For me!" With an unnecessarily harsh tone, Eve spun around to answer Paul's seemingly innocent question. Her mind was racing through all the infidelities that he had so cavalierly dangled in her face throughout the years. Eve's recounting of the incoming calls for Paul from women she didn't know and him never telling her who they were intensified. All she knew was that they were calling for him. But she knew two other things—Paul was a sex hound, and he was good at it. Somewhat attractive and sexually adept, Paul had succumbed to his base nature tending to overlook the fact that he was married with children. It was Paul's indiscretions that took a toll on Eve's psyche and self-esteem eventually driving her to drink.

"You know something, Eve? You're a disgusting bitch. Is it really all that difficult for you to figure out why I'd want nothing to do with you? You're always drunk, always looking and feeling bad, and you're always cursing and hollering. At this point, Eve, I wouldn't screw you with another man's dick. That's just how much you turn me off. You should be ashamed of yourself. I'm certainly ashamed of you." Paul knew how to deliver the most horrific comments in a low monotone. Typically, with a controlled delivery, he would find words to bluntly slice Eve in half without any apparent emotion. He taught Eve that indifference was the opposite of love—not hate. And that absence of emotion was the loss to dread. Paul could not have been any more indifferent to her feelings, her desires, and her need for emotional support towards getting the help she needed for her alcoholism.

Eve bellowed, "*You motherfuckin' bastard! You're the reason I drink. If you weren't screwing other women all this wouldn't be happening! Why do those bitches call this house? This is my house and I'm your wife! Your kids live here! Don't you have any respect for that?"* Eve had gone into a full-blown rant!

"Shut up!" Paul's voice was slightly elevated and undeniably commanding. He never appreciated Eve's sailor-like vernacular and found it even more distasteful when their children were within earshot. "No, I don't have any respect *for you*. Look at yourself, you don't have any respect for you. I give you money to do whatever it is that floats your boat. Unfortunately, it's booze. All you can expect from me is money which you should be spending on the kids. Other than money, I've got nothin' for you. I'm warning you, Eve. If you don't stop drinking and learn to control your filthy mouth, you'll be outta here. Only reason you're still here is because you're the mother of my kids. Nothing else!"

With Paul's concluding remarks, Eve found herself sitting on the kitchen floor in a crying stupor. Fortunately, the children had not come down for breakfast to discover their mother's state of being. She heard Paul's Toyota pull out of the driveway and her crying intensified as she concluded he was off to meet some woman. She realized she could call Cindy and promptly started dialing. No sooner than Cindy said hello, Eve went right into a dysfunctional monologue.

"Cindy—I just can't come right now. I—just—can't do lunch with you. Maybe never either. Paul is off with some woman and I'm home alone. He left me again, Cindy. I don't know what to…"

Cindy interrupted her, "Eve! You're not making any sense. We weren't doing lunch today." Shaken and not knowing what to think, Cindy continued, "I'm coming over there. It's been a while, but I still know how to get to your house. It'll take me about two hours—I've got to get dressed and all—but I'll be there. Okay?"

"Okay, Cindy. Thank you. I need you, Cindy. Please come."

"I am, Eve. Where are the kids?" Cindy asked.

"Upstairs, I guess. I haven't seen them this morning yet. I don't want to see them—I don't want them to see me either!" Eve replied.

"Pull yourself together, Eve. Have some coffee and a shower. Eve, don't drink anymore—please." Still shaken, Cindy hung up. Readying to prepare for her trek and thinking aloud, "What in the world has happened to that marriage? I sure don't know what to do, but all I can do is go see her for now." Cindy was somewhat relieved that she wasn't too emotionally close to Eve. For had she been and with what she'd just experienced, she would have been in a frenzy too. After her shower she'd throw on a pair of jeans and oversized tee. Going to Eve's was certainly not a dress-to-impress occasion.

Driving, Cindy recalled an ARSC meeting where the Fair Meadows Center representative brought in an alcoholism treatment representative from a neighboring State. The woman, whose name Cindy didn't recall, gave a presentation entitled *Alcoholism Treatment Efficacy—What Works; What Doesn't.* She made impressive points about why treatment facilities cannot be held accountable for the high number of returns amongst alcoholics. Her concluding remarks centered around the fact that if the catalyst for what caused or contributed to the alcoholism is still existent in the everyday environment the person is returning to, no matter what progress has been made at the facility, it is likely to be reversed. There must be a strong supportive network of family and friends awaiting the return of the recovering alcoholic. The battle is an everyday uphill climb back to functionality in a relatively dysfunctional world. Cindy specifically remembered typing the woman's last statement--- Life is tough anyway; trying to recover from alcoholism makes it tougher.

With all her thoughts, she found it somewhat difficult to keep focused on the way to Eve's. She was already at a slight disadvantage since it had been about two years since she'd been there for their housewarming.

Having arrived, the sight of Eve was enough to make Cindy want to cry. "Eve! You look –um—Oh, Eve! I'm so – it's so good to see you." Embracing, they were crying. Eve looked awful. Her hair was unkempt; she'd taken a shower, but her clothing was not fresh, her skin was pale, and she had dark circles around her eyes from all the whiskey and worry. She had on makeup but to no avail. In trying to get it together and sport stiff upper lips, they both took deep breaths and stopped the tears.

"You want a drink, Cindy?"

"No, Eve, *dammit*, and you don't need one either! Are the kids here?"

Now knowing that the kids were safely with neighbors, Cindy soberly walked with Eve to the living room and sitting across from each other, Cindy started, "Eve, remember when you first brought Paul to meet Mom and Dad? I was twenty, you were twenty-four. Remember that Dad didn't like Paul because he noticed how Paul looked at me, he noticed him looking at Bess when she left the room. Dad said to you then…Eve, don't keep going on with that guy. He's not going to make you a good husband… Do you remember how *pissed* you got with me because Paul kept looking at me? Remember how mad you were with Dad because he told you the truth? You swore it was everybody else's fault that Paul was the way he was."

"What are you saying, Cindy? Are you here to lecture me? I need something, but it damn sure ain't a lecture from you!" Eve was blatantly angry.

"What I'm saying is that you need to take responsibility for marrying a man that you and everybody else knew was into women. Eve, you pushed Paul into marriage because you wanted to leave home. He wasn't ready for marriage. You were determined to prove everybody wrong about him! Paul hasn't changed and your thinking you could change him with marriage didn't work.

Even more angry, Eve continued, "Cindy, you're so *fuckin'* self-righteous! You know everything, or you think you do."

"Well, what is it that I said that's wrong? I'm not the scapegoat here for your anger! I'm your sister who just wants to help you get through this. I'm going to do that if you give me a chance. I'm going to get you into treatment and I'm going to need you to help me help you. Is that clear, Eve?"

Eve had simmered down, allowing Cindy's spirit of compassion and words of truth to resonate.

They continued talking and reminiscing a while longer in a far more hospitable mood. Before leaving, Cindy embraced Eve and headed to the door. "Give my love to Corey and Noel. Next time we get together hopefully we'll be in better spirits. I'll bring pizza for us. I'm sure the kids will like that. Eve, keep in mind that I am going to help you and you're going to help me help you." With her point remade and Eve seemingly accepting, Cindy was on a mission. Her thoughts continued silently about Paul, 'Only decent thing about him is that he's not physically abusive. But he's got the market cornered on emotional abuse and selfishness! Bastard.'

Not wanting to think anymore she switched on the car radio. She scanned all her pre-set stations until coming upon a song that wasn't offensive at the moment…. Anita Baker's *Fairytale*. "How fuckin' appropriate," she said in agreement with the lyrics.

Start of the first week of August was hectic for all. Gina's husband fractured his ankle while coaching his little leaguers; Alonzo's older son fell out of a tree and broke his arm; Ted's wife had a slight fender-bender hurriedly on route to Wall Street; and Cindy was running around in pursuit of alcoholism treatment programs. She also started checking her voicemail a bit more frequently in case Eve had called with an emergency. Now that she'd decided to help Eve, she'd also decided to stay close at hand.

By Friday, everyone was exhausted from spur of the moment adjustments made to accommodate the needs of their loved ones, in addition to doing their own things. Walking into Claudia's office, it was apparent that something was different there too…Margie was missing.

"Hi, Claudia. Where's Margie? She's usually here before me every Friday."

"At the hospital."

"Oh! So soon? Wasn't the baby due next month?" a perplexed and concerned Cindy inquired.

"It's not the baby. It's her daughter. Around two this morning the child was complaining of stomach pain and vomiting. Probably appendicitis. Anyway, they rushed her to the hospital. I don't have any updates yet though."

"Well," Claudia continued, "since it had to happen, it happened at a good time. These were her last two weeks in-office and all her assignments have been transitioned. And I'm sure her daughter will be fine."

"Yeah, for sure. Is there anything you'd like to discuss with me then?"

"No, not especially. Um, just that you know August twenty-eight is HRRC at nine-thirty for you. And the following fourth week of September it's HRRC again on Monday *and* Tuesday same time. This begins those fast-track meetings Mr. Prier wanted."

"Absolutely, Claudia."

"That's it then. Have a nice weekend."

"You, too." Free at last, Cindy headed home, ate dinner and placed a check-up call to Eve. Nothing new there—Eve had been drinking, Paul was out, and the kids were somewhere doing whatever. Eve became belligerent again when Cindy began talking about her alcoholism treatment findings.

"I'm not going. I've had time to think, I'm feeling better now and I'm not going." Eve's cavalier attitude was another manifestation of alcoholism. Cindy had reached her at the point where she was feeling empowered by the alcohol. A few moments later, after she'd had more, she'd be at its disposal begging for mercy from anybody who'd listen.

But Cindy was relentless, "Yes you are going! You can't continue living life in the condition you're in. If I must, I'll call **D**ivision of **Y**outh and **F**amily **S**ervices! It's not just about you, Eve. It's not about Paul either. There are two children in that household that need two functional parents. You're not one and Paul is gone most of the time, according to you! You're going for treatment, or your kids are going to **DYFS!**"

Eve wasn't saying a word. Instead, she was polishing off the corner of scotch from the fifth she'd only started the day before. Suddenly crying again, she conceded. "I'm sorry, Cindy. I know you want to help. I do need it. I get—I just get so—oh, I don't know. What should I do, Cindy?"

"Let me help you. That's all. Remember? You said you would." Cindy was speaking to Eve as if she were incapable of responding to complex sentences.

"I remember. I'll try, Cindy."

"Good. I'm coming back Sunday. We'll talk about the programs I've found. See what you think. Are you hearing me, Eve?"

"Yes, Cindy. I hear you and I'm sorry. See you Sunday. I don't feel well. I'm gonna be sick."

"Bye." Cindy hung up knowing it was a waste of time to tell Eve to not drink, so she didn't. She'd hoped her system would keep her from not drinking by not tolerating it anymore. "Maybe she'll just puke her brains out until Sunday."

With the weekend now over and mulling matters over, she recognized a sense of purpose emerging. Her once thought boring life was now seemingly taking a turn for action. It was the kind of action that she had neither anticipated nor would have joyfully welcomed, but it was something. Her roaming thoughts momentarily interconnected with Eve. Had it not been for ARSC, she wouldn't have known what to do about Eve. Curiously enough, all the boring bullshit she studiously captured daily had provided a significant knowledge base, almost by way of osmosis. She never consciously paid attention to all that stuff; it just seemed to seep right in.

Continuing along her "acquired knowledge" thought, her next profound thought was, "Maybe that was a way the Universe brings a person their intended life purpose. Something out there doesn't allow for just sitting around doing nothing. At some point, there's something requiring action that can't be ignored." Still unsure but now thinking back, could it be her "I want to be tussled" thought about to bring some relevance to life?

Moving on, her next thought was to call Gina and place her lunch order for their next lunch session. No answer. She left a message.

At the conclusion of the PAAOC proceeding, the Secretary approached Cindy as she was packing to go. "Miss Jack, I understand this is your last PAAOC meeting. Claudia from Casten called to tell me that we're getting another stenographer. I believe she said her name is Kathy or Carol?"

"Yes, Mr. Lucas," Cindy cordially replied and continued, "I'm being replaced by Carol West. I've been switched to the Hospital Rate Review Commission. Those sessions start at nine-thirty and conflict with these dates and times."

"I see," replied Mr. Lucas. "Best wishes, my dear. From what I've heard, the Hospital Rate Review Commission has some serious issues on its plate. Good luck. We look forward to working with Miss West. Take care." In contemplation, Cindy thought how gracious Mr. Lucas was. Rather to the point and not overly talkative.

Now 11:50 a.m., Cindy headed over to meet Gina. In the South Broad Street building's cafeteria, she spotted Gina at the same spot they'd first dined. Gina had her lunch order she'd requested via voicemail.

"Hey you! How you doing? I see you got my message. Thanks."

"Yeah, Cindy. I would've called back last night but Dan and I didn't get in until late. His sister Cheryl felt sorry for me and cooked dinner for us yesterday. With the basketball game and wrestling match, Dan and her husband Bruce settled in for the night. We didn't leave there till almost one in the morning! *Shit*! I'm tired."

"Why'd she feel sorry for you?" Cindy asked.

"Oh! Cause Dan's a big baby with that fractured ankle he got coaching those little leaguers. Any kind of ailment reverts men back to babies. He's been such a pain! Suddenly, everything he's got hurts. And I've just had so much going on that Cheryl took pity and made us dinner. Of course, I drove. Marriage and men are no jokes –only the *strong women* survive. Careful what you wish for, Cindy."

"Damn, Gina. You sound a little peeved," sarcastically commented a smiling Cindy.

"Maybe because I'm pregnant. If he'd fractured his ankle when I was more in a mothering state-of-mind versus condition, I could handle it better. I don't know but Dan was not "the man" last week. His splint comes off in three weeks and girl, I'm on countdown! What you been up to?"

"A lot! I reached out to Eve following your suggestion to get a life. What a nightmare! Eve is an alcoholic, her husband is a Rover, and their kids are practically raising themselves. I'm looking into treatment programs for her thanks to all the info I got from one of my assignments. She and the kids need help!"

"Good for you, Cindy. You know, we're not totally in control of what we do. I'm not so sure that life isn't just one big Divine plan that has us all here together to help each other. You know, in a weird sort of way, your helping Eve, helps you too. You're not doing anything else on a personal level right now, so help Eve and her kids. They say you reap what you sow. Somebody somewhere is bound to do something good for you. It's coming for you, Cindy."

"I hope so, Gina. I'm coming to believe that we all do have a Divine purpose. We've just got to find what it is. There has to be some sought of groundswell beneath all this."

Focused on finishing lunch, Cindy and Gina became less talkative while pondering their own life's challenges. At the elevators, they continued to make small talk until parting. Back in the JHPTC meeting room, Cindy avoided looking at the little balding Secretary. He avoided looking at her but only when it seemed as though Cindy could have caught him staring—while she was striking poses.

With the meeting in progress at exactly one o'clock, all had come prepared for a lively discussion. The meeting would be particularly challenging since the time was drawing near for a vote. After the Secretary made his opening remarks and asked for public participants requesting to speak, he started the proceeding with John Waterston, CEO, Maytown Memorial.

"We're getting closer to the vote and seems to me, no closer to the answer. I'm going to start by throwing my hat in for quasi-regulation. I'm not willing to cut off the hand that sometimes must feed us in times of financial hardship. We all know Gary Numan is totally for deregulation. That could not be clearer. But Gary Numan represents a totally controlled State Hospital, and the public hospitals don't have a vote here. So please, let's put Mr. Numan's comments in perspective. Thank you, Mr. Secretary."

Thank you, Mr. Waterston. Mr. Fisher, COO, St. Charbel's Medical Center."

"I agree with Mr. Waterston, and I don't have any more to add. I'm quasi-regulation oriented too."

"Thank you, Mr. Fischer. Mr. Williams, CEO, Kingston Memorial."

"I agree with the former two hospital speakers. But I think Mr. Numan has some very credible points. Even being regulated to the extent we are now as private hospitals, which I already liken to quasi-regulation, is not going to get us to where Mr. Numan presents strong arguments for our future direction. We cannot be entrepreneurial with the Health Department even slightly holding our reins. It does not work! Mr. Numan is right. I vote deregulation. I think we must all come to that conclusion if we want to control the destiny of our respective private hospitals. Thank you, Mr. Secretary."

"Thank you, Mr. Williams. Ms. Plom, CFO, Ridgetown Medical.

"Yes, Mr. Secretary. As CFO, I like the entrepreneurial spirit. I'm looking to expand my hospital and do that by bringing in new ventures. Can't do that maintaining the status quo. There're so many antiquated rules and regulations to follow and we must wait until they come up for revamping. And that's if any changes are even proposed. Plus, it that takes years! Windows of opportunity on the entrepreneurial side can be lost by the time regulators dust off far-fetched regulations that are out of touch with forward thinkers. I applaud Gary Numan for his candor and ability to perceive the future. Let's step into the future folks. Thank you, Mr. Secretary."

Thank you, Ms. Plom. Mr. Cambridge, CEO, Waterloo Memorial Hospital.

"Well said, Ms. Plom. And thank you Mr. Numan for being so vocal about the woes of full regulation on State controlled hospitals. If this is a win for us privates, State hospitals get stepped down to quasi regulation, giving them some release. Their human resources and operations resources would not be as taxed by the burden of full regulation. So, I appreciate all of this. I would also remind everyone that the Health Care Financing Board, which by the way will never go away, still maintains essential monitoring for all entrepreneurial ventures because they must approve them. They know the ins and outs of every hospital's debt financing and debt service status. And if you're in too deep, they don't let you go any further out. That's enough regulation for me. I'm voting deregulation. I'm crossing the line. Thank you, Mr. Secretary."

"And thank you, Mr. Cambridge. Well, Mr. Numan, since you've received such a high confidence level, would you care to begin with the public guest hospital remarks?"

Mr. Numan began and ended with some extremely passionate and eloquently phrased remarks. It was as if he'd been told his life depended on getting the private hospitals to put an end to the Health Department's regulatory stronghold. Even if it meant that emergency rate relief the Health Department could grant at any given moment would end. Gary Numan's mission was to shut the door to the Health Department which would also end the Attorney General's Office microscopic introspections at the Health Department's request. If Gary Numan could end the regulation scenario, the HRRC would also dissolve, and his hospital would never again be before the Health Department sweating over monies that could not be readily accounted for. And good to know… no more Alonzo Prier for them either.

Cindy's day was over at 3:55 p.m. She'd have quite enough time to bring Eve back to her forefront. She placed a call to Mr. Kindler of Fair Meadows having the contact numbers for all the ARSC members. Hello, Mr. Kindler, this is Cindy Jack. Hope I didn't catch you at an inconvenient time."

"Ms. Jack. Good afternoon. How may I help you? Not an inconvenient time at all," Mr. Kindler politely said.

Cindy continued, "I have a personal issue, Mr. Kindler. My sister is an alcoholic who needs treatment as soon as possible. She lives in Willingston, and I'd like to find the closest and most effective program for her."

"I see," replied Mr. Kindler. "That's really tough and sorry to hear. Fair Meadows has an excellent outpatient program but we're too far away. There's a woman from Pennsylvania, Mrs. Camila Radke, who's associated with a program near the southern half of the State, not too far from Willingston. I suggest you give her a call. You may remember her. She did a presentation for the ARSC several months ago."

"Yes, I do remember her presentation, I just couldn't recall her name. Now that you've said it, I remember. Mrs. Radke. Linnear Foundation, correct?"

"Yes. Call her at 215-252-4357 and tell her I suggested you call. And all the best with your sister, Cindy."

She graciously thanked Mr. Kindler and began dialing thinking, "Why can't these phone numbers be something easy to remember like 252-2000. Everything's so damn complicated these days!" What she didn't realize was that the 252-4357 was user friendly as its alphabetic compliment spelled ALC-HELP.

"Good afternoon. Linnear Foundation. How may I direct your call?"

"Hello, I'm trying to reach Mrs. Camila Radke. My name is Cindy Jack."

"Hello, Ms. Jack. I'll connect you to her extension. Hold on, please."

"Hello, this is Camila Radke."

Cindy was ecstatic in having reached her. "Hello, Mrs. Radke. I'm Cindy Jack. Mr. Kindler of Fair Meadows and a member of the New Jersey Alcoholism Rate Setting Council suggested I call you."

"Yes, I know Mr. Kindler and that Council also. How may I help you?"

"I have an alcoholic sister who desperately needs treatment. I'm also the stenographer for the ARSC and I remember your compelling presentation. I don't know where to start so I'm calling for advice and an elementary discussion. My sister lives in Willingston not too far from your facility, according to Mr. Kindler."

"Well, Ms. Jack, you're on the right track." Camila Radke had a kind soothing voice and disposition, which Cindy picked up on during her ARSC presentation. In hearing the warmth of her voice emanating through the phone, she'd recaptured Camila Radke. "First, let me ask you a couple of pertinent questions. Has your sister acknowledged she's an alcoholic and recognizes she needs help? Has she joined an Alcoholics Anonymous support group?"

"No. She has not joined A.A., but she does know she needs help."

"Okay," Camila replied, "but by whose acknowledgement is she accepting of the fact that she has an alcohol problem and needs help?"

Cindy didn't grasp what the woman was getting at and was becoming somewhat impatient with what she'd regarded as unnecessary probing. 'What difference does that make? She's an alcoholic. She knows, her husband knows, her kids probably know, and I know. So, what do you mean 'by whose acknowledgement'?"

Mrs. Radke demonstrated tolerance and patience. "First, Ms. Jack, because of the high incidence of relapse amongst alcoholics, the first major hurdle is in the individual accepting and voicing they have a problem. That's the reason for the AA meetings as the first step in a twelve-step program. When that acknowledgment is made, that's when our facility can help with the treatment and counseling program."

"I see, so she goes to A.A. first," courteously responded Cindy.

Mrs. Radke continued, "Pursuant to our treatment modalities, yes. Let me advise you of one extremely critical component for the success factor amongst these types of programs. If the person has not acknowledged the fact that they have a problem, they're doomed to fail. You know Mr. Kindler can speak to the grueling episodes he's experienced in trying to get adequate reimbursement from the payor community when alcoholics have exhausted their benefits and still need help. It's because of the high incidence of relapse, which I can't stress enough. As concerned providers, for us to maintain integrity for our contributions to successful recoveries, we must do all we can to ensure that the people entering our programs are fully aware of what they are doing and dedicated to their own recovery. Get your sister through the first few steps of A.A. and we'll take it from there."

"Ok," Cindy replied. "I made note of three A.A. groups in her area. I'd hoped to bypass that since I don't think she'd be receptive, but you've confirmed the need for it." Feeling more comfortable with Camila Radke's advice, she continued, "Thank you for your time and advice and I'll be in touch."

Not totally surprised and now knowing undeniably Eve would need A.A. first, Cindy's thoughts continued, 'And just how do I make *that* happen? Eve barely accepts the fact that she's got to commit to a program. Now she's got to stand up in front of people and proclaim she's an alcoholic? Yeah, right.'

"Always Allies, A.A. Support Center. May I help you?"

"Yes, I have a sister who needs to join A.A. I was told that I also should come to some of the meetings first to help get her involved."

"Yes, transferring you to one of our counselors. Hold please."

The call didn't last long but lots of information was provided. She learned that Eve would not have to state her real name and proclaim her problem at the first meeting. They allowed people to come and observe for the first few sessions and hopefully build enough courage at some point to state some name before stating the problem. This was one of the "speaker" programs where those braving the storm gave accountings of their despair with alcohol induced impairment and professing their way to help and desired recovery. Cindy concluded that it was a non-threatening environment that Eve could probably handle, and especially if she were there for moral support. And just as Mrs. Radke had suggested, Cindy was encouraged to attend a few sessions first for acquaintance with what she'd be undertaking. Her next call was to Eve.

"Hi, Eve. It's Cindy. What's up?"

"Nothing. You?"

"Look, Eve, I'm not going to sugarcoat this, I'm just going to tell you point blank. For you to get into an outpatient treatment program, you first need to join a local A.A. support group."

"What? Why? I'm not doing any such thing!"

"Eve! We talked about the possibility of your having to go to Alcoholics Anonymous first! I'm just as horrified as you! This means that I must go to some of those meetings alone first so I can be an adequate support partner for you! You think I like that? You think I want to spend my evenings with a bunch of alcoholics? Here's a clue, Eve! I don't! But if I can make that sacrifice for you, you damn sure are going to make it for yourself! And if you don't, I'm calling DYFS on you like I promised! You've got no choice and you've run out of time! Are you hearing me, Eve?" Charged with anger and disgust, Cindy slammed down the phone; a startled Eve just stood in her kitchen holding the receiver in one hand, glass in other.

Good thing it was the weekend. Cindy's mindset was far from fantasy. Having ascribed to all people having a Divine purpose, that meant Cindy was exactly where she was intended to be, doing exactly what she was supposed to be at that time—helping Eve. And just as the definition of *tussle* had offered, helping Eve was proving to be a rigorous struggle.

Cindy had decided to find an Al-anon group in her vicinity to avoid that long trek to Eve's local for the *come-see-what-it's all-about* meetings. After work, Monday, Tuesday, and Wednesday, she rushed home, had salads for dinner, and rushed right back out. Burdened by those AA visitations, hearing story after story from alcohol and substance abusers she likened to being trapped in a confessional. The despair, desperation, dependency and disillusionment circulating in the room was heart-wrenching. But these people had dared to face the demon, and that was uplifting. Having come to that uplifting conclusion, Cindy found the conviction to call Eve Thursday evening.

"Hello, Corey speaking."

The kid was polite, somebody taught him something. "Hi, Corey! How are you? This is Aunt Cindy. You and Nicole been ok?"

"Hi, Aunt Cindy. Yep, we're good. Are you coming here and we're going out?"

"Sure thing. And soon too, I promise. Is your mom there?"

"Yep. Hold on." A playful little Corey took the cordless phone over to his mom where she was laying on the living room sofa. "Get up, Mom. It's Aunt Cindy!"

"If I felt like it, Corey, I would. Just give me the phone. Hello?"

"Hi, Eve. How you doing today?"

"I'm no different than any other day. So now what?"

"Good news. I went to three A.A. sessions, and Eve, it's not so bad. There're plenty of people suffering from the same condition as you. But Eve, they're all fighting back. They're all getting back in the game, taking back their lives. You've got plenty of company, Eve."

Eve was crying again. But this time when they hung up, Eve had settled down. Cindy had settled Eve on a date for next week. She would call Always Allies and get Eve and herself registered for the coming week's sessions.

Alonzo was working harder than usual. It was almost six o-clock Thursday evening. He was preparing for Harrington, reviewing some other outstanding matters, and had become involved with Steven's windstorm policy issues. Steven had researched it well, and now in the throes of a philosophical interpretation of seemingly a statue leaving loopholes.

Knocking on Alonzo's slightly open door he immediately spoke, "You know, Mr. Prier, I just don't like this. Why should a homeowner have to buy a rider for the works of nature? Isn't pretty much everything an Act of God when it comes to the elements, like wind, rain, snow, hail? All that. Folks should only need one homeowners' policy that covers everything."

"Steven, do yourself a favor," Alonzo, saying somewhat annoyed, "stop haggling over a battle that's been fought and decided. The Legislature decided in favor of Windstorm Riders to deal with Acts of God. Done deal. Let's just make sure the insurers are writing those riders in deference to the regulations. Thank you, Steven."

"But, Mr. Prier, don't you think...?"

Without hesitation, Alonzo summarily replied, "Doesn't matter what I think, Steven. And make sure you're not over at the Insurance Department trying to undo what's been done. Just read the regulations and make sure you understand how those riders are to be written and underwritten. You've got a good analytical mind, Steven, but don't get carried away."

"No, sir. I understand."

"Thank you. Good night." Alonzo was too busy to keep debating over Acts of God with Steven. He was more concerned with what was appearing to be works of the devil regarding Harrington and other pressing issues.

Before she left, Anna brought him the schedule for the hospitals appearing before the HRRC on Monday. Lindy had left him the fiscal year documents for those four hospitals and had also analyzed all the rate-review considerations. No major issues. 'Well, guess I'll call it a day now,' he thought looking at his watch displaying six-thirty. He headed home.

VII

The Week That Was

WHEN MONDAY MORNING ARRIVED IN the tone of beep, beep, beep. Cindy was already awake. She'd been staring at the ceiling trying to pass the minutes having awakened at five a.m.

She'd reset her alarm to five-thirty in deference to the HRRC starting a half hour earlier than her typical 10:00 a.m. proceedings. "Today, Monday, August twenty-eight is Alonzo Prier day and lunch with Gina. Umph! Can't be jittery or I won't be able to concentrate on what I'm really there for – to take down Alonzo! Fuck the dictation." In rare form again, she hastened to the shower. Her undergarment was already laid out...a new Victoria Secrets basic black teddy with lace. Her outer attire would be a soft yellow sexy blouse with a shorter than usual matching darker yellow skirt, newly acquired. She'd run the razor over her legs since she wasn't going to wear stockings.

Leaving the house almost an hour earlier than usual, everything was picture perfect. Her make-up, her hair, under and outer wear, her disposition, and her timing. Cindy was wearing Greta out! She'd drop by Casten, pick up her newly scheduled weekly roster and head back out. She recalled a befitting song but couldn't remember the group who popularized it. She sassily sung out loud, *"And nothings gonna stop us now!"*

"Oh, Cindy, you do know where the HRRC meetings are held, correct?" Claudia was on the case too, wanting to ensure she hadn't left any loose ends.

"Absolutely, Claudia. They're in the Health Department's second floor conference room." Raring to go, Cindy retrieved her roster and left. For the time being, the only difference in her assignments was the loss of the PAAOC in exchange for the HRRC.

It was now 8:45 a.m. with plenty of time towards the engagement of the nine thirty meeting. "This is cool. Maybe he'll arrive a little earlier since he knows today is my first day. I wonder if I should be standing or sitting. I want him to see my legs. Maybe I'll be standing and sort of booed over my machine. That way, he can get the full view. No. If I'm sitting, I can uncross my legs at just the right moment and get his undivided attention that way. And of course, I'm going to put my Greta moves on him. He won't be able to keep his mind on that boring bullshit for that entire boring meeting. This is going to be fun! I'm going to see Alonzo under pressure and fire! *Come on, baby, light my fire*! Now that's a good song." All the way to the Health Department, Cindy bombarded herself with outlandish commentary about capturing Alonzo's attention. She had her radio on so people would think she was singing along to songs if they happened to notice her lips moving. She'd overlooked the fact that no one could have heard the music anyway and she still could have appeared a bit off, even if was singing.

Now in the Health Department's second floor conference room at 9:12 a.m., she was the only one there. The room was constructed as an amphitheater with tiers of seats and an open area, somewhat elevated, where the HRRC members would sit panel – like. Directly in front of them would be another set of people...The Health Department's analysts and the hospital representatives coming before the HRRC for rate review. "This is deep", Cindy again thought. "Looks like these hospitals are coming before the judge and jury. And Alonzo makes a lot of judgement calls, I'd assume, since he's Senior Counsel. Think I'm gonna like this. At least I like the set-up." She quickly started setting up her apparatus. She'd also noted that the walk down to the area where Alonzo and others would ultimately take their seats, was a rather long plank-type walk. The only unsettling part was in which door he would enter. If he entered the middle or the extreme right door, her set-up would not be in his path. If he entered the extreme left door, he'd almost walk right up on her long legs. That's what she was hoping for. Since the HRRC table was already set up with nameplates, she'd also noticed that she was on the side that Alonzo's nameplate was on.

The Health Department was only a two-minute walk from the Alberson Justice Complex. In gearing up to take that walk, Alonzo sipped the last drop of his coffee, picked up his folder and briefcase and left his office. On his way to elevator, he stopped by Lindy's office. "Lindy, since this is a rather smooth meeting, don't bother to come. Just keep working on the Harrington stuff since that's more critical. Oh, by the way, I'm having lunch with Warren Lein after the meeting. If you want, join us. I want to get his perspective on Harrington. As a matter of fact, you should join us. See you around noon. We'll be in the Health Department's cafeteria."

"Sure thing, Alonzo. See you then."

It was now 9:20 a.m. and Alonzo was on his way. Cindy sat looking poised and professional. Her yellow outfit was stunning against her almond toned skin with the perpetual healthy glow. The meeting commission members and audience participants had begun to arrive and get settled. The HRRC Secretary arrived. He looked at Cindy and nodded. At nine twenty-seven, Alonzo Prier opened the middle door and began his stallion-like descent down the center aisle. Cindy's heart was beating a mile-a-minute as she sat frozen, mimicking composure. His direct field of vision focused him on the Secretary. They spoke briefly and Alonzo proceeded to his seat. He then looked over and noticed the stenographer. "Hey, Cindy. My goodness you look— different. I almost didn't recognize you there. That's right, today's your first HRRC meeting. Welcome aboard."

"Hi, Alonzo. Thanks. Yes, this is my first." Cindy didn't quite know what to say. 'You look—different' was echoing in her head. Did that mean he liked it or not?

Alonzo had now focused his attention to the business at hand pulling some papers from his briefcase followed by a document from his legal folder. People begun rushing him with questions. With the pounding of the Secretary's gavel at 9:32 a.m. folks started to move away from Alonzo and be seated.

The meeting was underway at 9:35 a.m. The Secretary read the same opening remarks as all Secretaries read. Nothing new so far. Then he announced that one hospital, Maynard Valley, scheduled for review would not be in attendance, therefore the meeting would conclude early. Mr. Secretary went on to announce Cindy Jack as the new recorder for the HRRC in having replaced Margie Wyndam. Cindy rapidly took down each and every word said. However, when he acknowledged her, she'd looked over at Alonzo, he looked at her, winked and smiled.

Mr. Secretary then introduced the HRRC members—Mr. Warren Lein, Department of Health; Mr. Lawrence Evert, Department of Insurance; Mrs. Dot Reinhold, Hospital Association; Mr. Damion Spears, Public Advocate's Office; Mr. Lyndon Grayson, Public Member; and Senior Counsel to the Commission representing the Attorney General's Office and the Department of Health, Mr. Alonzo Prier. He concluded with the Department of Health's Analysts for the day's proceeding—Ms. Candice Bremmer and Ms. Bernice Swartz. First hospital up is Jamestown Memorial.

The meeting went on for an hour and fifteen minutes. Cindy recognized some of the same players from her former PAAOC and present ARSC meetings. During the break she was somewhat disillusioned again as Alonzo either busied himself with paper shuffling or with people right back in his face. 'Damn,' Cindy silently thought, 'do these folks ever leave the man alone? Hell, I want a shot at him too!'

The meeting again resumed and was going in such a smooth fashion that Cindy noticed Alonzo seemed preoccupied or perhaps bored. Feeling more at ease and Greta-like, she decided to get playful. In decidedly aiming for his attention during the lull, Cindy did something with her legs. They were long enough to stretch out and at least catch his peripheral view. She swung around in her chair and placed both legs now crossed almost directly within his line of sight. Still typing away, she was moving her top foot in a slight circular motion. He couldn't help but notice. And he was preoccupied knowing that he had more pressing matters at his office awaiting his return. Her skirt was rather short, and he noticed that. Alonzo wasn't the type to avert his gaze. If he wanted to see something, he looked. Cindy noticed him looking but obviously didn't know his thoughts.

Having noticed Cindy's unusual posturing, Alonzo started thinking about the attributes he found sexy and seductive about a woman. As his mind wandered, he in fact was thinking about legs. Alonzo was a long, lean, sexy, shapely legs admiring man. 'Cindy's legs,' he thought, 'are too skinny. Lindy's got the legs. Shawna's legs set the bar for me, but Lindy's legs raise the bar, no pun intended. Damn, I think Lindy even has a skirt like the one Cindy's wearing,' he summarily concluded with a silent chuckle. At that point, he looked up at the ceiling as if to be in deep thought. Cindy looked up at the ceiling as if in thought of being on her back. A question was asked of him that brought them both back to the meeting.

Alonzo answered, "I understand that you're displeased with the delays of your Medicare reimbursements, but that's solely Federal. I can't authorize the Health Department to extend rate relief to your hospital because of Federal delays. Why haven't you called the Regional New York Medicare Office on that, Mr. Neeks?"

"Mr. Prier, we have. It's to no avail. They must go through their reconciliation process and sometimes the delays in their process give us significant shortfalls. Is there anything the Health Department can do to help us with that? Like raise our commercial payer rates?" Mr. Neeks of Bayville Hospital was almost pleading for the State's Health Department to rescue his hospital from the Feds by way of the Attorney General's Office.

"No. Precedent setting, Mr. Neeks. Let me advise you to do what you can by way of your own initiatives. Better budgeting and planning may help. Sorry."

"If there are no further matters, the meeting can be adjourned. May I have a motion to end today's proceedings?"

The motion was made and seconded. Cindy started to pack. Thinking she made progress with Alonzo, she felt rather accomplished, even though he hadn't bothered to glance her way again. She'd just assumed he might have been somewhat embarrassed that she'd noticed him noticing.

Now eleven-thirty and as Cindy had convinced Eve to keep her phone numbers close, she figured she'd find a spot nearby to check her voicemail in case Eve had called with an emergency. Outside the conference room where Alonzo was still engaged in conversations with various folks clamoring for his attention, she dialed her office number and entered her voicemail access code. "You have *one* new message, received today at 10:45 a.m. Press *one* to hear your messages."

"Oh, shit," Cindy grimaced, "I hope Eve hasn't freaked out while I still have another meeting to cover." She pressed one and the message played.

"Hi, Cindy. Gina. Sorry, can't do lunch today. Gotta take Dan to his doctor, his ankle hurts. *Men*! I'll be in touch. Hope you get this message in time. Bye."

Not having any plans for lunch, Cindy decided to take her time in moving to the South Broad Street building for a solo lunch before her next meeting. She was waiting for the elevator when Alonzo walked up. "So, Ms. Jack, how was your first Hospital Rate Review Commission proceeding?"

Smiling immensely, Cindy replied, "Fine! Not too involved though."

"Don't let today fool you, they can get rather heated. On your way to the cafeteria downstairs?"

Hoping that was an invitation rather than a question, she replied in the affirmative. "Yes. My next meeting is the Joint Hospital Payor Task Force Commission. I can just grab something here since my lunch partner stood me up." She was beaming.

Alonzo replied, "Oh, you have that Task Force too?"

"Yep. And talk about heated! That one gets pretty emotional."

"You don't say. Why?"

"It's Harrington Hospital actually. Gary Numan gets so emotional when it seems as though the other hospitals are not in favor of deregulation."

"Really! That's interesting." Alonzo was now looking at her with a pensive gaze.

And totally unaware of him, there was someone standing directly in front of them awaiting the arrival of the elevator intently listening to their conversation.

"Oh, yeah," Cindy continued, "Gary's extremely passionate about deregulation. He makes these long-drawn-out arguments about why deregulation is vital to the entrepreneurial spirit and critical to the upward mobility of the hospital industry. That's pretty much a quote. He even brings up other countries' free enterprise efforts in healthcare and healing that would never withstand regulation and that's why they're so much more progressive than we are."

"Certainly a deregulation endorsement. Are you sure, Cindy? It's Gary Numan of Harrington State General Hospital talking about free enterprise like that?"

"I'm positive. *He's all over those transcripts.* You should read them, he's interesting."

By now the elevator had arrived and the gentleman in front of them had gotten an ear full. Alonzo had turned on to Cindy for a reason other than what she'd perceived. She thought she had impressed him with her newly formed sex appeal and the Harrington stuff was just a pretense on his part. And she was willing to play along in the interest of fooling around. The gentleman previously in front of them, getting in the elevator first, positioned himself directly behind them. He could now observe Cindy's interaction with Alonzo. It was apparent that Cindy had struck a nerve with the man and was playing to every second of the sensation. Her body language and mannerisms suggested she wanted him to review more than just the JHPTC transcripts—obvious—even to a mere stranger on a semi-crowed elevator.

"Cindy, would you care to join us for lunch? Deputy Commissioner Lein and one of my deputies are meeting me in the cafeteria. These are the people you'll be working with during your HRRC days. I'd also want Warren Lein to hear your comments about Harrington. Would you mind?"

"No, not at all, Alonzo." Cindy was feeling heightened passion. The inquisitive gentleman was determined to not let any of this out of earshot. He surreptitiously followed Alonzo and Cindy as they made their way to a table. He usually had a sandwich for lunch, but today he'd follow Cindy's and Alonzo's lead. He placed his briefcase and jacket down at the table behind the one where Alonzo and Cindy had dropped off their belongings.

On to a lighter note, Alonzo asked, "So who'd stand up a charming young lady like yourself for lunch?"

"Oh, my girlfriend," Cindy chuckled. "Actually, you know her. She works for the DEP Commissioner. Gina Falcone."

"Oh, yeah, Gina. Ted's secretary. Nice lady. She's pregnant now too."

"That's right. We just reconnected and I'll lose here again when the baby's born."

"How so?" Alonzo nonchalantly asked.

"She'll be home at least three months, and the majority of our face-to-face time is on the second and fourth weeks of the month when I'm over at the JHPTC meetings."

"No worries. When she's back, you'll start having lunch again."

The conversation had deteriorated into nothingness and Cindy felt the need to revitalize it by being a bit nosey. "How many children do you have?"

"Three," casually he replied.

"That's a plenty," she said.

By now they'd moved to the point in line where the food processor was ready to take Cindy's order. "May I help you, Miss?"

"Yes, I'll have beef stew and a bottle of water."

"Make that two and I'll get them both." And yet another little thing for Cindy to blow out of proportion. Alonzo was buying her lunch.

The stranger was still on their trail. He'd ordered the same thing and proceeded to his table a few minutes after Cindy and Alonzo had settled down at theirs. Lindy Jewel and Warren Lein had spotted Alonzo and made their way over.

"You guys haven't ordered yet," was Alonzo's first observation.

"No. We just walked in," Lindy candidly replied. Something was wrong. Lindy and Cindy looked at each other and immediately exchanged vibes. A little female competition over a married man, maybe?

Warren responded to the food comment, "We'll go over and order and be right back."

"Fine. By the way, this is Cindy Jack. She's the new stenographer for the HRRC. I worked with her a few years ago. When you get back, we'll talk."

Warren Lein immediately said, "I know you from the PAAOC. Nice to formally meet you, Ms. Jack." Warren Lein was a rather social creature once out of context with the demands of public performance.

"Let's get lunch and get back, Warren," was all Lindy's offered. Not seeming to appreciate Cindy's guest appearance, she wanted to hurry back to observe Alonzo's looks at Cindy.

Lindy too had the hots for Alonzo. Not that she had ever said or openly done anything to display it, but the desire was there. Lindy was quite an attractive young woman herself—with legs to die for. She was a slender five-feet eight inches, with short-cropped dark hair and big green eyes, set against a fair and flawless complexion. Simply overall striking. And, she had a knack for the HRRC business. Alonzo was grooming her to replace him on that commission. With lunches in hand, she and Warren returned. Lindy made a point of sitting as close to Alonzo as possible. He unassumingly moved over a tad appearing to give her some needed space.

Cindy, in having observed Lindy's posturing and Alonzo's polite move, silently smirked thinking, 'He just backed you off, Bitch.'

Alonzo began, "I wanted to discuss something else, but I invited Cindy to lunch because she's also the stenographer for the JHPTC." The stranger's ears were perched again as Alonzo began stating the purpose of the lunch gathering. He continued, "She has some interesting knowledge about Harrington's Gary Numan and I wanted you both to hear this, unbiased, from the stenographer. Cindy, would you share with them what you told me?"

"Sure. What I've recorded for the open public record from Gary Numan is that free enterprise is essentially a valuable thing and if deregulation isn't achieved for the hospital industry, it won't make progress in health and healing, and the entrepreneurial spirit can't exist. He's extremely passionate about that. I was telling Alonzo that his comments are all in those transcripts. He's *very* emotional about the issue."

"Thanks, Cindy. Folks, I think there are some interesting elements to explore about Harrington's operations, and I think what Cindy has mentioned is close to where the answers are. What do you two think? We can discuss it more later, but mainly, I wanted you to hear that." Alonzo looked at his watch. "Damn! It's twelve forty-three; Lindy and Warren, think about it. I've got a one o'clock conference call with the Insurance Commissioner and I've got to briefly meet with Steven.

Cindy, thanks ever so much and see you on September twenty-sixth. Take care." Alonzo grabbed his stuff and hurried off.

Cindy, now feeling slightly uncomfortable, finished her food and excused herself too. Lindy and Warren continued eating while the stranger continued eavesdropping for whatever aftermath he could pick up and take back.

Warren resumed, "Well, I think he believes there's a smoking gun somewhere at the JHPTC level."

"That's obvious, Warren. But that means going through all those transcripts to find it. Alonzo doesn't follow blind leads. I'm not quite sure I get it though."

"Lindy, your boss is a maverick. When he's on to a clue, he's like white on rice. All over it! So even if we don't get it, let's see where he's going. Commissioner Morris thinks he can find the missing links and have this one done soon. And that's without the task force stuff Cindy mentioned. We'll see."

"Warren, this beef stew is not the best. I'm done." Pushing her plate aside, Lindy continued, "Do Harrington execs know they're about to be stripped down to their underwear?"

"The call should have been made this morning. By now they should know that September 26 is A-day. They've got a month to concoct some more nonsense. It's too bad we're required to give them prior notice. Anyhow, Alonzo will probably conduct that entire meeting so no matter what they concoct, he'll be ready."

"Yep, he sure will. The Health Department has given up on Harrington from what I hear. Now they've been bumped up to the AG's Office for a microscopic review."

"They're slippery bastards, though. Just when we thought we had a handle on them, they slipped right through our fingers."

"Warren, I'm heading back now too. Like I told Alonzo, let the games begin!"

"Take care, Lindy. This keeps getting bigger every day. I've got a bad feeling about this whole Harrington mess. There's something *critically* wrong there. No pun intended."

"None assumed. Bye." Lindy was up and on her way back to the Justice Complex.

The stranger was up and off about his business too. He quickly grabbed his stuff and headed over to the South Broad Street building where the JHPTC meeting was already in progress.

The little balding Secretary was in the throes of his eloquent pontification. "Since the formation of this task force was predicated on a sixteen-month basis to discuss the issue and decide the future direction, I think last session's preliminary vote polling was a good idea. We only have three more months, and we're almost int September. So, I would suggest we just keep on the discussion towards the ultimate vote."

Sue Morrison, Liaison from the Health Department spoke next. "Well, it's clear that Gary Numan has made such intense arguments for deregulation, that the industry is likely to vote that way. And Mr. Numan, as you've stated many times, your goal may be to someday end up in a private hospital and not have your entrepreneurial spirit usurped. But do recognize that the Health Department has authorized millions of dollars, on an emergency relief basis to private hospitals. That goes away with deregulation. So be careful what you vote for, and I urge you all to vote with the consciousness of your own specific hospital's needs."

The discussion continued back and forth. The Health Department and the private hospitals challenged each other with Gary Numan acting as a biased referee. The stranger, now co-mingled with the other audience participants, sat quietly towards the back of the room virtually unnoticed. He took a seat with rather good distance viewing of Cindy, intently watching her strike keys and occasional poses.

After the meeting ended and Cindy packing to leave, the stranger started heading Gary's way. In approaching he noticed Gary gazing at Cindy. A task force member, wanting to commend Gary for having helped her see the deregulation light, interrupted Gary's gaze. Cindy left, and the stranger immediately rushed Gary breaking up his premature commendation ceremony.

"Oh, hello, Denver. This is Ms. Plom, CFO of Ridgetown Medical." Gary was in his glory.

Denver replied, "Hello, Ms. Plom, pleased to meet you. Denver Simmons, Director of Purchasing for Harrington State Hospital." He extended his slightly clammy hand to Ms. Plom. He then turned to Gary and continued, "I'm sorry to interrupt, but I need to speak with you. It's somewhat urgent." Denver handled the situation politely as he was visibly anxious.

"Excuse me, Ms. Plom. And thanks for your support. I don't believe you'll be sorry in voting deregulation."

Walking away together, Denver begun to relay his earlier encounters to Gary.

"*What? What are you saying?*! A fucking stenographer is bending Alonzo Prier's ear about what I'm saying here? *Why?*" Gary was evidently stunned.

Denver continued, "I think Cindy Jack has the hots for him. He's the shit; Senior Counsel to the HRRC. And today was her first meeting there. She replaced some pregnant babe who went on maternity leave. Lawson's had me covering those rate meetings looking for new angles that the Health Department grants emergency money for. He thought my going to HRRC would be good for me to get some education in hospital business as the Director of Purchasing. You know Lawson's always looking to make good use of time to scope out new information."

An angry Gary replied, "I still don't get what the fuck that has to do with me and what I'm saying over here!"

"I do! The bitch is trying to get Alonzo's attention. If she can impress him with brains and beauty, she's in there! She went through some weird body contortions in that HRRC meeting. At one point, she had him in a dead stare. Everybody was checking her out. I was. That bitch is hot to trot, man, and she's good looking too! Shit! *I just saw you checking her, Gary!* But I think she wants to ride Alonzo's pony." Denver was laughing.

Gary looked horrified. "This is no laughing matter, Denver. Lawson needs to know about this right now! *What the fuck?*! So close to the deregulation vote I can feel it, and that simple ass stenographer horn-ball is about to blow us up because she wants to impress Alonzo? Ah, fuck her! That dumb bitch!" Gary's blood pressure had to have shot up by life-threatening degrees.

"Gary, that's not all either," Denver continued, "she's trying to get him to read the JHPTC transcripts where you're talking a lot about deregulation and being hospital entrepreneurs. Seems like a State hospital shouldn't be all that involved. I don't' know. But I followed them to lunch. Alonzo had Deputy Lein and one of his own deputies listen to Cindy spill the beans on you." Denver was relaying the details without skipping a beat. He continued, "I can hear her now: *Oh, Alonzo, I brought you the transcripts. Would you like a little pussy before I go?*" Unwittingly, Denver seemed to be enjoying the irony.

"Stop it!" demanded Gary. "I don't want to hear anymore. This is outrageous! We've got to get to Lawson with this!" Gary Numan was livid. His face was beet red and his heart rate rapid. Under much physical duress, he ordered Denver to meet him back at the hospital in Lawson's office.

Denver Simmons had just turned twenty-five. Another fine male specimen but nowhere near mature nor commanding. Looks wise, he held his own. Sporting the beachcomber look, with a nicely formed athletic body, about six feet with a strong hairline etching his dirty blondish hair, his rugged good looks cast him as a good catch. His attributes culminated into him having been caught. Last year, Denver married his college sweetheart. Only reason he was Director of Purchasing at Harrington was because they needed to fast-track him so he'd be of assistance with matters outside the scope of his job. Denver was outgoing and personable too.

Back at Harrington, Gary and Denver met at the elevator where they headed up to the executive hospital offices. "Good afternoon, Gert. Please hold Mr. Lawson's calls. Denver and I have urgent business to discuss with him and I know he'd want to give this his undivided attention." Gary was in full official effect.

"Sure, Mr. Numan. Will do." Gertrude Collins was Patrick Lawson's executive secretary. Patrick Lawson held the title of President and CEO of Harrington State General Hospital. He was fifty-six.

Numan, immediately walking into his office began, "Patrick, we've got big problems looming!"

Lawson immediately replied, "Well, I've got wind of one of them. Just got a call today that the HRRC is bringing us up on a full three-year rate review on September 26. This is going to be tough. I thought we would have replaced every dime by now. I'm not pleased that this venture has not panned out as expected! Gary, you're the CFO! Explain why we're not in such good shape right now!" A stern-faced Patrick Lawson sat patiently awaiting a credible answer.

Gary tried, "Well, as Denver can probably confirm, all I've been hearing is *production problems*. Have you heard or do you know anything different, Denver?" Gary was feeling a bit lost.

Denver was undeniably lost. "No, sir."

Lawson resumed, "I tell you this, gentlemen. My numbers indicate that we've expended five and a half million dollars on this nifty little venture, and we don't have a damned thing to show for it. And attempting to spread this out over three years in our rate-review sessions with the Health Department, hasn't worked. So, you know what? You both need to get busy constructing a plan to make this look good, because right now, it looks pretty damn bad. And if it looks pretty damn bad to me, it's going to look pretty damn criminal to Alonzo Prier *and* the Health Department. I don't need to know how you're going to clean this up. I just know that you guys brought this venture to the table, and you better find a make to make this motherfucker credible! And quick! We've got a few more weeks before we're in front of Alonzo Prier and that HRRC. Good day, gentlemen; time is money and time is a-waste-n." With that Lawson angrily watched Numan and Simmons scurry from his office.

Heading to Numan's office, a naïve Denver started talking keeping his voice low as they walked. "But we didn't even tell him what we came to see him about."

Gary's voice was equally soft-toned, "Are you really that stupid? The man is a pressure cooker right now. After what he said, could you really see yourself saying, and by the way, there's this stenographer bitch that wants to fuck Alonzo, and ready to blow us up with those transcripts where Gary's been advocating for deregulation to get the Health Department off our asses! Do you think that would be a good conversation for Lawson, Denver? Lawson's right! We need a plan to fix this shit!"

"Gary, I don't know what to do. I don't know this business and I'm just"...

Like a faucet, Gary cut Denver off. "You're just as involved as we are, Denver! You don't know what to do? I'm going to tell you what to do. First, you're going to call the motherfucker you introduced us to who got this grand scheme going in the first place. You're going to find out exactly when we can expect a return on our investment and when our shipment will get here. It they can't deliver within a reasonable timeframe, you're going to tell him we need our full investment back. You're going to lock him into some concrete answers about what the fuck went wrong and how they plan to fix it!"

Gary stopped to breathe…and started again, "And at the same time, you're going to start dating that stenographer bitch to get her mind off fucking Alonzo. She's going to be fucking you instead! That bitch needs attention and you're going to give it to her. That's the plan, Denver! That's the plan!"

Shocked, Denver resounded, "Everything's cool up until the fucking that stenographer bitch! I just got married! I can't do that kinda shit! My wife will divorce my ass! No, I can't…."

"There's no such thing as *can't*. I don't give a damn about any of what you just said. And don't tell me what you *can't* do. This ship is sinking and we're all dead rats if we don't find a way to keep our asses afloat! That includes you! We've got to clean this up before Alonzo Prier gets a stronghold on this. We've got four weeks. Once we're up before that HRRC, especially with that Cindy Jack bitch creeping around, it'll be too late!"

An astounded Denver replied, "I've got four weeks to make Cindy fall in love with me and forget about Alonzo? *Get real.*"

"It's a long shot, but it's all we got. Alonzo is high profile. He's not going to fuck some silly-ass stenographer no matter how good she looks or what she does. He'll pick her birdbrain till she's dead pheasant and heap her ass out the window. He's not playing the same game as the average fuckin' Joe. He's got a lotta eyes on him. But he's still a man with an imagination. In his mind, he's probably fucked every one of those attractive women in that Justice Complex twice over. But he's also got a heart and wouldn't want to see any of them get fucked over emotionally. And since he couldn't admit that or openly go to their rescue, that would probably fuck with him, you know, distract him."

"And so what? You think he'd be too distracted over some other man fucking Cindy to work on Harrington?" Denver was almost laughing at what he thought was ludicrous and ridiculous. "Didn't appear that Alonzo was bent outta shape over her, she was bent over him!"

"You got any better ideas?" It's something, Denver, you got nothing. A betting man can't bet with nothing. I've got to get Alonzo to leave us the fuck alone. If that Jack girl made such an impression on him, maybe he's taken her to heart. I don't know! But hopefully this deal comes in and sets us free! But in the meantime, this is what you're going to do, Denver…."

"Okay, Gary. You're grasping at fuckin' straws but, I'm in." And as if in the Witness Protection Program, a newly named and emerging Denville Seamons was born of Denver Simmons. Denville Seamons was on his way to the biggest performance of his life. In that regard he and Cindy made a perfect pair.

A few days later, Gary was questioning Denver again, "So, what have you got for me now? Did you call that Frank character?"

"Yep, sure did, Denver replied. "He said you all had the prospectus that spelled out all the terms and conditions of the deal. It was to be a three-year deal with provisions built in to call for additional money if shit went wrong. From Frank's perspective, shit went wrong, they called for additional money that you all provided."

"That's not acceptable! Just like Lawson said, we've got to clean this up! We can't keep accepting production problems shit as an excuse! Can we get any money back?"

"From what I understand, no. It was an at-risk venture. Didn't you know that?"

Angrily, Gary replied, "We knew that, but it didn't seem at the time that the risk was that great! What else?"

"If you want a conference call, Frank can get that, but all signatories to the deal must be present."

"Okay. Let me talk to Lawson and Imani. First, I need to make sure Lawson's calmed down enough to listen to this. In the meantime, polish off your moves to charm that wacky-ass Cindy Jack."

"Yeah. Got that. And good luck with Lawson and Imani" offered Denver. "Let me know when you want to make that call."

Denver left Gary's office with mixed emotions. He was headed towards big fun and a big challenge. And if his wife found out, he was headed to divorce court. In acknowledgement of it all, he simply said aloud, "Whatever's supposed to be will. Shit happens!" He scowled.

VIII

Cindygate

A T FIVE O'CLOCK CINDY HAD finished with her day's last proceeding and moved off to call Gina. Gina typically left at five-thirty and was usually in a better phase of her day to entertain a personal call.

"Department of Environmental Protection. Gina Falcone speaking. May I help you?"

"Gina! Hey, girl. I got your Dan message. Everything okay?"

"Yeah. He just needs to keep his foot elevated a little more than he does and try to keep off it a little more. Funny though, he's never up and around on it when I'm home! Other than that, that baby's fine. What's up with you?"

"Guess what? I had lunch with Alonzo yesterday. It was my first HRRC meeting, and he asked me to lunch!"

"Really?! Why?"

"Thanks for the vote of 'you're an attractive woman and he probably wants to fuck you, Cindy.' Gee."

"Well, you are an attractive woman, and he probably *still doesn't* want to fuck you, Cindy. So why did he really invite you to lunch?"

"Actually, I did tell him something about this man that's on the JHPTC who's really passionate over issues he shouldn't even be concerned about. He thought that was interesting. But you know what, I think my knowledge about that stuff makes me more interesting to him."

"Whatever. But you know what? I wish some guy would come along and sweep you off your feet! You need somebody who will make you forget all about that married man who's known for not fooling around. Maybe after your attention is taken up with somebody else, you'll stop this obsession with Alonzo. Every female that thinks she's going to wrap her legs around Alonzo ends up disappointed. And word gets out because these silly-ass women make all-out fools of themselves trying to get with that man. Anyway, I've got to get off and clean up my desk. Ted is walking over here, so I'll see you for lunch—when—September eleventh?" Gina was looking at her calendar, tracking Cindy's hopscotch schedule.

"Is that the second Monday of the month?"

"Yep."

"That's it then unless Alonzo has something better in mind. Just kidding!"

"You better be! See you, girl. Take care."

Even though she said she was just kidding, Cindy was still hoping that perhaps by some outlandish stroke of fate, Alonzo would find some use for her. She wasn't ready to throw in the towel though. She just decided to make herself more useful to him. Just at that moment, she decided on another course of action towards her ideal man. "That's it! I know what he's interested in, and I can deliver. Then he'll have no choice other than to see me in a whole different light! Ha-ha, maybe moonlight." Frolicking towards a new plan, Cindy was off and running. She would keep this one a secret too; much like her decision to mimic Greta, but she thought that this new plan would at least be beneficial for whatever reason Alonzo was so hell-bent on Harrington.

"Let me head home. I've got to call Eve and make sure she's ready for tomorrow." Cindy's thoughts continued quietly. She had much to accomplish within the coming weeks and more than willing to get it all done.

Wednesday was a particularly long day. She arrived at Casten at 8 a.m. towards her new plan. Claudia hadn't even arrived. If they crossed paths it would only be in leaving to get to her ten o'clock assignment. By then she'd be in a hurry and could just breeze through.

Now in Casten's Documents Storage department, Cindy greeted Arlene Snares, files storage supervisor. Arlene was about fifty and like Claudia had been with Casten since its inception. Arlene somewhat reminded Cindy of the older lady at the library during her Greta track down. Arlene was reading the paper and having her morning coffee. She liked to arrive a little earlier than her usual starting time.

"So, Arlene, is the file retrieval policy still the same?"

"Sure is. We have our permanent file storage hard copy, a duplicate hard copy that can be removed with sign-out, and the microfiche copy. Which committee are you looking for?"

"The JHPTC. I'm interested in eleven months' worth." Arlene kept Casten's hard copy files in alphabetical order by the unclever initial descriptors that Cindy despised.

"Those meetings are held twice a month, aren't they? That's twenty-two transcripts you'll need. Well, just make sure you sign each card for each one you remove. What are you looking for?"

"I'm the stenographer for them; it's going to be over in three months and I was just looking for testimony where I think some of the members were trying to extend the length of the time they could be in existence." Cindy was lying, but it sounded reasonable to Arlene. "If they do extend their life, my schedule will have to be changed."

"Oh. I see. Happy hunting."

"You know what? I'm not going to take all twenty-two at one time, I'm going to review these over a couple of weeks at most. Today I'll just sign out four."

"Whatever. The section for the JHPTC files is to your right." Arlene couldn't have been more disinterested.

Cordially, Cindy replied, "Thanks, Arlene. I'll sign out what I want now, I've got to get on the road. See you later." Cindy hurried over to the appropriate section, retrieved the files and signed them out. Silently thinking headed back to her desk, 'that was a good lie I told Arlene. If Claudia sees me with these files, I'll give that snoop the same story!'

Claudia didn't see her. She wasn't in her office when Cindy passed by on the way to her desk; she still wasn't in when Cindy left.

That evening while Cindy patiently sat through Eve's Always Allies meeting, she re-directed her attention towards Alonzo's interest. She'd taken two of the four transcripts along to the AA meeting to keep herself occupied while Eve was involved.

Those documents were typically about two and a half inches

thick and were neatly bound in manuscript form. The speaker was always identified prior to speaking, making it easy to find the speaker being sought. Cindy made little pencil stars on the pages she'd later photocopy. She also paper clipped those slightly-pencil-marked pages for easy identification later.

The AA meeting lasted two hours and Cindy completed two documents. She'd rediscovered the JHPTC and, having stepped outside the role of stenographer by reading what she'd typed, she was discovering some remarkably interesting information.

Eve had emerged from her meeting a little annoyed, "I can't believe that this was my very first A.A. meeting, and you're sitting in the back going through some bullshit from work."

"Eve this is something I must get done. And I am here for you, not participate. Anyway, how was it?"

"Not bad. I certainly wasn't ready to stand up and say I'm an alcoholic, but maybe next time. You were right about one thing; a lot of people have this illness. I feel better already. Even in knowing it's an illness. Somehow that makes it a little easier for me to cope. I know I need to get well. And that thought helps. Thanks, Cindy." Eve held her arms out to embrace her sister. This was a breakthrough moment for them both. "Oh, I'm not really mad you were working on that shit," Eve sarcastically said.

"Oh, good, Eve. Thanks. And when's your next session?"

"Friday. I don't want to keep imposing on you, but I'm not ready to quite go it alone yet. I'll get to that point. I haven't even told Paul. But I told my friend Peggy since she's watching the kids. She's a good friend too. She's so glad that I'm doing this. So have another set of your documents for Friday."

"Will do."

Cindy dropped Eve off and continued her forty-five-minute drive home. It was 11:15 by the time Cindy got home and by then she was exhausted. "I've been going non-stop since five-thirty this morning! I'm going straight to bed. Tomorrow after work I'll finish those other two transcripts and be ready to photocopy. This is going great. Friday morning, I'll return the four and get six more for the weekend."

IX

The Prier Party

A FTER WORK THURSDAY EVENING, ALONZO got home around 6:30. It was the night of the private fashion showing that Shawna was all hyped and getting ready for. Her parents were already there entertaining the kids and Shawna was up in the bedroom deliberating over a few different party dresses. She'd finally decided on a fitted red sarong-type dress that could only accept a thong as reasonable underwear. When Alonzo opened their closed bedroom door the thong was all she was wearing.

"Ah! Looks like my timing is impeccable! We should have a set of parents here all the time. I like coming home seeing you like this." He was smiling while becoming aroused.

"Hi, honey," she replied with a sexy enticing smile. "Azo, don't let your eyes take you there right now. We don't have much time and everybody's wide awake."

"Oh, come on. How often do I get to come home to this? I'll be quiet and quick! Besides, it heightens the intensity when you know you're only a knock away from being caught! Let's go for it," he pleaded.

"We deal with that enough with the kids around," she replied.

"Yeah, but they wouldn't know what they were looking at even if they did catch us. Your parents would!"

"Alonzo, you are out of your mind. But okay, really quick!"

By the time Shawna and Alonzo emerged from their bedroom, it was 7:35 p.m. They both looked great. Shawna was wearing that red dress out! Alonzo was sporting casual male attire showing off his well-structured physique.

They arrived at Reeve Rouse in New York's upper Manhattan district at 9:20 p.m. The music and the hors d'oeuvres were piping hot. The champagne and wine were flowing fervently. Stronger drinks were being served by the minute. The guests looked fabulous. The models were gorgeous! Alonzo and Shawna fit in ever so well with the select crowd of beautiful people. In a nutshell, it was a beautiful thing. Moments before the fashion highlights of the night were about to grace the runway, Shawna's former boss and host of the event made his way over.

"I'm so glad you came! I was a little worried that you wouldn't make it!" Vladimir Ustaci was at the height of his fashion industry career. He'd always admired Shawna for her appealing physical attributes that paid great tribute to his highly sought designs.

Shawna was glowing. "Are you kidding? I still live for your private parties! We don't get out much, but when you call, we come. We know it's going to be a fabulous thing. Who's your new designer? That is the reason for this celebration, correct?"

"Yes! We're only presenting ten designs tonight and they're all his. I thought it would be a great time to have a party and show him off. His name is Roman Gustav; he's lived in Sweden, Paris and Bolivia, and he has some of the hottest, most sensual designs I've seen in quite a while. Shawna, I know you'd look sensational in his pieces. So tonight, I'm doing this in welcome of him to my shop. My friend over at WorldWind Productions sent me a new song too. It's the perfect runway song for sensual, sexy pieces. I'm going to use it as the feature song for Gustav's collection. It's called 'Makin' Love With Our Eyes'."

Ecstatic, Shawana said, "Can't wait! And like you usually do, you've taken yourself up another notch."

"Yes sir, Vladimir. This is really fabulous." Alonzo had just been listening, but as Vladimir was about ready to move on, Alonzo at least wanted to say something cordial.

"Thanks, Alonzo. And I thank you both again for coming. Shawna, we'll probably call you next week to come in and give us your opinion on a few fabric shipments we just got in. Did you get your check for the last consultations you did?"

"Yeah. Thanks."

"Good. Hopefully later tonight I can introduce you both to Gustav. I've got to get the fashion show underway. I had a small dinner prepared for tonight too that I've got to check. Gotta go! Talk later."

When the theme music hit the models began strutting down the platform runway choreographed to the song. The fabulous crowd of beautiful people became speechless! Vladimir Ustaci really knew how to put on a show with elegance and pure grandeur. The sex appeal and sultriness that Gustav had woven into mere pieces of cloth had seemingly captivated his audience.

"Wow! That song is certainly the answer to safe sex; just use your imagination and get off!" An aroused Alonzo, caught up in the rapture, whispered that little remark in his sexy wife's ear. And that Thursday night, August thirty-first, was the perfect end to the grueling month of August for Alonzo.

X

Game On

B Y THE END OF THE first week of September, Cindy had completed
her review of nineteen of the twenty-two transcripts. She was
so dedicated to completion of her self-imposed assignment that she'd
made all the necessary adjustments to handle her business. By arriving
early at Casten she'd avoid Claudia completely. That was the perfect
week to review the additional transcripts towards the completion of
the task during a rather uneventful time. Plus, that was not a week she
was scheduled to lunch with Gina; hence no guilt trip, even though
she'd never planned to share that little Alonzo tidbit anyway. There
was a decision to be made about the last three transcripts; one reflected
that Gary Numan had to leave early that day, and the other two were
the most recent wherein the discussion of moving towards the vote
had started. Gary Numan had already made his contributions to the
JHPTC —she had gathered enough for Alonzo to hang him out to dry.

During the weekend, with yellow marker in hand, Cindy highlighted
the significant comments from the various photocopied pages that she'd
collected. For the novice, that would have been akin to accomplishment
of a feat. But Cindy, being a seasoned stenographer with good recall,
and especially attuned to those meetings, knew exactly where to look.
By Sunday afternoon Cindy had a bound dossier on Gary Numan.

And again, it was the second Monday of the month. September
eleventh would hold many splendors for Cindy. She arrived at the
HRRC at 9:15. Alonzo and Lindy entered the Department of
Health's amphitheater-type conference room about ten minutes after

Cindy's arrival. Cindy was set-up and waiting; Alonzo immediately acknowledged her and smiled, as Lindy barely looked at her but managed a slight 'good morning'. Cindy immediately picked up on her aloof behavior and silently thought to herself, 'I guess you can't handle the competition, Bitch.' Cindy pretentiously smiled at Lindy.

Meeting now in progress, Lindy sat taking notes on various points about the scheduled hospitals' reviews. Alonzo was essentially quoting rules and regulations. From Cindy's vantage point, it seemed as though Lindy was Alonzo's private secretary; little did she know that Alonzo was grooming Lindy to replace him at those meetings. His main goal was to stay in the process until he could finalize the Harrington matter and then pass the baton. That way he'd be free to focus on the labor strike ordeal. Even if deregulation became a reality, Lindy was certainly competent enough to handle the fallout.

Not forgetting her celluloid marvel, Cindy made a point of going for Alonzo's attention with her gracefully displayed Greta stylized poses. She caught his attention, but his thoughts were more along the lines of, 'what the fuck is up with that action?' She was somewhat subtler but being as observant as he was, he'd noticed the difference from the Cindy Jack he'd known years before. 'Oh well, people change,' was his concluding thought, silently chuckling.

During the break, Cindy made a beeline to Alonzo. "You know, I was thinking about when I joined you and your associates for lunch two weeks ago. The more I thought about it the more I really think you should read the JHPTC transcripts."

"Oh, Cindy—I'm so overloaded right now I couldn't even take a message, much less, read through all those transcripts. I'd have to go from day one to discover all the relevant comments that individual made. Too much, too late. I trust your perception about it though. I only wish I did have the time to read them."

"Well, what if I could get them to you with the relevant information highlighted?"

"Excuse me? When? Why would you?" His full attention was now on Cindy. "You know, or you probably don't, this is a rather serious matter. For you to involve yourself to that extent is commendable, but I wouldn't want to see you get drawn into this situation. Your comments were quite fine. Going beyond that, I don't think you'd want to."

She didn't let up, "Oh, but I do. I've already highlighted them for you. It registered with me too, even before our conversation, that there must be something wrong there. I've recorded emotional testimonies before, but he was still beyond that. So, I started reading the transcripts and just made copies of what I thought you'd be interested in."

"Cindy, that is commendable! Remarkable. This break is almost over. Tell you what, call my office and we'll talk. Um, let me give you my office number. Call me. Thanks." He was smiling—pretty much in disbelief. And no sooner than Cindy was about to walk away, Lindy began walking up. Cindy noticed him noticing her lengthy legs as she sashayed towards him. Cindy looked at them too. Lindy's legs were admittedly notably nice.

The meeting ultimately ended at 11:40 a.m. and as Cindy was on her way out the door, someone from the audience pleasantly interrupted her. "Hello. Let me get that for you." It was Denver Simmons about to introduce himself as Denville Seamons. He'd entered the meeting about thirty minutes prior to its conclusion. His only business there was Cindy. Because the circular room was so large, it was virtually impossible for anyone in Cindy's location to notice late-comers.

Denville looked and smelled great. He had on a splash of a full-bodied cologne that captured Cindy immediately. Gary was right about one thing; if anybody could give Alonzo competition, it was Denver. "I'm Denville Seamons and you're Cindy Jack. I'm psychic, so my psychic abilities gave me your name. I attend these meetings here and there. I was just waiting for the opportunity to say hello." Denville was a smooth operator.

A charmed Cindy replied. "It's nice to meet you, Denville Seamons. This is only my second HRRC meeting. I started last week, so I wouldn't know if you're a frequent or infrequent flyer. Do you work for a hospital or are you a public observer?"

"I work for all the hospitals and I'm a very private person. Just joking. I'm a private observer as in work for a privately held company. I don't even too much like the word public. Kinda implies that everybody knows your business. Speaking of business, I know it's none of mine, but you are such a lovely lady, can I ask if you're involved with anyone? I'd like to know if I could perhaps take you to dinner?"

"No and maybe." Cindy was smiling, completely enthralled.

"No and maybe. I've gotten a 'yes and no' to that question before. I understood that, but I don't get 'no and maybe'."

"So, you've asked that question a lot?"

"No not a lot, but I have asked it before. Anyway, are you going to explain 'no and maybe'?"

"No, I'm not involved with anyone, and maybe you can take me to dinner if you're not involved with anyone."

"Well yes and no, then. Yes, we can go to dinner because, no, I'm not involved with anyone." Denville was lying, but it wasn't the first time, and it certainly wouldn't be his last. Cindy accepted.

"Well, I've got to get over to lunch and my next proceeding."

"Let me guess, the JHPTC meeting in the South Broad Street building."

"How'd you know that?"

"I attend that meeting too occasionally. There's no mystery. I'm in hospital supplies sales and I must attend the relevant hospital business meetings to see what's going on with specific hospitals and the industry overall. I've noticed you as the stenographer for the JHPTC for over the last eight or nine months. I just started working for MedExpress about a year ago. Monitoring those two meetings became one of my assignments. Other than that, I'm on the road all over the state. So, Ms. Jack, shall we go?"

"Yeah, we shall go. We'll head over to the South Broad building together and then we'll go from there. I would ask you to have lunch with me but I'm meeting a girlfriend for lunch. We have this standing lunch routine when I'm doing the JHPTC. Unless you don't mind two lovely ladies?"

"Thanks, but no thanks. I've got to make some quick calls before the meeting. I probably won't get there until late. I usually just grab a quick sandwich and return calls because most people I deal with have lunch at one, so I can get them at twelve. Anyway, give me some digits on you. Let me give you mine."

They exchanged numbers and agreed to have dinner. Denville

commented to Cindy that he would wave to her from the back of the room when he'd finally arrive at the JHPTC.

They parted ways, and Cindy, delightfully impressed, hurried off to share her good news with Gina. She'd met a man, a fine man, who was totally available!

Rushing into the South Broad building's cafeteria at 12:10, Cindy spotted Gina already eating. "Hey! Sorry I'm late. But guess what? I met a guy! He's so fine! That's why I'm late. He's a hospital supplies salesman, and he attends the HRRC meetings. Occasionally he stops by the JHPTC meetings. This was only my second HRRC meeting, and poof!" Cindy was talking so fast that Gina had stopped eating. She couldn't simultaneously digest her food and what Cindy was speedily rambling on about.

"Hey that's great! Oh wow! How old is he?"

"I don't know. He looks to be no older than thirty if that, but he's certainly one good-looking guy. And he's got a great body too. He's tall and dirty- blonde-ish. Sort of like a Don Johnson look. His name is Denville Seamons. He asked me to dinner."

"Well, all right! You go, girl! Didn't I tell you that's what you needed? Somebody to get your mind off Alonzo. You are so excited. I'm happy for you, Cindy."

"You know, Gina, Denville has moved Alonzo to the side. And I just met this guy today! I admit it; you were right." And even though Cindy believed in what she'd just said, she had already promised Alonzo the documents and a call. Being that she was a woman of conviction also needing to prove her self-worth, she felt obligated to deliver. She didn't feel compelled to share that little nuance with Gina.

"Well since you were late, at least you were late for a good cause. When are you going to dinner?"

"I don't know. We exchanged numbers so I'm sure he'll call and let me know. He'll be at the JHPTC meeting today. I wish you could sneak down and see him. Gina, he's a hunk!"

"I wish I could sneak down and see him too. For your benefit, of course." Gina sheepishly laughed.

Cindy having picked up on the sly remark, replied, "He'd take one look and know you're not available with your wedding ring and pregnant self." They both laughed; Cindy continued. "Is everything still okay—with you and your pregnancy?"

"Yes, I'm fine, thank God! Me and the baby are exactly on schedule."

"Great!" Both Cindy and Gina were headed towards the conclusion of lunch hour.

Cindy was anxious to get to the JHPTC and Gina appeared anxious for her.

Seven minutes ahead of time, Cindy was gearing up. The little balding secretary was shuffling through some papers but made a point of greeting Cindy. Gary Numan entered the room with a scowl that could kill, but Cindy never paid any attention to his appearance anyway. The meeting began on time with all the participants in place and with Cindy occasionally glancing towards the back of the room.

All the meeting panel participants were engaged in lively discussion and Gary Numan was appreciably less talkative. Denville made his entrance about thirty minutes before the meeting concluded.

With the meeting finally over, Denville and Gary made it a point to not acknowledge each other as Denville sat patiently in the back of the room waiting for Cindy to collapse her apparatus for the evening. Denville walked out to the hall area to greet her when she came through the door.

Seeing him standing a few feet beyond the proceedings room exit, Cindy smiled. "Hey, I was getting worried you'd forgotten all about the meeting."

"No, couldn't do that," he said walking over. "Besides, the most productive part of my coming to these meetings is pretty much when they're almost over. I hear the concluding remarks, and then get to network with people. I'm in sales sweetheart."

"I see," she admiringly replied, and with a cagey tone asked, "So, you're networking with me?"

He bluntly said, "No. I'm trying to socialize with you. So when would you be free for dinner? Would tonight be too soon?"

"Tonight? It's Monday. Don't most first dates happen on a Friday night?"

"You have to eat dinner on Monday night and Friday night, don't you? If you're available, what's the difference?"

"None, I guess. And yes, I am available tonight. Okay, fine. Where shall we meet?"

"I usually like to pick my date up. I'm harmless. Hey, a maniac wouldn't be coming to these boring meetings. I must be here for my job, so I'm sane and safe. Why don't I pick you up around 6:30? Where do you live?"

"I agree. A maniac would be more imaginative and could never tolerate sitting through this business." As Cindy was in the process of writing down her address, Gary Numan slowly passed by, surreptitiously noting Denville's moves. Their eyes met but they didn't speak.

Denville took the little slip of paper from Cindy and commented. "Oh, you don't live too far from me—um—that is, from where I used to live." He'd momentarily forgotten that he now lived at Gary's condo.

"Oh, where do you live now?"

"South Mountain."

"South Mountain? That's about an hour and a half from here! Why so far?"

"You keep forgetting I'm in sales—I'm all over the State. What's far for you is nothing in comparison to where some of my clients are. There's not one spot that I could really say is close to my job. I do a lotta roadwork, my darling." And the die was cast.

Sounded reasonable. "True. I'll just have to adjust to the life of a salesman."

"See you at 6:30 then. My parents live about forty minutes from you. I'll just hang out there until I'm ready to pick you up. Anything comes up; you have my numbers. Call or page me. I've got some other stops to make. See you later." He kissed her on the cheek and departed.

Denville was off to his wife. He had to get home and deliver a fabricated hospital business meeting that he had to return to work to attend. As he drove home, he was thinking that he should make his trumped-up story lasting. He'd need to establish a missing-in-action status as far as his marital duties were concerned. He decided to tell his wife that the BandRxStat shipment was about three months away from delivery, and as Director of Purchasing, he was on a special project at the hospital warehouse making space for the incoming delivery. This was a big deal; so much so that a preliminary strategic planning meeting was called, and he'd have to get back to the hospital frequently to oversee the project. Also, it was something that had to be done after normal business hours, as it would interfere with his daily responsibilities, and other assigned employees' too. To add more credibility to his story, he'd show his wife his new pager. His boss could possibly have the urgent need to contact him. He would not mention the cell phone and other Gary-given amenities.

"Cool. Shit, I even believe my own bullshit. Damn, Denver, you're the man with the plan!" Denver was essentially having a ball devising his own game within the game. "Let me run this by Vicky now. She won't have a clue!" He parked on the street; knowing he'd be right back out he didn't bother to drive into the apartment complex lot. He was careful to lock his new cell phone in the glove compartment.

After hearing his fabricated story, she replied, "Seems like they're asking an awful lot of their employees. Do you get more money for these extra hours?"

"Baby, you just don't understand the business world. I'm management, so no I don't get overtime pay. But the union guys moving all the stuff around freeing up space for the shipment do. You're a first-grade schoolteacher. That's so different from what I do and who I deal with. I deal with decision-makers. You deal with little kids. Trust me, there are many things that go on in big business. But this hospital business won't last too long. Maybe about a month. Then we'll be back to normal."

"That's not bad. I'll miss you at nights, but I can handle a month." Vicky bought it. "I made chicken cutlets for dinner. Do you want to eat now or a little later?"

"Actually, I'm not really hungry. Tonight's our big kick-off meeting so I've got to get back to the hospital by 6:30. Here's my new pager number if you need me—for an emergency only though."

Having sold his story to Vicky, Denver was now kibitzing around. "Anyway, I'm going to change and head out. I should be home no later than eleven. These guys are cool though; dinner's on them tonight." Having changed his tune completely, he continued. "Can I at least get a kiss before I go?"

And he did love his wife. It was in being young and still somewhat mischievous, that he was turned on by Harrington's happenstance.

121

As for Cindy, she wasn't really his type. Although he thought she was a good-looking lady, he preferred his own race. His wife Vicky had recently turned twenty-four. And albeit he was going to enjoy the pleasures of frolicking around with Cindy, he wouldn't have gone out of his way to get in bed with her either.

A ready to go Denver kissed Vicky goodnight. On his way to Cindy's he stopped by an out-of-the way supermarket and broke in his new credit card purchasing a bouquet of fresh mixed flowers. Back in the car, he thought aloud, "Unlike that Alonzo character, I know I can't dazzle her with brilliance, but I can baffle her with bullshit. And charm her panties off too. Gary, you're gonna be one happy man! You can live again—through me!"

He arrived at six-thirty sharp. Cindy was ready *and* raring to go. She was wearing another one of her recent shopping-spree expedition ensembles that was rather short and sassy. And of course, she was sporting one of Victoria's Secrets underneath.

When he rang the bell, Cindy answered immediately. "Whoa, you look hot! And these are for you."

Delightfully charmed, Cindy accepted the flowers. "Thank you. This was very nice of you. And you look hot yourself." He was wearing a pair of casual pants and a short-sleeved shirt that donned his nicely structured frame. "One minute while I put these in some water, then we can go."

"No problem. Take your time."

During the drive to the restaurant, the conversation was light and airy. It had been many moons since Cindy had been on a date, so naturally she was somewhat nervous. Denville made sure to keep the gab flowing by asking her questions to draw out what appeared to be a somewhat reticent personality. It was more that Denville was friskier than what she was accustomed to or had attached to in lust of Alonzo. Alonzo was more polished and laid back. But Alonzo was forty-something. "How old are you Denville?"

"Twenty-five. Is that a problem for you? How old are you?"

Before she answered, she felt a twinge of nausea. 'Damn,' she silently grimaced, 'I'm going to hit the big three-o next month. What if he thinks I'm too old for him?' But she managed to get it out anyway. "I'm twenty-nine."

"Oh, big deal. But I hope you don't think I'm too young for you. Some women have problems with that—you know—dating a younger man. I think that's bullshit myself. Age is only a number. Besides, younger guys admire older women. But you're only four years older than me, that's nothing." He slowed down the car, turned to her with a sincere expression and asked, "The age thing is not going to be an issue for you, is it? It's certainly not for me." And at that point, Denver realized he wasn't just lying again. With Cindy, he'd picked up on that it really wasn't her age, it was born of her job as a stenographer. She always sat up straight, stayed focused, listened well so she could precisely hunt and peck. Thus, it was more of a presence versus disposition that made her appear older. But whenever she was in position to let her hair down, he suspected Cindy could be a blazing fire!

Feeling more at ease she responded, "Absolutely not."

"Now that's what I'm talking about! Meeting of the minds—and hopefully hearts. I like you, Cindy. I really do."

They drove into the top-choice Italian restaurant's parking lot. It was a great little hide-away spot that he used to frequent prior to his marriage. He enjoyed indulging in Italian food but made a point of not taking his wife to too many places where his glory days had left trailblazer memories.

"Pompeilio's has the best food you could imagine, if you're into Italian."

"I'm into Italian."

"Then you're in for a treat. As you've said before, shall we go?"

"Absolutely."

Dining together for the first time was accentuated with small, getting to know you; getting to know all about you, talk. Cindy was holding her own and returning each romantic and comedic serve Denville threw her way. He kept the Merlot flowing like spring water as the candlelight playfully danced their shadows around the wall. The main course was scrumptious, and the dessert was erotic. By the time they got back to her house, the comfort zone had been maximized. He could now passionately kiss her goodnight, and whatsoever else.

"Well, we're at that awkward moment where guy wants to kiss girl. If you're not comfortable with that, I'll understand. If you are, I'll be gentle."

"Umm, this was a really nice evening. I'd be disappointed if you didn't kiss me goodnight." He was so handsome. And his smile was just as intoxicating as Alonzo's smile and the wine, combined.

He pressed in for it. Hard! Cindy was so taken aback that she longed to ask him to stay the night but dared not. It was undoubtedly too soon. And he had to get home to his wife!

That night, Cindy went to bed among the stars. She'd come so alive by way of Denville that Alonzo was no longer much of a romantic illusion; but he was still an intellectual property to which she had willfully committed. Moments before she laid down to sleep, she remembered her promise. "I'll call him tomorrow. That's my HCPC meeting day; and I pass by the Albertson building on my way home. I know he's probably at the peak of his workday by that time. I'll drop off this Gary Numan shit then." Without further ado, feeling the effect of Denville and the wine, she was off to dreamland.

Tuesday was just another workday for Cindy. Since she was so tremendously unoccupied after her HCPC proceeding, she decided to reach out to Denville and thank him again for such a delicious evening. 'I'll try his cell phone first. If he doesn't answer, I'll page him.' Her silent thoughts had her inwardly beaming. The warm feeling the new man in her life brought was immeasurable and long overdue.

It was 4:20 p.m, and the first call on his new cell phone. Somewhat startled, he suddenly recalled Gary's words of wisdom: a sincere lover was accessible twenty-four/seven. He always kept the phone and pager at his side.

Challenged by this challenge and not in a mood to deal with Cindy's gaiety, Denville answered with a non-discernable, "Hello?"

"Hey you! Just wanted to call and thank you again for last night. Hope I didn't interrupt one of your client meetings. And I did want to hear your voice," she whimsically said.

"Cindy. Oh no, you didn't interrupt. I'm in my office today doing paperwork. How are you? I was going to give you a call this evening.

It's probably impossible to reach you during the day, but I was thinking about you, love."

"Really?"

"Really. I don't want to come on too strong, but I want you to know you're a beautiful woman and I want a lasting relationship with you. Is that possible?"

"Anything is possible, so they say. But I like that thought, so it's possible."

"Cool. So when can I see you again? I was going to call you tonight and ask you if you had any plans for Wednesday night."

"Wednesday will be tough. I go to AA meetings with my sister. I told you about her."

"Yeah, you did. But you know, she's got to start going to those meetings without you as a crutch."

"I know. And so does she, but for right now, she needs me there. We've come so far. I just can't let her down, or my niece and nephew. They're all depending on me—whether they know it or not—to pull them through this."

"I hear you! The commendable Cindy Jack. Hey! I'll still call you tonight before I start calling hogs, and maybe Thursday we can get together—for a quick dinner and a movie. Okay?"

"Sounds good. Okay. See you Denville."

"Yep! Sure will, Cindy. Talk to you later, sweetheart." And unbeknown to Denville, Cindy was about to do the very thing he was sent to ensure never happened!

She hung up the phone and looked at her watch. It was 4:45 p.m., perfect time for her next call.

"Good evening. Alonzo Prier's office. This is Anna. May I help you?"

"Hello. This is Cindy Jack. I'm the stenographer for the HRRC and I have some transcript excerpts for Mr. Prier. He told me to call him. Is he available?"

"Hold on please, I'll check."

Anna buzzed Alonzo who was on another line, three-way conferencing with Michael Neely and Debbie North about the proposed labor strike. Debbie was in New York at McCarther & Parks with Michael. She thought it would be a good time to go over some of the financial implications of the issue. "Hold on Michael and Debbie, Anna's buzzing me. Yes, Anna?"

"A Cindy Jack is on line one. She has some transcript excerpts for you. Should she mail them?"

"No, ask her if she can drop them off. I'll be in my office pretty much until I'm ready to leave. I've got to finish up this call I'm on, but I'll be done in about fifteen minutes. See if she can bring them by. Thanks, Anna."

"Ms. Jack, Mr. Prier would like you to bring them over. Is that possible? He's on a conference call now but can see you in about twenty minutes." Anna always added a few extra minutes for Alonzo's sake. He was always so busy going from one fiasco to the next that she scheduled a little breather for him in between appointments.

"That's fine. What floor are you on?"

"We're on the fifteenth floor. This building has two elevator banks. Get off the elevator on the third floor; turn right; walk around to the other side of the building to the second elevator bank. Those elevators run from three to twenty. When you get off on fifteen, make a left and head to Section H&I. We're the Health and Insurance section. That's section fifteen hundred. Come through the double doors and you'll be at my desk. I leave at 5:30, hopefully you'll be here before then."

"I sure will." She recalled her CRFC meeting had been booted over to that building and the two distinguished men discussing Alonzo by the third-floor elevator. 'Oh,' she thought, 'so the employees have separate elevators for floors four through twenty. I guess that's how they protect the AG's employees from the unpredictable masses of JQ public who enter that building. All public conference and meeting rooms are on floors one through three. Interesting.'

Cindy was on a mission! That morning of September twelfth, she had placed her bound and highlighted transcript excerpts in a legal-size envelope from Casten. She tucked it safely in the trunk of her car before packing her other stuff for the day. It was now 5:15 Tuesday evening.

After the security guard's clearance, when Cindy arrived at the Albertson Justice Complex's elevator, she was its only passenger. Once inside elevator bank number one, she thought aloud, "I wonder if there's any numerology significance to this? At 5:15, I'm headed up to the fifteenth floor; section fifteen hundred; with one hundred fifteen pages of bullshit straight from Gary Numan's mouth! The only thing that could have made this more mysterious is if it were September fifteenth! Then I'd just turn around and go. Too spooky; couldn't have done this."

Her mouth suddenly shut like a trap door when the second elevator bank's doors opened at the fifteenth floor. She was about to come face-to-face with the Ace-man behind his closed office door! Package in hand, she stepped off the elevator and followed Anna's directions.

"Hello. I'm, Cindy Jack."

"Hello, Ms. Jack. I'm Anna. Alonzo's in his office. He's just been so busy lately. The guy gets home so late, it's a wonder his beautiful wife doesn't come down here and get him. I would if he was my husband. Just a moment."

Anna got up and went over to Alonzo's door. Before she could knock, he opened it. "Gee, you must be psychic!"

"Nope. Just blessed with fairly good timing." He looked over towards Cindy and unexpectedly she had a lust-rush! Alonzo was back in the romantic forefront of her imagination. She managed to suppress it as she quickly re-focused on why she was there, and on Denville. Alonzo was standing in his office doorway, flashing his sexy smile. "Cindy, so you believe there's something looming at the JHPTC level that I should be aware of, huh?"

"Absolutely. You know, I've recorded emotional testimonies many times where public and private representatives almost come to blows but Gary Numan's arguments are from someplace else. And it's obvious." An impressively articulate Cindy had Alonzo's undivided attention.

"I just want to give Anna a few things I'll need for tomorrow. Do you have a few minutes?"

"Yes."

"Great. Then, have a seat in my office and I'll be with you in a few. This is interesting, and I want to talk with you some more before I read the transcript excerpts."

"No problem." Cindy entered Alonzo's office and sat in a chair facing his desk. His office was huge and plush, housing two sofas configured in an L-shape, separated by a table in the middle. Many neat piles of documents accentuated his desk and table. As Cindy gazed around awaiting his return, she fixated on his family pictures displayed on the cadenza behind his massive mahogany desk. There were five beautiful high-gloss Kodak moments. There were separate pictures of Shawna, Erik, Thornton and Chloyee. The fifth picture captured him and Shawna, in the company of another couple, with the Governor in the middle. 'That must have been the picture that Gina mentioned,' she thought. And now, Cindy too was thinking how gorgeous Shawna was, and how cute the kids were. Nope, it didn't seem like a man with all that was going to give it up for anybody else. 'How could anybody else upstage and uproot that closely held situation?' Her thoughts stopped just before he re-entered his office.

"Now that Anna's all squared away, I'm all ears for you, Cindy." He sat in the matching chair next to her. He'd left the door ajar. She also noted that he didn't say, 'I'm all yours.' "So, you think there's something funky going on with Gary Numan? Truth be told, I know something funky's going on with Gary Numan and crew. I just don't know exactly what it is. They'll be before the HRRC September twenty-sixth. I already have enough information to start heavily interrogating them, but I don't have the motivation for their actions. Point blank, that's what I'm looking for. So, what do you think I'll find in the JHPTC transcripts?"

"It's like there's some bigger picture that he's got to make sure everybody sees. And if they don't get the picture, he's angry, excessively emotional, and he throws in a couple of expletives here and there! He's out of control. You'll sense that in reading these transcripts. I even inserted exclamation points during the proceedings when he was really bent out of shape. He talks a lot about foreign countries' ventures and how they're much more advanced because of the nature of their healthcare system. He's always making arguments about how hospitals must be deregulated; it's like the cream can only rise to the top if it's free to do so. He even talks about this foreign organization, UKing. His point is that when healthcare is rationed, the system and people do more to keep healthy. They're remanded to their own hands. And I've highlighted all those comments for you. I went through nineteen transcripts; there were twenty-six in total since the time that task force was started to discuss deregulation. But these nineteen tell the whole Gary Numan story."

"Cindy, I'm remarkably impressed. But I hope you realize that as I didn't ask you for any of this, and because of my position, there's absolutely nothing I can do to compensate you for your time or efforts. You did this purely of your own volition."

"I understand and I'm not asking for anything. You seemed curious and interested in Harrington Hospital; and so have I, just in being the stenographer for the JHPTC. Gary Numan is so obviously stoked by this deregulation issue even Stevie Wonder would see it. Maybe it was just meant to be that I deliver this information to you—no expectations." With that, she handed the stuffed legal-size envelope to him marked: CONFIDENTIAL—Alonzo Prier, Sr. Counsel, Section Chief, Attorney General's Office.

Before she left, she commented on his family pictures. "They're all such beautiful pictures. But you don't have a family group shot."

"No, I don't. I got that from my dad. When my brother and I were growing up, my father always kept single pictures of us. He said it helped him focus on us as individuals, not as a pair. I think it helped in developing our unique personalities and individual differences. So, when I focus on Thorton for example, I just see him. I don't see any possible expression of Erik."

"That's an interesting concept."

"Well, it worked for us. My brother's an Electrical Engineer; we have no idea about what either of us do career-wise, but we have much respect and admiration for each other's choices."

"Is your brother older than you?"

"Yeah, three years older. He's forty-seven. He's got two daughters and he keeps his household pictures the same way."

"Wow." Feeling the need to move on, Cindy and Alonzo exchanged handshakes as he thanked her once again for such a commendable undertaking. He was now smiling with what appeared to be an expression of admiration. Although that would probably be the end of her Harrington involvement and the extent of her after-hours Alonzo involvement, she left with a feeling of accomplishment and mutual respect.

Just as Alonzo was about to tear into Cindy's envelope his private line rang. "Hello?"

"Hey, Azo. How you been, buddy?"

"Knee-deep in bullshit with a shit-load of work! What's up, Ted?"

"Same problem. Major asbestos problems brewing in pockets of the State once again. New Jersey was such a highly industrialized State that this asbestos thing just keeps rearing its ugly head—never gets resolved. Anyway, I just thought about you and that barbecue we were supposed to have. What happened, man?"

"Ah. Erik broke his arm. He was irritable and kept Shawna so damn busy around that time, I just didn't have the heart to ask her to plan the Labor Day thing. And me too. I've been running non-stop with all my issues."

"Well, I'm working late tonight. Just thought you might want to grab a quick brew and steak, before we start round two. I'll probably be here until nine tonight."

"You know, Ted, yeah. I'll meet you at the Brewsky again; give me twenty minutes. That work for you?"

"Sure does. See you then."

Alonzo called home to inform Shawna that it was his turn to bail Ted out. Ted now needed a little tea and sympathy, in much the same way as he did when Harrington had him running helter-skelter.

Now at The Brewsky, Ted was about to educate Azo on one of his critical issues as the Commissioner of Environmental Protection. "Man, you think you've got problems with that one fuckin' hospital, you should see and hear the shit I'm going through right now. This asbestos thing is bigger than ever; my problem dates to when God created Adam!"

"What's happening?" Alonzo questioned with concern.

Ted replied. "A load of complaints and lawsuits from cancer victims of major corporations that exposed people to asbestos. About six counties major league affected and four marginally. Good news for you though is that Compton and contiguous counties were not impacted by this round. But for those that were, the investigation alone—is driving us to the limit. Problem is that those who were victimized, were victimized ages ago, and the damages are just beginning to surface."

Alonzo curiously followed up with, "What are the considerations now?"

"First we've got to get a handle on all the accusations. Then we've got to dig up all the stuff that passed through the DEP when those corporations were requesting approvals for what they were manufacturing and installing. Then there's the medical analyses. There's so much quagmire there, I don't even want to discuss it. Really, I just came out to have a quick dinner with a friend. The thought of what I've got to go back and face is disgusting. What's up with you? How's Harrington?"

"Oh, I think I might have a lead on what's been motivating their shit. And that's good to know that asbestos wasn't a problem for their vicinity. I've got some transcripts to review first before I can say. Guess I'm in the same boat as you—I'm looking for skeletons too. Anyway, to hell with all that. How's the family?"

Alonzo and Ted continued conversing on lighter terms for almost an hour. When dinner was over, they'd be on their respective ways. That evening, versus returning to his office, Alonzo opted to take the document Cindy had prepared home for perusal.

Cindy had only been home for about fifteen minutes when her phone rang at 6:47 p.m. "Hello?"

"Hey, sweetheart. Hope I didn't catch you at a bad time."

"No, you didn't, sweetheart. I was just deciding on dinner, so your timing is perfect. I haven't even undressed yet."

"I can imagine the visual—you undressing. Umm. Anyhow, I'm tired and I'm not a phone person after business hours. But I did want to touch bases and let you know I was thinking about you. So will you keep Thursday open for me?"

"I certainly will. You want to do a movie, right?"

"I really want to do you. But I'll behave a little longer. I like you, Cindy, and I want to be close to you. Are you feeling that way too?"

"Yes. I'm starting to. It's really been a while since I've been involved with anyone."

"That's what you say. I don't understand that though. Anyway, we'll talk about it. I'm changing that! I'll talk to you tomorrow and I'll see you Thursday. Love you."

They hung up. "Damn!" she said aloud. "He used the L-word! This guy is hot! Now I'll have someone, beside myself, to show my Victoria's Secrets too. Look out Denville! I think I love you too."

Since the prior Wednesday, Cindy had waded through all the documents by which she needed to convince Alonzo of Gary's personal agenda. When she picked Eve up that evening, she would be free and clear to give Eve's dilemma her undivided attention.

Wednesday came and went uneventfully for Cindy, other than a few "I love you; and I miss you" voicemails from Denville. Denver was doing his best in making his romantic intentions known.

By Thursday, Cindy was in the mood for love. When he picked her up for dinner and a movie, they'd become so stimulated over the main course that the side dish being the movie wasn't needed. Cindy yearned for Denville to serve up dessert at her house, and he was undoubtedly obliged to accommodate her.

It was about 8:30 when Denville and Cindy returned to her house. "I didn't want to see a movie. I'd rather make a movie."

"Oh really, Ms. Jack? Well let me just see what I can do to make that happen." Denville was reflecting to his hay-days when he could have easily been regarded as stud-like. He'd buried those tendencies in deference to marriage. But dredging up that capacity would not a problem.

Behind closed doors in the serenity of her apartment, Cindy turned on her stereo system's radio to a pre-set romantic lite jazz station in a dimly- lit living room. She waltzed back over to Denville who was getting ready for the conquest. Just thinking about being with a new woman, as part of the Numan conspiracy, was a newfound reason for the fictitious Denville to shoot for the stars. And little did he know that he was playing amongst the stars. For Cindy Jack had taken on the essence of the late-great Greta Garbo.

They started seductively dancing to Basia's *Crusing for Bruising*. It got a little bit jungle and steamy in Cindy's serene apartment. The next selection the disc jockey played was more 'embrace me now' oriented. Feeling the heat of the moment, Cindy and Denville were in each other's arms. She felt his erection; he felt her desire. He didn't have to ask. Knowing that he knew all the right moves, he just got busy. He started with the sensual neck kisses while running his hands fluently over her back and down around her butt. She was wearing a short skirt that he unbuttoned and unzipped. It fell to the floor. She stepped away from it; he followed her movement. He unbuttoned her blouse; she took it off. Now all of Victoria's Secrets were exposed. And the music was getting more sensual with each selection. He started to undress. He took off his shirt and then his pants. His body was even more perfect than his clothes suggested.

"*Umm*," was all Cindy expressed. They were both down to their underwear and thrilled with the sight of each other. Within a matter of moments their relationship was consummated. Smack dab in the middle of her living room floor. And Cindy was hooked. Denville was a sensitive, well-endowed aiming-to-please lover. He made sure Cindy climaxed twice, before he even dared to go there once. The game was invariably on; Cindy remained clueless, but sexually gratified, nonetheless. "Umm! Oh yeah," were her concluding sentiments sealed with a smile.

"Did I do it for you? Did I make you feel good?" He wanted to know.

"You couldn't tell?"

"Nope. Don't know you well enough yet. But if you need something from me, tell me, I'll perfect my act. I care about meeting your needs—at least the ones I can, Cindy."

"I just want you to hold me. Everything was perfect," she genuinely offered.

"Done. Name it, you claim it." With a sigh of accomplishment, a deceptively sensitive Denville held her passionately.

Knowing an endearing sign from a lover is when he remains cuddled close, embracing, as if to not even be able to tolerate the intrusion of a hairpin is exactly what Denville did, long after the act was over. It was about eleven thirty when he was about to head home.

"Hey! Sweetheart!" Cindy had drifted off into a slight blissful sleep; he awakened her. "This has been one helluva evening. We've got to do this again. Real soon. But—I've got to go—I've got a long drive; I'm going to split."

"Oh, absolutely. South Mountain is a long trek from here."

"Yep. Cindy, I'll call you tomorrow. I'm falling in love with you. I want you to know that. Oomph! Maybe I'm just intoxicated by you. Whatever; I'll call you tomorrow." Denville had dressed and was on his way out. Cindy laid there in the comfort of her carpeted floor.

"Denville, will you call me and let me know you got home okay?"

"Sure will. No problem." He gently kissed her forehead on his way out.

Cindy arose to walk about fifteen feet to her bedroom. She plopped herself atop her bed and gave way to the best sleep she'd had in years. Denville/Denver drove all about twenty minutes home. Before he entered his house, he dialed Cindy's number from his car. He let the phone ring three times. Figuring she'd need more time to answer, he gratuitously hung up. He didn't really want to speak with her. He only wanted to give the impression that he did. He was now home. He securely locked his cell phone in the glove compartment, ensured that his beeper was in place, and proceeded to enter his apartment. It was now twelve-thirteen a.m., and a soundly sleeping Vicky was none the wiser about her husband's illicit activities. She'd accepted his overtime hospital business story as gospel truth. That story made it convenient for him to come home and go directly to the shower! After all, he'd been working amidst a taxing environment; at the very least, he'd be sweaty. A totally refreshed Denver slid into bed next to his unsuspecting and unconscious wife. He spooned her and moments later, drifted off to dreamland.

Around the same time, Alonzo too was headed up to bed. What he'd read the previous night from Cindy's highlighted excerpts' package was so compelling, that he felt the need to re-read it on Thursday night after all in his household were sound asleep. Late Thursday night, he'd devoted total undivided attention to what those transcripts alluded. He'd focused on the specificity of certain aspects of Gary Numan's comments—all excerpted and highlighted by Cindy Jack. On the way up his spiraling staircase, he inwardly admired Cindy's tenacity for having plowed through those documents and pulled together a scenario well worth his scrutiny.

XI

More Rounds

F RIDAY MORNING, EVERYONE WAS BACK to work as usual. Denver was
ready to give Gary an update on his progress; Alonzo was ready to
update Lindy on his discovery; and Cindy was raring to update Gina
about her wildly romantic interlude.

"Denver, come in. Close the door; have a seat. How's that Cindy
Jack bitch? Have you made any headway yet?" Gary was anxious to
know if his little seeds of divisiveness were bearing any fruit.

"Oh yeah, man! I told you she was hot to trot. She wants it, and I'm
giving it to her. But I don't want this woman to fall in love with me,
Gary. She's really a nice person, and if I wasn't married, maybe I could
go for her. But Gary, I can't afford to have Cindy wanting me forever
man. I just can't..." And Denver was cut off again!

Gary was emotional as usual. "You just can't what? You're in this as
deep as we are! Don't you realize that you don't deserve a position in this
hospital as Director of Purchasing? You have no experience! The only
reason we put you in that position is so you'd be the one controlling the
arrival and warehousing particulars for BandRxStat! You introduced us
to the guy who helped bring this BandRxStat deal to the table, so we
brought you on board. That's it! And now you're standing in my office,
telling me that you can't do something that's going to help get our asses
out of deep shit! Look at it this way, Denver—if we sink—you're history
too! So, I don't think you want to keep talking about what you can't
do—do you?"

Recognizing that Gary wasn't fooling around Denver cowered to the occasion. "No. And I'm sorry, man. It's just that she's really a nice person. I don't love her, but I don't want to hurt her or my wife. But I'll do what I have to do. It's working. Cindy's going for all of this."

"Good. Have you taken her to my condo yet?"

"No. I was planning to do that this weekend. That's a long way from here; I'm glad I know where it is. I figured that would be a weekend thing. This weekend will be good. My wife's sister is having an engagement party on Saturday, and Vicky's going to be busy with all that bullshit. I'll run Cindy up there then."

"Good. Good. Keep this moving, Denver. Don't let your emotions get in the way. This will all be over soon. Remember you're going to dump her. I just want you to get her all worked up! That way her fall will be really hard. And we don't have much time anyway. You've got to work long, hard and quick!"

"Will do. See you later, Gary." Denver left Gary's office; both unaware that Cindy had already done the deed they were aiming to sabotage.

Meanwhile, Alonzo was updating Lindy Jewel on Cindy Jack's contribution to the Harrington hodge-podge. Lindy had already constructed a rather large file of fact-filled information based on the considerations he had previously asked her to investigate.

"After you've read this, add the relevant testimonies to Harrington's file for me please. I've marked the excerpts that I want to further question Gary on when they're before the Commission on Tuesday. I like what you've prepared so far Lindy—and this puts the lid on it." He handed Lindy the bound dossier Cindy had prepared. "She did an outstanding job on this. If the fallout from the September twenty-sixth meeting is what I think it will be, some of the credit will be due to Cindy Jack."

"I see. I'll get busy on this immediately, Alonzo. Anything else?"

"No, Lindy. That's it."

Feeling a little bit jealous of Alonzo's obvious admiration for Ms. Jack's efforts, Ms. Jewel left his office, document in hand. Mr. Prier was oblivious to the two females' underlying sentiments towards him and resentments towards each other. Both would have done anything to impress him.

"Department of Environmental Protection. Gina Falcone speaking. May I help you?"

"Hey girl, it's me! I'm on a fifteen-minute break, and I wanted to tell you first!"

"Cindy! Hey! What's up?"

"Gina, you're not going to believe this but, I've really got a great guy in my life! Denville is great! We made love last night! Gina, he was awesome. I'm in love! And so is he! I feel great! He's even started using the L-word. He told me he was falling in love with me!" Cindy was so excited.

"Wow! I'm so happy for you! And I don't doubt anything you're feeling. But Cindy—it is a bit soon for love. I certainly don't want to burst your bubble, but lust happens a lot sooner than love. Are you sure you're both just not in lust? You're a great looking woman and you say he's a great looking guy. You know?" A somewhat skeptical Gina was somewhat leery of true love so soon.

"Yeah, I know what you're saying. But he's so persistent and consistent. He's not letting up and he's always following through. He's not like the other fake-ass guys that just want to screw you and say goodbye. This guy has staying power—in many ways! For the first time—in a long time—I'm happy, Gina! Even Eve's AA stuff is working!"

"Well, you sound great, and I'm really happy for you. But just keep your wits about you. It's still early in the game of love for you two. Anyway, we'll talk at lunch. We're on for the twenty-fifth, right?"

"Right. So, I'll see you then. Are you and the baby still fine?"

"Yep. The bambino and me are fine; the old baby and I are fine too. Thanks for asking. See you in two weeks."

"Sure will. See ya."

An electrified Cindy charged back to finish her morning proceeding. Afterwards, she would grab a quick lunch and page Denville before her next session. He'd return her page via her office voicemail and leave a steamy message. She knew he preferred reaching out to his clients around noon, so she wouldn't bother telephoning him then.

True to form, after her last proceeding when she checked her voicemail, there was a message from Denville. "Hello my lady. Just wanted to check in and say I love you. I'll call you tonight. Don't make any weekend plans; I'm making them for us. Later."

A love-locked Cindy hung up the phone. Her next call would be to Eve to ensure she was ready to be escorted to her sixth AA session. She'd hve a banana and a bottle of water before she picked up Eve for the night's meeting.

By the time Cindy got home that Friday night, she was still on an emotional high. Everything in her world was going right for a change. She'd decided that she finally was exploring the caverns of her innermost "tussled" thoughts. Life had now begun to manifest as the exhilarating journey it was intended to be. She recalled that song again and sung it aloud as she placed the key in her apartment door's lock— *"And nothin's gonna stop us now!"*

Denver, knowing about what time Cindy would be home, called her five minutes later. He had excused himself from his lovely wife's company to attend to some nonsense about his car. From there, he placed the call to Cindy via his cell phone. "Hello, lovely. How are you and how was AA with Eve?"

"All is well. And you?"

"All is well."

"What did you mean about the weekend?"

"You've never been to my house. I'll pick you up tomorrow morning about ten thirty. You know I live about an hour and a half away from you. We'll get started early, spend the day and possibly night here. Is that okay?"

"Absolutely. That's fine. I can't wait."

"Cool. I'll see you tomorrow morning then. Love you."

"I love you too." Cindy had now committed. She'd returned his serve.

Denver committed his cell phone to his glove compartment and returned to his wife.

"You know, all this hospital shit is really keeping me hopping. I've got a full schedule tomorrow in the warehouse. Only good thing is that I don't have to be there until 10 a.m. I'll probably work until ten or eleven tomorrow night, though."

"It's Saturday for goodness sakes! The hours are ridiculous. Don't you think?"

Vicky was curious but not distrusting.

"Yeah, they are. But I've got to go where the money is. Honey, when all of this is over, it will truly be over. And the payoff will be there too. You can believe that! Just hang in there with me a little longer. Okay?"

"Sure. Denver, if you're okay with this, I'm okay. My sister's shower is tomorrow, so I'll be busy anyway. I guess all of this couldn't have happened at a better time. At least I'm not sitting around waiting for us to get some time together. It would have been worse if it was a few months ago—when I was off for the summer. But I'm back at school now and I've got my sister's engagement thing to do."

"Timing is everything. I love you, Vicks. Come here—I'll prove it to you." Denver began embracing his wife. Her youthful beauty and innocence always aroused him. Within seconds, they were in the passionate throes of their marital rites.

Meanwhile, Cindy was rambling through her closet for her weekend rendezvous. She'd certainly bring along a few of Victoria's Secrets. But she was a little unsure of whether she'd be a weekend guest for one or two nights; requiring one or two outfits, and what types of outfits? "I'll just call him and find out for sure." Cindy called his cell to no avail. "Gee, he didn't mention he was going out. Umm, maybe he's out with some of the guys. It is Friday night. I'll just page him then." She did.

It was eleven forty p.m., and Vicky was closest to his pager. He had placed it on the night table when he undressed to make love to her. By now, Denver was sound asleep. "Honey, wake up. Your pager is beeping."

"Ah shit. What?" Still rather hazy, Denver reached over to turn on the light and check the number appearing on his beeper. Vicky wasn't much of a gadget person; she had no interest in or use for the thing.

Seeing it was Cindy's number, he quickly deleted it and laid there quietly wondering what to do next. He certainly could not call Cindy while lying in bed with his wife; he couldn't get up and run out to the car, that would raise suspicion; and he didn't really want to ignore Cindy's page.

"Aren't you going to call them back? It was the hospital folks, right?" Vicky casually asked.

"Yeah, it was. But I'll just call first thing tomorrow morning."

Vicky replied, "Maybe they don't need you to come in tomorrow."

"Then they'll just tell me that tomorrow morning. Let's go back to sleep. Come here."

Decision made. He'd just tell Cindy he had gone out, left the phone in his car and his beeper at home. Plan concocted. Perfect.

Cindy was up way past midnight awaiting Denville's return call. She didn't believe that she should be suspicious especially not so soon. But she did find him not calling back to be somewhat curious.

Saturday morning around eight-thirty while Vicky was showering, Denver snuck out to his car to call Cindy. "Hey, lady. Hope you're wide-eyed and bushy tailed. I didn't wake you, did I?"

"No, you didn't. Everything okay?"

Yep. And we're still on for today. Unless you can't."

"I can. In fact, I paged you last night to ask you how long we'd be together. The weekend or just the night?"

"Oh. Last night I hung out with some friends. I don't take my cell phone in clubs, and I left my pager home. I had on a different belt my pager might have fallen off. But um—regarding the night or the weekend, I was thinking more of just the day. I've got to go out of town Sunday evening for an early Monday morning sales convention. And, I've got something to drop off at my parents' house. So, I'll just get you back tonight—around ten or eleven."

"Oh. Okay. Just wanted to be sure." A beaming Cindy was none the wiser.

"Great. I'll see you around ten-thirty?"

"Fine. See ya." A little less together time than Cindy had hoped but it was still reasonable. They had just started to get involved, and perhaps she shouldn't want so much, so soon. Perhaps being together for an entire day was more than enough for the time being. "Yeah, I think I'm rushing things now. We've got time for more time together." Expressing those thoughts aloud gave Cindy a restored sense of comfort. "And if he'd been with another woman, he certainly took her back early enough." She realized it was only eight-thirty in the morning and he was calling her; by ten-thirty he'd be at her door.

"Did you call the hospital back?" Vicky was now doing her make-up and getting ready to fix a quick breakfast. She too would soon be headed out to attend to her sister's party details.

"Yeah. It was nothing; just wanted to confirm that I'd be there. I've got to get started a little earlier though. I'm going to shower, get dressed and just have a glass of juice. Don't fix me any breakfast."

"Okay. But it wasn't like I was going to fix a full course meal. I was thinking tea and toast."

"No thanks." Denver quickly headed to the shower.

Cindy had already showered. When Denville called earlier that morning, she was lounging around in her robe, having decided to not get dressed until nearing the time he would arrive. Having squared away that their togetherness would only last for the day, it alleviated the pressure of having to pack attire and matching accessories. She became more comfortable with that as time passed.

He arrived at ten-thirty-three. Cindy was dazzling! She had on another sporty short skirt ensemble with low-heeled matching pumps. Both were dressed in rather nice casual attire. "Gee! You're always a sight for sore eyes! And I'm three minutes late because I had to stop and get you some flowers. So that's what held me up before you ask." He presented her with six flawless red roses. "Wantta put these in some water before we go?"

"They're absolutely gorgeous! Denville, my goodness, the first bunch of flowers you gave me are still alive. I can't believe you've done this again!"

"I don't think a beautiful lady can ever get too many flowers or too many kisses."

"Okay. I guess that means you're ready to roll out the next bunch of kisses too."

She playfully smiled as she stepped closer in towards him.

"Umm, you're a mind reader too." He kissed her passionately for about one non-stop minute. She was overwhelmed, overjoyed, and in over her head. "Let's hit the road, lady." And as fate should have it, Denver was familiar with the route to Gary's condo. Ironically, his parents had friends who lived in South Mountain three blocks from Gary's condominium development. Even more uncanny is that they were Frank Balone's relatives. Denver and Kenneth frequently met Frank in South Mountain to frequent some of the posh clubs there prior to Denver's marriage. The women were upper class and outlandishly beautiful. Those three guys always felt like they'd died and gone to heaven whenever they hung out up there in God's perfect territory.

The drive was relaxing amidst the great weather. And Denville did think of everything. To acquaint himself with Gary's condo in the presence of Cindy he thought to bring a blindfold along. A block before Gary's development Denville pulled over. "Cindy, put this on. Turn around, I'll tie it for you. I want to surprise you. Okay?"

"I like surprises, but what's this? And why?" She was playfully curious.

"Listen, I stayed up and cleaned all night after I got home. I've got a few surprises for you and I want to heighten the moment. Can't I just make this extra special for you? Why do you have to question everything? Just relax and enjoy. Now, put this up to eyes; turn around and let me tie it. No peeking!"

"Okay. No peeking."

Cindy was now looking most ridiculous wearing Vicky's black and white bandanna cast as a blindfold. But it was a needed nuance to help Denville fumble his way through Gary's hide-away. He didn't even know which way the key went into the lock. Luckily, Cindy could not observe that! And Denville had no idea what he was about to see. He needed time to first adjust his vision and response to the visual.

Having opened the door he was speechless. The one level over-sized dwelling was like a little mansion. It was exquisitely decorated and spotless too. It was done up to the tune of—it's a man's world after all! 'Damn', silently thought Denville, 'this place must have cost a fortune! When Cindy sees this she's going to freak out! Hell, I'm freakin' out! Gary, you son-of-a-bitch!'

"So, Mr. Seamons! How much longer do I have to stand here in this damn eye gear?" Cindy was becoming a tab anxious.

"Just a little bit longer. I need two more minutes. Please!" He desperately needed to quickly run through the house to see it through once himself. "I need to set up a few things!"

But everything was set up. A big box of chocolate candy tied in a pink, satin bow was on the living room coffee table with a card addressed: To Cindy. Silk and dried floral arrangements accentuated the contemporary décor throughout. All kinds of exotic fresh fruits were in the refrigerator, with the more common apples and oranges in the kitchen fruit bowls. A variety of wines were filling his over-sized wine rack to capacity. The king-sized bed donned satin sheets underneath a huge plush satiny matching comforter. There were about ten pillows on the bed! And then there was the Jacuzzi and a thirty-some-odd inch television; not to mention the gas fireplaces in the living room, kitchen and master bathroom! Denville's quick tour was over. He rushed back to Cindy to do the unveiling honors.

"Whoa! This is fabulous. I don't believe this! You're in hospital sales with all this and you're only twenty-five? *You must be one hell of a salesman.* Damn, I wonder where the CEO of your company lives if you live here with all this! This is incredible, Denville!"

"Well, it's not just sales related." Even Denville was overwhelmed. "Um—my parents are really the owners. I just—um —I live here. And it's just me. My brother is not into being way out here and my parents have a more modest single-family house too." Denville nor Denver could have ever been prepared for all that luxuriousness. "But I've done a lot of re-furnishing in here."

"So, you regard yourself as the caretaker?"

"Well yes. I am. I pay rent though. Plus, I pay the utilities. This place can be mine if I want it. But for now I play it by ear. Come on, I'll show you around."

Taking Cindy on a guided tour throughout, Denville was now feeling more rejuvenated. He'd gotten his equilibrium back after having been knocked off his feet from the first-time viewing of Gary's digs. Ending back up in the kitchen, he opened the refrigerator. "Can I get you a drink?"

"For now, I'll just have some water."

"The real thirst quencher. Sounds good. Me too." Now it would be potluck since he didn't know what cabinet in which the glasses were kept. He hit the jackpot. He opened the cabinet over the dishwasher. A couple of sets of glasses and dishes were there.

"It's quarter after twelve. Let's go have lunch. I'll show you the town, and we'll come back here and hang out."

"Sounds good. Let's do it."

And that's what they did. When they returned, they made love—a few times. Before they left, he deliberately went into Gary's garage and picked up an empty box as Cindy sat in the car watching and waiting. He locked it in his car trunk. During the long drive back, and since they'd discussed practically everything else, Denville thought to broach the subject of the HRRC and Alonzo.

"So, how's it going with your new HRRC sessions?"

"Fine. They're pretty much like the others actually."

"It's just that I know Alonzo Prier can keep those hospitals hopping if he doesn't believe what their cost reports are showing. He's tough. I've seen him in action—many times. That could make your life harder."

"No; not really. I'm somewhat familiar with Alonzo's style. I worked with him a few years ago."

Not knowing how else to approach it, he simply asked, "Do you like him?"

Not knowing what he was really getting at, she simply replied, "He's married with children." Her lack-luster response threw him a curve ball. He didn't know where to go from there, so he dropped the subject.

When Denville dropped Cindy off at her apartment, it was almost eleven o'clock. He told her what a great time he had, hoped she was equally pleased and kissed her again—a little less passionately since they were in his car. He didn't go in, since he had to get that box to his parents, as he'd promised. And since he was going to his parents, it was perfectly reasonable for him to have taken a shower at Gary's and be refreshed before greeting them. Hence, no need to run past Vicky and shower once he got home. Denville had pulled off the perfect date, which fit in perfectly with his wife's plans that day. Everybody was happy! As he put the key in his apartment door lock, he thought silently, 'I'll be glad when this nightmare is over. Keeping this kind of shit up over time is pretty risky business!'

With the lights still on in the living room he figured that Vicky was probably still up. As he walked through to the dining room, she was exiting the kitchen. He playfully grabbed and kissed her. She didn't even notice that he was freshly showered. He'd made a point of no cologne and a lot of Gary's secret bar of unscented soap.

"Hey, honey! I just got in about ten minutes ago. I brought you some food from the festivities; Lasagna and cake."

"Thanks, Vicks. You're my honey, baby. So how was the party?"

They talked until bedtime. A contented Denver went to sleep with his unsuspecting wife. Cindy went to sleep content with the suspicion that she and Denville were on to something real.

That following Monday morning was the week of September eighteenth. This was the big preparation week for Gary Numan and crew, as well as Alonzo Prier and staff. The Health Department personnel were also gearing up to assist Alonzo in wading through Harrington's hocus-pocus. Gary had arrived at work earlier than usual that morning and had already left a message for Denver to come to his office immediately.

At nine-ten, Denver was knocking on Gary's half-closed door. "Yes. Come in."

"Morning, Gary. I got your message."

"Yeah, Denver. Tell me about the weekend. Did you take that crackpot to my condo?"

"Oh yeah! The place is fabulous! Man, I had no idea that it was like that. She was real impressed too!"

"Great. But is she in love with you? Are you impressing her with all the right moves and royal bullshit?"

Denver relayed all the sorted details. He even told him about the blindfold which Gary found clever. He mentioned the brief conversation he'd initiated about Alonzo and Cindy's lackadaisical response.

"That's good news, Denver! Sounds like the bitch might be enjoying your loins right about now and her mind's off Alonzo's. Good job! Oh, I've also talked to Lawson and Imani about the conference call with the Germans. See if Frank can set something up this week. We've got to know more before we deal with Alonzo next Tuesday. This shit has gone haywire, and we don't have much of a clue as to where he's going to be coming from. Alonzo is one tough and tricky son-of-a-bitch."

"You're going to talk about the BandRxStat deal?" Denver innocently inquired.

"Hell no! Are you fuckin' crazy? But we've got to know what's going on with it! We need to have at least an inkling as to when we can expect to start replacing that five and a half million. It would be great if those Germans have worked out the bugs with that fuckin' bandage! And besides, Alonzo wouldn't know to specifically ask about that. He's good, but he's no damn psychic!"

"I've been checking him out at those HRRC meetings. He's heavy! He knows all those rules and regulations. And he gets right to the point. Well, I'll call Frank when I get back downstairs. Any particular dates and times you want me to suggest?"

"Any day and anytime this week. All three of us will be here from sun-up to sundown. We've got to pull our act together before next Tuesday. We've all got our key employees pulling information together too. I've got to reach out to our hospital's independent counsel so maybe they can help brainstorm us through this. They don't know about BandRxStat either but they do know about our financial irregularities."

Denver left to call Frank; Gary had his secretary place a call to Iverson & Roth, Harrington's independent counsel.

"Iverson & Roth; Katelynn speaking; how may I direct your call."

"Martin Roth's office. This is Gary Numan calling."

"One moment please, Mr. Numan." While on hold, Gary sat fidgeting; thinking how to best present the circumstances to the hospital's outside counsel, who were totally unaware of Harrington's unscrupulous inside job.

"Gary? This is Martin. How's it going? I understand you're coming before the HRRC on September twenty-sixth. We got the schedule last week. From my assessment, that's going to be one hell of a meeting."

"Yeah. You're right. I was thinking that perhaps we need your expertise before we go in. You know, some legal advice probably? It's my best guess that Alonzo Prier is going to be the driver of this meeting for the Health Department."

"You're right. But I've been telling you guys about your financial discrepancies and what appeared to be extreme irregularities for quite some time now. Quite frankly, Gary, I'm not sure I wouldn't have some of the same questions and concerns Alonzo may have."

"So, what are you saying?"

"I'm saying that if you want us to come in and represent you at this meeting, we need to know more about why these problems are occurring at your hospital. We also need to have a possible corrective action plan to put on the table; even if it's just a talking points document."

"All of that is definitely reasonable and doable. Can you get in here sometime this week and what data do you need us to send you in preparation for the meeting?"

"Gary, this is very spur of the moment. But I'll give my secretary a list of items I want to see. Have it sent by courier and either I'll try and get there or have you guys here by the end of this week?"

"Thanks, Martin. We'll owe you."

"And you'll pay. Get me that information soon. We'll be in touch."

The law firm of Iverson & Roth was well respected by the Attorney General's Office. They were thorough, knew the hospital rules and regulations, and were ethical. They represented twenty-three of the ninety hospitals operational in the State. It was because of their reputation that Harrington State General Hospital sought I&R as its independent counsel. I&R had little interest at first since their client roster was comprised of private hospitals only. They thought it a little unusual that a public hospital would seek them so arduously. At any rate, they acquiesced. Hence, Harrington became their worst nightmare.

"Frank! Hey man, how's it going?"

"Denver! I'm fine, man. Guess you're calling back for a conference call with the Germans. Or do you have a babe or two you want to set me up with?"

"It's your first call. The Germans."

"Okay. When?"

"Anytime this week. Are they on the same time schedule as we are?"

"No, man, they're six hours ahead of us. It's ten fifteen in the morning here; it's four fifteen in the afternoon there. So, this is about how I'd set up the conference call. You guys would be on at ten in the morning; they'd be on at four in the afternoon. I wouldn't go past eleven and five. Know what I mean?"

"Yep. Got it! So could you set it up for any day this week with those times in mind?"

"I'll try. Everything else okay?"

"Man, you wouldn't believe what I'm going through with this BandRxStat shit. We'll have to get together for a few drinks. I need to tell you about this stuff man. It's bizarre. Anyway, let's get together after this conference call."

"Sure. I'll get back to you. I'm not promising anything, but I'll try."

"Thanks, Frank. Later."

And the rest of the week schlepped on. The only one who remained in gloriously high spirits was Cindy, as Denville continued to shower her with endearing voicemails, unexpected evening visits, fresh flowers, and great sex; all the ingredients that create love. Denville was surely working overtime.

Thursday morning, Frank called Denver to tell him he was successful in having gotten the Germans to agree to a Friday morning conference call.

"Whoa! That's great! Thanks, man. Are we talking ten and four or eleven and five?"

"Eleven and five, Friday, September twenty-second. Let me give you the telephone number. Get the international operator to place the call exactly at eleven o'clock Friday morning. The company is Helblien R & D and the number is 0711/24 75 53."

"That's a weird phone number."

"It's a German phone number. Anyway, gotta go. Call me afterwards and let me know how it went. Oh, Gary's got the guys' names in the prospectus."

"Will do. Thanks again."

Denver rushed to Gary's office with the good news and number. Gary rushed to Lawson's office, and Lawson called Imani. They would all gather in Lawson's office for the Friday morning telefon call.

Denver was awaiting Gary's return to his office. "Am I supposed to be in Lawson's office too Friday morning?"

"No. We'll take it from there. By the way, you haven't said anything to anyone about our little CJ project, have you?"

"Not a chance, man. You told me to keep it under wraps."

"Absolutely. Everything still on target?"

"Yep. She's falling harder by the minute. I've seen her every night so far this week. Tonight, she's going to an AA meeting with her sister, so I'll just call her. When should I break it off with her?"

"That depends on Mr. Prier. We'll know better after that meeting. If it only takes us a couple more visits to the HRRC to wrap things up, I'd say anytime around then. But if he starts asking a lot of questions and starts digging for answers, I don't know. What I don't want is for that bitch to push him towards those JHPTC transcripts! If you ditch her too soon and she's got nothing else to do she'll be back on Alonzo's trail —trying to get laid. And God only knows what she'll say to him in the process. That stupid bitch!"

"Well, if it's any consolation I think her mind is off Alonzo. She's not looking for love from him. Not now, anyway."

"Good! Keep it that way until this shit is over. Thanks for getting the call arranged."

And Lindy had completely arranged all the supporting information Alonzo would need towards his inquisition of Harrington Hospital's officers. She'd organized the file by three major categories of concern. Alonzo would begin with the outlandish financial irregularities appearing on Harrington's cost reports; he would next cover the curious organizational and personnel changes that had recently been put into effect; and finally, he would shift to the peculiar comments flowing from Gary Numan excerpted from the JHPTC transcripts!

She sat on one section of his L-shaped sofa with her long, lovely legs crossed; he sat on the other, attentively going through the file. "You've done an excellent job in organizing all this stuff. And there's no way the Numan bunch can lie their way out. The facts speak for themselves and those JHPTC transcripts speak to how the money disappeared!"

As she had been sitting awaiting his response, she'd been dangling her shoe by her perfectly manicured toes. Her shoe fell off and landed over by him. As he leaned forward to pick it up, her long sexy legs with one bare foot were right beneath his nose. She purposely uncrossed her leg at just the right moment; he could see all the way up to her panties. He felt a slight twinge. 'Damn', he silently thought, 'don't wantta be feeling this.' He took a deep breath, handed over her shoe, and quickly got up from the sofa.

Walking to his desk, he continued, "Yep, Lindy. This was quite an effort. And Candice Bremmer was quite helpful too. I'm going to call Warren Lein and update him on all this."

"Okay. Should I stay for the call?" She looked at him with an almost non-detectable lustfulness.

"No. You should go call Candice and let her know I've reviewed all the facts. Please thank her too. Oh yeah, you might also want to tell her I'll be conducting the full meeting Tuesday. Harrington's danced around the Health Department long enough. I'm about to take their little road show off the dance floor." And, he wanted Lindy to get the hell out of his office. He didn't like feeling that little feeling he'd sometimes feel around her.

As Lindy was exiting, Anna was entering Alonzo's office with a rather official looking package from Washington, D.C. "This just came for you. Special delivery."

"Thanks, Anna." He relieved her of the package, looked at its return address, and smiled. "This is what I've been waiting for. Would you close the door on your way out?"

"And how long would you like to not be disturbed?" Anna asked.

"It's ten-twenty now. Give me at least until noon. Thanks again."

A rather curious Anna closed the door behind her and proceeded back to her desk silently wondering 'what's going on in Washington? He's been there a few times within the last six months; he's gotten a few phone calls from people there, that he doesn't discuss with me— Umm—I wonder.'

Before tearing into the sealed package, Alonzo dialed Ted's private line from his private line. "Ted Garretson."

"Hey, Ted, its Azo. I got my Washington stuff today."

"And once again, up all night!"

"Yep. That's what it looks like. Well, I'm not going to even mention this to Shawna. If it's meant to be that's when I'll talk with her about it. In the meantime, it's like you said. Up all night, once again!"

"You've got my sympathy, man. Get some toothpicks to hold those eyes open."

"Thanks for the tip. How's your asbestos crisis?"

"Still in crisis. Hasn't moved one freakin' inch."

"Alright, Ted. We'll talk later. I definitely need to get back to the grind."

"Right, Azo. Later."

"Yep!." Alonzo tore into the special delivery package. He began reading the very nicely constructed letter from the independent health care policy and consulting law firm to the Health Care Financing Administration.

Dear Mr. Prier:

As you are aware, any person may upon proof of good moral character as it relates to the practice of law, be admitted to the Bar of the District of Columbia without examination provided such person has been a member in good standing of a Bar of a court of general jurisdiction in any state or territory of the U.S. for five years immediately preceding the filing of an application. As you are such a person, we sincerely hope you...

Just at that moment, Anna buzzed him. "Sorry. I know you wanted privacy but the Health Commissioner's on your line."

"No problem. I'll take it." He stuffed the Washington stuff back in its envelope. "Dr. Morris! What may I do you for?"

"Counselor, first you should stop with the formalities when we're not in public or else I'll just have to keep calling you counselor."

They both laughed. "I'm just messing with you, Gwen. What's up?"

She replied, "Harrington. I wanted to have a briefing with you and Warren before Tuesday. Is that possible for your schedule?"

"Absolutely. I was going to call Warren, but I got the Washington information we'd discussed a few months ago. It came this morning just as I was about to call Warren and tell him I've discovered the truth about Harrington."

"First, what are your thoughts about Washington?"

"I just started reading the letter. I haven't gotten through it yet; when I do, you'll be the first to know."

"Thanks; I'm holding you to that promise. And Harrington?"

"Can you get Warren in your office in the next ten minutes? If you've got the time now, I'll head over and brief you both. I'm not wasting any time with these characters. All the facts and figures point to gross mismanagement and misappropriation of five and a half million bucks."

"My goodness. I'll get Warren; we'll be waiting." Before leaving, Alonzo finished reading his letter. Quite pleased, he replaced it in the envelope with its remaining stack of papers and made certain to lock the package in his cadenza. He neatly positioned the Harrington file in his overly laden briefcase and stopped at Anna's desk before leaving. "I'm going to brief Dr. Morris and Deputy Lein on Harrington. We'll probably have a bite to eat so I'll see you when I get back. I don't think any of my deputies will need me, but if they do, you know where I'll be. See you." With that, he left. Anna went searching for his Washington envelope.

Anna thought, 'I know I shouldn't do this but I can't help but wonder what's going on with him. What was in that package from Washington?' Her curiosity had gotten the best of her, but to no avail. Alonzo knowing Anna as well as he did knew to lock up the envelope before he left.

Meanwhile, Gary Numan was returning Martin Roth's call. "So, Martin, I assume you've had an opportunity to look through all the information we sent you. We sent what we thought might be called into question by Alonzo."

"Yes, Gary. I reviewed it all; it's still the same financial information that hasn't made any sense for the longest. What you're presenting here is exactly what we've repeatedly said seems unreasonable. Your facts and figures are non-credible and highly suspect. So, what is it that you're asking I&R to do as your external counsel? Like I told you before, we've got the same questions Alonzo Prier is likely to have."

"I understand, Martin. There are a few issues and we need you to frame our argument."

"And what exactly would we frame an argument for?"

"It's rather complicated and difficult to explain over the phone. Can you arrange to be here for an international conference call we've got scheduled for tomorrow morning at eleven? Also, I need to invoke client/attorney privileges here. This is highly confidential at this point."

"What? An international conference call?! Gary, I don't like the sound of this. What in the hell is going on there?"

"The call will explain everything and at this point we desperately need your representation. This was just a matter of perspective, I guess. We thought we had all the answers to critical and futuristic health and healing initiatives. Can you just be at this conference call meeting tomorrow?"

A more than curious but certainly less than eager Martin Roth—Esquire—agreed to show. "I can't imagine what's going to manifest tomorrow, but I can arrange to be there. Eleven o'clock; whose office?"

"Eleven o'clock in Lawson's office. And thanks, Martin."

"Don't thank me yet, Gary, but I'll be there. Have a good day."

Gathered Friday morning at eleven o'clock in Patrick Lawson's office, Martin Roth was the only person not about to have a conniption. He sat calmly amongst three frightened and anxious men, waiting for the international operator to connect the call. At five after eleven, all parties were in touch via voices emanating through Lawson's speaker- phone. On the other side of the international waters were Uwe Haselmeyer, Hugo Kleinhammer and Adam Ulm, the creators of BandRxStat.

After all parties identified themselves, Gary Numan began the discussion. He presented to the German developers that they desperately needed to see some progress quickly, or they needed to bail out. The German developers quickly informed Numan and associates that they should have read the terms and conditions of the prospectus before committing to the funding—especially since it was an at-risk venture. Nonetheless, BandRxStat was presented as a three-year deal from point of investment due to clinical trial and testing requirements; patent and trademark considerations; production, warehousing and shipping logistics; and overall market receptivity.

"*auf Wiedersehen, gentlemen.*" That was the last they heard from the Germans.

"And just what the fuck did that mean?" A rather irate Imani asked now hearing dial tone after the forty-minute call.

"Until we meet again," concluded Martin Roth about the exchange. "And in other words gentlemen, no wine will be released before its time. And you're not getting any money back either!" A horrified Martin Roth looked at all three men in utter amazement. "Gary, may I see the prospectus?"

As Martin scanned the pages, he quickly noted key phraseology that confirmed everything he had just heard over the phone. His summation was accurate. As they all sat quietly for about five minutes while Martin thumbed through the document, Patrick Lawson resumed discussion.

"Well, Martin, how would you suggest we position ourselves for the HRRC meeting with this in mind? I doubt seriously that Alonzo has any knowledge of this. And I'm not certain that this really needs to be discussed at the meeting. Is that the forum to introduce this venture? I mean it hasn't exactly failed. It's just that we've got two more years before there's any possibility of return on the investment."

"Point blank, Patrick, this is not a simple bad business decision here. This is a case of a bad decision that exposes all the signatories to the BandRxStat deal on behalf of Harrington Hospital to criminal prosecution. You manipulated the State's rate-setting system to get funds to invest in a foreign product they weren't made aware of, and still aren't. And when were you planning, *or were you planning* to tell them? And who was your counsel on this deal?"

Patrick Lawson, visibly shaken, continued," Martin, you haven't answered my question."

"Patrick, I think you need to ask your questions from the gravity of what has transpired here. You're facing public embarrassment if this is presented at the meeting; private embarrassment if it's presented in a closed meeting with Alonzo. And you know if you call for a closed meeting at this point, he'll bring in the Attorney General. That's his boss!"

Gabriel Imani, visibly anxious responded, "Neither of those approaches sound good to me. I don't want to drag the Attorney General into this if there's another way out! Since Alonzo doesn't know about BandRxStat, let's just go to the meeting and see what he comes up with as a corrective action plan for us. If they fine us for sloppy cost reports, we pay the fine! Whatever he says, we'll just do. That's my approach to cleaning up this fucked-up mess." Gabriel Imani had been relatively quiet until that moment.

"So be it, Mr. Imani. But if you're wrong, you'll have just thrown a torch on a highly flammable situation," replied a calm Martin Roth.

"I believe we'll just have to take our chances," concluded Gary Numan. "We'll talk among ourselves and vote."

"If you want me to attend Tuesday's meeting as your external counsel of record, I can do that. But on behalf of I&R, I must invoke recusal; I'm biased towards the Health Department and AG's Office on this one. My firm cannot represent you and your BandRxStat deal. You'll need the firm that handled that for you. And for our mutual protection, I don't want to know anything more about BandRxStat. If offered by the Health Department, I'll represent you going forward on a corrective action plan for what appears faulty on your cost reports. Considering the circumstances, gentlemen, that's my best offer. I'll see you Tuesday at the Health Department unless you call and tell me not to bother. Have a good day." Martin Roth left immediately in total disbelief of the debacle in which Harrington Hospital's three major players were ensconced.

Back at Alonzo's office, there was a surprise visitor. "Shawna! Hello!"

"Hi, Anna" she replied. "How are you?"

"Fine. What a surprise! What brings you and little Miss Chloyee to these trenches? She is just adorable. And you just missed your husband. He's not far, he's tracking down his boss on something."

"Oh okay. Not a problem, we'll just wait a few then."

"Is everything okay?" Anna pleasantly asked.

"Oh yeah, everything's fine. Chloyee just had her check-up today with her pediatrician. Since she doesn't get to hang out much with her 'always working overtime Dad', I thought I'd bring her by so she could see him for a minute and get a hug."

"That's so sweet. She's so pretty. She looks just like you, Shawna."

"She's got a lot of Alonzo in her though."

"Can I hold her?"

"Sure. She might be a little bit irritable. She's at her best when she's been spending time with her Dad. Lately, that's been impossible. When he gets home, she's asleep; when he leaves, she's asleep. It's a tough life, right Chloyee?" As Shawna was handing Chloyee over to Anna, Alonzo was rounding the corner towards his office. Chloyee spotted her Dad. She got so excited!

"Hey, Chloyee! How's my precious little baby girl?" Alonzo got just as excited with the surprise visit. He genuinely loved both his lovely ladies. "Honey, hi! Is everything alright?"

"Yep! Everything's fine."

He gently kissed her and walked over to Anna to retrieve his kicking- up- a- ruckus little girl. "Come here, precious." Anna wanted to hold her a little longer but that was not possible since Chloyee had beheld her Daddy.

"How old is she now, Shawna?"

"A year and eight months."

"Oh. So, we're not telling her age in terms of just months anymore, huh?" Alonzo inquired while being charmed by Chloyee.

"No. I haven't since she was a year and a half; she's almost two. At a year and a half we weren't saying Erik or Thornton were eighteen months. Remember? You always want to think of Chloyee as months old; you don't want her to grow up." Shawna teasingly said.

"Maybe you're right, Shawna. I just told somebody last month she was nineteen months old."

Anna contributed her two cents, "I'm sure she's right, Alonzo. Look at you! You're in seventh heaven holding your little girl. You'll always want her to be Daddy's baby."

"Yep. I totally agree, Anna." Shawna and Anna were both teasingly laughing at Alonzo's fatherly sentiments. And the little one was basking in the security and comfort of her father's strong arms.

"Well, we should be going. I've got to pick up Erik and Thornton. Since Chloyee misses you so much, I figured I'd get her to you while she was still awake and could get her little hug and kiss."

"Shawna, you're the best. Thanks, and Chloyee thanks you too." He was still holding her. "I'm leaving early tonight. Let's eat out. I'm leaving here about four."

"Four?" Anna was impressed. "You never leave early."

"Tonight I am. My little ones need me too—all of them—and that includes you my Lovely," Alonzo playfully said, having turned directly towards Shawna.

"And honey, you've got a few needs I attend to also," Shawna playfully replied.

"O-kay! Let me walk you two lovelies out."

"Bye, Anna. Nice seeing you."

"You too, Shawna. Bye, Chloyee." Anna was pleasantly surprised when Chloyee waved bye-bye.

"And Anna, you're leaving today at four also. We've all been doing more than enough around here."

"Thanks, Alonzo. What about your staff?"

"They can decide for themselves. I'll be back in a few." It was two-twenty p.m. when Alonzo holding their little girl, proceeded to accompany his wife down to her car.

Accosted at the elevator. A spirited Steven Bowman was on the loose in the corridors. "Mister Mom! Go for it! Hello, Mrs. Prier; you're looking ravishing as always! And what a beautiful little girl!"

"You know, Steven, if I didn't like you so much, I'd have you locked up. You are one loose cannon." Alonzo and Shawna couldn't help but be entertained by the wilds of Steven Bowman.

"Just trying to keep it light in a real heavy world, Mr. Prier! I'm still trying to get a decent perspective on that Acts of God windstorm business. I still don't like it! It's a money maker for the insurance companies selling those additional endorsements. It's not right."

"And that's the way it remains Steven, on this twenty-second day of September. Give it a break! Go home early this evening—I'm leaving at four, Anna's leaving at four, you leave at four too. Don't think about windstorms over the weekend and come in refreshed Monday. Have a good one, Steven."

"Thanks, Mr. Prier; good deal! Take care, Mrs. Prier."

The elevator had arrived. "Bye, Steven. Good seeing you." A slightly amused Shawna stepped into the elevator first.

Alonzo entered next, holding Chloyee. "He's something else! But I like that guy. He's a deep thinker, believe it or not."

Shawna still amused, said, "He's funny enough."

XII

No Way Out

WHAT WASN'T FUNNY WAS WHAT was going on in Patrick Lawson's office. After lunch, Lawson, Numan and Imani had re-convened to continue discussing the pros and cons of having Martin Roth at the Tuesday meeting.

"I understand his point of view. I&R wasn't involved with this BandRxStat deal, our approach was unethical, and his law firm won't touch this. That's clear and not likely to change." Lawson was now summing things up himself. "But they are one of the best and most respected firms representing hospitals. If we go in with Roth, using Imani's approach, we'll take our whipping, get sanctioned and commit to a corrective plan. That's our best shot."

Numan had all sorts of sorted thoughts, recanting with one significant comment. "I agree with Imani's approach too. But what if Roth is right and by not addressing BandRxStat we've just thrown a torch on a highly flammable situation." Numan's thoughts were with the JHPTC where he had planted seeds towards the exposure of his interest in entrepreneurial ventures. What if Alonzo, by courtesy of Cindy Jack's meddling had decided to dig through those transcripts? And worse, it was a bad time for Numan to introduce those previously harbored concerns to Lawson and Imani.

"Well, let's not over-react. Admittedly we fucked up. We fucked up bad! But there's no reason for Alonzo to have found BandRxStat mixed in with our dirty laundry! Shit, we've already taken the low road. We'll just keep an even lower profile. We'll go in and get our asses kicked and get the fuck outta there! Roth will be there to support the Health Department's concerns with those damn reports, and he's got credibility with Alonzo. In a way, he's good cover." Imani finished up where Lawson left off. "Hey! It's not rocket science."

Numan chimed in once more. "I just want to be certain we haven't overlooked any possible areas where we might be vulnerable."

"Like what?" Imani was becoming annoyed. "I can't sit here all day playing this *what if* shit! What if the fuckin' world ends tomorrow? Then all our worrying will have been pointless. We've decided a course of action and that's it! I'm outta here. I'm going back to my office." Gabriel Imani, as the hospital's Chief Operating Officer was the youngest of the three. He was forty-nine years old and more of a risk taker. He was decidedly more in favor of the German deal than Lawson when Numan brought the possibility to the table. Imani was also the one who sought out the law firm for the deal. His fiery attitude and abrasive style were about to do him no justice.

Numan decided he'd had enough too and didn't want to be alone with Lawson. He went in search of Denver.

Denver was sitting in his office reading a fitness magazine when Gary walked in. "Denver, got a few minutes? Let's take a walk outside, I need some air. Wantta run some things by you."

Outside and pacing the length of the hospital premises, a worried Gary was almost pleading with Denver to reassure him that Cindy was no longer desirous of whispering sweet nothings in Alonzo's ear.

"Gary, from what I can tell, I'm in there! I know women. And from what I've heard about Alonzo, he doesn't have time to be fuckin' around, or interest either. I told you from the beginning, she was hot for him. Now I keep her busy so she's cooled off. If she hasn't, she's doing a damn good job of keeping it from me. How'd the conference call go?"

"They're not budging. It is what it is. And it's all spelled out in the prospectus. That fuckin' prospectus is going to be the death of us all."

"It's going to be the death of whomever signed the bottom line." Denver retorted. He didn't appreciate Gary lining him up on death row. He was not a signatory to the deal. He also knew that Gary could not have possibly known what Frank had shared with him about who was going to crash and burn. And Denver's name was not on that list.

They continued walking about fifteen more feet when Denver spoke again. "You know, Gary, I'm glad we took this walk. I'm glad we're outside your respectable office and outside my token office. You keep saying things like I'm going to sink with this ship; and this is going to be the death of us all. Gary, I'm twenty-five. I had no parts of this BandRxStat deal, other than to introduce you to a friend of mine. And I didn't hire myself at Harrington. If this thing blows up, man I can get another job. My reputation won't be tarnished. Shit, I don't even have a professional reputation yet. And you know what else, Gary? I don't like what I'm doing to Cindy, and I don't like what this could mean to my marriage. I don't love Cindy, but she doesn't deserve this kind of deception. She's good people. And I'm not going to keep doing this deception thing to her or my wife. No disrespect intended but, if you keep trying to make me feel like I'm part of the problem with this shit, I'll bail, man. I want to help you out, but don't try and make me feel like I own some of the responsibility for this shit- gone-wrong. I didn't sign squat. And you know that as well as I do."

With a totally changed attitude, Gary responded. "I'm sorry, Denver. I'm sorry. This has gotten the best of me. It's gotten the best of Lawson, Imani, and me. We really are in deep shit, and maybe it's just human nature to try and spread the disaster. But you're right. I had no right to draft you into this as far as I did. But I need you to just hang in there with me for a few more weeks. The meeting's Tuesday, and you'll be in the audience. You'll decide for yourself how much further you can go from there. I just hope and pray you won't bail on our sorry asses just yet. There's still a real good chance we can work this all out! And I'll owe you. Big!"

XIII

The Rules & Regulations

M ONDAY MORNING 9:15 SEPTEMBER TWENTY-FIFTH, Cindy was already at the Health Department setting up for the first of her two-day HRRC sessions. Having only spoken with Denville over the weekend due to his feigned debilitating migraines, she was wondering whether he'd show for the day's meetings. It was the JHPTC meeting day as well. She was also wondering whether Alonzo had gotten around to reading her excerpts from the JHPTC transcripts. Within the next few minutes, Alonzo and Lindy were walking down the long center aisle headed towards their select seats.

"Cindy! Good morning." Alonzo branched off from Lindy and was approaching Cindy's select area. He lowered his voice considerably. "I want to thank you for all the effort and diligence you put into excerpting those transcripts. The work you did helped me discover the missing link. I've already put a good word in for you with the Health Commissioner. She'll probably say something to you tomorrow after the meeting. Great job, Cindy. Thanks." He smiled again.

Cindy smiled in acceptance of his gracious comments. "I'm simply happy they were useful to you. Thanks for the compliment too." She wasn't quite feeling the lust she'd been feeling since Denville had been handling that. But he'd have a long way to go before he could eradicate her admiration for Alonzo.

And just as Alonzo was about to be seated, a supposedly not feeling well Denville arrived. This time he walked down closer to where she'd stationed her set-up and waved. She smiled, comforted with the knowledge that he was back in business.

The meeting began and ended as usual. The hospitals slated for the day's proceeding had no financial irregularities or major concerns for the Health Department to bring before the HRRC; the HRRC had no issues with those private hospitals.

Denville waited for Cindy to finish packing her equipment. They walked out towards the elevators together. "Cindy, I'm sorry about this weekend. I couldn't have made it down to your place on a jet plane. My head kicked my ass all weekend!" More accurately, it was his conscience kicking his ass.

"Oh wow! You should have called me. I would have come to you!"

"Oh no! When I get those headaches I'm better left alone. I'm not good company for man, woman, or beast. I just took some medicine and slept mostly." His disposition was certainly down. And that's not the way in which Cindy had become accustomed to him.

"You don't seem quite like yourself. Maybe you should have stayed home today."

"I'll be alright. Don't you meet Gina for lunch today?"

"Yeah. Wantta come? I've told her all about you and I'm dying for her to meet you. You'll like her too."

"No, I can't—you know I,"

Cindy cut him off. "I forgot you call your clients at noon. Well, we've got to arrange for a double date. Gina and her husband, you and me. It's got to be soon. Her baby's due soon and the closer to the arrival, the less likely she'll be to go out. She's already complaining about getting too fat."

"For now, you need to get going. It's five minutes to twelve."

"You're right. Are you coming to the JHPTC meeting?"

"I don't know—maybe—I'm not sure yet. I've got to run. I'll call you later, Cindy." He kissed her on the cheek. He left her feeling somewhat perplexed, but she chalked it up to him not feeling well.

An explicitly detailed-packed lunch conversation with Gina had Cindy back on top of the world. Talking up a storm about the new man in her life overshadowed her intuitive persuasion that something seemed different about him. "But he's still not feeling well. That's why he didn't join us for lunch. And he calls his clients at noon. Anyway, you think we can do a double date soon?"

"I'd love too. It's not like me and Dan do a whole helluva lot these days. But really, let's do this soon. I'm not getting any smaller, you know."

Cindy and Gina parted ways when Cindy exited the elevator in route to the JHPTC proceeding. While she was setting up, the balding secretary entered the room. His entrance was oblivious to Cindy, but he certainly noticed her on the way to his podium seat.

As she sat waiting for the meeting to begin, she kept focused on the doors watching for Denville's entrance. Throughout the overly extended testimonies, intermittently she visually scanned the room. He never showed. Gary Numan never showed either. Gary was back at the "all-wrong-chorale" tuning up for their HRRC show. Denver had gone back to his office too. As Cindy was preparing to leave the JHPTC proceeding, Denver was on the phone with Frank, singing like a canary.

"Do you want to meet for a drink after work tonight? Or is tonight no good?"

"Frank, I can be out whenever. If you can meet me tonight that's great! I need to talk about this. This shit has spun completely outta control!"

"I'll leave here at five then. I'll meet you at Brady's Bar-N-Grill around six-thirty. How's that, Denver?"

"Frank, you're the man, buddy. I'll be there." And little did Frank know he was about to become a confessional. Denver needed to unburden himself of a relatively heavy load. He needed to talk with a trusted friend who would understand and be able to offer some credible advice.

It was six-thirty exactly when Denver sat down at the bar in Brady's. "What can I get you?"

"Coors Lite."

"We have it on tap."

"Cool." Denver did not want to strike up a conversation with the bartender. He certainly didn't want to start some worthless exchange that he'd want to abruptly end when Frank arrived. And being the only patron at the bar on a Monday night at six-thirty, Denver's assessment was correct.

The bartender was back with his beer. "So, guy! How's it going? Weather's not too bad. As a matter of fact I was just saying to my wife" ...

Denver cut him off. "I've got to make a call. I'm waiting for someone but I'll pay this now."

"Oh okay, certainly not a problem. That'll be three bucks. Seen any good games lately?"

"No." Denver put four dollars on the bar, picked up his beer and split. Inasmuch as he had his cell phone he simply went over to a vacant table near the door and sat there. He was now in view of the entrance and out of the bartender's range. About five minutes later, Frank arrived.

Denver bought Frank a beer and within moments he rapidly took him through every painstaking detail of his Gary Numan/Cindy Jack ordeal. Frank held back his laughter in relation to the serious comedy of errors.

"Man, everything involving this BandRxStat deal gets deeper by the minute! When you told me that they had somehow used the State as their venture capital pool, I knew it wouldn't be long before some other dumb shit surfaced. Fuckin' around with that stenographer, under an assumed name, is that some other dumb shit! If I were you, I'd be looking for another job in another State—like yesterday!"

"Yeah. I think that's about the only answer. And damn, if Vicky finds out about Cindy, that's another crisis."

"And what's worse, you don't even want this babe you're screwing. Shit man! If there's a chance your wife could find out, at least be fuckin' a woman you chose to fuck around with! That's one of the widely held rules of the game!"

"Ain't that the fuckin' truth."

Having become more serious, Frank continued. "Denver, the only thing for you to do is move on. Start looking for another job; break it off with this Cindy person; and tell Gary that you're at the finish line. You said he doesn't want anybody to know about you two's little CJ operation. That tells me that he knows he went way over the line. I bet he doesn't even want his boys to know! I don't have happy-ending vibes about this, Denver. You need to hurry up and get the fuck outta Dodge."

After a few more beers, Frank and Denver parted company. Denver knew Frank's assessment of the situation would support what he'd already decided was necessary. He was going to ease out of his pretend relationship with Cindy whether his timing suited Gary's needs or not. And Frank was correct. Since Gary wanted to keep the C.J. sting covert, he obviously had good reason. It was as Frank said. He didn't want his partners-in-crime to know that he was stupid enough to drop hints at the JHPTC meetings about their unscrupulous entrepreneurial venture. After all, if a disinterested stenographer could pick up on it, where would a principled and seasoned counselor from the Attorney General's Office go with what Gary had said? A tangled web of deception was beginning to unravel.

9:33 p.m., Denver was almost home when his cell phone rang. He answered with a pensive "Hello?"

"Hey you! Just wanted to check up on you and your migraines. Are they gone for now?" It was a sincerely concerned Cindy calling her duplicitous lover.

"Yeah, they are."

"Great. So, can we hang out tomorrow night? You know, I should have asked you to stay at my place tonight. That way you'd be closer for the HRRC meeting tomorrow. You'll be there, right?"

"Yeah—yeah, why?"

"It's going to be a pretty steamy meeting. Alonzo is hot on this one particular hospital."

"Really? Which one?" Cindy had peaked Denville's interest.

"Harrington. Seems like they've had some issues for a while that the Health Department hasn't been able to resolve. So now it's moved to the Attorney General's territory and the ball is in Alonzo's court." Cindy was beginning to act cagey. Reverting back to her Greta Garbo steamy 'actress-ing' and 'every man's fantasy mistress' thoughts, she'd try to impress Denville with a little mystery. Also, subliminally she was uncomfortable with something. He hadn't left her one message during the day. Something felt different. Even if not feeling well, he still could have called. So, she'd just be mysterious too. And it was working. He was getting worked up. She continued, "the Health Commissioner will be there too."

He pulled over and parked. He was too close to home to continue without having uncloaked Cindy's veil. "How do you know all that? And what do you think Alonzo's going to do?"

"You've been to more HRRC meetings than I have, I just started. But I think Alonzo is going to come down on Harrington tomorrow."

"But why would you think that, Cindy? Did somebody tell you that? You said you worked with Alonzo before. Did he say something to you about Harrington?"

"He didn't give me any specifics, he just implied it was going to be an interesting meeting."

"And why would he go there with you? You don't know anything about the Health Department's rules and regulations for hospitals?"

"And why are you so overly concerned?" Cindy had noted that Denville's enthusiasm for the facts and nothing but the facts, seemed peculiar.

He toned it down. "I'm concerned with all my clients. Harrington is a big State hospital, they purchase a lot of medical supplies from me. If they're about to be run up the flag-pole—yes—I'm concerned." His voice still carried a detectable unpleasantness.

"Why are you getting angry with me? I don't know all the facts!"

Denville snapped back, "You brought it up! If you don't know what the fuck you're talking about, then you shouldn't be talking about it!"

Cindy angrily recoiled, "What? You know more about the HRRC than I do! You're the one who deals with all the hospitals. I tell you there's going to be an interesting meeting with one specific hospital, and I'm supposed to know every damn detail? That's ridiculous! What's the matter with you, anyway?"

And it was the heat of the moment that Denver used to begin fueling his way out. "Well, I figured Alonzo might tell you a little bit more than others, especially since you want to give him a little bit— don't you? You got the hots for him." Denville low-balled her hitting beneath the belt!

Foul play! Cindy's hurt feelings gave way to her reply. "Obviously, your migraines left you with some brain damage. Call me when it's been reversed." She hung up the phone, devastated by her smooth guy's crass comments; Denver hung up the phone, relieved that Denville was on his way out of the box.

It was the truth that hurt. Although harsh, Denville's words were not untrue. Cindy just never knew that he had picked up on her interest in Alonzo. She obviously never knew about the Denville assignment either. And at this juncture, she wouldn't know since Denver was planning to look for a new job.

By 9:40 Denver was home. He stashed his phone in the glove compartment and hurried to his apartment. It was late, but not enough for Vicky to be concerned, considering his overtime hospital business. He did smell like beer, but so what. He and the guys had stopped for a few after a rough evening in the warehouse.

Cindy was almost in tears. Continuing to replay Denville's interrogation of her about Harrington and Alonzo, she desperately tried to figure out the motivating factors. Nothing came to mind. But she knew his words were telling—saying he'd somewhat lost interest in her. Her thoughts were now aloud. "He thinks I want to sleep with Alonzo. How could he have known? But, I don't want Alonzo in that way anymore. I know that's not going to happen. I'm sure Denville lusted for women he never got. So, what's the big deal? Maybe he's jealous? But if he is, that's crazy! And I don't recall ever saying anything much about Alonzo." And she kept on, until the wee hours of the morning— searching her mind—looking for Denville's love-gone-south. She wasn't ready to give him up. She'd see him at the HRRC and give him a chance to explain. She finally drifted off to sleep, slightly comforted by her last thought.

Tuesday morning was September twenty-sixth! Cindy turned off her alarm and sprung forth. As she showered, she aligned the line-up. Alonzo would take center stage; the HRRC members would be his supporting cast; Harrington Hospital officials would be in the spotlight; Denville would be in the audience; and she would have a small, but nonetheless important role. The Health Commissioner would be there to critique Alonzo's show.

By 9:15, the Health Department's meeting room was getting full. People from miles around filed in. As Cindy was setting up, she intermittently watched the gathering crowd. About five minutes later, four men walked in together. They sat in the front row, facing the HRRC platform setup, which faced the Health Department's set-up where the hospital representatives were also required to sit. Within another few minutes, Alonzo and Lindy walked down the center aisle.

At nine-thirty sharp, the HRRC Secretary called the meeting to order. He gave his canned speech and called for the Harrington State General Hospital representatives to take a seat with the Health Department representatives. The four men stood up and approached seats in the Health Department's domain. Just at that moment, Denver inconspicuously walked in and found a seat in the audience.

"Mr. Prier, it is my understanding that today's proceedings in accordance with Harrington State General Hospital's financial review will be conducted by you. Is that correct?" The HRRC Secretary was setting him up for the record. Cindy was taking it down.

"That is correct," replied Alonzo as all attention focused on him.

The Secretary continued. "Representatives of Harrington State General Hospital, would you please state your names and titles please."

Patrick Lawson, Gary Numan and Gabriel Imani did as requested. Martin Roth stood up and announced himself last. "Mr. Secretary, I would also like to state for the record that my representation of Harrington today is related only to going forward with a corrective action plan should one be offered by the Department of Health. Thank you." Martin Roth sat down.

"Duly noted," the Secretary replied. Alonzo noted that odd remark. "If there are no further comments, would the Health Department representative please announce herself.

"Candice Bremmer, Department of Health Analyst for Harrington State General Hospital."

"Thank you, Ms. Bremmer. Would you care to begin now Mr. Prier?"

"Yes, Mr. Secretary. I don't intend to have a long drawn-out meeting today. My staff, in concert with the Health Department staff, have thoroughly researched Harrington's situation. We've identified three major areas of concern that I'm requesting further information about; then we can finalize this matter. Gentlemen, I know for a fact that there's no way your hospital could have housed the sickest people in this State over the past three years at the length of stay rates presented in your cost reports. That would be utterly impossible. Plus, your hospital is located in one of the environmentally cleanest counties in the State. Therefore, no reason for you to have such a sick patient population. And even if you had, your corresponding variable costs don't support your financials either. For example, your utilities' costs remained flat; your medication costs never increased proportionately; your overtime budget never went up, etcetera. Get my drift? It's obvious your cost reports were altered. So, I'm just going to cut to the chase and follow the money trail. Before your next scheduled HRRC meeting, I want your bank statements delivered to my office. I want to see every single monetary transaction made by Harrington over the relevant timeframe. Money in and money out—deposits and disbursements—for the last thirty-six months—sequentially. You're not to skip a month. Is that clear?" Alonzo was articulate in making each sticking point.

All three Harrington men looked to Martin Roth, who responded to Alonzo. "That's clear to me. When exactly are the bank statements due in your office?"

"Why'd he say that? Shit," silently thought Numan, "that's no fucking help!"

Alonzo continued. "I'll have my secretary call your office before the end of the day with a date. In representation of your client, will you accept the call or shall we speak directly to the hospital officers? And we'll need time to review those statements before the next meeting is scheduled. Anything else?"

"Yes." Gary had a question before Martin could respond. "We've been working most cooperatively with the Health Department. Is there any reason why we now must start working with the AG's Office? We're willing and always have been, to provide any information the Health Department asked for."

Alonzo replied, "The Health Department has asked the Attorney General's Office to intercede here in an investigation mode. The Health Department has been working towards the resolution of your long-standing problems and the data your hospital staff keeps providing makes no sense. So now you've been bumped up to the AG's Office. Does that answer your question, Mr. Numan?"

"Yes, Mr. Prier."

Lawson and Imani, continued to sit motionless; hoping that Numan wouldn't ask any more pointless questions. Roth responded to Alonzo's prior question.

"Yes, Mr. Prier. My office will accept the call on behalf of Harrington."

"Big fuckin' whoopee," silently thought Imani, as he looked at Roth.

Alonzo continued. "And with no further questions about the bank statements request, that brings me to my next item. I've been looking over your personnel records and organizational charts. You had a slight restructuring within the past year. And Mr. Numan, yes, your staff has been quite responsive to the Health Department's requests for information. I'm sure Ms. Bremmer can attest to that."

"Absolutely. When Ms. Jewel asked us to request Harrington's organizational chart and personnel files, Mr. Hammer, got them to us timely."

"Thank you, Ms. Bremmer. Let it also be recorded for the record that Mr. Hammer is Director of Human Resources for Harrington Hospital," interjected the Secretary. Cindy was taking it all down—and all in—as well.

"Thank you, Mr. Secretary. Duly noted, I'm sure." Alonzo looked over at Cindy, engagingly smiled, and continued. "And some *occurrences* or perhaps I should say *placements*, don't make any sense either. Ah—maybe both terminologies are accurate. In your revamping of personnel and responsibilities, I noted that you created an Assistant Vice President of Accounting position and hired a new Director of Purchasing."

At that point, Denver's ears perked. Gary's blood pressure climbed another notch. Imani and Lawson sat quietly listening, not necessarily knowing where Alonzo was headed. Roth just sat listening attentively.

Alonzo continued. "Both those positions report to you Mr. Numan. What I find particularly curious about that, is why would a Chief Financial Officer & Treasurer, have direct reports of an AVP of Accounting and a Purchasing Director. Why doesn't the AVP of Accounting report to your Vice President of Finance? And why in the world wouldn't your Purchasing Director be a direct report to your Vice President of Operations & Inventory Control? In having looked at these gentlemen's resumes, I don't get it. So, I'm personally inviting these two young men to come before the HRRC at your next scheduled meeting. I hope Clayton Mantis and Denver Simmons can impress me as much as they impressed you, Mr. Numan. I need to know that these gentlemen warrant their positions at Harrington."

'Oh shit! What the fuck?! I can't go up there and have Alonzo Prier breathing down my back! Damn! I hope fuckin' Gary says something to get Alonzo off my ass!' Denver was sweating bullets. And his silent thoughts were anything but subtle. He'd turned beet red.

An extremely nervous Gary was trying to rescue them both. "Well, I can vouch for both of them, Mr. Prier."

"And I thank you very much Mr. Numan, but that won't be necessary. I'd prefer that they speak for themselves. I'm requiring them to appear before the HRRC at your next scheduled meeting. Regarding the time, shall my office inform you directly Mr. Numan, or will Mr. Roth handle that as well?"

"Mr. Roth's office is fine, Mr. Prier." Gary shakingly said.

Denver's quiet thoughts resounded again. 'That motherfucker! He gets no respect from Alonzo, and he's just going to float Clayton and me down the river! What in the hell could we ever say to Prier that would be convincing? And then there's fuckin' Cindy! How can I testify before the HRRC as Denver Simmons? DAMN!' Denver really did have a headache now! And it was only going to get worse.

Alonzo summarized, "So that concludes my agenda for today. I have one final issue to put on the table, but I won't bother with that until I've completed due diligence on the two issues presented today—your cash flow and personnel considerations. Any further questions gentlemen?"

"Before we conclude, may I take a moment to confer with my clients?" Mr. Roth had something to say to them—finally.

"Be my guest, Mr. Roth," Alonzo graciously replied.

With a barely audible voice, Imani, who was sitting closest to Roth said, "I wondered what we'd be paying you for. You haven't said a damn thing that would back Alonzo down! So what's the stall here?"

All three men huddled in to hear the wisdom Roth was about to espouse. "Don't you see where Alonzo's going with this? Why don't you all bite the bullet and call for a private meeting? You're not going to survive this."

Cantankerous Imani was a live wire once again. He managed to keep his voice low as they caucused. "Is that all you've got to say? Fuck that! I heard exactly what you heard. We're sticking to having had reporting problems and we manually adjusted the data. We were wrong, so he'll sanction us! Once we get the reporting data together, the money should be there. Right? Listen, there's so much money traveling in and out of a hospital—legitimately—that he's really going to hone in on any particular transactions? Come on! You disappoint me, Roth."

Roth conceded, only because he'd seen the light. He was dealing with assorted fools. "Thank you for the time out, Mr. Prier. Mr. Secretary. I have nothing further."

"Fine, Mr. Roth. Mr. Prier, do you have any further remarks?" asked Mr. Secretary.

"Only closing remarks. The Attorney General's Office will be in touch with Mr. Roth of Iverson and Roth for what we've requested in further consideration of Harrington State General Hospital." Alonzo's closing remarks were quite concise.

"That being so, the meeting may be adjourned. May I have a motion for conclusion," Mr. Secretary concluded.

Mr. Evert, in representation of the Insurance Department made the motion. It was seconded by the public member and concluded.

Cindy was hastily packing to leave to catch Denville when Dr. Morris approached her. "Hello, Ms. Jack. I'm Dr. Morris, Health Commissioner."

"Oh, yes! Pleased to meet you." Somewhat taken aback, Cindy extended her hand.

Alonzo had mentioned that Dr. Morris would say something to her, but she was more interested in what Denville had to say.

"I'd like to thank you. Your diligence and conscientious work ethic brought much clarity to this situation. And Mr. Prier speaks very highly of you."

"Thank you, Dr. Morris. As I told Mr. Prier, I was glad to be of assistance."

Both ladies smiled, and Dr. Morris turned back to converse with Alonzo. As usual, swarms of people were buzzing around him. Cindy chuckled to herself as she thought about the power that Dr. Morris wheeled. All those folks covering Alonzo would have to buzz off and let Dr. Morris through. 'Must be nice', she thought, in pushing towards catching up with Denville.

But Denville had pushed off. He was so upset with knowing that he'd be served up at the next HRRC meeting, it was best that she had missed him. Hence, Denville disappointed her again!

Curious, puzzled, anxious and suspicious, Cindy somehow made it through lunch. She knew not to call him at noon. He didn't want to talk to her either. Her next session had nothing to do with hospitals, so there was no chance he'd be there. Therefore, she'd go through the rest of her day feeling as if she'd committed a crime.

Imani, Lawson and Numan had returned to the hospital and were all in their respective offices, when Denver went barreling into Numan's office and slammed the door! "How the fuck am I supposed to go before the HRRC with Cindy there?" Denver was unhinged. "It's bad enough I'll probably have to answer questions about my job here; then Cindy Jack who knows me as Denville Seamons is recording my shit? No way Gary; no fuckin' way!" Denver paced the length of Gary's office with nervous anxiety.

"Denver! You can't ignore the Attorney General's Office request for you to be there. I hope you realize that. He could put a warrant out for you if you don't show up!"

"What would you suggest I do? Wear a wig and buy a mustache?" Denver's sarcasm, Gary ignored.

"The only thing to do is make sure Cindy isn't there. I thought about this driving back. You're going to give her a dose of Ipecac!" Gary was the answer man,

"What? Now I'm supposed to poison the bitch? Have you totally gone crazy?"

"No; no; no! My daughter had to give it to her son last month. Ipecac just makes you vomit. But it makes you vomit a lot. My little four- year-old grandson swallowed some cleaning shit. The label said if swallowed, induce vomiting. When you have kids around you know these things!

174

You can get Ipecac without a prescription from the drugstore. That's how common and safe it is."

"And that's disgusting."

"You got any better ideas? If she's sick the night before the proceeding—I mean really vomiting bad—there's no way she'll make it in to the meeting. She'll be weak and have to stay in bed a day or so; they'll have to call in another stenographer. I'll go down to Ben in pharmacy here and get you some. You'll have it when you need it. No problem."

"That's an awful thing to do to somebody, but I see I don't have a choice. How much of that shit do I give her, and how?" Denver had calmed down somewhat.

"I'll get you the proper dosage in a little vile. Just pour it over her food or mix it in a soft drink. It works within twenty to twenty-five minutes after taken. Make sure you don't have that bitch at my condo when you give it to her!"

"Oh! But I should, Gary. One disgusting act deserves another!"

They both just looked at one another. Gary was clearly looking more like a scoundrel and Denver was looking more closely at himself. In reflection over how he'd gotten so entangled, he recalled the initial thrill of the game. Now he was facing the dementia borne of deception.

Going back to his office, Denver was thinking of yet another dilemma he had to face. He'd started booting Cindy out. Now he'd have to reel her back in, only to string her along, until he could blow her off again—forever. "Shit! I'll call her tonight," he said aloud as he entered his office.

By the time Alonzo had returned to his office, Lindy had already worked up the follow-up particulars for Martin Roth to relay to his client. She'd need to run them by Alonzo first. He was in his office making changes to a memo Anna had previously typed.

"Hey! How was lunch?"

"Great. We went to this Italian restaurant about forty minutes from here. It's one of Gwen's favorites."

"Why'd you go so far?"

"Didn't want to run into anybody. We had a few confidential issues to discuss."

"Oh. Did Warren go too?" Lindy was a little inquisitive; feeling a little slighted, by not having been invited.

"Nope, just me and Dr. Morris. What can I do you for, Lindy?"

Still standing in the doorway of his office, she responded, "Alonzo, if you've got a few minutes, we can go over what I've prepared for Martin Roth to tell the Numan crew."

"Sure, come on in. Just give me a minute." He continued to make the edits to the memo. She entered and closed the door behind her.

She sat there in silence as he continued working. She started scanning certain things about him. His hair was thick, dark and well groomed. His mustache perfectly graced his mouth. He had the sexiest bottom lip, which he'd infrequently gently bite. His skin was flawless and adorned by year-round perfect coloring. He wasn't wearing his jacket, so his well-formed upper torso and muscular arms made her yearn to know what it felt like to be held by him. He stood up; he was tall, and his designer belt hugging his waist, focused her around his tight mid-section.

"I'll be right back. Let me get Anna started on this." He walked from behind his desk and headed for his closed door.

Her eyes followed his nicely shaped tight end and slightly bowed legs. When he re-entered, he left the door ajar and returned to the chair behind his desk. This time, if Lindy's shoe fell off, she'd have to get it herself and he wouldn't be close enough to see.

And it had been decided from what Lindy had worked up. Harrington's thirty-six months of bank statements should be in Alonzo's possession within two weeks; Clayton Mantis and Denver Simmons should be in front of the HRRC's second Harrington Hospital meeting scheduled for October twenty-fourth. Since Alonzo knew exactly which two financial transactions he was looking for and the point- in- time at they would have occurred, his staff would need all of ten minutes for discovery. The other bank statements would only be analyzed for whatever else might appear questionable.

"Fine. The circus clowns will be back on October twenty-fourth then. You can let Roth know. Thanks. Oh, ask Anna to call Casten and advise them that we'll need Cindy for overtime on the twenty-fourth and for an Executive Session, probably that following Friday. Also, on your way back, would you ask Debbie to come to my office with her labor strike file, please?"

"Sure." As Lindy got up and was walking away, Alonzo was noticing that she was probably wearing a thong. He gently bit his bottom lip and picked up another memo from his in-box.

Debbie was next up in Alonzo's office. He relayed to her the tactical approach that he and Commissioner Morris had discussed over lunch. They had proposed to offer the hospitals an alternative to avoiding the proposed strike.

"Debbie, after I reviewed all the analyses that you and Michael Neely prepared, there seems to be a reasonable point where everybody wins. Commissioner Morris agrees. I want you to call the Hospital Association President and have him run this by his hospital members. The numbers and facts suggest nurses and nurses' aides are entitled to an approximate seven- percent wage increase from last year and forward. In the interest of avoiding a strike and in good faith, hospitals agree to a five- percent increase going forward; of which three- percent, is retroactive to last year. All calculations are to be based on this year's economic index. The three percent is to be issued in lump sum and calculated in accordance with the labor market area profiles of each hospital. Any hospitals that find themselves impaired with this action; upon reasonable proof of harm, may appeal to the Health Commissioner for an emergency rate relief grant."

"Wow Alonzo! That works for me! But I have one question. When did you get the time to look at this labor strike stuff? You've been all caught up with Harrington; Steven's windstorms; routine HRRC meetings; deregulation issues; I'm impressed!"

"Don't be. I've been working too much; that's all. My wife alerted me to that when she brought my little girl here the other day. Chloyee's growing up and changing from month to month, and I'm somehow missing it. That's a sign you're spending too much time away from the really important things in your life." And there was more. Alonzo was studying his Washington stuff too.

"Oh! That's right. Steven saw them! You know he thinks Shawna is awesome and Chloyee is adorable. But you know Alonzo, you're right. When you realize that the important things in your life are passing you by, that's when you recognize it's time to rearrange your priorities. Anyway, I'll give Raymond Masters a call and run your proposal by him—sounds good! Have a good evening."

"Thanks, Debbie. Give my best to Michael Neely. You two make a good team." And Alonzo realized what he admired about Debbie all over again. She had a strong work ethic; she had a stronghold on the realities and truths of life; and she was a quick study too. Alonzo himself, was obviously a quick study.

By now it was 4:15. Cindy was headed home; Denver was caught up in thought; and both Gina and Eve wanted to catch up with Cindy. Eve didn't have a problem; to the contrary, she wanted to let Cindy know that her life was getting better. Even Paul was beginning to take notice of the changes in her and responding positively. When Cindy got home, she arrived to three messages via her voicemail....

"Cindy. It's Eve. You are the best! Call me! I'm ready to do these AA meetings and next step stuff alone now! I love you Cindy. Bye." ....
..

"Hey Cindy, its Gina. I mentioned this double date thing to Dan. He's fine with it. Call me and let me know when. Make it soon though. Bye." ....

Hello Cindy. I'm sorry about my behavior. Some of it I can't explain; some I can. Anyway, I'm sorry. I'll try you again later. Bye.".........

Feeling a little better after hearing her last message, she decided to change her clothes before returning Eve's and Gina's calls.

"Hello."

"Eve, it's me. I got your message. Sounds good."

"Cindy! Hi! I'm feeling good. I know I've got a lot more ground to cover, but I'm handling it. And Paul is responding well to all of this too. I want to do the outpatient thing soon."

"Eve, I couldn't be happier for you. That's great! I'll call Camila Radke and let her know. How's Corey and Noel?"

Eve had detected something in Cindy's voice. She didn't sound as jovial as she had been. Eve naturally assumed correctly that it probably had something to do with Denville. "They're fine. How's your boyfriend?"

"I don't know, Eve. He's started acting peculiar. Like maybe he's got another woman. I don't know. Something's wrong. We haven't spoken in a couple of days. He was at one of my meetings today, and he didn't even hang around to speak."

"Men can be so unpredictable. Well, the good thing is that you haven't been with him all that long. If it's over at least you haven't invested a lot of time in him."

"Yeah, but I love him."

"Oh God. Well then for your sake, I hope it works out. But Cindy, remember to practice what you preached. Don't slip into denial. If you sense there's something wrong for no reason, then there's something wrong for some reason." Eve had begun thinking more clearly.

"I guess…And you sound different."

"I am different. Going to those AA meetings made me realize that I needed to take responsibility for my own actions. And I owe you for that. You helped me get to where I could see what I'd started doing to myself and my kids. And I'm ready to go to my sessions alone now. Well, I've got to finish fixing dinner. Talk to you soon. Love you. Keep me posted on Denville."

"Will do. Love you too. Bye." Fixing dinner was something Cindy needed to do as well. She hung up the phone happy to know that her sister was on the road to recovery; anxious to know what was ailing Denville.

Before she'd return Gina's call with a tentative date, she wondered whether it would even be appropriate in light of the present circumstances. She busied herself fixing dinner, anticipating his call.

"Vicks, I'm heading down to the park. I need to round the track a few times. I need to unwind. This hospital shit has me pretty tense right now." Denver had changed into sweats and was headed out.

"Dinner will be ready in about an hour. Or should I make it later?"

"Give me about an hour and a half, Babe. I'll be back."

"No problem. Do a few laps for me," she jokingly said.

"Sure will," he jokingly replied.

He was going to the local park but not to run. His main purpose was to get some privacy so he could get on the phone with Cindy. In the privacy of his car, he'd crack the window for a little fresh air while he delivered some foul bullshit cover story.

It was six-twelve p.m. when her phone rang. She was both apprehensive and excited.

"Hello."

"Hello, Cindy. It's Denville. Look—um—I'm sorry." That was good for starters, he thought.

"I don't understand. We're having problems because of a hospital's rate review meeting?"

"Um, no. It's just that I've got a lot of things on my mind, Cindy. Shit happens. Sometimes it happens the way you want it too, sometimes it doesn't." Trying to make light of it, he continued. "Hey! Sometimes ya feel like a nut—sometimes ya don't!"

Not yet ready to let him play it off, Cindy continued. "Yeah, but you've been acting like a nut. Just because I said Alonzo implied it was going to be a hot meeting, that says to you I want to sleep with the man? What's that all about? Are you jealous of him?"

He'd be reaching, but Cindy had talked just enough to give him something to latch onto.

"No, I'm not jealous of Alonzo. But remember when I asked you if you liked him?"

"Yeah. And I said he was married with children."

"Right. And that's my point. If you didn't want him, or if you hadn't considered him at some point, the fact that he's married with children wouldn't matter. As a matter of fact, you never would have said that!"

"That he's married with children? He is!"

"You don't get it. Let me explain. You know Gary Numan, right? From the JHPTC meetings? If I asked you—do you like Gary Numan—what would you say?"

"I'd say I don't know him. I'm aware of him, but I don't know him."

"Right. But you could probably guess that he's married with children too, right?"

"Right."

"Well, you just proved my point. Because you have no interest in Gary Numan, it doesn't matter to you that he's married with children. I guess I'm territorial—I don't want my girlfriend wanting some other guy—and the only reason she can't have him, is because he's married with children. So, I'm sorry. I apologize. Now can we get past this?"

Cindy bought it. "I guess so. Just don't keep acting like a nut. There's no reason. And my territory is your territory."

And it was at that moment that he was supposed to say something like—I love you—but he didn't. "Well good. So um, I'll call you tomorrow. I wasn't sure you'd accept my apology, so I made a few plans with some buddies of mine. But maybe this weekend we can do something?"

"Oh yeah—sure." Not overjoyed with his response, Cindy continued. "Gina and her husband are game for a double date. What about that?"

Hell no! He didn't want to be introduced to anybody else as Denville Seamons, and he didn't want to meet Cindy's friends. "I just think we should spend some more time alone together for now. Let's get a little further beyond this episode we just had. I've got to start studying up on this new product line my company has. Anyway, I'll call you tomorrow. I'm going to run a few laps before I shut down for the night. So, I'll see you—sweetheart." And that single solitary "sweetheart", was the only term of endearment he'd offered throughout that entire conversation. She chose to ignore that.

Now what was she going to tell Gina? Should she tell her that her Mr. Wonderful had made a jackass of himself and wanted to hang out in seclusion until he was Mr. Right again? Wrong. Denville was her man, and their relationship deserved loyalty and some privacy. Besides, if she told Gina that story, she'd say it was ridiculous.

Cindy went to bed that night feeling slightly out of kilter. She always liked to believe she was in control of her emotions, but now they seemed to be controlling her. Even when she was in the throes of her Greta Garbo days towards the captivation of Alonzo, she still maintained a sense of balance. She never went out of her way to try and accidentally bump into him. As a matter of fact, she'd made it a point to keep her distance until ready to role-play. She certainly wasn't headed towards any romantic interlude with Alonzo. She didn't know it but she didn't appeal to Alonzo in that way. Luckily, Denville came along to obstruct her efforts before she'd embarrassed herself. She shifted her pent-up longings and desires from Alonzo to him. And he swept her away with all the right moves. Suddenly, he was coming up short. And in such a short time, she had fallen fast and deep. And funny too that

Eve should call that evening. It was only a few short months ago that Cindy was reminding Eve how everybody tried to warn her about Paul. When Eve had fallen fast and deeply in love with Paul, everybody, including Cindy, was trying to convince Eve how wrong he was for her. Now Eve was mirroring back pretty much the same advice. And her best friend Gina—her sentiments were always—to just beware.

"When I said I wanted to be tussled, did I tempt fate? I don't understand any of this! He says we'll do something this weekend, but it's only Tuesday. Why doesn't he want to see me before the weekend? Don't two people who're supposed to be in love get together and make up after an argument? Why aren't we?" Again, her thoughts had come aloud. And again, she was up most of the night being grilled by her roller-coaster soliloquy about Denville's inconsistent behavior.

The days and nights dragged on for everybody. Denver was hard at work, studying the Harrington State Hospital Center Purchasing Policy and Procedure Manual. It was the second time he'd looked at it since he'd secured the job. It was a ninety-page document, containing highly specific and critical details.

Cindy, due to her insecurity over her love-relationship gone south, found herself dialing Denville's number a bit more than usual. He'd make pit stops at her house only to keep up appearances. He was only keeping up appearances in the interest of taking her down with a dose of Ipecac at the appropriate time.

Eve was keeping up with her AA meetings and Paul was beginning to live up to his marital vows.

Gina was trying to keep Cindy's awareness level up, as Cindy's only choice was to now confide in her trusted friend. It was the night of October tenth; the evening after Cindy's JHPTC meeting. She'd lunched with Gina as usual the previous day but was still trying to protect the privacy of her slip-shod relationship with Denville. Even though Gina had picked up on some of the irregularities in Cindy's recounting Denville episodes, Cindy was still trying to remain loyal. The night of October tenth, Cindy broke down and called Gina with what she believed to be—the truth.

"You know, Gina, I think he has an intimacy problem."

"You're kidding, right? Cindy, this is the guy you said is personable;

great in bed; well endowed; handsome; outgoing; he's in sales making a fortune; lives in a mansion; hangs out a lot with his friends! How does all that add up to intimacy problem?"

"He doesn't seem to want to meet my friends and he hasn't introduced me to his friends either. It's like he doesn't want anybody to know the true him—you know—the Denville-in-love, side of him."

"No, I don't know. It seems to me that he's the Denville-in-hiding. You've only known him since the end of August. I've been pregnant longer than you've known that guy. I know my unborn baby better than you know Denville!"

"But I love him. I know that."

"Based on what? What you've created in your mind about him? It's like I told you about wanting Alonzo. All you knew about him was that every woman who sees him wants him. The only woman that really knows him, is his wife. Hell, he could be a workaholic—that sucks; a sex fiend—that's a hassle; demanding—that's no fun! Shit, Dan is lazy! And that's gotta change when the baby comes. Point is, you only know a man after you've lived with him. You can't possibly know Denville after only two months! Stop telling yourself you're in love with somebody you really don't know."

"You've certainly got a point there—but my emotions are already there. I know I love him. I think we just need time to get closer. You know he's only twenty-five. I hit thirty last week! I kept it from him because—well—I didn't want him to know I'd turned thirty."

"I thought your birthday was last week! It slipped my mind to ask you. Damn, Cindy. Not only did you keep it from him; you kept it from me too! You're both keeping secrets! That kind of relationship is headed nowhere. It's even got you keeping things from me! Cindy, take some time out to re-evaluate your situation with Denville. I've got to go. I've got a new baby book to read. But I'll see you on the twenty-third for lunch. Think about easing up a bit with this guy. You're in too deep, way too soon. Sorry, but it doesn't sound like he's going all out for you anymore. Take care." Despite the consequences, Gina was a true friend who would only tell her what appeared as the truth. "See ya."

"Yeah. Thanks, Gina. Bye."

It echoed in her mind thrice over. 'You're both keeping secrets!'

Gina was right. She had her Victoria Secrets; her longings for Alonzo secrets; and her recent birthday secret. And although not necessarily a secret, she'd never mention the JHPTC transcripts she'd excerpted for Alonzo to anyone. If she had secrets, Denville had secrets. And essentially, her secrets could even be considered irrelevant. But could his? It was her enlightening conversation with Gina that brought that consideration to light.

The week of October sixteenth, things were not much different. Cindy did manage to reach out to Camila Radke who was most ecstatic that Eve was gracefully moving onward. She scheduled an evaluation appointment for Eve. Camila would personally interview Eve. If all went well, Eve would enter a well-recognized outpatient alcoholism treatment program for a period of fourteen weeks— two sessions per week. After twenty-eight sessions at the Linnear Foundation, coupled with her prior AA sessions, Eve would emerge as a long-term survivor in the ranks of recovering alcoholics.

By Monday October twenty-third, the AG's Office was hopping! They were almost in celebratory mode that the bank statements had arrived, and Alonzo immediately zoomed in on the two offending cash transfers. They were wire transfers to Germany in the amounts of three and a half million dollars, and an additional two million dollars eight months later. The first transaction was made two years immediately after the Health Department's approval of an emergency cash infusion to Harrington; the second wire transfer was made two weeks after the same kind of emergency relief. Neither of those cash transfers should have ever taken place—irrespective of when.

Also, the Hospital Association President had called Debbie North back with the results of his canvassing the hospitals with Alonzo's proposed labor strike remedy. It was a good report! The hospitals agreed his strategy was reasonable and acceptable and would probably ward off the strike. They'd of course need to wait for the feedback from the labor union representatives, but they were anticipating the best. No doubt the Health Commissioner was pleased—Alonzo's win would mean a win for her too!

Steven's windstorm policies' study also blew in good news. The insurance companies had complied with all the underwriting requirements and the Insurance Commissioner could now feel comfortable in having his Enforcement Unit ease the minds of the angry homeowners that they weren't being ripped off! "Well, Mr. Prier, they pulled it off." A still unduly concerned Steven was in Alonzo's office delivering his legal review results.

"Steven, you may not like the law, but the property and casualty companies have abided by the letter of the law, and most important, are following the underwriting regulations. We've done what the Insurance Commissioner commissioned us to do. It's over, Steven. I'd like you to get beyond this towards your new assignment. I don't want to hear any more about windstorms and acts of God. Good job and move on."

Steven heard it in Alonzo's voice and the look on his face, that he'd had it. Steven vowed to never discuss windstorm riders with Alonzo— ever again.

It was both HRRC and JHPTC day for Cindy. She was still in the throes of turbulence, as Denville had her emotions running amuck. When he would show up, sometimes he was nice enough, but he wasn't showing up as much anymore. The passion was certainly not as high. She had become annoying to him by always asking, "What's wrong?" There was a lot wrong that he obviously couldn't divulge. She had sensed he was winding down and upsetting her. And she wouldn't get the opportunity to latch onto him for another few stolen moments before meeting up with Gina for lunch. He didn't come to the day's HRRC meeting.

"How's lack-lover boy?" Gina had talked with Cindy a few other times after the keeping secrets conversation and was now a little annoyed that Cindy was still so enamored with this character.

"He didn't show up for the HRRC meeting. That's unusual."

"How do you know? You just started those HRRC meetings at the end of August. You've only done four. So how would you know whether it's unusual or not for him to miss a meeting?"

"I don't really. But he didn't tell me he wasn't coming. You know, I just don't know what's wrong. Why's he acting different? Do you think he's involved with another woman?"

"I keep telling you to ease up on yourself about this guy. He's twenty-five years old, Cindy. Hell, guys at that age are likely to cancel a romantic date just to bungee jump! He's young, adventurous and probably not commitment ready. And if he's all of what you say he is, he probably is seeing other women. *Duh!*"

Cindy was now angered by Gina's insensitivity. "You don't have any right to be so down on him. You don't know him!"

"And apparently, neither do you." Gina didn't back off. "When you tried to get us together on a double date, he backed out! I'm your friend, Cindy. And I also recognize the warning signals. You are constantly distressed over this guy. He's started letting you down. If you're not ready to tell him goodbye, at least move him to back-burner status and start dating some other guys. Enough of Denville already! How's Eve?"

"Better, actually. She's got an appointment today for a good outpatient treatment program. It's at one-thirty, so I'll call her tonight to see how it went."

"That's great! You really made a significant difference in her life. Well, time to head back up."

"Yeah, time to get back to the grind. Glad I made a difference in somebody's life."

Lunch was over. Cindy and Gina remained relatively quiet on the way back to their separate destinations. Cindy was a little disturbed with Gina's candor; Gina was a little frustrated with Cindy's naivete.

And a distinct parallel had surfaced. Frank, who functioned as Denver's sounding board spoke as candidly as did Gina. Denver remained unemotional and able to hear the voice of reason. Cindy however, having become so emotionally entangled, was prone to refuting Gina's reasonable insight. As she approached the entrance to the JHPTC meeting, she recalled some of Gina's remarks about Denville and grimaced. But she couldn't totally ignore some of the realities about Denville. She couldn't help but notice he wasn't calling as much, not leaving the steamy messages to which she'd become accustomed, and just somewhat distant. She'd stopped checking her voicemail whenever she had a break. But fatefully, Denville had left her three messages by one o'clock that fateful day of October twenty-third.

Upon having arrived at the spot where she'd station her set-up, the little balding Secretary immediately approached her. "Ms. Jack. How are you today?"

"Fine. And you?"

"I'm quite well, thank you. Casten called with a message for you. Claudia Hoosier asked me to have you contact her immediately. She's sending over another stenographer for today's session. It's an emergent situation, but you shouldn't panic. Don't bother to set up—just go— please go and call her now."

With a message like that, she couldn't help but panic. She immediately left the room and headed towards an area for privacy. Her fingers were trembling as she made her call. The phone only rang twice, but it felt as if it had been ringing forever.

"Claudia Hoosier speaking."

"Claudia! This is Cindy. I got the message to call you! What's wrong?" Cindy was almost hyperventilating.

"Cindy, please don't panic. There's been an accident. It's your sister. Apparently, she was headed somewhere on the major highway to Philadelphia when a car side-swiped hers. She's at Wilingsboro Medical Center. Luckily, she hadn't made it to Philadelphia, so the ambulance took her back into Wilingston. And her husband's away on a business; that's what the hospital folk said. It's not life threatening, but she has a concussion and a fractured rib, so they want to keep her overnight for observation. She'll need you to pick up the kids and get them off to school tomorrow morning."

"Oh my God!" Cindy was still shaking despite Claudia's not a life-threatening statement.

"Please get yourself together, Cindy. This is not extremely serious. It could have definitely been worse. I've also got Laura on her way to cover your JHPTC meeting. She should be there by now. Anyway, just calmly get yourself to Wilingsboro Medical and see your sister. Then go pick up your niece and nephew from school. I'll be here until about six tonight. Call me immediately after you've attended to everything and let me know your situation for tomorrow. Remember I told you last Monday that Alonzo Prier would need you for overtime on tomorrow's HRRC session and a possible Executive Session on Friday. So let me know if I need someone to cover his meetings after you've assessed your sister's needs."

"I most certainly will. And thank you, Claudia. I really appreciate your concern." Cindy hung up the phone with a newly found respect for Claudia. She'd comforted her, and was handling Casten's business, simultaneously.

Cindy returned to the JHPTC meeting room to retrieve her belongings. Laura was there, ready to roll. Cindy politely nodded her head in acknowledgement of the little balding Secretary's apparent concern, as he still couldn't keep his eyes off her.

Claudia had done a good job calming Cindy down. She was still somewhat anxious in moving towards Wilingsboro Medical. And speaking of anxiety, Denver was worse than Cindy. He'd been desperately trying to reach her. It was D-day. Denville was supposed to dose her so she'd be unable to take dictation—tomorrow! By now he'd left three voicemails at work and a couple at her house. No return calls did he receive from Cindy, nor did he know her whereabouts. An obvious twist of fate loomed. Cindy was not consumed with thoughts about Denville.

"Damn! Where the fuck is she? What do I do now?" It was twenty minutes after one, and Denver was sitting in his office alone, deliberating over his dilemma out loud. "Gary didn't go to that JHPTC meeting. I've gotta tell him this shit!" With one giant leap he was headed to Gary's office.

Gary's door was closed, "Oh! Denver, you can't go in there right now. Mr. Numan's on a conference call." Gary's secretary was most studious.

"Oh, yes I can. He can call his conference call back! He'd wantta know what I need to tell him." Denver rudely proceeded into Gary's office closing the door behind him.

Gary was speaking with detectable agitation, "*Martin*, I don't share Imani's sentiments on this whole thing either! But he's convinced Lawson that Alonzo won't discover BandRxStat! Just a moment." Gary was looking at Denver, visibly wondering what the hell he'd burst into his office for.

Visibly nervous Denver spoke, "This time bomb is about to fuckin' explode, and I'm getting outta harm's way!" He was so rattled. "Martin, I've got to call you back. I've got another urgency here. How late will you be in your office?"

Whatever Martin said, Gary responded by begging. "No. Please Martin. You don't understand! I'm willing to do what's necessary, but I need to know what to do!"

It was suddenly clearer to Denver that the ship was sinking fast. Martin gave Gary a time to call him back towards which Denver intuited was probably the time he'd be gone. Anyway, Gary was now Denver's captive solo audience. Stressed, Denver said, "I can't find Cindy! I've left her several messages at work; at home; she's not calling back! I was going to do the romantic dinner thing at her apartment tonight and give her that vomit shit! Now what?"

"What the fuck do you mean now what? And why the fuck can't you find her?" Gary was now even more rattled than before. "If you were keeping on her trail like you were supposed to she'd be putty in your hands *and* stuck like glue! You know that! Tell me you're not serious. Tell me that you're just shittin' me and you busted in here to say you've got it all planned for tonight! I need some good news right about now, Denver!" Gary was furious.

"Well that's too damn bad—'cause I got nothin'! I can't find her, and I'll be damned if I'm strolling down that aisle tomorrow for that meeting."

"I'll tell you what's too damn bad! You decide not to stroll down that aisle tomorrow, Alonzo will have your ass sitting up in one of those State cars. He'll have you personally escorted in! Need I remind you again that the man is second in command to the Attorney General? And he's required you and Clayton to be at tomorrow's meeting?! You're on at ten-fifteen! Right after Clayton! All you had to do was be ready to spend fifteen minutes on Alonzo's witness stand and have Cindy out of the way. For just one day; one freakin' meeting! How'd you let that bitch get away? I thought you were on top of your game!"

Dead end. Gary was totally useless. A thoroughly disgusted Denver, with nowhere to turn, turned and walked out. He'd do his best in recalling the rules and regulations he'd recently gleaned from the

Purchasing Policy and Procedure Manual, but his performance would unquestionably be hampered with Cindy there. And on having an AG's car arrive for his pick-up the morning after the meeting before his wife left for school? No way!

Cindy had reached the hospital. Eve was still in holding in the ER. All her insurance information had cleared; it was just more advisable to observe her from ER for a while longer. Her head was neatly bandaged; bandaging had been wrapped around her upper torso; the whole incident had understandably frightened her. She was cognizant and coherent.

"Eve! My goodness! What on earth happened?" Cindy was understandably still alarmed.

"Hi, Cindy. Thanks so much for coming. I'm so sorry to keep putting you through so much drama."

"Don't be silly. This wasn't your fault. What happened?"

"This woman was drinking a cup of coffee. It must have slipped out of her hand or something. Anyway, she dropped a steaming hot cup of coffee in her lap and lost control of her car and sideswiped me. That's what I was told. You know I was on my way to my appointment with Camila Radke."

"Yeah. Yeah, I know. Don't worry about that. I'll call her and let her know what happened. Anyway, what time do I need to pick up the kids from school and where? I'll get them, take them out to eat, and run back to my place to pick up some clothes. I'll stay at your house with them, since I can drop them off at school on my way to work. Paul's out of town, right?"

"Yeah, he's in Chicago. We're doing better, Cindy. It's really been nice having him around like a husband. He's trying now that he sees I'm trying. The kids get out of school at three-thirty. What time is it now?"

It was almost three o'clock. It would take Cindy about fifteen minutes from the hospital to Wilingsboro Elementary with Eve's directions. Her head was slightly pounding, even with medication to ease the pain. But she was nonetheless lucid enough to be explicit about matters. And she was not under the influence of alcohol.

"Don't worry about anything. I'll stay at your house tonight. Do you wantta call Paul to let him know what happened and that I've got the kids?"

"Yes. When he goes to Chicago, it's usually not long. He'll be back Wednesday night. He'll call me around eight tonight. I'll tell him everything. My cell is in my bag. Can you get it for me?"

"Sure. I'm going to get the kids now. They'll probably move you into a room in a few. I'll bring the kids to see you tomorrow after school. You certainly won't be here long. That's good. Anyway, I'm going."

"Thanks again, Sis. You're the best."

"Who knows, maybe somebody will do something for me along the way. That's what Gina believes anyway. You reap what you sow." In having expressed one of Gina's sentiments, Cindy was now smiling in gratitude of Gina's friendship.

And so she went. She picked up Corey and Noel; took them for hamburgers, french-fries and shakes; and stopped by her house to call Claudia and pick up clothes for her stay at Eve's. It was now about quarter to six.

"Claudia Hoosier speaking."

"Claudia, hi. It's Cindy."

"Is everything under control?"

"Yes. And it was like you said. Not life- threatening, just frightening. Anyway, I can do my meeting tomorrow. Since it's going overtime, it's the only one you scheduled me for anyway. I'll even be able to do Friday's executive session; Eve's husband will be home Wednesday night. The kids must be at school by eight-thirty, giving me an hour to get to the HRRC meeting. It's only a thirty-minute drive from Eve's. The kids already know to go to the after-school program and wait if I'm late."

"Well, good news on all counts. Take care, Cindy, and give my best to your sister. We'll talk more Monday morning. If anything else comes up don't hesitate to call."

Corey and Noel had settled in with pieces of fruit and their favorite TV show while Aunt Cindy packed. When she picked up the phone to dial Claudia, she'd received a stutter dial tone, indicating that she had voice messages waiting. She had four messages, all from Denville starting from one o'clock that day.

"Cindy. It's Denville. I've been trying to reach you. Thought maybe you'd be home for some reason. Anyway, call me. Thanks."………

..

Cindy. It's Denville again. What's up lady? Why haven't you returned any of my calls? Call me. Please."………

.

"Cindy. Hope you're not upset with me. Let's do a romantic dinner tonight. I'll bring a feast to your place. Listen, I know we need to talk. So let's do it! But, you gotta call me! Call! Bye."………

..

And his last message was left five minutes before she'd walked in with Corey and Noel.

"Cindy. Where are you? I know things have been strange with us lately, but what else can I say? I love you? Does that help? Call me. Please. Let me bring dinner over tonight. Call me."………

Denville sounded more desperate with every plea. But in reflecting over her conversations with Gina, she finally felt compelled towards her best friend's advice. She remembered Gina saying, 'ease up with this guy; you're in too deep, way too soon; you've only known him two months; put him on back-burner status; you're both keeping secrets!'

She deleted his messages, finished packing, rounded up Corey and Noel, and was headed back to Eve's house. She felt good about no longer being a contender in an emotional tug-of-war with Denville. She silently thought to herself, 'let him feel the heat now. Let him see how it feels to want somebody to respond and all you get is totally blown off!'

She called out to the youngsters in her living room. "You guys want another piece of fruit for the road?"

"Nope. Mom has fruit at home for us. We'll see her tomorrow. Right, Aunt Cindy?"

Corey was especially close to his mother.

"Sure will. Right after after-school. That'll be our first stop."

"And maybe we can take her some *fresh* flowers." Noel candidly said having observed the dead flowers Aunt Cindy's apartment was hosting in homage to her impending dead Denville relationship.

"Yeah. We can do that too. Come on; let's go."

No more than five minutes after she drove off, he drove up. He

192

figured he'd make one last-ditch effort to find her. By now, she should be home, he thought. But for Cindy, fate had prevailed. Denville had just missed her! "Damn," he thought aloud returning to his car after having rung her bell, "wherever the fuck she is, I hope she stays there. At least until that damn meeting is over tomorrow. I will never do anything like this again! That's for sure." Denver got back in his car and drove home.

Obviously not being in such good spirits, Vicky caught some of the brunt of his sour disposition. His attitude was not nice; his behavior was notably different.

Vicky unassumingly asked, "What's bothering you? You've just seemed so restless over the past few weeks."

He snapped! "And what don't you understand about working hard? I told you this hospital shit was the pits! What else should I say? What do you want me to say? You want every little stinking detail, Vicky? You wantta put me under a microscope too now? Just leave me alone!"

Vicky countered back, "I'm not trying to put you under a microscope. I don't need a microscope to see there's something bothering you. We can't talk about it?" Vicky had a way of being rather matter-of-fact, not overly emotional. As an elementary school teacher, she was accustomed to occasional bad attitudes and behaviors.

He softened, "I've got to start looking for another job. I don't like what I've had to get involved with at that hospital. It's not worth it, and I just might quit before I find another job. We can make it for about a month if it takes me that long."

"We can make it about three months, if need be," she sympathetically replied. "But the bottom line is that you're happy with yourself and reasonably happy with what you're doing. Lately, you don't seem to be either. So maybe you should quit. But I don't appreciate your taking your problems out on me. If something's wrong let's talk about it. If we can't discuss it now, fine. But I'm not the problem; so, don't take it out on me."

"Understood. I'm sorry. I don't wantta talk about all the details just yet, but Vicks I do need to tell you some things. This really sucks—and it sucks big." He'd realized he didn't relish keeping the secrets Numan had forced on him. He didn't like how it had begun to affect him, and

193

possibly next, his marriage. And Cindy was yet another force to be reckoned with.

Vicky was supportive. "Honey, whatever it is, we'll get through it. You know what the saying is, 'bad times don't last always!'"

By 11:00 p.m., all characters were in bed and two of the leading men in the next day's proceeding were engaged in intercourse. Denver was anxiously replaying getting fucked by Gary; Alonzo was making love with Shawna. In the morning, one would arise with nervous anxiety; the other, confident and self-assured. One would be operating via the disgrace of divisiveness; and the other, by the valor of integrity.

After dropping Corey and Noel off at school, Cindy sat at a major intersection red light, deliberating over whether she should turn on the radio. If she did, she'd be distracted from mulling over her thoughts; if she didn't, she'd only have her thoughts frequently tainted by harsh realities. The vehement horn blowing behind helped her quickly decide. The light was green. "Let me just pay attention to driving. That's all I need to think about right now."

And she was there. It was nine-fifteen on the Health Department's clock when she walked into the room. She strolled down the extreme left aisle pulling her stenography gear along. Again, she took note of the many people already seated. Many more were still to come. As she was setting up, Numan, Imani, and Lawson were stepping off the elevator heading towards the meeting quarters. Imani and Lawson proceeded in to get situated. Numan hung outside awaiting Mantis and Simmons. Prier, Morris, Lein, and Jewel single-filed down the center aisle.

Mantis spotted Numan on his way in. "This is going to be one hot session, I imagine."

"Yeah. And I'm sorry I couldn't get you guys off the hot seat," Numan offered, "but you'll hold your own. Have you seen Denver? Did you notice if he was in the parking area anywhere?"

"No, I didn't. The meeting starts in five minutes, right?" Mantis uncomfortably asked. It was now nine-twenty-five, and pretty much everybody had arrived.

Roth had entered from the extreme right totally avoiding Numan and Mantis.

Responding to Mantis, Gary said, "That's right. Well, I guess we should go in now too. Sit up in the front with" ... At that moment, Denver walked up. "Denver!" Gary resounded, "Gee, what a relief! For a moment there I thought you weren't going to make it."

"According to you, I had no choice. Anyway Gary, I talked to my wife about some of this nightmare. She said a few things that made me see this whole mess in a new light." And Denver wasn't sharing. Gary was wondering what the new light revealed but there was no time to coax Denver into exposure. It was show time.

All three—Gary, Clayton and Denver—single filed down the center aisle with their heads down. They joined the other two face down players who were holding seats for them in the front row. Cindy was busy fiddling with additional rolls of paper knowing that she'd need them readily accessible in deference to the proposed overtime proceeding. She didn't notice "Denville's" entrance.

The Commission Secretary called the meeting to order at exactly 9:30 a.m. He read his canned speech and called for the Harrington officers, along with counsel, to be seated with the Health Department representative. He then asked them to state their names and titles for the record, as per usual. Clayton and Denver remained in their front row seats. Cindy still had not noticed Denville as she was actively engaged in the proceeding herself.

Alonzo was next up. He recapped Harrington's first session details and proceeded.

"So that brings us up to date." Alonzo paused momentarily to discern the crowded room.

"It's quite interesting that so many private hospital representatives are in attendance today which leads me to assume that you're here to observe the controversial Harrington dilemma outcome, especially since Mr. Numan was such a powerful voice at the JHPTC meetings, I'd suspect." Alonzo's statement particularly resonated with many of the participants, especially Numan, and crew.

Cindy had now taken a moment to scan the full house. Now that he'd mentioned it, she recognized many familiar JHPTC- goers' faces too.

Alonzo continued. "So, in moving forward, I'd like to have Mr. Clayton Mantis, Assistant Vice President of Accounting, answer a few questions regarding his position with Harrington."

Clayton approached the Health Department's area and took the open end-seat next to Gary.

"State your name and title for the record please," interjected the Secretary.

"Clayton Mantis, Assistant Vice President of Accounting for Harrington State General Hospital."

Alonzo continued. "Thank you for coming, Mr. Mantis. We secured a copy of your resume through the Health Department. You were an accounting clerk for a department store before you joined Harrington as an Accounts Payable Supervisor two and a half years ago. Correct?"

"Yes, sir," replied Clayton.

"And two years ago, you were promoted from an Accounts Payable Supervisor to Assistant Vice President of Accounting reporting to Mr. Numan. Before your promotion, you reported to the Accounting Director. The Accounting Director is also currently a direct report to the Vice President of Finance. Is that correct?"

"Yes, sir."

"So, Mr. Mantis, tell me exactly what it is you do, in your AVP capacity?"

"I handle suspense accounts—that's accounts where we've had significant vendor or supplier-related problems. I assure our accounts are paid timely, I get involved with vendor negotiations and I handle budget overrides."

"And especially since there's no AVP of Purchasing counterpart, I would assume your position requires you to interact with the Director of Purchasing. I mean there would be some sort of relational job activities between you two, since you both report to Mr. Numan. Is that correct?"

"Yes, sir."

"After having spent two years in your current capacity, responsible for various and sundry cost centers, and an encyclopedia's worth of explicit rules and regulations, would you say that your former accounting clerk position in a department store adequately prepared you for your AVP position in a regulated state hospital?"

Clayton was stumped. He had no idea what to say so he simply told the truth. "No, sir."

"Thank you, Mr. Mantis. That's all." Alonzo sympathetically smiled.

'Damn,' Cindy silently said to herself, 'Alonzo's no joke!"

The Numan crew and Denver Simmons were all being held hostage by their own underhandedness. Now the hand of justice was about to come down. Denver was up next.

"Is Denver Simmons present?" The Commission Secretary followed up for Alonzo, whom at that moment was jotting down a few notes.

He didn't have far to walk in exchange of seats with Clayton before he'd quickly arise, he'd decided to momentarily wait for Clayton to be nearing the point where in passing, his full view would be obstructed. It didn't work. Cindy was watching for Alonzo's next victim.

As he cagily approached exchange place, Cindy was steadily zooming in on him. Her eyes were starting to widen in disbelief! What wasn't making sense was that he was being referred to as Denver Simmons— not Denville Seamons—although the names sounded similar. Also, he was a hospital supplies salesman! How the hell could he be Director of Purchasing for Harrington?

The Secretary continued. "Please state your name and title for the record."

He did as requested.

Cindy was shocked! She blurted out in a most unusual manner; "I need the spelling of the name!"

The Secretary reinforced her request. "Would you please re-state and spell your name for the recorder please, Mr. Simmons."

His knees buckled and he felt faint, but he complied. "Denver Simmons. D-e-n-v-e-r S-i-m-m-o-n-s." He immediately sat down.

First numb, now horrified, Cindy recorded his name. After he had taken his seat and Alonzo still jotting down notes, in the silence of the proceeding she'd begun to become rattled. It was taking Alonzo forever to finish writing what he was writing. She was becoming more anxious and physically agitated with every stroke of his pen. She was perspiring, her heart was pounding, her breathing rate was increasing, and her hands were trembling.

Alonzo spoke. "Hello, Mr. Simmons. Thank you for coming. Mr.

Simmons, you're Director of Purchasing for Harrington State General Hospital?"

"Yes, sir."

"Unlike the two-year stint served by Mr. Mantis, you've only held your position for about a year. Is that correct?"

"Yes, sir."

"According to your resume, Mr. Simmons, you were a former fitness manager for a health club. Let me just cut straight to the chase here. Mr. Simmons, what are the three major objectives for state hospital purchasing efforts?"

"Um, to um—ensure the best prices."

"Not exactly. Quality assurance; on-schedule deliveries; and best efforts towards *reasonable* prices, is the answer. What's the scope of your jurisdiction?"

"Excuse me?"

"How many hospital departments do you make purchases for?"

"All of them."

"Okay. What's the on-hand supply objective required for a hospital?"

"I believe it's ninety days."

"Wrong. The inventory control system is based on a thirty to sixty days supply-on- hand objective contingent on the types of supplies, controlled by minimum and maximum inventory levels and reorder points, based on need, predetermined standards and available space. What are the criteria for requests to add inventory?"

As Alonzo grilled Denver, Cindy was becoming more nauseous with every question and wrong answer. Tears began streaming her almond complexioned face, as water filled her mouth. She was going to vomit! Pushing back from her stenography apparatus, her chair hit the floor. She bolted down the aisle to the exit. Heads jerked—all those in close proximity—in an effort to glimpse the streaking through Cindy! Inquisitive minds wondered what was wrong?"

Lindy had zoomed into an obviously stunned Alonzo. He beckoned for Lindy to come up to the platform. He said, "Running like that, she must have needed the ladies' room, badly! Would you mind seeing what's wrong? If she's ill, call Anna and tell her to call Casten. We'll need a backup here ASAP. We'll take a twenty- minute recess now. Hurry back; let me know what her problem is."

Lindy rushed to see about Cindy; Alonzo quickly conversed with the Commission Secretary, who announced the following...

"Ladies and gentlemen, we are required by law to have open public meeting proceedings recorded. Since our stenographer apparently had a difficulty, we're taking a twenty- minute recess. No comments or questions are allowed at this time. We'll reconvene at eleven o'clock. At that time, we'll either resume or postpone until another time." The Secretary delivered that dialogue, which he probably never had to do before as related to the present unsavory circumstances.

As Lindy entered the ladies' room, Cindy was exiting a stall. She indeed had vomited and without the Ipecac inducement. She was headed to the sink to wet a cold paper towel for her warm head. "Cindy; my goodness, you're apparently sick! What's wrong?"

Unable to deny appearing ill, but unwilling to talk about its cause, Cindy simply agreed with Lindy's assessment.

Lindy continued. "Alonzo asked me to find out what happened. We're in a twenty- minute recess right now, and we can certainly call Casten to have someone here to cover for you. Do you think you'll need to go home?"

Lindy sounded sincere enough, but Cindy didn't know her well enough to confide in her. So, she stalled. "Can I just take a few more minutes to get myself together? I'm sure I'll be fine. I must be coming down with a virus or something. Would you tell Alonzo I'm sorry— and –I'll be okay? I just need a few minutes alone."

"Sure. Is there anything I can get you? Pepto Bismol, Tylenol, tea?"

"No thanks. I just need some air and a few minutes."

"Well, the meeting is to resume at eleven o'clock. But I'll get Alonzo to push back another fifteen minutes. So come back at eleven-fifteen. But just to follow up, I'll be back at eleven to check on you. If you're not better by then, we're going to have to call Casten for a replacement and you should go home. If you're sick, you're sick; it can happen to anybody."

"Thanks so much, Lindy. I really appreciate your concern."

"No problem." Lindy went back to relay the details to Alonzo. He was agreeable to the additional fifteen minutes; so was the Secretary. It would have taken more than thirty-five minutes to get another stenographer there. Alonzo was also relieved to hear that Cindy's situation was not critical.

The ladies' room was all of about fifteen feet from a spot where Cindy could make a private call. Gina was the only one she could call and confide in about what had happened.

"Department of Environmental Protection. Gina Falcone speaking. May I help you?"

"Gina! It's Cindy. My God! You'll never believe what just happened!" She sounded frantic.

"My goodness, Cindy. Calm down. What could possibly have you so upset?"

"Denville! Denver! I just found out his name isn't even Denville Seamons! It's Denver Simmons. Gina, he's been lying all along! He's no salesman either; he works for Harrington Hospital as a Purchasing Director!" Cindy was crying.

"What!? Cindy, please calm down and stop crying. First, none of this is making any sense. Where are you?"

"I'm at the Health Department. I found out because Alonzo called Harrington Hospital before the HRRC, and because he's investigating them, he called in people that were in positions that they didn't seem qualified for. Denville—or Denver, was one of those people."

"What the fuck? Wow! That's deep. He was lying about his own damn name so how the hell would he have known those job responsibilities?" Gina didn't want to laugh, but the matter did seem funny. "So, Alonzo called him before the HRRC? Exposed that ass on the carpet. Then what?"

"Not only did he have to face Alonzo—me had to face me too! I can't believe that guy lied like he did! But why? I don't get it! I fell in love with him, Gina. I didn't go out of my way to get him. He came after me. And it was all based on a lie! I'm so embarrassed. I feel so sick, I should probably just go home."

"No way! You pull yourself together and make that stinking bastard feel sick! You walk back in that room with your head up and take down every word that miserable low-life says. He's the varmint, Cindy. Not you! Don't let him embarrass you; he's the son-of-a-bitch that should be embarrassed. And he doesn't even know what the hell he's supposed to be doing in his job? Hell, he should be arrested too! You should be laughing at him yourself. Get back in there! Don't let him off easy! Stand up in his face, if necessary. Tell Alonzo on him! Let him fry that bastard to a crisp!" Gina was pissed! Her Italian temper was flagrantly wailing Denver's ass.

"You're right, Gina! Thanks. I guess I needed to hear that. I'm feeling better already. I'm going back in there and do exactly what you said—face off to that lying bastard! I can't believe he did this!"

"I told you it was too soon to be so involved. You didn't know him, or anybody who knew him either. Obviously, he's a damn dog carrying secrets! Call me tonight when you get home. In the meantime, go back in there and do your thing."

"Oh, I'll call you from Eve's. She had a slight car accident Monday and I'm staying at her house with the kids until Paul gets back tomorrow."

"Is she alright?!"

"Yes, thank God. It wasn't all that serious. Anyway, I'll call you from there tonight."

"Fine. Keep your spirit up, girlfriend. Chin up and get back in there!"

And once again Gina's words of wisdom reigned. Although neither of them would ever know, it was Gina's vocalized suspicions about Denville that caused Cindy to ignore his desperate voicemails that infamous Monday —the evening of which she would have been subjected to his truly unromantic dinner plans. It was also fate that had required her assistance for Eve that afternoon. It was the unmistakable hand of the Almighty that gently pushed her beyond the undeserved divisiveness that Denville was about to heave her way.

As Cindy was returning to the proceeding, she spotted Lindy approaching. "Lindy, I just went over to make a quick phone call. I'm better now. Gee, it's eleven o'clock already."

"Yep. And are you sure you'll be okay to continue? This meeting is supposed to go into overtime, so if you're not really sure, let me know now."

"Yes, I'm fine. I'll be okay to handle overtime too. Well, overtime up until about three o'clock—I must pick up my niece and nephew. Does overtime mean like Executive Session hours?"

"No; absolutely not. Our regular session overtime is usually one or two hours at most. I'd say this should conclude around two—two thirty at the latest."

"Oh, I'll be fine then. Don't worry. I'm feeling much better now."

"Well, we still have a little more time. Alonzo was most cooperative in adding an additional fifteen to recess. And he was glad to know that there was nothing serious about your situation. See you back in there in fifteen then."

"Yes. And thanks again, Lindy."

Lindy left Cindy to return to Alonzo's side. Cindy roamed the outside corridors for another ten minutes, talking herself into knowing that she could rise to the occasion. She also had Gina's supportive comments ringing fresh in her mind.

Heading back to the proceeding, Imani, Lawson, Roth, and Mantis were still in their own deliberation as to what happened to the stenographer. Numan and Simmons had chatted surreptitiously about same.

All folks back in and situated, including Cindy, the Commission Secretary reconvened the meeting. It was eleven-thirty a.m., when Denver Simmons was asked to be seated again with the Health Department; and re-state his name and title in deference to the unforeseen break in the proceeding. He did as requested.

Alonzo continued. "I don't have anything else for you Mr. Simmons, other than the same last question I asked of Mr. Mantis. Do you feel that your former position as a fitness club manager adequately prepared you for your current Purchasing Director position with Harrington?"

"No, sir, I don't."

"Thank you for your honesty, Mr. Simmons. That's all." Denver went back to his front row seat. He certainly didn't want to draw any more attention to himself by strolling up the long aisle to the exit. He had indeed avoided Cindy's eyes, as he felt her watching him dejectedly scuffle back to his seat of about twenty feet away. Still a little shaken, Cindy was holding her own.

Alonzo continued. "Without any further ado, I'm ready to conclude this matter. Analysis of Harrington's bank statements revealed that there were two wire transfers made to Germany in the total amount of five and a half million dollars. Both transfers occurred within two weeks after the Health Department granted and issued emergency relief funds to the hospital. By the way, as per our further investigation with the bank, Mr. Mantis handled both wire transactions as authorized by Mr. Numan. So not only does Mr. Mantis handle budget overrides, but he also handles transactions that should never occur!" Looking directly at Clayton Mantis, Alonzo focused his next comment. "That's one little nuance you forgot to mention as a job responsibility, Mr. Mantis."

Clayton was looking pitifully distressed; Numan was looking terribly panicked; Imani and Lawson just sat looking guilty as sin, as Denver just sat looking down. Alonzo refocused his attention back to the Health Department platform where the ring- leaders sat. He continued.

"And in further analysis of your bank statements, the other numbers you tried to manipulate—like your supplies and medications costs— although they remained flat in comparison to your feigned length of stay numbers—payments made to those vendors were even lower than what you reported! And then, you have two people; both of whom by their own admissions, are in positions they're not qualified for, reporting to Mr. Numan. What's even more interesting is that these two positions strategically link. I believe that Mr. Mantis' position pays for what Mr. Simmons' position receives and warehouses. And I was even more convinced of that in having read Mr. Numan's comments from the Joint Hospital and Payer Task Force transcripts. Would you care to take the stage and tell us all about UKing Corporation, Mr. Numan? You certainly spent enough time talking about them at the JHPTC meetings." Alonzo was sternly and squarely looking right at Gary Numan.

"Uh—I can explain that this really doesn't look like what it *appears* to look like. Um—this was a healthcare and healing project—that um—would have resulted in better healing rates after surgeries—and um, we would have pioneered this with this new German development company." An extremely nervous Gary was grasping for words that just weren't flowing coherently enough.

Alonzo ignored Numan's chatter and continued. "UKing Corporation is a global world organization and leading provider of information and cutting-edge solutions for healthcare and healing. It's a $1.9 billion dollar organization operating in ninety countries with over fifty years' experience. They're sought by medical technology development companies that have new medical breakthroughs for which funding is needed. Essentially—venture capital funding. And mostly all these ventures are at- risk. Isn't that correct, Mr. Numan?" Alonzo had his staff follow-up on every detail Numan had elaborated on at the JHPTC meetings.

"Yes, sir."

Roth was now scanning the appearances of all three gentlemen who all appeared to be most uncomfortable. Cindy was holding up well, as she kept a stronghold on Gina's wise counsel. Denver was barely holding on—as he continued to sit wedged between the focal points of Alonzo and Cindy.

Alonzo continued. "So, as we're all in agreement with the essential facts, would someone from Harrington care to tell me why the two previously noted wire transfers were made to a German company by the name of Helblien R&D?"

The three Harrington officers were speechless.

Alonzo spoke again. "Cat got your tongue, Mr. Numan? What about you, Mr. Lawson? Mr. Imani? Mr. Newman, you were quite talkative and highly informative at the JHPTC meetings. I'm sure you gentlemen realize that you had no right to authorize five and a half million dollars of the State's money to go floating off to Germany. Likewise, I'm sure you know now—you have no other recourse than to tell us exactly what it was for! Speak up—gentlemen." Alonzo was demanding, articulate, and explicitly clear!

Imani spoke up. "Mr. Prier, may we confer with our counsel?"

"Yes, you may. As a matter of fact, I'd like to call for a ten-minute break."

"Granted", announced the Secretary. "The meeting will resume at twelve thirty."

Alonzo headed straight over to Cindy. "Cindy, how're you feeling?

Lindy told me you got sick. I certainly appreciate your hanging in here but I hope you haven't put yourself through too much agony."

"Oh no, Alonzo. I'm much better now. It was just a momentary thing. I'm okay."

He again beckoned for Lindy to join them, who was looking in their direction anyway.

She was only too pleased to join. "Yes? I was just on my way down to get some juice. Do either of you want anything?"

Alonzo continued, "Would you like some juice or anything, Cindy?"

"Thank you. I'll take some orange juice," Cindy replied.

"Lindy, would you please get Cindy an orange juice and an apple juice for me? Here's ten—get whatever you want too. Thanks."

"No problem." Lindy headed out to the little concession stand outside the main event.

Before he headed back over to briefly chat with his colleagues, he again thanked Cindy for her JHPTC excerpt efforts and for hanging in. He returned to Dr. Morris and another gentleman whom Cindy didn't recognize. The three of them engaged in a conversation that alluded to do not disturb.

Lindy was back with the juice. She proceeded to give Cindy hers, and on to Alonzo next. He gave her a high-five; followed by an immediate clinched-fist, as if to indicate he'd take his juice later, and the present conversation was closed to her as well.

Imani, Numan, Lawson and Roth had all moved to the front row seats to caucus. Roth had just finished reminding them again that he'd recused himself of anything to do with them in relation to their overseas exploit.

But Imani wasn't hearing him. "Well, what should we tell him now? Should we go into all the details here? Would it be better if we had the prospectus so he could see what a great thing this BandRxStat shit is? But Gary, why the fuck did you talk so damn much about this shit at the JHPTC meetings? And how the hell did Alonzo find out? What the fuck happened here? He doesn't go to those meetings! It's a task force—an open exchange of ideas about deregulation or not! It's not a forum that Alonzo would attend!" Imani was all over the map. Before anyone could answer one of his questions, he was on to the next. He'd finally shut up!

And all Roth could advise them of was one of the two options he had previously mentioned. Now it was even clear to them, that all they could do was ask for a private meeting to avoid further public embarrassment. Roth also stated that he could not ask for the private meeting on their behalf, as again, he was not representing them by way of Germany.

During the break, Denver and Clayton had decided to transplant themselves to the back of the room. They found seats way up near the entrance, so that when the meeting finally adjourned, they'd be the first ones out.

It was time to resume. The Secretary re-convened the meeting. Alonzo was up again.

"We left off with Mr. Imani having asked for time-out with counsel, after I asked what exactly Harrington bought in Germany with the State's five and a half million dollars. I'd like an answer now—please."

And it was Patrick Lawson who responded. "Mr. Prier, we recognize this is a most unusual situation. At this time, we would like to ask for a private meeting with your office to further discuss this matter."

"And Mr. Lawson I can most definitely appreciate your circumstances. However, I'll have to defer to my boss for an answer to your question."

At that point, the unfamiliar gentleman that Cindy had noticed Alonzo and Dr. Morris conversing with earlier, stood up. He was in the front row separated by the center aisle, across from where Denver and Clayton were previously seated. The Attorney General was in the house.

'Damn.' Lawson silently thought.

'Oh shit!' Imani silently bellowed.

'For cryin' out loud!!' Numan silently screamed.

Trapped by their tales, three blind mice had finally seen the light.

"My office, three o'clock, tomorrow afternoon." And it was official. Attorney General Raymond Chandler had spoken. He gave Alonzo a thumbs-up in acknowledgement of a job-well-done. He didn't sit back down. Instead, he started walking out, which turned into a studious ascending stride up the center aisle to exit. He didn't look at anyone, nor did he break stride. Raymond Chandler was fifty years old, a well-seasoned, long standing Attorney, who was well respected and admired by the Governor and everyone reporting to him. He too, was a man of upstanding character brandishing a regal handsome appearance. There was no ill-repute blemishing his track record. He and Alonzo made a good team.

The Secretary reiterated the AG's Office meeting details. He then asked of Alonzo, "Do you have any other questions or considerations for Harrington Hospital staff, Mr. Prier?"

"No, but I have a question for Mr. Roth. Was Iverson and Roth counsel to Harrington State Hospital regarding UKing and Helblien R&D?"

Mr. Roth stood up and answered. "No, sir. When I learned of that matter only on September twenty-second of this year, I recused my firm and myself. We had absolutely no knowledge of the matter until then."

"I am relieved to hear that, Mr. Roth. I suspected your comment about only serving as counsel going forward meant you weren't involved with this most disgraceful scheme. Thank you." Alonzo then asked one of the three, "Mr. Lawson, who was your counsel in this outrageous undertaking?"

"Bender and Binds, sir. They're an investments type legal firm in New York."

Alonzo wrote that down too. "Thank you, Mr. Lawson. I have nothing further."

The Secretary called for any additional remarks. No one offered a mumbling word. Accordingly, the Secretary called for a motion to conclude. It was made, seconded and ended. Denver and Clayton were the first ones up—and out.

And Cindy had made it through! At 1:53 p.m., she'd have more than enough time to continue re-grouping, as she unwound from the day's drama. She'd also have more than enough time to pick up some "fresh" flowers and be on time for Corey and Noel. She would also have too much time to think about the injustice that Denver had leveled against her. But nonetheless, she would handle it.

XIV

Extra Innings

COREY AND NOEL WERE SO happy to see their mom! Eve was doing so much better too. She'd been moved to a double-occupancy room and was due to be released by five o'clock that evening if her attending physician concurred with the head nurse's findings. She would need some follow-up, but nothing drastic. As the kids busied themselves out at the nurses' station in search of a container for mom's flowers, Eve had zeroed in on Cindy's downheartedness.

"Cindy, is everything alright? You look upset."

"I am. I didn't want to say anything in front of the kids—but Eve—I've been dating a guy, who lied even about his name."

"What?"

"Denville Seamons is really Denver Simmons." Cindy went into explicit detail about how she discovered the truth and how Gina's words of encouragement helped her to "get back in there" and finish the day's proceeding. She was still none the wiser as to why Denver had done such a deplorable thing, as he obviously didn't hang around after the meeting to explain. Cindy was desperately trying to fight back the tears.

"Oh, how horrible! You know Cindy, Paul and I have certainly had our problems; and I'm not trying to justify any of his past bad behavior, but he's not a liar. It wasn't until I started getting grounded with those AA meetings that I realized we're all responsible for what we do and what we accept, no matter what. I accepted Paul's behavior by getting drunk and staying in denial. That part was my fault. But you had no idea what Denver was up to. And that's got to be even worse. I guess it feels like being hit by a Mack truck when you thought the coast was clear. So go ahead and cry, Cindy. I'm sure you're hurt and feeling a lot of pain right now. But once the pain is gone, it's over. If he could do such a miserable thing, to such a beautiful person, he's got problems. And you may not ever know why he did what he did, but he's not even worth trying to figure out. Just be glad you didn't have years invested in a liar. You deserve so much better than that!"

Tears were streaming Cindy's face. She reached over to embrace Eve for such a touching soliloquy, both crying.

The kids were back with the flowers in a container, accompanied by the head nurse. She would check Eve's vitals, and if all were well, she'd get her prepped for the doctor's send-off.

"I just hope those are tears of joy! This accident could have been a whole lot worse, you know." The head nurse had noted Cindy's peculiar condition. "And I'm fairly sure I'll be giving her a good report for the doctor. He should be here in about an hour. She's been doing fine."

Cindy managed a weak smile. The kids were happy to hear mom was on her way home.

He'd decided against going back to Harrington after the meeting. He instinctively felt that if he went back, it should rightfully be to clean out his desk. Thus, he opted to spend the rest of the afternoon in seclusion with his innermost thoughts—and turmoil. He drove to the County park. 'I've got to tell Vicky about this. But how? I need to say something to Cindy. How? What made me think anybody could ever do anything like this and pull it off? If I had just minded my business! I shouldn't have ever told Gary about hearing Cindy talking to Alonzo. Truth is that those hospital fuckups got just what they deserved. Alonzo, steam-rolled their asses. Shit, he steam-rolled mine too. But it's going to get worse for them. And I'm glad Cindy really didn't get hurt—just heart-broken a little—maybe. Damn, this whole thing got way out of hand.'

It was four-thirty and Alonzo was back in his office on his private line. He was in discussion about his Washington business when Anna buzzed... "Could you hold on for a moment, Peter? My secretary's buzzing." He depressed the intercom button after placing Peter on hold. "Yes, Anna."

"Mr. Lawson from Harrington State is on line one for you. Shall I have him call back?"

"No. Have him wait one minute. I'll take it." He took his private call off hold and continued. "Peter, I've got one of the bumbling brothers I told you about on my other line. Anyway, I'm quite pleased, and I'll see you soon. Thank you and I'm really looking forward to this."

"Great! Call me if you think of anything along the way that you want to chat about."

"Will do, Peter. Have a good evening." He took a deep breath; exhaled and smiled; and suddenly grimaced, in having remembered Lawson was on hold.

With a matter-of-fact tone, he spoke. "Yes, Mr. Lawson—and the purpose of your call is?"

"Gabriel Imani is here with me. In reference to tomorrow's meeting, our counsel for our German matter will not be available. Is it possible that we can"…

Alonzo cut him off. "Change the date? No. Let me tell you something Mr. Lawson; and put me on speaker for Mr. Imani's benefit if you like, but there isn't one attorney on the face of this earth that can devise a defense for—or shield you from—the unethical stunt you and your comrades concocted. If it's an attorney that you need—look no further, gentlemen. I'm an attorney; the Attorney General is an attorney, and we'll even have a doctor in the house for you too—Dr. Morris will be at the meeting. You have a right to counsel, but you have a requirement by the Attorney General to be here tomorrow at three o'clock. And make sure you bring all the pertinent facts about what you sunk five and a half million dollars into in Germany for. Good evening, gentlemen."

Lawson and Imani didn't get an opportunity to respond. Dial tone was all they heard coming from the other end of the phone.

"I guess we should all really go through that prospectus and highlight the healing values of BandRxStat. That's my best shot for this shit." Imani got up and headed back to his office.

"Close the door on your way out," ordered Lawson.

Numan was hiding out in his office. He was trying to avoid being grilled about what Alonzo was talking about—that JHPTC meeting dialogue! His plan failed. Imani suddenly recalled that piece of unfinished business and burst into Numan's office in route to his.

And Alonzo was about to give Ted a news flash! He took a moment to call his buddy's private line.

"Ted Garretson."

"Ted! What's up man?"

"Azo! This job is one headache after another. We're finally making a little headway with this asbestos crisis, and then I find out we've got a 'too-much-Mercury-in fish' crisis. It's more of a problem for pregnant women though. I'll tell you! If it's not land, it's some shit at sea! Never a dull moment! What's up with you?"

"We've got the three dancing bears coming in tomorrow for their final show. They did some deal in Germany with the State's five and a half mill. Amongst the three of them, they've got all the brainpower of a single flea."

"So, it's closed curtains now, huh? Hey! What about your Washington stuff?"

"That's really what I called to tell you."

And while Alonzo continued chatting with Ted, Shawna was chatting with Vladimir Ustaci. He had another fabrics/fashion consulting assignment for her in relation to his new location. He would now have distinctive designer stores in New York, Florida, Chicago *and* Washington D.C.

"Vladimir, you certainly are a shaker and a mover. We really had a great time at your Making Love with Our Eyes debut. It was really a great theme and his designs were fabulous. How's he doing anyway—that new guy—what's his name again?"

"Roman Gustav. He's fine. He's doing great actually. But he's the more sensual, erotic clothes designer. I've got him mostly working the New York and Florida circuits. But for my new shop, I want to introduce the working woman's line—you know—the high-power, woman-of-the-hour look. I'd like you to consult about the fabric selections for some of the designs. I want to put some seductiveness in the sedate working woman's wardrobe. I'd like to do it with the fabrics versus the designs. Know what I mean?"

"Yeah. But I'm not sure I like it! My husband is in that working world too! I don't want you dressing these women up too sexy, now. I've got a husband to keep! Know what I mean?" She was certainly kidding. And they both knew exactly what each other meant.

"I saw your husband looking at you that evening. Girl, that man loves you, with your beautiful self! You don't have one thing to worry about. He may look at other gorgeous women, but he's got Betty Davis eyes for you, girl! Plus, you're the mother of his three kids. Honey, other girls may get the bone, but they'll never get the meat. He can't afford all of you all, and a little piece on the side."

"And that's not comforting, Vladimir." They both laughed, as Shawna was quite familiar with Vladimir's risqué sense of humor.

"You know that man is yours—like forever, girl. So shall I get the stuff to you, or can you come into New York next week?"

"I'll come to you. I'll divvy up the kids between my mom and Azo's mom, and I'll see you next week. Either Tuesday or Wednesday, and I'll let you know for sure on Monday. How's that?"

"Perfect. And we'll do lunch! Thanks so much, Sweetness. Love you."

"Love you too. See ya next week."

And she cherished her occasional consulting assignments with Vladimir. The high fashion and modeling world were deep seeded aspects of Shawna's sensuality and persona. In addition to the fact that she was also intelligent, she was a sweetheart too. And although Alonzo didn't view Lindy as a sweetheart-type, he did find other things about her to be like Shawna.

And after he hung up from Ted, he immediately called Shawna. "Hello, my love. And how are you this evening?"

"Fine, Honey. And you?"

"I'm just dandy! Kids okay?"

"There're just dandy too. Thorn and Chloyee had a little tiff though."

"Really? What happened?"

"He snatched her doll, and she hit him in the head. They've been at it ever since. They're too funny!"

Rather amused, Alonzo chuckled in saying, "I have to teach him not to do things like that."

"That's true, but Chloyee also let him know not to do that again. So, are you calling to tell me you're meeting Ted for drinks and dinner?"

"No. I'm calling you to tell you I love you and I'm bringing dinner home for us tonight. A chicken pasta dish would be good for the kids, right?"

"Sure. That's fine."

"And I'll decide on a romantic dinner for us, and the wine. Is that okay with you, Love?"

"That's absolutely a-okay with me, Love. I'll see you soon then. Hey, what's the occasion?"

"Ah, now you're looking to know too much. Later."

"You mean you're leaving at a reasonable time, too?"

"Yep! It's five-fifteen now; I'm out the door as soon as I call the restaurant and place my order. And, I'll get to hang out with my little Chloyee before her bedtime. I've got to teach her how to box off Thorn properly."

"Don't you guys mess with my little Thornton now! He was just being a boy, having a little fun. Chloyee took it personal! Love you. Bye."

And before he stopped at the delectable Italian restaurant to pick up his order, he had stopped by a local florist and the liquor store. At the florist, he purchased a half dozen flawless red roses. At the liquor store he bought a bottle of vintage Parisian Merlot. By the time he got to the restaurant, his order had just been packaged for pick-up.

And since he was doing so much, Shawna decided to re-do the kids and herself too.

She quickly bathed Erik and Thornton; lotioned them down; and got them in their nighties so that chore would be done when Daddy arrived. Chloyee was up next. Shawna swooped her from her playpen, bathed and lotioned her, and dressed her in her little bedtime attire. Shawna breezed through the shower, brushed back her lioness locks, spritzed her favorite body fragrance, and coated her luscious lips with a clear gloss. She slipped into a thong, and a long slinky housedress! Alonzo arrived within moments of the grand finale.

And the Prier family spent a wonderful evening at home. Shawna was impressed by all that Alonzo had gone way out of his way to do, during his recent demanding work schedule. After dinner, he played with his kids a while, and then helped her get them off to dreamland. And now the rest of the night would be intimately theirs.

"You know, this was a great night. Thanks. I wish it could be just like this more often. Not every night—then it wouldn't be special." Her head was in his lap as he stroked her lengthy thick tresses. They were in the living room, on the sofa, with a few candles strategically lit throughout. No music, no television; just their intimacy sufficed for entertainment.

"Shawna, I have something to tell you."

She abruptly sat up. He sounded mysterious. "Is something wrong?"

"Nope. Things couldn't be better actually! You know the Health Care Financing Administration meetings I've been to in Washington?"

"Yeah. HCFA."

"Right. Remember I told you I was attending those meetings regarding the independent legal and policy advisors to HCFA?"

"Yeah."

"Well, they made me a job offer. The salary is double what I'm making now, and I'd be up for partner status in a year. The job is in Washington D.C.; and a couple of weeks ago they sent me the policy proposals I'd be responsible for if I took the job. I'm hoping that you're not going to be turned off to this, Shawna. I know it means leaving your parents and relatives and our friends, but"...

"But what?" And this time, Alonzo was cut off. She continued. "You've decided that's the best move to make? Well, Mr. Prier, let me tell you a couple of things. First, I don't have a successful legal-eagle track record like you, but I do enjoy my occasional fashion consulting. And since I talked to Vladimir today, who has another assignment for me, your new job offer—is the best news in the world! *Azo, that's great!* Vladimir's new shop is in Washington too! And with Erik only in first grade, we don't have to go through that changing schools nightmare! Honey, when do we move? I can't wait to tell Vladimir. I'm meeting him next week for lunch and my Washington project. Oh honey, I'm so happy for you—and me—and the kids! This is great, Azo!" She was smiling.

He was speechless. The way Shawna started out, scared him; the way she concluded, shocked him! Nonetheless, they ended up on the same page.

"Honey, for a minute there, you had me worried! But I'm so glad you're happy. Let's blow out these candles, check our little ones, and hit the sheets. You think you could make love to an old, tired guy tonight?"

"No. But I know I can make love to a remarkably brilliant and handsome man, whenever! Let's go, you!"

And the die was cast. His best friend had suggested he go for it; his wife was supportive of it; and it was Dr. Morris and the Governor who put him up to it in the first place. Now he'd only need conclude the Harrington matter and announce his departure to his staff. Raymond Chandler, his boss, was also already in the loop. Alonzo's attendance at the HCFA meetings in representation of his home state was highly political posturing and favor for the Governor. And the Attorney General, was a direct report to the Governor. Alonzo's first order of business for the morning would be twofold; he would call Dr. Morris with the news and tell his boss too. Or vice-versa.

The next morning, before Cindy left Eve's house with Corey and Noel, she mentioned to Eve that she would probably leave after Paul got home that evening. Eve was mobile and capable of functioning about the house, she just couldn't drive, nor did she have a car to drive anyway. It had been hauled off for repair.

"You don't have to leave because Paul is coming home. You sure you want to be alone now?" Eve could still see Cindy was upset over her recent Denver discovery.

"I've got to be alone at some point. But if you need me, I'll stay."

"No. I'm okay. But if you need me for emotional support, I'm here. Must be the silver lining in the cloud—me—being able to offer you emotional support. Funny, huh?" Eve smiled.

"I'll call you later. I'm off to drop the kids at school and get on to work. Bye."

"Bye. Keep your chin up," advised Eve.

By nine o'clock, Alonzo was in his office on his private line.

"Department of Health, Office of Commissioner Morris. Diane speaking. May I help you?"

"Good morning, Diane. It's Alonzo. Is Dr. Morris in?"

"Oh hello, Mr. Prier. She's in. Please hold."

As he sat waiting, he thought about how he'd deliver the news. It would certainly be with mixed emotions.

"Alonzo?"

"Yes, Gwen. Good morning."

"Hi! How are you? Ready for those Harrington folks this afternoon?"

"You bet! Isn't it amazing how ridiculous people can be and how low they can go?"

"It's frightening. I'm bringing Warren to the meeting. He'll be working the follow-up details for the Health Department with Candice."

"That's fine. And I also wanted to let you know I made my decision about Washington. I decided to accept the offer. My wife is supportive; it's good timing as far as my kids are concerned, and it's one hell of an offer!"

"Oh, my goodness! Alonzo, my heart just broke. You are surely going to be missed! But for all the reasons you just mentioned, I certainly understand. It's a wonderful opportunity and no one is more deserving than you."

"Thanks, Gwen." He took an emotional pause. "I need to run up and tell Raymond now. You know it was a toss-up between telling you or him first."

"How'd I win?"

"Ladies first—and he wasn't in his office earlier this morning. Anyway, I sincerely want to thank you for all the support. You made it difficult for me to not consider this!"

"And I'd do it all over again! I suppose you and Raymond will tell the Governor together—huh?" Dr. Morris was almost in tears.

"Probably."

"Anyway, congrats—and I'll see you at three."

"Thanks, Gwen. Three it is."

He hung up; took a deep breath; exhaled; and moved on! In heading up to share "the news" with his boss, Alonzo stopped at Anna's desk.

He asked her to set up a staff meeting for his direct reports for nine o'clock Thursday morning.

Denver was moving towards an emergency meeting Gary had scheduled for Harrington Hospital personnel. He got the message that morning since he hadn't returned the day before. Already in progress in the hospital's huge cafeteria, Gary was holding his disingenuous meeting. He was attempting to downplay the fact that there would undoubtedly be some buzzing amongst the industry people about the prior day's meeting.

Gary was diligently explaining that, "the Attorney General's Office at yesterday's HRRC meeting, didn't understand the dynamics of Harrington's initiatives. And I'm not at liberty to discuss that now either. But that's why we had to request a private meeting, so that the critical concerns could be discussed in a more intelligent and confidential manner. So, if the AG's Office didn't get it—it only follows that the private hospital folks didn't get it either. So, disregard any backlash you may hear—from your friends at other hospitals—or wherever. It's all clatter!" He was on a microphone and podium setup.

"Yeah! Right." Clayton chuckled in whispering to Denver who was standing beside him at Gary's innocuous meeting. Late comers had been remanded to standing room only.

"He's totally off the fuckin' wall," was Denver's candid soft-spoken reply.

Gary continued his spiel, "And that's it in a nutshell. We have a three o'clock meeting with the Attorney General's Office, but I suggest you all not discuss this among yourselves and let us handle it. Are there any questions?" Gary was trying to simultaneously hold the fort and diffuse the possibility of job security anxiety.

Of course there were no questions. At that point, none of the other employees had the slightest clue what was going on. The meeting began at nine forty-five; it was over at ten o'clock.

Lawson and Imani just remained seated in awe of Numan's stellar performance. They were all in agreement that the full personnel meeting should be held, but neither Lawson nor Imani had a clue that Numan would spin the matter so well. Now Imani realized Numan's ability to spiff up the facts and talk too much! That was exactly how so much information about their venture ended up in the JHPTC transcripts. Numan loved to grandstand! Imani and Lawson were now in agreement that it was one of the private hospital people at the JHPTC meetings, who dropped the proverbial dime on them!

Denver and Clayton had returned to their offices. On the way back, they discussed what they thought the next move might be. They concurred that Alonzo would undoubtedly deliver the final edict at the three o'clock meeting.

Shawna was on the phone with Alonzo's mom, talking gleefully about her recent developments! She'd also ask her mom about her availability for next Tuesday or Wednesday to baby-sit Chloyee. Nan would take the boys, since the grandsons always rejuvenated Azo's dad.

"Hello."

"Hi Nan. How are you?"

"Shawna! Hello darling. How are you all? I was just saying to Pop, I needed to give you a call. What's going on?"

"Oh, we're all fine, Nan. Couldn't be better. Alonzo has some pretty big news, but I don't want to steal his thunder. I want him to tell you, so I won't. But it's great news!"

"Oh, come on! You can't be serious. You can't say something like that and leave me in suspense! What is it?"

"Well—he got a new job offer. But that's all I can say. Act surprised when he gives you the news and all the details. I've probably said too much already."

"Oh, that's wonderful! That's great! My son is such a good guy! And I'll act surprised. I'll wait until he tells us. I won't say a word to Pop, either."

"Thanks, Nan. Oh—would you and Pop mind keeping Thornton and picking Erik up from school on Tuesday or Wednesday for me? I've got a fashion consulting assignment next week I'm trying to schedule. I need to go into New York for this."

"Sure, Honey. Either day is fine. What about Chloyee?"

"My mom will take her either day also; I didn't want to overload you guys. So then let's do Tuesday."

"Fine. And thanks for the news about Alonzo! See you soon. Love you all."

"Love you too, Nan. And thanks."

Cindy was on a fifteen- minute break. She decided to call her Casten voicemail to see if Denver had mustered up the decency to at least try and explain. Nothing. Carrying the burden of disillusionment, she returned to the proceeding chambers to wait out the rest of the session break. Those few more minutes seemed like a weighted eternity.

Meanwhile, back at the hospital the three quasi-protagonists were busy at work—working up a believable story for the three o'clock meeting. The AG's Office main characters, in conjunction with the Department of Health's leading lady, were awaiting the performance. And when the clock hands rolled around to three, the requisite cast and crew were ready for action.

"We're going to dispense with the formalities folks. We all know why we're here."

Raymond Chandler's style was even more deliberate than Alonzo's— he was a busy man, with no time to waste. "So why don't one of you begin with exactly what it was you purchased in Germany with unauthorized State funding."

Lawson replied, as he begun distributing the document, "We've brought copies of our prospectus for everyone. We've also highlighted certain aspects of this prospectus so it would all be perfectly clear. We invested in a miraculous new discovery. The German Company that conceptualized and created BandRxStat was looking to launch their product in this country. We sincerely believed this would be an excellent health and healing initiative, which would definitely get people out of the hospital—happier and on the road to recovery sooner!"

Alonzo confirmed that, "Helblien R&D is the German Company—correct?"

"Correct." And in a rather calm and collected manner, Lawson continued. "And if you turn to page five of the prospectus, you'll see we've highlighted the description of BandRxStat. It's a bandaging, which when applied after surgical procedures of any degree, promotes rapid healing without scarring. It's like a plastic surgery immediately following an invasive surgical procedure! It's a miraculous revolutionary discovery and development that's not available in the USA. People would be extremely receptive to it too! Especially those who've had major surgical procedures like arterial bypasses for example, even third degree burn victims would benefit tremendously from this new bandaging technique. It almost erases the tell-tale scars of surgery and skin-grafting."

"I see. And does this new bandaging technique require application of a topical solution, or is it all wrapped up in the bandaging?" Raymond Chandler was not buying into the hype.

Numan responded. "Well, the attending surgeon would have to apply the serum type solution in specified dosages, as per type of surgical procedure and patient toleration."

Chandler followed up. "Mr. Numan, who would the surgeon and nurses following up on changing these post-surgical dressings receive instruction from? I'm asking about the training for use of this rare find."

"We'd have a video presentation from the Germans. It's a two-hour presentation of the product and it's healing properties. It's also instructional, and all those handling BandRxStat would be required to see the video and certified in its application as well."

"Do any of you gentlemen recognize the fact that environmental considerations; diet considerations and the overall differences in people from one corner of the world to the next, dictate response patterns to various and sundry healing techniques and medicinal properties?" Dr. Morris had now started her inquisition of the Harrington trio.

Imani answered. "Yes, we do."

Dr. Morris continued. "If you do, then what provisions had you discussed with the German innovators towards the efficacy of BandRxStat in America? And even more important, who was to be responsible for acquiring the appropriate regulatory approval to use BandRxStat in this country?"

"The Germans were. They were going to obtain the necessary approvals to have the product in use here. I think we highlighted that on page twelve." Numan replied.

Alonzo spoke next. "Well, I'm reading what you've highlighted on page twelve. Verbatim, it reads… 'Inasmuch as Helblien R&D maintains responsibility for clinical trials and requisite approvals for use in Germany, the patent for BandRxStat will be obtained in Germany, by its developers. In addition, since trade marking is essential to protect the trademark name, Helblien R & D, in Germany, as required, will perform all the necessary considerations. Use outside Germany, will be contingent on the necessary regulatory approvals in other jruisdictions.' Even a strict interpretation of that Mr. Numan, implies that it's anybody's guess as to whom will be responsible for approval to wrap folks up in BandRxStat, in the U.S.A. Do you know what regulatory agency is responsible for such a thing?"

Numan replied, "Well, after we received it, we were going to bring it before the Department of Health."

"Oh really? I don't quite believe that Mr. Numan. I think you were going to piggyback on what was done in Germany. And the Health Department couldn't have helped you with use approval anyway. That's FDA territory. Ever heard of the Food and Drug Administration? According to your document here, the accompanying solution is a vital consideration to jump-start the miraculous non-scarring healing process. The Health Department doesn't do the clinical stuff that would authorize such a thing." Alonzo was becoming more flustered with their every ridiculous answer.

Dr. Morris had further concerns. "In addition to what Mr. Prier just pointed out, were you intending to make the Harrington Hospital surgical patient aware that they would be bandaged in BandRxStat? Would you offer the patient a choice? Or were you just intending to use it at someone else's discretion? Like perhaps the attending surgeon who had recently seen the video. And what if a patient had an adverse reaction? And since you're obviously not versed on its usage requirements in this country, who would you call for urgent BandRxStat complications?"

No one from the Harrington bunch had an opportunity to respond. It was obvious they didn't have answers anyway. And Deputy Health Commissioner Lein, who had been quiet throughout, asked a few other damming questions. "You're hopefully not using BandRxStat now, are you?"

"No," replied Mr. Lawson. "We haven't received it yet."

Mr. Lein continued. "When were you supposed to receive it and planning to start using it?"

"BandRxStat's release is scheduled within another twelve months. They're in the clinical trial phase with it," was Lawson's response. "We hadn't decided on when to use it."

Lein continued. "And if this product was supposed to promote such miraculous healing and accelerated recoveries from surgical procedures, what did you assume that would translate into regarding your outrageous ALOS days? Were you intending to lower them after you started using the healer? And were you going to lower them to what's acceptable or to the ALOS commensurate with BandRxStat—if it worked?

Imani fielded that question. "Well, we would have a better healing rate at our hospital. People would be released sooner, so our ALOS days would have been reported at what BandRxStat rendered. In effect, we would cost the State less for our surgical patients."

In other words, you were intending to repay the State the five and a half million you manipulated the Health Department into authorizing for your bogus emergency rate relief needs, by suddenly reporting even lower than generally accepted stays for surgicals? I don't believe that! You never would have been able, under reasonable considerations, to explain the drastic drop. We all know that! Why don't you?"

Before any of the dumbfounded trio could answer, Alonzo interjected, "And that's the five and a half million-dollar question. Plus interest! Thank you for asking it, Deputy Lein. Their manipulation of the Health Department suggests that after they'd started using BandRxStat; assuming it did all the wonderful things it was supposed to do, they would now profit from the windfall. They'd send post-operative patients home a few days earlier; and pocket the excess from what's normally reimbursed at acceptable length-of-stay rates. Seems to me that they would report some of the drop as just an overall improvement in operations. No pun intended but, Mr. Imani, that seems like something you'd say, as Chief Operating Officer."

Mr. Chandler spoke again. "But what if it didn't work—and worse yet—people died from it? If you started using this product without the necessary clinical trials and approvals in this country—where your hospital is, gentlemen, what remedy would you have had for that travesty?"

Brief silence. No subsequent answers. They were done; none of them had anything else to say. The Regulators had capsized the Harrington crew. All three men— face down.

Attorney General Chandler continued. "If this wasn't so disgraceful, it would be hysterical! In my seventeen years of dealing with corporate and civil criminals, this act tops the list—from men who, if not wise enough, certainly old enough, to have known better! You've just emerged as the three stooges of white-collar crime. All three of you have just successfully gotten yourselves disgracefully terminated from your positions at Harrington.

"And we're sending those two guys—Clayton Mantis and Denver Simmons—out with you!" Alonzo added.

Dr. Morris carried on. "The Health Department has arranged for Deputy Rehabilitators to be at Harrington tomorrow morning at eight thirty. Justin Reamer and Winston Title are from the independent hospital- consulting firm of McBride & Furst. Mr. Reamer will be working out of your office Mr. Lawson; Mr. Title will be working from yours Mr. Numan. Mr. Imani, you need only return to clean out your desk. Mr. Numan, your ability; along with Clayton Mantis, to transact any financial business on behalf of Harrington was seized this morning. All three of you gentlemen are officially terminated as of Friday, October twenty-seventh. Do not make the further mistake of trying to conduct any business on behalf of Harrington State Hospital. Further details concerning charges of misconduct will be provided by the Attorney General's Office. As for Mr. Mantis and Mr. Simmons, the Attorney General's Office will also provide them with the details of their dismissals by tomorrow afternoon. Any questions?"

None of the three had need of any clarification. It was clear that everything they needed to know, in addition to things they'd never even wanted to consider, had all been made crystal clear. And the few remaining uncertainties? They could wait for.

And what a disgrace. The only other information Alonzo offered was that they seek criminal charges counsel. And even the best of the best would fall short in relation to what the charges would be. Alonzo would begin preparing his legal brief that evening. Meeting dismissed.

Prior to leaving, Dr. Morris informed Prier and Chandler that the Hospital Association President had called her earlier that afternoon with great news. The hospital labor union accepted the proposed remedy. Thanks to Alonzo, the labor strike had been averted!

It was now five o'clock. Alonzo would head back to his office; share the great news with Debbie North; and spend thirty minutes on Harrington's legal brief. He would then head home. On his way out, he'd check his desk calendar. Anna had penciled in the staff meeting he requested she arrange.

Cindy was back at Eve's. Paul was scheduled to arrive later that evening, and Cindy was feeling an intensified need to be alone. Eve didn't want her to leave, fearing that her emotional status wasn't up to par. Denver's deception was bad enough; to totally ignore her now, only added insult to injury. But Cindy insisted on privacy and headed home.

Denver, now also at home, had begun to share the sorted Harrington story with Vicky.

He chose his words carefully though. He didn't want to intimate that he had been intimate with another woman—no matter what. He side-stepped the issue by insinuating that all he was supposed to do was date this woman and get her to the point of desiring him. Vicky, astounded by his story tried to keep an open—and trusting mind.

When Alonzo got home, which was now in deference to his final stint with the AG's Office, his kids were still bright-eyed, bushy-tailed, and ready to rumble! Shawna remarked about his new home coming hours. "Hey! You're spoiling us with this, you know! We could get use to you coming home early."

He replied, "That's my plan."

Then he whispered something in her ear, to which she playfully responded, "You're just too kinky!"

"And with you—I've got the right one—Baby!"

They both knowingly laughed.

The next morning Cindy arose to beep, beep, beep. Not a single call did she receive the night before, not a single good feeling did she awaken to. The only good thing was that she had fallen asleep somewhere along the line. She showered, put on some understated cotton underwear, and headed for her coffee. "I'm right back where I started from—only worse," she grimaced. "Like I really needed this shit! Guess I got my wish. I got roughed-the-fuck-up and fucked over! Thanks for the tussle, whomever!" In defiance, she scowled at 'whomever'. She completed her morning matters and headed out to yet another proceeding with an acronym that couldn't be pronounced.

At nine o'clock, Alonzo's staff was filing into the small conference room for his staff meeting. He was about a minute late since he'd stopped by Anna's desk to ask her to come to his office after his meeting for about fifteen minutes.

All were in place when he walked in. "Good morning, guys. How are you?" And as usual, he was flashing that sexy smile.

"Fine," they all seemed to say in unison.

"We've got a lot of ground to cover within the next few weeks, or perhaps I should say, I do. Um, first let me start with the good news. The labor strike has been avoided. I told Debbie yesterday, right after Commissioner Morris told me. Again, Debbie, you and Michael Neely are to be commended for pulling all the facts and figures together so that the solution was apparent. Great work."

"Thanks." Debbie replied. "Glad this is over! And I'll reach out to Michael today too."

"Yeah. And tell him he can bill us now. He'll like that part even more. And the next big issue off the agenda is Harrington. We concluded that matter yesterday and I've already started preparing the legal brief. I intend to send them up before the Supreme Court on charges of defalcation, willful negligence, and bad faith. Thank you graciously, Lindy, for all you brought to the successful conclusion of the Harrington saga. You may also want to reach out to Candice and thank her as well."

"Damn!" exclaimed Steven. "That's a mouthful of some serious charges, Mr. Prier."

"I couldn't agree more—and they deserve all three of them! And Steven, even though you didn't agree with the law, you did a great job completing your windstorm assignment."

"Thank you, Mr. Prier. Glad to have been of service."

"And the last order of business takes me through to my last days with the Attorney General's Office."

"Whoa, Mr. Prier—that doesn't sound good!" Steven was candidly concerned.

"What?" Lindy was curiously concerned.

"Are you leaving, Alonzo?" Debbie cut straight to the chase.

His other deputies remained speechless.

"Yes, I am leaving. I officially gave my resignation to Raymond yesterday."

"Why?" Lindy solemnly asked.

"It's all good! I accepted an offer from HCFA's independent policy consulting firm. I'll be involved with Federal considerations towards the establishment of new health care policy initiatives. From the legal perspective, it's essentially a 'think-tank' position."

"Isn't that highly political? I mean, wouldn't you be subject to get booted with party changes?" Steven was on the money.

"That was one of my first questions, Steven. But no, this firm has been retained by HCFA for the last ten years. They've got a stronghold on their position since they created it. And it's not party driven; its agency responsive. There's a compensation structure from HCFA, which can't be altered by party contributions. As a matter of fact, the firm is prohibited from accepting platform contributions. To make a long story short Steven, I'm safe."

"Well right on, Mr. Prier. All the best!"

"Thanks, Steven. And that brings me to my last items. Lindy, since I've been grooming you to take over the HRRC meetings, you'll be fine. In about two months the deregulation vote will be in—and that will determine whether those meetings are continued or not. But since Gary Numan was the main driver of 'vote deregulation', and after we finish with his delirious ass, the industry may reconsider. But even if they don't, I've proposed a 'Word of Warning' speech from Dr. Morris. That, and my Harrington brief, will be my last orders of business here. You've been a tremendously supportive staff, and I'm appreciative of having had the opportunity to work with each of you. Any questions?"

For the most part, everyone was too emotional to speak. But tears had welled up in Lindy's eyes. She had questions, but her emotions and tears, blocked them.

And then Tyler Cordon rose to the occasion. "Mr. Prier, sounds like you're headed for a great opportunity! Congratulations. But how much longer will you be here?"

"Oh! I'll be leaving here November twenty-second, right before Thanksgiving. I'll be starting my new job right after the New Year festivities. I'll need about a month for my wife to settle on a new house! And then the Christmas holiday is wedged in there too."

Lindy remained uncharacteristically quiet. She wasn't handling his departure news well, at all.

Alonzo continued. "Well, if there's nothing else, I need to tell Anna now. I wanted to tell you all first, now I need to let her know. There'll be a new Section Chief here in about three weeks; I'll spend a week grooming him; and then I'm out. Give me fifteen minutes alone with Anna, and if you think of any questions, my door is open. Thanks."

In approaching his office, Anna looked up in the nick of time. "Should I come in now?"

"Absolutely, Anna."

She hurried over as his crew filed out. He smiled at Anna entering his office. "Close the door, please."

Unassumingly, she said, "Okay. What's on your mind?"

"Anna—I'm leaving. I resigned, effective November twenty-second, and I wanted to tell you in private. I just told my deputies—that was the reason for this morning's meeting. I'm going to work for a private law firm in Washington D.C. They're long-standing independent counsel to HCFA."

Anna stood motionless next to the mahogany chair in front of his desk. She was ill-prepared for the news, and completely overwhelmed. "I don't know what to say. I feel like you're my son, and I'm losing him."

"Oh, Anna, please don't go there. I can't deal with this from you and my mother too." Now Alonzo was bearing the brunt of detachment.

Anna continued now seated, "You know I don't mean to make you feel bad; and knowing you, it's probably a wonderful opportunity. But I've grown to love you as a son and respect you as my boss. But you've got to do what you've got to do. And us moms, we'll just have to get over it. Just call us occasionally and let us know you and the family are okay." Tearfully, she got up to leave.

Before she could make it to the door, Alonzo was on her heels. He hugged her momentarily as if she was his mother. "Anna, I will most definitely call to check on you. You've been like a second mom. You've also been a wonderful secretary. But I'm sure you'll like Lawrence Stangle. He's the new Division of Law Section Chief replacing me, and I've got two weeks with him. I'll make sure he's Anna- appropriate before I leave!"

And the emotional gravity was lifted when she sarcastically responded, "Oh right—thanks! It took you a year to get there!"

Feeling somewhat relieved, he closed the door and returned to his Harrington legal brief preparation. He also remembered he was due to place a call to Clayton Mantis and Denver Simmons. It was only ten fifty-five a.m. now; he would make the displacement calls after lunch. And notwithstanding that, he again refocused and continued working on the brief.

"Come in," was his instant response to a brisk knock upon his door.

"Alonzo, do you have a moment?"

"Sure. I only needed a few for Anna. What's up?"

"A few things. I wanted to ask you a few questions about—Harrington."

"Sure, Lindy. I'm working on the brief now. But don't worry, I'll certainly have this prepared for Supreme Court submission before I go. I'll make sure this albatross isn't hanging around your neck."

"Okay. But I'd just like to discuss the charges. Is it okay if I close the door?"

"Yeah."

"Thanks." She began to take deep breaths towards her soliloquy, "So, defalcation is the premise of the brief, correct?"

"Absolutely," he candidly replied. "Financial misconduct by officers of a state hospital, where specifically an act of misappropriation of funds and failing to properly account for them has occurred, is an act of defalcation."

"Umm. Sinful, and without any benefit whatsoever," she replied and continued in a most odd fashion, "unlike fornication, huh?"

"That's an interesting parallel," he innocently replied.

She seductively continued, "Umm. The words rhyme too. The second charge you mentioned—willful negligence."

"Right," he said. "The intentional performance of an unreasonable act in disregard of a known risk, making it highly probable that harm could be caused. I'd say that the Harrington team actions, fit that description." Noting that her questioning was going to some offbeat territory.

Lindy continued, "Isn't it sorta hard, to willfully neglect something?"

He'd been sitting at his desk and in deference to Lindy's lusty line of questioning, beginning to feel a uncomfortable. He got up to go open his door. Halfway between his desk and the door, Lindy stepped in front of him. In awareness of the morning meeting, she'd purposely worn an excessively short skirt. She was also aware that he admired her legs, as did most men.

Standing almost in his face and practically atop his shoes, she repeated her question, most seductively. "Isn't it hard, to willfully neglect something?"

"Lindy, you're making it hard for me right now. And I know you can feel it, cause you're right up on it!" And he was trying hard to keep an erection from happening, but it wasn't working.

So, she toyed with him a bit longer. "We've got one more to go—bad faith. As for the Harrington bunch, there was intent to mislead, deceive, and a conscious refusal to meet accurate reporting requirements. I'm guessing you'd believe it was bad faith towards your wife if you slept with me before you left?"

"*Oh, damn*! Lindy, my goodness! Why are you behaving like this? What's up with you?"

By now she'd eased off one shoe and was running one bare foot around his pants leg. And if her skirt had been any shorter it would have doubled as a necklace. She had Alonzo so high he could almost touch the ceiling without hands. And just as she was about to seduce him into a kiss, s swift knock on his door. He bolted back to his desk chair. Standing was not an option,

Lindy immediately stepped back into her pump.

"Come in." He was desperately struggling to calm down. Glad for the interruption—from Anna. He was hoping she wouldn't sense the tension.

"Here's another special delivery for you from Washington. Gee, can't they let us have you until you're officially supposed to be there?"

"I second that emotion," interjected a sensually charged Lindy.

Still discombobulated, he responded. "Guess not, Anna. Thanks."

"You're welcome. Should I close the door?" Anna asked.

"No. Leave it open," he replied.

And after Anna left, Lindy had begun walking towards the door.

"Don't close the door, Lindy. This isn't—I mean I can't—um—you know I'm working..."

She cut him off in mid mumbo-jumbo. "Look, I know how you feel about your marriage and your children." Honoring his request, she turned from the door and headed back towards his desk. Continuing quietly, she said, "You have a beautiful wife, and I know you'd never do anything to separate yourself from her or your children. But I want you for one night. Sex with you, one time. I'm not playing for keeps, just a keepsake."

He sat stunned. Unable to speak, he listened as Lindy continued, "I'm heartbroken you're leaving. I've learned so much from you and we'll probably never see each other again. Is it really bad faith towards your marriage, when neither of us have any intentions to mislead or deceive? Bad faith, as you well know, suggests active ill will. There's no ill will here, just an element of strong attraction that I know you feel too. You have my home number. One night, before you leave, call me—unless you're just not feeling this."

She was confident, intelligent, secure, articulate, and sultry. He had been feeling it for quite some time but had always made a conscious effort to ignore it. Now he sat speechless pretty much having maintained his composure throughout Lindy's soliloquy. But he wondered if he'd be able to hold out until final departure. She tore a post-it note page from his pad and jotted down her phone number as a reminder. She folded it and stuck it in his shirt pocket, as he sat totally mesmerized by the unexpected exchange. As she sashayed out, he had a single thought – the kind of underwear she was wearing—if any. He gently bit his bottom lip and continued to just sit there. His private line rang.

"Alonzo Prier."

"Azo! What's up?"

"Ted! Man! Damn!"

"Sounds like you're under some pressure there, Azo!"

"Whoa! You hit it right on the head! Man, I've got a tale you won't believe! You up for lunch?"

"That's why I called. Figured we'd get a few lunches in before you start getting all your farewell invitations. You did drop the news, right?"

"Yeah. I did. Everything okay with you? Asbestos; Mercury under control?"

"Both those issues will be around for an awfully long time. Anyway, meet you in an hour."

"I'll pick you up. Let's take a ride out for lunch. I need to talk."

"Sounds good. Later."

He tried to refocus on the legal brief, but Lindy had made that difficult. 'Damn' he silently thought, 'never in a million years would I have associated Harrington's criminal charges with sexual innuendo. She's *sizzling* hot, probably smokes in bed!' Alonzo was under pressure and fire, for sure. Putting his pen down and finding various other busywork to do, he looked over some files, cleaned out a few desk drawers, and made a few calls. Soon he'd be off to lunch.

Upon arrival at the South Broad Street building, Ted was coming through its huge double doors. He spotted Alonzo's car immediately. Headed to some obscure restaurant, and after exchanging a few meaningless woe stories, Alonzo started telling Ted his steamy Lindy story.

"Man, she just point blank offered it. I was about two seconds away from granting her wish, when Anna knocked on the door. Ted, I tell you; she's beautiful. She's a vamp, man! She's got my collar tight right about now."

"Let her loosen it up for you then," Ted replied.

"I've never been outside my marriage. As a matter of fact, it's only been Shawna since we got married. It's been seven years now."

"You mean there's some truth to the seven-year itch?" Ted asked in jest.

"Ah, come on Ted; I don't know. But it's not like I was looking to go elsewhere, it's just that there's—something about Lindy."

"Well, I tell you Azo. My advice to you is to remember and forget."

"Remember and forget? What the hell does that mean?"

"I'll tell you in the restaurant. Let's go." They'd pulled in the parking lot of Sabatino's little obscure Italian place about twenty minutes from their offices. Once inside, they immediately found a table. The waitress was just as timely, hurrying over to recite the specials and take their orders.

Ted continued their conversation, "Let's face it, Azo, laying the pipe in the same building for seven years is a long time. And no doubt you're the proud owner of a beautiful building. But sometimes you see another beautiful building, and you want to do a little prospecting. You're not looking to buy it, you'd just like to check out the insulation, and be on your way. That's what I mean by remember and forget. Remember Shawna is where your heart is; she's the woman you love, have kids with, and made a commitment too. But don't forget you're a man, subject to human frailties. So, you prospect, and forget about it!"

"It's something like there's a flaw in our design, huh? Something about the psychology and physiology of a man—that just makes our heads inter-changeable. So, you're saying you believe it's forgivable to cheat on one's wife?"

"No. From what you said, this would be a one-shot deal with you and Lindy. It's not a wine-dine and call-her-all-time thing. So, to that extent, it's not about Shawna; it's about you taking care of a fixation. You know you mention Lindy, a lot. Do you even have any other female deputies?"

"Oh shit; really? I do have one other. I mention Debbie North too. It's just that Lindy and Debbie are vastly different, and I work more with Lindy since she has the HRRC stuff. I guess."

Alonzo had a little more time to digest the reality byte. The waitress was back with their orders. As she diligently placed their food and drinks down, Alonzo continued to ponder if he had in fact been fixated on Lindy.

Ted took up where he'd left off. "Well Debbie doesn't get too much honorable mention. Anyway, Azo, don't make the mistake of not banging Lindy, and then start chasing her in every other woman that reminds you of her in some nonsensical way. You know, some shit like, someone wears her hair like Lindy or someone walks like Lindy—shit like that. Too much of that leads to cheating on the wife. You're better off fuckin' the one you want and forgetting about it. If you're lucky, another Lindy won't come along for another seven years."

Alonzo looked at Ted in disbelief. "I gotta hand it to you buddy, you made me see this in a whole new light. I'm certainly not in love with Lindy; she's just sexy as all get-out. I did a pretty good job of holding it down, up until today. It's that new building thing! Guess I'd wantta do a little prospecting before leaving town."

"Well, whatever you do, don't put Shawna in the middle of it. Don't set her up to shoulder the blame if you decide not to do Lindy because you're married. You know that human frailty thing has a way of making us shift blame to others for the things we own responsibility for ourselves. Hey, remember and forget, Azo! That's my best advice. And if you dare taste the wine, soak your mustache in a little vodka before you go home."

"Damn Ted. Let's eat. Sounds like you've been doing a little wine tasting and remembering to forget, yourself. You motherfucker!" It was now comical, as Alonzo's burden had been eased, and Ted had seemingly shared the secret of his successful eleven- year stint with Janice; eight of which were wedded.

"Ah but nothing serious. One every seven years or so! And it always reminds me just how settled I am—in the old building."

Both laughing, they ate, Ted picked up the check, and they headed out.

Back at the South Broad Street building, Alonzo dropped Ted off. In exiting the car, he provided his buddy with one last tidbit of advice, "And if you do go prospecting, protect yourself—B.Y.O.C.!"

For a second, he had to think about it. And then he laughingly replied, "Ted, you're a madman!"

Upon entering his office, Alonzo had become serious again. It was almost three o'clock; time to place the displacement calls, to Clayton Mantis and Denver Simmons.

"Anna, would you get Harrington Hospital on the line for me please. I'll start with Clayton Mantis."

"Sure."

By the time he got settled at his desk with his 'Clayton Mantis' folder, Anna was buzzing to let him know his party was on hold.

"Hello Mr. Mantis, this is Alonzo Prier, representing the Attorney General's Office, Division of Law and the Department of Health. This is certainly not one of the more favored calls I must make, but nonetheless, it is in line with the call of duty. Your position with Harrington State Hospital has been terminated. Harrington's Human Resources Department received the full details of your dismissal by courier from us this morning and will be in your office by three-thirty today. You're entitled to three months' severance. Based on your testimony before the HRRC, I'm sure you understand the reason for your dismissal. Best wishes in your future endeavors."

A somber Clayton replied. "I understand. After I've spoken with Human Resources, how long do I have to be here?"

"You should begin clearing your office of any personal effects now. After you've spoken with Human Resources, you are to vacate the premises," Alonzo replied.

"Okay then. Goodbye, Mr. Prier."

Without emotion, Alonzo simply said, "Goodbye." The State already had their trusted Deputy Rehabilitators in place to police operations and oversee Harrington's routine business.

It was three fifteen; with one more call to make. "Anna, could you get Denver Simmons on the line now? Still Harrington."

As he sat waiting, his mind was back to Ted's 'remember and forget' logic. His thoughts suddenly flipped to Lindy…

Anna buzzed, "Denver Simmons is holding."

"Thanks." He regained his Harrington consciousness. He went through the exact same dialogue he'd just had with Mr. Mantis. However, that call turned into a soul baring session for Denver.

"Mr. Prier, I can certainly accept being terminated from this job, because like you said, I had "no commensurate or applicable knowledge to perform the requisite duties'. But there's something I'd just like to get off my chest. I really owe someone an apology because of what I personally did in this whole Harrington mess. I believe that um—well I don't really know for sure—but I think that I was the reason that um—that stenographer—Cindy Jack, ran out of the room."

"Excuse me?" Alonzo was totally thrown with Denver's odd admission of guilt.

And Denver, a.k.a. Denville, told him the whole sorted story!

"And you're not kidding, are you?" Was Alonzo's only question, asked in sheer amazement.

"No, sir. I only wish I was. I feel terrible and I can't face Cindy. It was tough enough to tell my wife most of this."

"You know, Denver, termination from your position is one bitter pill to swallow. But I could draft you into the State's criminal charges against Harrington, with the story you just told. You were an accessory to fraudulent misconduct, which in your case, translates into malicious intent. Whether you knew it—or not!"

Denver was now overtaken by the onset of the Blues! Alonzo had reduced him to an updated version of that old song—Shake, Rattle... and Roll! Alonzo had him scared.

And while Denver sat shaking, Alonzo continued. "Because you were just plain stupid, I'm going to pretend your soul-baring never happened. Your behavior towards Cindy, and your wife, was nothing less than despicable. Maybe your confession is tantamount to unburdening, but you still better hope and pray, that one doesn't always reap what he sows. And just what do you intend to do about Cindy?"

He took a deep breath, and wearily exhaled. "I don't know. I feel worse about that, than being fired. Could you—I mean would you—please apologize to her for me?"

"No! She deserves and explanation and I'm more than willing to do that. But me— apologize to her—for you? Grow up, Mr. Simmons! Facing Cindy, and apologizing yourself, will help." Alonzo hung up the phone.

And Cindy continued to mope along. Life was back to the grueling nightmare she had assessed it to be before any of this happened. Denville was gone with the wind; she'd concluded that romance with Alonzo was truly a figment of her imagination; and Greta Garbo really wasn't signaling from beyond. Her only truisms were Gina's friendship and

Eve truly on the road to recovery. "How Great Thou Art!" she bellowed sarcastically.

But it was Thursday evening, and on Friday evening; around that same time, she'd be in Executive Session with Alonzo. Even though he was off her Richter scale of romance, she still found him admirable, charismatic and outlandishly handsome.

Come Friday morning, Cindy dragged herself out of bed with the sounding of her alarm. For the moment, the only good thing was that her first session started at ten. Anyway, she got through her morning particulars and in heading out the door, she vocalized yet another amazing revelation. "Time surely drags when you ain't having any fun."

During the day, her mind aimlessly wandered back to Denver and the times they shared when he was Denville. It was so very mind-boggling, almost to the brink of insanity, how someone could be so duplicitous. Being so removed from the reality of the root cause of their involvement in the first place, Cindy continued to dig her emotional pit. From her first morning session break until her usual evening quitting time, she'd checked her office voicemail three times, only to discover two messages. One from Eve, the other from Gina. They were both concerned with her emotional well-being, asking her to call back. Cindy ignored them both.

It was approaching five o'clock and she now needed to head over to the Health Department for the HRRC Executive Session. She recalled Margie telling her that with those sessions, the Health Department always had some decent sandwiches and soft drinks for the participants. On the way over, she grappled with her residual embarrassment from the last HRRC meeting. Alonzo and Lindy were nice enough, but nonetheless, it was still embarrassing. There would be a few others present that had only stared at her that God-awful day. "And now I've got to break bread with them too," she softly thought aloud entering the building.

The routine was the same, but this was not an open public meeting—no audience. She sat up her apparatus, ignored the food, and awaited the arrival of all participants to the HRRC Executive Session. The Secretary was the only one present when she arrived; about ten minutes later Alonzo, Lindy, Dr. Morris, and Warren Lein arrived. Mr.

Evert, from the Insurance Department; Mr. Spears, from the Public Advocate's Office; and Dot Reinhold, from the Hospital Association, entered last. They had a quorum, so it didn't matter that the one Public Member couldn't attend.

It was now about ten minutes after five. With all present, they all proceeded to the sandwiches and soft drinks area. Cindy was just sitting alone when Alonzo approached her. "Cindy. Hello. How are you? Aren't you having something to eat, or drink maybe? That's what it's there for. Are you alright?"

"Oh, thanks Alonzo. Yes, I'm okay, I guess. Thanks. Yes—um—maybe I will—have a sandwich."

He noted that she sounded a little strange. Feeling sympathetic in his awareness of the Denville story, he continued. "Definitely. Get yourself something to eat. And after this session is over, I'd like to speak with you. That is, if you can hang around for a few. This session should be over at six-thirty or so."

"Oh sure. No problem." She somewhat wondered why but didn't place too much emphasis on it. She didn't have the requisite enthusiasm to build up to heightened curiosity.

On her way to a sandwich she and Lindy exchanged brief pleasantries. Lindy politely asked if she was feeling better to which Cindy simply responded in the affirmative.

About ten minutes later, the session was underway. The Secretary opened with the order of business for the meeting, which included three agenda items. They would discuss the averted labor strike; the conclusion to the Harrington mess, and legal brief preparation; and the Health Commissioner's Word of Warning speech to the hospital industry regarding deregulation. Alonzo proposed that considering the Harrington matter, if the hospitals had any thoughts of voting deregulation only to follow in Gary Numan's footsteps, they should be advised that Numan was not to be regarded as an entrepreneurial genius and role model—but more appropriately—a parole model. He would further confer with Dr. Morris towards those efforts, since the speech should be delivered by the Health Commissioner, who would continue jurisdictional watch over the State's ninety hospitals—rate-regulated or not. The meeting concluded at six-forty p.m.

Cindy was busy packing up when Alonzo approached. "Remember I said I wanted to speak with you for a moment?"

"Yes. Sure. I was just packing up my stuff. But I remember."

"Fine. Let's grab a seat in the back of the room."

"Okay." She felt slightly uncomfortable, not too sure if her appearance was pleasing. But she followed with all the exuberance of a flat liner.

Now seated away from the remaining few, Alonzo began. "Cindy, what I'm about to say to you is actually none of my business, and then again it is. Someone told me something yesterday that I regard as most unethical. And what made it even worse, is that the person on the receiving end of this display of indecency, is someone that I have utmost respect for, and view as a highly intelligent and nice young lady. Denver Simmons told me that he was the reason you ran out of Tuesday's HRRC meeting. He admitted that he'd been led astray by his own stupidity. He said he'd deceived you into thinking that you two had a relationship; and right now, he just can't face you."

Cindy was shocked and had started crying. To give her some needed space, Alonzo went over to the picked over food display for a few napkins. He returned and sympathetically continued. "I know this sounds ridiculous. But you deserve the truth, and you need to know that the guy you probably thought was your knight in shining armor was only there to deceive you. According to Denver, he was drafted into Harrington's plan to divert our investigation. He'd overheard our conversation at the elevator the day you told me about Numan and the JHPTC meetings. He told Numan, and Numan set him up to date you. Numan was hoping that you would lose interest in talking to me about those meetings and transcripts if Denver had your attention."

"What a horrible thing to do! I am so embarrassed! I'm hurt, and embarrassed! He told you that? He never said anything to me at all about anything like that. I mean, we never talked about the JHPTC. And Alonzo, I only found out who he really was—I mean his real name at the meeting! Oh my God! This is the.."

Alonzo cut her emotionally charged rambling off. "Cindy, I'm so sorry this happened to you. But don't focus on the small stuff. And that's exactly what this is. Denver is worse off than you are right now.

His actions reduced him to someone less than respectable! He's been terminated from Harrington, and his wife is"..

"He's married too?! He said he was single! Oh my God!" Each detail became more traumatic for Cindy.

"You wouldn't have known that either? Cindy look—don't focus on the weak, focus on your strengths. You helped the AG's Office hone in on an outlandish scheme; you're very conscientious—you got those transcripts to me just as you'd promised; you're very bright—most stenographers don't pay attention to this stuff; and you're an attractive young lady. You got roughed up a little in this game of life. But you know what, Cindy? That's a part of life. And what doesn't kill you makes you a better fighter. Don't sweat the small stuff; walk with confidence in the bigger picture. And if Denver could take this all back—I know he would. He was wrong, and he's paying for it—in many ways."

"But it hurts, Alonzo. And I would never do what he did—to anybody!" She was still crying, but she'd consumed every word he'd said.

"Sure, it hurts! But allow yourself to recognize that your integrity is greater than his shallowness. This isn't worth your continued grief, Cindy. You've got too much to offer. I've got to go. You do too. Give me a minute and I'll walk you to your car."

And although she was still feeling the grief, she was also feeling touched by an angel. In having so eloquently walked her through her despondency, Alonzo manifested as "the" knight in shining armor he had always been touted as. Up until now, she'd never known the reason for Denver's departure other than the exposure of his identity. But most important, thanks to Alonzo, she would now begin to recognize her own true worth.

Crying along the way home, she suddenly remembered having heard that crying was a way of cleansing the soul. If that were true, she'd soon be spic-n-span. With the spic-n-span thought, her grief had begun to lift. And this was the last day of the month of October she would have cause to interact with Alonzo. The next HRRC meetings were scheduled for November twenty-seven and twenty-eight. But Alonzo's final Attorney General's Office business would be concluded on November twenty-second.

The following first week of November, things were hectic in the AG's Division of Law. The first draft of the Harrington legal brief had been completed and was in Anna's in-box for typing; his Health and Insurance Deputies were vying for as much of his time as possible; the Attorney General himself was spending more time with him; his phone was constantly ringing; etcetera. By noon on Friday, everybody was practically rejoicing that after lunch, there would only be a few more hours to some much-needed R&R. But at noon, Lindy had a brilliant R&R suggestion of her own.

"Alonzo, can I interrupt you for a moment?" She was properly attired and standing in the doorway of his office.

Rather pensive, her replied, "Sure, Lindy. What's up?"

"You've been avoiding me, and I want to apologize since I obviously took you through a loop. But I would at least like to take you to lunch before you leave. It's only two and a half more weeks before farewell." She had on a two-piece tailored navy suit, with a skirt that fell just at her knees.

He looked up from the file he had been reviewing and responded most engagingly. "I apologize, Lindy. I wasn't purposely avoiding you, but if your lunch offer is good for now—let's go." He smiled.

She accepted. "Great! Is American Cuisine, okay? I know this fantastic place called The Dining Room. It's about twenty-five minutes from here though."

"You invited me. It's up to you." He flashed that sexy smile.

"Cool. Now?"

"Yes." He silently started replaying Ted's remember and forget advice.

Lindy drove. In route to the restaurant, they made small talk. Once seated and after having ordered, they made eye contact.

"So why haven't you called? I know I'm not wrong about this, Alonzo."

"A few reasons, Lindy. I would need to know, beyond a reasonable doubt, that you'd not be expecting a love relationship. I'm in love with my wife; my career choice and all associated jobs demand integrity and ethics, and my personal conviction to doing the right thing keeps me from momentary indiscretions. And with marriage and three kids, I'm all tapped out in the love department. All I could offer is a base instinct encounter, sex —that's all it is. And you deserve more than that. You deserve a man who can make love to you because he's in love with you- -- not just have sex with you."

"And I don't understand—why you don't understand—that I know that. I've already told you I just want a keepsake. One night Alonzo, and then it's goodbye—and probably, forever. What's the harm?"

"Under those conditions, maybe no harm. I don't know." He didn't say it, but he was rather intrigued that she seemingly thought like a man.

"So, you kept my number then?"

And he chuckled to himself that she now had him responding like a woman. "Yes."

"Cool." She knew she had him and not to press further. "How do you like the food here?"

He smiled. "It's good. Really. good."

XV

The Finale…Done Deal

THAT FOLLOWING MONDAY, SCHEDULES FELL right into the hands of fate. Alonzo and Debbie would be in New York, settling with McCarther and Parks. They had been an excellent independent analytical resource for the issues they were retained for. Their deregulation points would be drafted into the proposed speech to the hospitals 'Words of Warning' to be delivered by Dr. Morris. Shawna would need to be in New York about an hour after Alonzo's departure to assess the fabrics' shipment for Vladimir's new professional Women-in-Washington designs.

It was about three-fifteen p.m. when Alonzo called Anna to check his messages. "Hey there, how are you? Anything urgent?"

"Hi Alonzo. Nope, not on the business front. But Shawna just called. She wants you to pick up the kids from your parents' house this evening on your way home. Chloyee is spending the night with her mom and dad. She's got to run into New York to do a fabrics review. She's leaving the house around four, and she won't get home until around eight or nine tonight. All your other callers said they'd call back tomorrow."

"Okay. Thanks. Um, Debbie and I are about to head out now then. Oh, is Lindy in? Transfer me to her please. If I don't get back today, I'll see you tomorrow."

"Okay. And I'll transfer you to Lindy."

"Lindy Jewel speaking."

"Hello. How are you?"

"Alonzo? Hi. I'm fine."

"Good. Listen, I'm on my way back from McCarther and Parks. Would you care to meet me for drinks?"

"Sure. Where?"

"I'll meet you at—The Dining Room—five o'clock. I should be there by five; I'm leaving New York now."

"Sure thing. I'll see you then. Bye." She hung up; gently bit her bottom lip; and smiled—wickedly.

Alonzo and Debbie walked out of the huge Fifth Avenue building where McCarther and Parks leased offices. They would take the train back to New Jersey together, and pick up their separate cars around four thirty.

Now back in New Jersey's Penn Station, Alonzo broached the parting words. "Debbie, I'll see you tomorrow. Job well done and have a good evening."

"You're not going back to the office, are you?"

"No. I've got to pick up my kids. My wife, quite coincidentally had to go into New York on some business. See ya."

"You, too. Bye."

Off to their cars they went, and on down the highway to The Dining Room, he proceeded.

It was at least a forty-minute ride, but the savings grace was that he had just beat the height of rush hour traffic.

When he pulled into the parking lot it was five-twelve. He saw Lindy's car, quickly parked, and rushed in.

She was seated at a table for two, facing the entrance, so as to be immediately visible.

She'd been sipping a glass of red wine; an empty glass and the half-corked bottle on the table.

"Hey! Sorry I'm a little late." He'd left his jacket in the car. All that he had to do, was simply sit down.

"No problem. I was prepared to wait, you were coming from New York." She was graciously seductive. She continued. "I took the liberty to order a bottle of Cabernet Sauvignon. It's from Chile. Have you ever had Chilean wine?"

He was now reading the label. "Umm, no. No, I haven't, but it looks official. What is it about Chilean wine that you like?" He had now begun to re-fill her glass and pour himself one.

"That's it's just as full-bodied and full-flavored as any of the other more widely favored imports or domestics, but not as pricey. I noticed that you usually drink wine. That is, the few occasions we've had lunch or at some after-work meeting."

"Yeah, I don't much drink strong alcohol. But I'll add Chilean wine to my list. Thanks." He picked up his glass to toast her. She reciprocated.

And for about thirty minutes, they chatted about various and sundry official things. He looked at his watch and at six-fifteen, Alonzo changed the direction of the evening. "I've got to be on my way soon. But I really want to switch gears and talk about this sexual tension thing. I thought about it; I've thought about how we've shared a successful work history, and how stunning, attractive and intelligent you are. But we're not on the same page where intimacy is concerned." He gently bit his lip and offered an endearing kind of smile."

Lindy, now more attentive to his every word, began to uncomfortably shift in her seat. Sensing that he was veering off her desired course, she asked sensually, "Would you like more wine?"

"No thanks," he cordially replied continuing unphased. "I haven't gotten past sex versus making love being just a base act, the demand of integrity and ethics of my chosen career path, and most importantly, my marriage. You know, Lindy, my wife and I have been married almost seven years and we're still like newlyweds. And I attribute that to us not having skeletons of infidelities in our closets. Infidelities cause the dynamic between people to change. Doesn't matter if the offended party knows or not. The offending party knows and starts acting different." His thoughts had shifted to Cindy and Denver now both in the agony of despair from betrayal consummated by a man who had also cheated on his innocent wife. Without divulging who he was referencing, he emphatically said, "I'm not willing to compromise my wife or my career for anyone. I'm a man and I find you awesomely attractive, but I will not act on that." Decision made.

Lindy sat motionless, uncomfortable with tears and unable to shrug off Alonzo's cutting words that sliced to the chase. She handled herself and after sipping her wine said, "I'm sorry, Alonzo. I didn't mean to offend you, I didn't know your views but I get it." She smiled.

Not wanting to belabor the point, he switched gears again, "We're going to be working closely on the commissions I'm transitioning to you and bringing the new section chief up to speed on all this stuff. You've been tremendous on all your assignments, Lindy, and I want to get you and Lawrence Stangle together for some briefings before I leave. Anna's going to schedule us over the course of the next two weeks." Adding a bit of levity, he continued, "Can I count on you to be on your best behavior?"

She replied sarcastically, "I don't know, Alonzo. Is he married?" The Lindy he liked was back. He felt good about that and his decision to not go there.

He beckoned the waitress and paid the tab. "Let's go. I gotta pick up my kids. I'll walk you to your car."

XVI

Redesigned Lives

H E GOT HOME WITH HIS little boys about twenty minutes before
Shawna. Since they'd already been fed, he began readying them
for bed.

Shawna pulled up alongside Alonzo's BMW, and quickly proceeded
inside. She hurried up the spiral staircase to her loved ones. "Hey guys!
I'm home."

"Mommy!" Erik exclaimed, "I'm helping Daddy get us in bed!"

Amused, she responded. "I can just imagine! Erik in charge, huh?"
She kneeled to kiss him and Thornton.

"Hello, sweetheart. How was your day? Did you get through all
the fabrics?"

"Yep! And they're great! The designs Vladimir is about to premier
for the working-woman-in-Washington are fabulous! I've selected some
pretty hot fabrics too; with the designers, of course."

"Of course!" He didn't' know a damn thing about that stuff. He just
loved going to the showings and hearing his wife so excited.

"Anyway, I'll tell you later. Let's get Erik to bed, and we'll talk—
in bed."

An inquisitive little Erik responded, "I wantta talk with you guys
too. I don't wantta go to my bed!"

"Oh, but you are, Erik!" Shawna had taken command. Erik looked
at her, and realized she meant business too.

With the boys down and out for the night, Alonzo and Shawna
were off to their private habitat.

After giving him all the details and in feeling the glory of the moment, Shawna wanted to celebrate. She wanted to co-mingle her Washington assignment with his. Sensuously and half-naked walking up to him in their master bedroom, she sat out to turn him on.

"Let the good times roll, huh, Shawna. I don't have to ask for it?"

"Nope. I'm gonna wild you out tonight," she seductively said.

"Sounds good to me," said Alonzo, excited as could be. His excitement was two-fold; he was still turned on by his gorgeous wife and thankful he hadn't sexed Lindy. Home run!

Throughout the course of his remaining weeks, Alonzo spent his time finalizing the criminal charges the AG's Office and the Health Department would bring against the Harrington officers. He wouldn't be there for their final day in court. But in having done an outstanding job in pulling it all together, he'd made it possible for whomever Raymond Chandler would turn the file over too, would get through it with smooth sailing.

Having reflected over her quest for Alonzo, Lindy had become a little less visible around his office. Despite what she'd said, he could only imagine that women really didn't have the ability to separate the issues in terms of love versus lust. In reflection back to his single hay-days, he remembered feigning love to get sex; while the women feigned enjoying sex, to get love. 'But that was then. He thought, 'I really do love my wife and kids, and maybe this thing with Lindy helped to reinforce that. I'm so glad I didn't take the plunge!' His silent thoughts ceased, and he got busy again.

About fifteen minutes later, Anna buzzed him. "Yes Anna?"

"Alonzo, Cindy Jack is here to see you. Can you see her now for a few minutes?"

Surprised by the unexpected visit, but certainly receptive, he responded, "Cindy's here? Sure. Have her come right in." He got up from his desk and headed over to one of his L-shaped sofas.

Cindy was now in the doorway of his office. "Hi, Alonzo."

"Hello, Cindy. Come on in. Have a seat. This is a surprise!" He graciously extended his arm to imply that she should be seated on the other side of the L. This was obviously not a formal meeting, and recalling her recent upsets, he wanted to be supportive. "What may I do for you?"

"Well first I wanted to thank you for the advice you gave me. I see things in a whole new way about my life, and having gone through that episode with Denver, was exactly what you said—not worth the continued grief and look within for the greater things I was a part of. And really, if it wasn't for Denver's stupidity and your support after it all blew up, I wouldn't have recognized some of those greater things." Cindy was smiling with gratitude and sincerity.

"Exactly. You have too much to offer to get hung up on the small stuff. Count the pebbles as steppingstones and move up and onward. There're a million Denvers in the world, but there's only one Cindy Jack. Remember that."

"I wanted to say thank you, Alonzo, and now that I've had a chance to think and get back on track, I've decided to go to Law School. I've been thinking about becoming a prosecuting attorney."

"Good for you! In tribute to Gary Numan, maybe? It's too bad you don't have your credentials now, so he could come up against the likes of Cindy Jack, prosecuting attorney. You've certainly got the mind for it!"

She was feeling at ease and smiling now. "Yep. Gary Numan and company certainly set the stage for me to want to go after white-collar crime." In getting up to go she noticed something was different. "Gee, I've only been in your office once, but you had pictures and plaques— they're all gone."

"Oh, that's right. You don't know. I'm leaving. I accepted a position with a firm in Washington D.C. I'll be working on health care policy drafting for the Health Care Financing Administration."

"Oh really? When did you make the announcement? Who's going to replace you?"

"For as long as the HRRC lasts, Lindy will. The hospitals will probably vote deregulation and the HRRC will go away after a year. There's a new Section Chief, Lawrence Stangle, replacing me. He starts next week. I'm out November twenty-second."

"The twenty-second is next week! Oh, my goodness!" She'd just been tussled again. She felt a queasy feeling in the pit of her stomach. "I'll sure miss you—at those meetings, I mean."

"Well, one never knows, Cindy. With your newly discovered ambition, who knows? You could end up in Washington one day—as President. You're a crackerjack, Cindy Jack! Take care and best wishes to you. I'm so glad you stopped by, and I'm most happy to see you're smiling." He hugged her and kissed her on the cheek.

And it was all she could do to keep from crying. The news of his departure was a shocker!

And on her way home that evening, thinking about now losing Alonzo, it dawned on her that Alonzo had completed his assignment in her life. Their paths crossed so he could further clarify what Webster's had seemingly inadequately defined. It was Alonzo who helped her to realize that going through rough struggles in life, toughens you up so you can move up to your next level. Yes, she wanted to be tussled. Her life was boring because she hadn't yet discovered the authentic Cindy Jack. The incessant 'I wantta be tussled' thought was about Cindy Jack discovering the calling on her life to put her mind, her skill-level, and her deep seeded commitment to integrity, to good use.

Damn right she was going to law school—and she was now determined to succeed as a successful prosecuting attorney!

And like Alonzo said—what doesn't kill you makes you a better fighter. You find out who you really are when life roughs you up. And Gina said, get back in there, Cindy! Stay in the game and fight back. And she got her desire…she wanted to be *tussled*.

The End

AFTERWORD

The State of New Jersey grappled with a few rather challenging issues during the mid to late 1990s that kept the Department of Health, the Department of Insurance, and the Office of the Attorney General hoping. The issues presented are factual; the Commissions and Task Forces with the lack-luster acronyms existed; many of the storylines embellished for levity; and the characters all fictionalized for the storytelling of CrackerJack!

Lightning Source UK Ltd.
Milton Keynes UK
UKHW011836280621
386319UK00001B/42